BLOOD BROTHERS

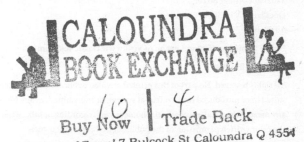

CHARLES BEAGLEY

JoJo
PUBLISHING

Blood Brothers
Charles Beagley

Published by Classic Author and Publishing Services Pty Ltd
An imprint of Jo Jo Publishing
First published 2015

'Yarra's Edge'
2203/80 Lorimer Street
Docklands VIC 3008
Australia

Email: jo-media@bigpond.net.au or visit www.classic-jojo.com

JoJo Publishing Imprint
Editor: Ormé Harris
Designer / typesetter: Chameleon Print Design
Printed in China by Inkasia

National Library of Australia Cataloguing-in-Publication entry

Author	Beagley, Charles, author.
Title	Blood brothers / Charles Beagley ; editor: Orme Harris.
Edition	1st edition.
ISBN	9780987609564 (paperback)
Subjects	Engineers--Western Australia--Fiction.
	Brothers--Australia--Fiction.
	Aboriginal Australians--Fiction.
Other Authors/Contributors:	
	Harris, Orme, editor.
Dewey Number:	A823.4

For my late wife, Glenys.
This one is for you, dear.

CHAPTER 1

It was 3:30 am when the alarm on Martin Dexter's mobile started vibrating under his pillow. He had no intention of disturbing his wife, Kate, at such an early hour and his expensive piece of technology did not fail him. He lifted the corner of his pillow, took out the mobile and reset it for another fifteen-minute sojourn. He felt he needed that to steady his nerves before his long flight into the Sandy Desert.

It was the first week of December; the first week of the wet season in northern Western Australia, but Martin's uneasy feeling was not to do with the weather. According to the meteorologist, the storm front that occupied his thoughts was not due until eight-thirty; plenty of time to get well out of its way. Martin and his family had lived in Broome this past five years and to date only one wet season had arrived early, all the

1

rest having the good sense to stay quiet until January, allowing everyone to enjoy a peaceful Christmas.

Martin lifted his head off the pillow slightly and looked over towards Kate snuggling under the doona. He smiled, wistfully recalling how Kate grumbled about the Australian Christmas. It was too hot, she would say. Not like the Christmas back in England when they would wrap up against the winter wind and cold snow; trudging through drifts on Christmas morning to church, struggling home with a real tree, and hot chestnuts on the open fire.

The mobile vibrated again. He eased his body towards the edge of the mattress, made sure Kate was still asleep and rolled out of bed. He tucked his feet into his slippers, made his way across the room to the door and out onto the landing. He moved from a darkened bedroom into the faintest orange glimmer permeating across the landing from the staircase window. It was not quite sunrise yet; the sun was still struggling to climb above the Durack Ranges, but it was not far off.

When Kate and Martin were choosing their house in Broome they were particular about its orientation – at least Kate was. The last house they'd had in England followed a line from east to west. It was a happy house; full of good luck; so she would settle for nothing less. Here the sun rises at the back of the house, is directly above at its hottest and sets at the front. This way they can sit on their bedroom balcony overlooking Cable Beach with a glass of riesling and watch the sun change into every shade of vermillion as it melts into the Indian Ocean.

Martin continued on to the bathroom, where he had laid out his clothes the night before on the rattan chair in the corner, and closed the door. It was almost four o'clock, an unearthly hour by anyone's standard, except for Mr Rudd, the newsagent. Martin could hear his old transit van through the open bathroom window, hopping from house to house with its door pulled back for the lad to toss the paper onto the front lawn. Martin hated looking for it amongst the flowerbeds, and he was glad he paid extra so that Mr Rudd would wrap it in Clingwrap. Others not so lucky had to settle for an elastic band.

After his shower, Martin dressed, went over to the bathroom cabinet mirror and wiped away the condensation. He stared at the gaunt image staring back at him. 'What on earth are you doing?' he questioned as he lifted the electric razor to his face. He paused and studied the forty-five-year-old reflection and wondered where all the years had gone. According to Kate he had been the catch of the café set back then.

Martin managed to keep himself fit. He had to, climbing over giant mechanical contraptions designed to tear the heart out of the Australian outback. The last five years and the relentless climate had reduced his English complexion to no more than the texture of a burlap sack. At first the bushmen employed by AMINCO had laughed at him and cracked jokes at his expense, saying the Pom wouldn't last five minutes in the outback. Yet here he was, five years later.

He shook his head, attempting a wry smile when he saw his wife's moisturising cream at the end of the bath. Right from the first day she'd had an aversion to the Australian sun. She would avoid it at any cost, lathering her face, arms and legs with a liberal amount of sunscreen and moisturiser, a wide-brimmed hat and huge sunglasses. When they were in England there was never enough sun; they would travel for miles on a weekend searching for a blue sky. And now she has it, she avoids it to a degree her Aussie friends find hilarious. Yet everyone always compliments her on the smoothness of her English skin.

Martin realised time was passing as he brushed his fingers sensitively across the greying stubble, inspecting yet another line in the craggy texture of his outback skin. Even his once-clear blue eyes were now beginning to lose their colour with the addition of fine veins gathering at the corners. His light-brown wavy hair had become a mixture of white and grey patches thinning on top at an alarming rate.

Almost finished, Martin caught sight of his Dunhill

cologne. Normally he avoided using any scented toiletry for fear the men on the sites he visited would acknowledge his arrival with a wolf whistle. In the early days his stylish English clothes caused such a stir that he began wearing the standard orange overalls. But today, for some inexplicable reason, he decided 'what the heck'. He was sick of the smell of desert sweat, diesel fuel and burnt grease. Then the mine itself had its own individual smell, whether it was opencast or underground.

Martin was still preoccupied by the ravages of time as he prepared his breakfast when he was distracted by a movement on the other side of the kitchen. He looked up just as Kate wandered through the door and stood for a moment inspecting him. She looked ravishing. Knowing how vain she was, he was aware she would have checked in the mirror before she came down; just as she always did even if it was no more an occasion than someone at the door. She would have wiped the moisturiser off her face, combed her hair and checked her appearance.

"How do you do it?" Martin remarked.

"Do what?" she asked as she sat down opposite him and poured a mug of tea.

He shook his head. "Here I am looking like something the dog dragged in and you breeze in looking like you did the day we first met."

She reached across the table and touched the back of his hand before taking one of his pieces of toast. "Oh, how nice," she said. "If I didn't know you were about to fly off somewhere I'd think you were after something." She stared into his puzzled gaze and bit into her toast.

"I wish," Martin acknowledged, finishing his toast and washing it down with the last of his tea.

Kate sat back drinking hers and studied the mixed expression on Martin's face. He was not usually bright and cheerful at this time in the morning, but there was something different in his manner. She could see he was preoccupied.

She leaned forward and took hold of his hand again, "What's on your mind?" she asked, squeezing his hand for an answer.

Martin knew his twenty-five-year marriage to Kate had equipped her with an uncanny sense of knowing when he was telling a lie or exaggerating the truth; years of experience had alerted him to the signs. It kept him on his toes. It meant he had to be sure of his facts or face the consequences.

Martin looked up and let out a long sigh, collected his breakfast dishes and placed them into the dishwasher. Then glancing at his watch, "It's just this trip, Kate," he finally answered. "Getting up at the crack of dawn, just to fly out to another godforsaken site in the desert; and what for? Just because some cretin has fouled up." He picked up the checklist from the table. "You see," he cried out. "I even have to make a list now so that I don't forget anything." He stared at the list. "Oh Hell…"

"What is it?" Kate asked, picking up the paper Martin had dropped on the table.

"I forgot to book the taxi."

"Is it too late now?"

Martin glanced at the clock on the wall opposite; it had just gone five. "You're joking…at this time in the morning? I'll just have to drive myself and leave the car at the airstrip. I can collect it on my way back."

"No, you don't…not in your mood," she said, standing up and moving back to the door. "Give me five minutes to throw something on and I'll take you."

Martin had no intention of remarking on how long her five minutes usually was. He just stood to one side as she passed him in the doorway.

She stopped. "Why are you wearing your Dunhill?"

"I don't know," he said. "I just fancied a change."

To save time Martin went out to the garage, hoping his faithful old SAAB would start first time. It did and while the engine was warming up he stowed his holdall on the back seat. It was still dark so he switched on the lights and changing into reverse, he backed the car out onto the drive. To his surprise Kate was waiting for him.

She opened his door. "Come on…move over," she said, leaving room for him to step out and walk round to the passenger side.

"I could have managed," he said, jumping in and fastening his seat belt.

"I'm sure you could, dear, but I need you to relax before the flight."

"What on an empty road?"

Kate reversed into the street and then followed it round to the main road running along Cable Beach. As Martin had said, it was empty and she turned right onto Gubinge Road to the first roundabout. Martin saw the right indicator light go on.

"Not here…straight on," he yelled.

She shot him a savage glance, switched the indicator off and continued on.

"I thought you were going to the airport," she said, regaining her composure.

Martin tried to stay calm, "No, dear. AMINCO has its own airstrip. It's about nine kilometres northeast of Broome."

"I wish you had told me that," Kate remarked.

"There was never any call to. And in this rush I didn't think."

She continued on for a few kilometres to the next

roundabout, which would take her to the other side of the airport. Martin said nothing and waited, but she passed straight through and he breathed a sigh of relief.

"I heard that," she said. "How far now?"

"Another few kilometres and you'll come to a fork on a bend. Keep following the road left onto Broome Road. Then it's a straight drive for fifteen minutes before you have to turn left onto Levesque Road. Another kilometre or so and you'll see the airstrip lights on your right."

"Okay...I don't need all that now. Just point out when I have to turn."

Martin settled back in his seat and tried to relax. When they'd left the house the sky on the Indian Ocean side had been still in darkness, but as soon as they'd crossed the last roundabout and turned east onto Broome Road the sky ahead of them began growing lighter. It was an eerie light. Traces of orange and gold seeped between the trees and suburban rooftops until they reached the outskirts of Broome, heading towards open country where it began to outline the undulating features of the distant hills.

He pointed out the left turn into Leveque Road and within a short distance Kate was turning into the lighted AMINCO airstrip. She pulled into the car park close to the main building and switched off the engine. They got out. Martin grabbed his holdall and they walked over to the double doors of a single storey weatherboard structure. This was all new for Kate. Martin preferred saying his goodbyes in bed or like this morning, after breakfast.

Just as they were about to enter the building there was a sudden gust of wind that shook them on their feet for a moment. It was followed by a few heavy drops of rain and Martin pushed Kate through the doors. Inside they shook the rain off and Martin led Kate across the main foyer, past the unmanned desk and left down a long corridor lit only with emergency lights. He had made this trip so many times before it was like a second home. At the bottom of the corridor he turned right and right again into a room full of easy chairs and coffee tables. It was just as dim, lit only by a couple of lights: one next to an exit out onto the airstrip and the other over a small kitchen set-up in one corner. According to the red light on an apparatus on the bench, coffee was percolating.

Kate walked over to the glass wall with the exit sign. She could see the runway and a small single engine plane standing out in the open. Two men were doing something under the wing while a third was heading in their direction.

She turned to Martin, who had dropped his hold-all on an easy chair. "That's not the plane you're flying out on…is it?"

He didn't look happy. The expression he'd worn in the house had returned. "That's the plane," he replied.

"What happened to the Lear Jet?"

"It appears our mighty American boss has commandeered it."

Kate turned around and threw her arms around Martin. "So that's why you were looking so glum. Why didn't you say something?"

"There was no use two of us worrying."

At that point the man walking across from the plane pushed open the doors and started brushing the rain off his leather jacket. "I was hoping it would hold off until we were in the air," he said, in a distinct Australian accent.

"What would hold off?" Kate remarked.

"The wind and rain," he replied. "I'm Joe Cirano... your pilot. "There're usually a few gusts of wind and some rain before the storm front comes through," he continued, removing his baseball cap and knocking it against the doorframe.

"Storm front?" Martin exclaimed, looking nervous.

"Do you mean to tell me you're about to take off with a storm about to hit?" Kate interrupted, looking as if she was about to throttle the pilot.

"Hold on," he said, putting his cap back on, "I assure you, Mrs Dexter, I've just been briefed by the meteorologist that the storm front isn't due until 0:830...that's eight-thirty." He glanced at the massive watch on his wrist. "That's at least two hours away. We'll be at the site by then."

While Kate was arguing with the man who was about to take her husband's life in his hands, Martin's mind had slipped back a step. In the Lear Jet he had noticed the aircrew, two pilots and a steward, wore smart, light-blue shirts with epaulets for their insignia, dark-blue trousers and matching peaked hats. But glancing across to his pilot on this trip, Martin thought he looked more like one of those flyers that spray crops. His only reference to the company that employed him was a large round badge on the breast pocket of his leather bomber-jacket. And all that had was the word AMINCO across the middle. There was other wording radiating around the circumference, but that was too small for Martin to read.

Kate looked at Martin's dismal expression. "I suppose that's not so bad...is it, Martin?" she said, turning her attention back to him.

Joe grabbed Martin's holdall. "Come on, Mr Dexter. If you want me to get ahead of this storm, I must take off now."

Martin turned to Kate and putting his arms around her, he gave her the most passionate kiss he could muster. He could feel the chemistry between them. He had a feeling that this kiss might have to last her for some time.

As Martin stepped out into the morning chill he could sense something was different. This morning was the first time Kate would see him off on the plane. It would be the first time he'd flown in a Cessna, and his first experience of a storm front chasing his tail.

Martin was becoming a little paranoid. He sensed the runway was alive. The trees at the end of the airstrip were swaying violently; the very trees the small plane would be flying over on its way south-east to the Sandy Desert. He stopped to watch them. Joe noticed and stepped back to take his arm and urge him on.

"Don't worry, Mr Dexter; we'll be well out of the way when it comes through."

Martin turned back to the plane. It was standing on a concrete apron close to the buildings. A gust of wind caught it, lifting it on its wheels like a young bird about to take its first flight. This was Martin's first real sight of the complex. Usually he was driven directly to the Lear Jet standing out on the main runway and missed all the detail. With the glow from the rising sun lighting up the eastern side of the AMINCO outbuildings he could see, other than the new glass extensions protecting the passage from one building to the next, the company had spent little on improving the tin-roofed hangars and operations buildings.

Joe was waiting for Martin beside the open door on

the passenger side of the Cessna. He had already placed his holdall on the two rear seats, firmly strapped down with the harness. He helped Martin up into his seat and as soon as he was comfortable, he hooked up his harness and snapped the buckle in place, stepped back out and shut the door. Martin heard Joe lock the handle, which Martin had to try as Joe ducked under the wing on his way around to his side.

As he jumped into his seat, buckled up his harness and slammed shut the door, he reached onto the centre console and retrieved a pair of headphones.

"Put these on," he said. "It's the only way we can talk to each other."

Joe's headset was already in place when Martin slipped the earphones over his head, retracting the narrow stem with a microphone on the end, just as Joe had.

There was a sudden deathly silence that reminded Martin of the time he'd had his ears tested. He glanced in Joe's direction as he adjusted his seat. Then the headset came alive. Someone was asking Joe if he was ready for a flight check. Joe realised Martin was listening and he pressed a button, which returned him to silence.

The silence gave Martin the opportunity to focus on the activity around the plane. Even at this hour there were two mechanics busying themselves under the wings. Martin noticed they also had headsets on and the man on his side came out from under the wing and made a gesture with his hand in the air. Joe's lips were moving all the time. He was checking off the instruments, flipping switches, turning the control column in his lap and jiggling his feet. Each action was followed by a gesture of acknowledgement from one of the men.

All the time Joe had been reading from a card. He placed it somewhere beside his left leg, flipped another switch and pressed something that started the engine. Martin flinched with shock. The whole plane came alive as the propeller in front of him disappeared in a whirling fury. After a scraping sound under the plane, the two men appeared again, this time standing out of the way with large metal objects in their hands. They were the chocks, the last vestige of equipment that had been holding the small plane in place on the concrete apron. One of the men raised his hand in a circular movement and Joe let off the brakes.

As the Cessna taxied along the short parking lane, Martin instinctively turned his head towards Kate. She was standing close to the window, waving her hand, looking as forlorn as she did when they saw their relatives off at Broome airport. At the last moment before Joe turned left onto the main runway, Martin blew her a kiss. She waved and the engine increased its power.

Martin's headset came alive. "I'd put your sunglasses on if I were you, Mr Dexter," Joe said, pushing the throttle lever forward. "We're heading east and the sun is just about to break out of the trees."

Martin took them out of his breast pocket and covered his eyes and instinctively clenched his hands together on his lap. Despite his earphones, his ears were popping, beads of sweat were breaking out on his brow and he had the awful feeling he was in a food blender. The sensation became more pronounced the higher the speed until suddenly the vibrations stopped. Less than halfway down the runway the Cessna lifted off and climbed into the salmon pink sky; high above the dreaded trees and east towards the rising sun.

Even with his sunglasses Martin could hardly look into the smouldering mass poking above the distant hills. "Why are we heading east?" he asked.

"Relax," Joe said, amongst a jumble of aircraft jargon as he communicated with the AMINCO operations crew. "In a few minutes I shall bank right on a south-east heading of 123 degrees for Site 21. You might as well get your head down and catch up on that early start."

Despite the gut-wrenching anxiety of taking off in what he considered a machine hardly more powerful than a lawn mower, they were in the air and still climbing. Martin was uneasy. It brought back a distant memory he thought he had forgotten; an equally traumatic flight in a Tiger Moth that was also too close to the elements, and the near proximity of that single propeller. Even with his eyes closed and his determined concentration on the memory of Kate's last anxious expression, Martin could not stop the flashbacks of that fateful day in the RAF.

Kate watched the small Cessna until it mingled with the drawn-out clouds rushing across the eastern skyline. They had started to accumulate into worrying columns, rising and falling in the same pattern she had seen from her balcony. It had started raining again, heavier now and she thought of Martin.

As it was out of her control, she let out a sigh and turned away from the window and made her way along the corridor trying to remember if it was left – left or right – right. Either way she managed to pass the familiar windows of the operations complex, turn into the last corridor that led into the administration block where she let out a sigh of relief on seeing the main entrance.

Suddenly she was surprised when a door on her left opened and Philip Hastings walked out. She remembered him immediately from an AMINCO party to which Martin had taken her. She stopped in her tracks.

"Oh Kate…on your way home?" he remarked.

"Yes, Philip. I had to see Martin off," she replied simply, not wanting to get involved at this time in the morning about why she was there.

"Of course you did," he said smartly. "I'm sorry I wasn't able to see you both when you arrived. We've got a big-wig flying in this morning." He glanced at his watch. "In fact he should be landing soon."

"Let's hope he arrives before the storm."

"Oh…you heard about that," he said in a matter-of-fact way. "That's not due for ages and he's arriving from the opposite direction."

Kate made a move to pass him. "Well, don't let me keep you."

Suddenly there was a loud bang that echoed along the corridor: a gust of wind hit the front doors, opening them slightly and clashing them together again. They both looked towards the entrance.

Kate jumped. "Oh dear…I'd better get a move on."

Philip walked her to the entrance, opened one of the doors for her and watched as she hurried across to her car. Despite his assurances, he could not help glancing in the direction of the Indian Ocean. It was a good ten kilometres away, but even from that distance, he could see the sky was looking ominous.

CHAPTER 2

There was no need for Martin to open his eyes to know Joe was making his south-east turn. It was like being the bubble in a spirit level. Despite being strapped in, or maybe because of that, his insides responded to every movement of the plane. Then there was a profound click and Joe's voice echoed in his headset.

"You can open your eyes now, Mr Dexter."

Martin opened his eyes and stared out of the windscreen. It was a strange experience as wispy clouds formed, evaporated and reformed again in front of his eyes. He had not summoned enough nerve to look out of his window yet, but he did manage to unclench his hands.

"I'm sorry, Joe…I didn't mean to offend you with my anxiety."

Joe laughed before replying. "Oh, that's okay, Mr

Dexter. It happens to everyone when they fly in a small plane for the first time."

Martin tested himself and glanced to the right. The wing was directly above his window so, regardless of the narrowest of struts holding it up in front of his seat, he had an unrestricted view of the ground.

"It's just so different to the jet," Martin replied.

Joe paused for a moment before replying as if that had ticked him off. "Yeah…I wish. You should try flying in a helicopter sometime. That would make you appreciate the Cessna. They have luxury jets too. It's just that AMINCO likes to have a wide range to choose from. You know…different tools for different jobs. Being an engineer, Mr Dexter, you can appreciate that."

"Oh, I can, Joe…and stop calling me Mr Dexter. It's Martin."

"Okay, Martin…thanks."

"It feels as if I'm sitting in one of those chairs on top of the Ferris wheel looking down on the fairground with all the people moving around like little ants. God, how I hated that, but my wife Kate couldn't get enough. And do you know what? She hated the dodgems. You know…the cars you drive around bumping into each other."

"I know what they are, Martin. We do have them in Australia."

"Sorry...I'll get used to the Cessna."

Joe started his customary instrument check. All seemed well but Martin was so on edge he just had to talk. It was a bad habit that Kate was always trying to cure him of. What he needed was some questions answered. That always worked.

"Joe...I never got a satisfactory answer about this storm front."

"What's your problem, Martin? You're an engineer. Surely you can understand the basic formation of storm-front windows?"

"Pass it by me again."

"Okay. We have a storm front coming in from the Indian Ocean. We have a window, that's a respite of approximately two hours before it hits Broome. We're travelling at 230km/h. We took off at about six, so by seven we shall be three-quarters of the way through our three-hundred-kilometre journey, and the storm hasn't even hit Broome yet. It still has another hour, by which time we shall have landed."

"Is that so?"

"Yeah...that's so. Martin...the storm is behind us. When it arrives it will be travelling at around 100km/h. Do the maths; it can't catch up to us."

Joe was suddenly distracted by a smell and started sniffing the air. Unusual smells in a confined space like a plane at three thousand feet concerned him.

"What's that smell?"

"Oh that," Martin said under his breath. "That's my Dunhill."

"Dunhill?"

"Yes…you know – the people who make the cigarettes."

"They do scent now?"

"It's not scent…it's cologne."

Joe shook his head and appeared to be satisfied it was not something he should be worried about. Martin forgot for the moment that he was the passenger and Joe was working. This was what he did, and going about his business of flying the plane needed his full concentration; not listening to an idiot that needed to talk to take his mind off where they were. In the jet Martin could relax, go to sleep, read his report, totally oblivious from what was happening outside the plane.

Joe went quiet again. He seemed preoccupied with his instruments; tapping dials, checking LED figures against his card again and glancing out of his window. Joe was in the early stages of the flight, making sure everything was as it should be. Then after another check below his wing he seemed to relax.

Martin had no need to check his watch. Suddenly a bright orange shaft of light burst out of the window behind Joe's seat and rapidly moved along the plane's side until it broke through his window and remained fixed there, passing across the instrument panel and onto the side of Martin's face. He could feel its warmth as it penetrated the gap between the rim of his glasses and the bridge of his nose; then just as quickly it disappeared as the Cessna continued to climb.

"Sunrise at last," Martin noted.

Joe glanced sideways at the distraction.

"Not quite," Joe corrected him. "Down below, sunrise was at its usual time of six-fourteen. I don't know if you were aware, but we've been climbing through clouds and what you experienced just now was the plane breaking out of the clouds' thousand-foot ceiling, and, as you can see...we're in a blue sky."

Martin looked about him. "So I see. I didn't notice."

"It wasn't a thick cloud. It was more of a scattered variety; common enough towards the desert. It keeps the vegetation alive."

"I thought the desert was all sand dunes."

"Oh no," Joe replied with a slight amusement in his voice. "They're further south. The northern Sandy Desert is mostly scrubland: mainly spinifex and a scattering of acacia shrubs and small trees. This low cloud is barely enough to sustain them until the rains. They can be very heavy, like that storm front that's following us. It'll dump about a 100 mm as it passes over."

"As much as that?" Martin questioned.

"Oh yes…sometimes more, right across the desert to Alice Springs and depending on what's driving it, even into Victoria."

"Yes, I remember now. I remember seeing the weather forecast showing the long white trail across the country."

"Anyway…as the sun heats up, all this lot will evaporate and within fifteen minutes it will be gone and you'll be able to see the ground."

Martin's apprehension began to take over. "I'm not so sure about that. I was just getting used to the distance between us and those clouds down there."

The cockpit soon began to feel uncomfortably warm and Joe reached over to his console and adjusted the airflow. It soon settled back to its earlier temperature and Martin was happy again. He turned to Joe. It was his first opportunity to see his companion in daylight. Not that he could see much past his sunglasses and baseball cap. But his name was sufficient to guess his ancestors were Italian.

"So, Joe," Martin opened the discussion, "when did you arrive in Australia?"

At first Joe looked aghast, as if the question was alien to him; then he realised it was a typical opening gambit between immigrants. "I was born here," he replied.

"Oh…sorry; it was your name that threw me."

"It was my father that emigrated from a small town on the Adriatic Coast called Rimini. It was back in 1948 when things were bad."

"That must have been very hard for the family."

"I wasn't born then and my father seemed to avoid talking about that part of his life. For me everything started when he joined the Australian Army. Not that he talked much about fighting in Korea; not many do. He was more open about his time flying a helicopter. You know the Bell that looks like an insect with a big glass bubble in front. He got shot down in the hills and had to walk back. It took days. I certainly wouldn't want to go through what he did."

"So he survived then?"

"Oh yes. When he got back from Korea, he found it difficult to settle, so he moved from Sydney to Queensland to become a cane-cutter."

"That was a mammoth decision to make."

"At the time it was the only way he could make any money. Within a year he had made enough to buy a second-hand helicopter and he started his own crop-spraying business. Then he went into partnership with an old army buddy, flying sightseeing trips up and down the Barrier Reef. They were doing really well until the Australian Aviation Authority pounced on them, saying they couldn't use the same helicopter they sprayed crops with to fly passengers; something about the toxic chemicals."

"Isn't that just like it?" Martin sympathised.

Joe seemed to appreciate that as he checked his altimeter.

"For my dad it was. Then his buddy had the brilliant idea of taking out a loan to buy a plane. It was a Cessna – an earlier version than this. And that's when I learned to fly. My mother was furious. 'Isn't it enough to have one madman in the family?' she would say. But she came round when I got my licence."

"So why are you not flying in your dad's business now?"

"The plane was just too much for them. They weren't getting enough passengers to pay its way."

"That's too bad after all the bad luck your father had already had."

"Not really. It led to my father finding out his buddy was cheating him."

"So what happened then?"

"His buddy disappeared, leaving my dad with all the bills to take care of. Almost broke he was about to sell the plane when he saw an advertisement in the paper. It was a new American mining company in Australia looking for pilots with their own planes. The deal was: they would rent the plane, pay for the expenses as well as a bonus if the pilot completed his targets. Piece of cake my dad thought until he realised he had to move to Broome and fly workers to and from mine sites in the Sandy Desert."

"And obviously he accepted the deal," Martin interrupted.

"He did. He also introduced me to the boss. Told him I had my licence and got me this job, which I've been doing this past eight years."

"I suppose your father is retired now?"

Joe went silent again. It was as if he needed a moment to find the right words, but there were none and he just continued. "He died two years ago…cancer of the lungs. The bloody idiot; I told him to stop smoking."

"Oh, I am sorry, Joe," Martin replied. "I had no intention of opening up old wounds. How terrible for your mother."

"Yes, but time heals all wounds, so they say."

Martin nodded and the conversation ended. Or so he thought.

"So you're an engineer then?" Joe asked.

"I'm afraid so."

"I usually only get the workers; you're my first executive."

"I wouldn't class myself as an executive…more an overseer."

"It's all the same to me. I wouldn't be flying you to

27

the site if his lord all mighty hadn't commandeered the Lear Jet."

"Yes, well that may be true, but I'm getting used to the Cessna now."

"I knew you would. But I bet next time you won't say no to the comfort of the Lear Jet. I persuaded the head pilot to give me a run around the hills once. I got to sit in the padded seats, enjoy a hot beverage and even took control for a few minutes. I have to admit, I'd choose the jet any day over the Cessna."

"All right…I was being tactful. And yes, I would choose the jet if I was given the choice. But in this instance I wasn't…so that's that."

Suddenly, Joe became attentive to the plane's performance. Every now and then the Cessna was buffeted with a cross wind that threw it off course. The left wing lifted and they gained height, dropped back and then began climbing again. Joe tried to look nonchalant, as if the turbulence was a common occurrence, but Martin noticed he was gripping the control column tightly.

Just as suddenly everything returned to normal and they were back on course. Before Martin was able to ask what all that was about, Joe continued their discussion as if nothing had happened.

"So Martin…you've squeezed all my history out of me; what about you?"

"I like that," Martin rebuffed him. "I couldn't stop you after I asked about you coming to Australia."

"I got the impression you wanted me to take your mind off the flight."

Martin laughed. He felt relaxed again after the turbulence.

"All right I admit when we're having a conversation I feel at ease…okay?"

"So what sort of an engineer are you, if you're not an executive?"

"I suppose you could call me an expert in mining equipment. They call me in if a problem is too great for the resident working engineer, or they need to know if a particular machine can tackle a new type of terrain."

"That sounds important. Have you always been a mining engineer?"

"Good heavens, no; I had to learn like everyone else."

"So what led to that?"

Martin reached over to the tray above his legs and retrieved a bottle of water. He broke the seal and removed the cap and took a couple of mouthfuls. After returning the bottle he contemplated how to simplify what seemed to him a convoluted journey over several years.

"I have to go back to the early fifties when I took

an engineering course at Willesden Technical College in London. When I finally got my Diploma in Mechanical Engineering, my first apprenticeship was at Battersey Power Station working on turbines. Some years later, in 1993, we decided to immigrate to Australia, and as we had relatives in Melbourne, that's where we headed."

"So your first experience of the big country was Melbourne?"

"Yes…and I soon found out about the rivalry between Sydney and Melbourne so don't say anything. We thought it was pathetic."

"Sydney should have been the capital."

"What did I say?"

"Sorry…carry on."

They laughed, but not enough to stop Joe from checking his heading.

"Right…where was I…oh yes. I soon found out that the only power station in Victoria had more engineers than they wanted, a union problem, and they had different turbines than the out-of-date ones at Battersey. So I pottered around taking engineering jobs far below my diploma level, which I might add was not accepted in Australia, until I saw an advertisement in the paper, not unlike your father did."

"Isn't that funny?" Joe said. "It's the same all over again."

"Yes, that's true. This was for the same company, only they wanted to retrain experienced engineers. We had a big family discussion. The money they were offering after the training was out of this world. So that was it…Broome was our next destination. Oh, and another persuasive factor was that they were going to pay for all our removal expenses, even accommodation assistance until we found our new home. And as an added bonus, should I meet their requirements, help with our loan."

"Bloody Hell…no wonder you accepted the job."

Another turbulent spell seemed to push the plane sideways. Joe struggled with the control column, keeping an eye on the instruments all the time. He was concentrating on the heading. They were well off course, by the curses he was uttering under his breath. Then he relaxed; all was well again.

"Sorry, Martin," he eventually said. "I can't understand what's going on." He glanced out of the window in the direction of the gusts. "It looks pretty clear."

"It's not that storm front coming through?" Martín asked.

"No, Martin. It's only six-forty-five. It's behind us." He paused a moment as if he was going through the scenario. "Sometimes the weather is unfathomable despite all the information the meteorologists manage to get hold of. You can get a freak circumstance like a build-up of warm air that is forced out of the way by a cold front. This might be what we're experiencing now."

"Do you really think so?"

"I don't know what to think. Anyway, it's calm enough now. So…what made you decide to immigrate to Australia?"

Martin thought he had finished his history, but was happy to continue, if only to take his mind off the turbulence. "Oh, it was a number of things. Don't get me wrong. We loved living in England, especially in Yorkshire, but back then it was literally going to the dogs. The final clincher was the massive unemployment, the changing social structure and the constant rise in the cost of living; there seemed to be no end. What sort of an environment was that to bring up children?"

"How did you know it wasn't any different in Melbourne?"

"Actually, that was the changer. We have relatives in Melbourne. They came over in 1953 and they supplied us with mountains of information: newspapers, pieces copied from job ads and would you believe, they even sent us some junk mail, giving Kate an idea of the food prices. We were astonished. Our assets were going to be worth twice as much on the exchange rate, the cost of living was cheaper and we could buy a house outright with what we got for ours."

"And is that what you did?"

"No. The interest on a loan was so low compared to back home we took out a small mortgage and banked the rest in case of an emergency."

Martin was not sure Joe was listening to his last remark. He expected one of his terse quips. He had only known Joe for a short while, but in these close confines he had learned Joe seemed to have a sharp retort to just about everything. There was no content in it or any sign of malice; he was just trying to be clever.

He was back to checking the weather as the Cessna started climbing and falling again. Martin could see things were getting worse; he was gripping the control column just as he had done before.

"I don't like the look of that, Martin," he said with his head turned to the left.

Martin tried to see what was capturing his attention, but Joe's body was in the way and the window behind his seat was covered in rain drops streaking backwards. He had been so preoccupied with Joe that he had not noticed the rain.

"What can you see?"

"There's a nasty black cloud coming up on our tail."

The black cloud was the least of Joe's worries. Since he'd left Broome he'd been forced to make several heading corrections. The small light plane was being buffeted about by the sudden gusts they were experiencing and forcing the Cessna alarmingly off course. It was not equipped with a GPS system like the Lear Jet and all he had to rely on was his compass and some quick dead reckoning.

Joe knew if he brought out his heading calculator it would alert Martin to the possibility that something serious was brewing behind them, so he did the maths in his head. By all accounts he might be twenty kilometres off course and would have to choose a new heading. He decided he needed help from the wise guys in AMINCO; they would know what to do.

CHAPTER 3

After Philip Hastings escorted Kate off the premises he returned to his office to finish off the reports he was preparing for his American boss, Larry Kingston. It was an irritating task, as he listened to the metal window frames rattle each time the building was hit by a gust of wind. He began to wonder if there was any validity in Kate's fear that the storm was a little premature. He had no reason to doubt his meteorologist's earlier report, but at the same time there was something brewing outside.

Philip made his way to the operations room to check if there was a fresh weather update on the storm front. Other than the low hum of the monitors the room was deathly quiet. For obvious reasons operations was soundproofed against any extraneous sounds that might distract the technicians formulating flight plans, watching the weather over AMINCO's various sites and monitoring radio traffic.

Having experience in all these areas, Philip was the operations manager. It was his job to oversee the smooth running of the company's communications, safe transfer of workers and consultants to and from the sites and if it was possible, the administration of the departments and employees of AMINCO.

Philip was an easy-going boss; he had to know the sweet way to get the best out of his technicians. Not an easy task here in the laid-back atmosphere of Broome. He obviously had to maintain some level of officialdom, in his blue company shirt and grey trousers. Then again he would have looked silly meeting clients in a sweat shirt and shorts. That was the attire of the nerds, as they were called, in the controlled environment of their computerised haven. The computers had to be kept at a constant temperature and that was difficult in Broome's climate.

Philip crossed the room to the chart table where two figures were bent over a large map of Western Australia. They were on the side of the table adjacent to the top end, as it was referred to: the Timor Sea on the upper edge, the Indian Ocean down the left side and the irregular coastline of the north-western corner; with Broome on the left, the Durack Ranges on the right and the Sandy Desert below.

Their focus appeared to be on the Sandy Desert, particularly on the coloured strings radiating from the AMINCO headquarters. They were casting shadows across the table because of the overhead lights and Philip's arrival added another. They looked up at the man with greying hair; he could give each of them at least a decade.

Max Wendeler was closest to him. He was probably the most Australian of any of the company's personnel, despite his name, descending from Dutch settlers back in 1850. He still bore the distinctive blue eyes, blonde hair and Arian features, even if somewhat tanned from his sailing obsession. He was Philip's meteorologist, the obvious one to explain the present conundrum.

Then again his colleague, Bryce Chandler, may well become their saviour before the day is out. He is the introvert navigator of the team; also the tallest. Probably why he is bald with thinning hair and brilliant at what he does.

They had that look of collusion on their faces, as if they knew why Philip was there and were in the process of coming up with an answer to suit him.

"I know that you're pretty-well protected from the elements in here, but have either of you got any idea what's happening outside?"

"We've heard," Max replied. "Elsie rang through a few minutes ago."

"Have you got an explanation or is this another storm you missed?"

"It's a cyclone," Max nonchalantly advised him.

"A cyclone? What are you talking about?"

"This isn't a cyclone, Philip…it's the original storm front. The cyclone is in the Timor Sea. It just sprang up out of nowhere and it's pushing energy into our ordinary storm. The cyclone's like a vacuum cleaner; it's come up against this cold front and it's trying to push it out of the way, and in the process it's changing our storm's course and pumping it full of extra energy."

"Describe the energy for me," Philip asked.

Bryce jumped in. He was the mathematician of the team and he had already worked it out. "We got confirmation last night that a grade two storm was heading for Broome at about 100km/h. Everything was going to schedule; the storm would arrive over Broome around eight or eight-thirty, which meant it would be well behind our flight to Site 21. Then this cyclone sprang up suddenly and it's heading west along the Timor Sea. We're not sure yet, but it looks as if it's merging with our storm. If that's true, we have an out-of-control monster travelling at an estimated 200km/h. And it's following the same path as our plane."

"And it's going to get there faster," Philip commented.

"It's already arrived," a voice from the radio section shouted.

Josh Mackenzie was the hermit among the bunch. His array of radio equipment was tucked away in the far corner of the building for fear of interference from their computers and long-range weather devices. He was so wrapped up in his own little world no one paid much attention to his part in the overall picture. Not until they wanted to communicate with one of their pilots or, like now, monitor the radio traffic coming in from distant sites and commuting planes.

Another reason for his reclusive nature was the difficulty understanding his thick Scottish accent. It made little difference to his credentials when he applied for the position way back when AMINCO first set up their headquarters in Broome. They were looking for more than his ability to communicate; which he could do when he needed to. They were looking for a radio operator with experience in the desert and his service career in North Africa clinched that.

Philip turned his head and stared down the room into the darkness. "What's that, Josh?" he shouted.

"I've got ALPHA, TANGO, ZULU on...he sounds upset."

"Who's that, Josh?"

"It's Joe...heading for Site 21."

"Oh, damn...put him on speaker, will you?"

There was a loud click and Joe's curses could be heard clearly. "What the hell's going on?" he ranted. "I thought this storm was two hours away."

"Calm down, Joe. It's Philip and I've got you on speaker."

"Oh…hello Philip. What's happening?"

"I'll let Bryce explain. We're still trying to work things out."

"Okay…what am I in for, Bryce?"

"Joe…calm down and listen. Everything I briefed you on last night was still in place until after you took off. What has changed is a cyclone has popped up in the Timor Sea and altered everything."

"How come?" Joe questioned.

"You've got a 200km/h monster wagging the 100km/h tail of your storm. It's pumping massive energy into what was only a moderate wind and some rain."

"I can see it racing up on me, Bryce. What do I do?"

"Get out of there. If you can't fly around it and get back on your heading later, climb above it. How high are you now?"

Joe checked his instruments again: "Twenty-three thousand feet."

"Oh well, you've got plenty of leeway. Take her up to five thousand and see if that gets you out of harm's way."

"It's Philip again, Joe, how's your passenger?"

"He doesn't look too good."

When Kate opened her front door after leaving the AMINCO airstrip she saw an explosion of orange light streaming through the glass patio doors across the family room and into the hall. By now it was bucketing down outside and the terrible thought of what it was like in the small Cessna caused her to stop and look back towards the Indian Ocean.

It was six-forty-five. She had plenty of time to have a shower and a hot drink before she had to leave for work. She had to be quick. Jennifer, her daughter, would be up soon and she would commandeer the bathroom right up till she had to set off for her Chemistry class at the university. Kate contemplated ringing Philip but quickly abandoned the idea, thinking it was too early. This bad weather might only be the cloud rushing in front of the storm like Philip had explained.

Following her shower Kate saw to her make-up, changed into her light-grey working suit, collected her briefcase and went down to the kitchen. She had hardly put the kettle on when she heard Jennifer moving about upstairs. Then the hot pipes in the larder began to rattle as she ran her shower and the kettle popped.

41

Ten minutes later Jennifer walked into the kitchen and dropped her satchel down by the door as she did every morning. Kate glanced up at her from the edge of her mug of tea. Jennifer looked different somehow. She looked too casual for a girl in her first year at university.

There were no uniforms as such anymore. Once you went to university it seemed anything was the order of the day. Jennifer was comfortable in a tee-shirt and jeans, a cardigan or jumper if it was cold, but that was not what had Kate scrutinising Jennifer's appearance. There was definitely something different this morning.

"Good morning Mum," Jennifer said, walking around the table, checking the kettle and switching it on. She then prepared her breakfast of cereal and a sprinkling of blueberries and pineapple chunks and placed them on the table opposite Kate before she returned to make her mug of tea. She brought the mug and the jug of milk back to the table. All the time Kate had said nothing.

"Good morning Mum," she said again, sitting down.

Kate broke from her stare. "Oh, sorry. Good morning dear."

Jennifer looked across to her mother. "What?"

"There's something different about you this morning and I can't fathom what it is," Kate said, continuing to examine her daughter.

Jennifer ran her fingers through her light-brown hair, teasing the shallow waves that fell onto her shoulders.

"Your hair isn't straight anymore," Kate said.

Jennifer waggled her fingers again. "*And,*" she emphasised, "you've changed the colour."

"No, Mum. I've added highlights. Don't you think it makes my hair look more golden? You should see it in the sunlight. It actually radiates."

An expression of relief crossed Kate's face. She had no idea what was different, but the little change Jennifer had made to her hair was fine with her. "You look beautiful, dear. I only hope this isn't going to entice the boys."

Jennifer laughed, "Oh Mum…they don't need any enticement."

"I beg your pardon," Kate said over her mug of tea.

There was a quiet moment as Jennifer got on with her breakfast and Kate pondered on a classroom of boys bursting with testosterone. It was a fleeting fear that was quickly superseded by the rain pounding on the kitchen window.

"Did I hear you get up early or was it a dream?" Jennifer asked.

"It wasn't a dream, dear. Your dad forgot to order a taxi to take him to the AMINCO airstrip, so I had to drive him there."

"I bet that was interesting. What was it like? I bet it was one of those mysterious hangars at the airport," Jennifer said, finishing her breakfast.

"That was the mistake I made, thinking it was at the airport. But it wasn't. It was nine kilometres outside the suburbs. It was quite big, what I saw of it. A little run down, but adequate for their needs."

Jennifer glanced at the clock on the wall but then turned her attention to the rain still falling in sheets. "I'm going to get soaked on my bike," she said.

"Don't worry. I'll take you."

"Thanks, Mum. We don't have to leave so early then."

Jennifer helped Kate clear the table and they wandered into the family room. There were no bright orange rays from the sun like earlier; they had been enveloped by a grey overcast sky and she walked to the patio doors and stared out at the rain.

Jennifer dropped into an easy chair and watched Kate pace back and forth in front of the mass of glass, looking this way and that, shaking her head.

"What's wrong? You've been on edge ever since I got up."

"It's this weather."

"What about it? It's the wet season. It rains most of the time in the wet season. It's never bothered you before."

Kate glanced at her watch. It was seven. "It wasn't supposed to come through for an hour, and look at it! Your dad won't even be halfway there yet."

Jennifer suddenly looked concerned. "What are you talking about?"

Kate realised Jennifer had no idea how her dad travelled to his job. She was never involved in the life he led outside the home and the recreational activities the family was involved in. He never thought it was necessary. She had her life with her friends and that was all right by him. Now if his son, Adam was here, instead of on the other side of Australia studying to be a doctor, he would have told him everything. Engineering was a male enterprise. Girls were not interested in smelly machines.

"Your dad didn't think you would be interested in his job. Yes, you knew he was an engineer, but that was the limit of your knowledge. He is a mining engineer and he has to travel hundreds of kilometres to isolated sites in the desert and work on massive dangerous machines."

"I thought he flew off to a city somewhere. I thought he was a consultant."

"He is, dear, but he doesn't fly off in a large airliner like the ones we go on holiday in. That's why he takes off from the AMINCO airstrip. If he's lucky he'll get a lift in a Lear Jet. If he isn't, he has to make do with a small Cessna."

"And what is it today?" Jennifer asked.

Kate looked back at the weather. "It's the Cessna."

"What? In this weather?"

"Now you know why I'm so anxious. This lot wasn't supposed to come through for an hour yet. What must they be going through?"

CHAPTER 4

As soon as Joe switched Martin's headset off he knew something was wrong. He could see by his body language that Joe was irritated about something and it was easy to guess that it was about the approaching dark mass behind them.

Martin tried to stay calm. He was not going to give in to his habit of predicting a situation before it happened. This time he was going to wait for Joe to tell him in his own good time. He glanced in his direction. Joe's lips were still moving, with short respites as he listened to the response, his free hand gesturing flamboyantly as the Italian temperament dictated.

There was a loud click and Martin knew he was back in touch. He remained calm and silent, waiting for Joe to collect his thoughts. Once again Joe had both hands firmly gripping the control column. Then he turned and faced Martin.

"It's not good news," was all he could say.

Martin had to draw the information out of him.

"Well, are you going to tell me?"

"Have you ever seen a storm drain turn into a torrent when an inlet suddenly dumps its contents from a higher source?"

"Of course. What does that mean?"

"Well, that's the situation behind us."

"What situation behind us?" Martin exclaimed impatiently.

"Believe it or not, that mass heading for our tail is the storm that wasn't supposed to arrive for another hour or so. Apparently a nasty cyclone suddenly appeared off Papua New Guinea, headed west along the Timor Sea and bumped into our storm at 200km/h. You add that to the original 100km/h and you've got one hell of a monster heading our way."

"If this cyclone is bigger and faster, why doesn't it just push past and continue on its way?" Martin questioned reasonably.

"It did…but I gather from our whiz-kids, that in doing so it not only altered our storm's course, it pumped masses of energy into it as it passed.'

"So where does that leave us?"

"Apart from being behind us, as I keep repeating, its course from the Indian Ocean was south-east towards the Durack Ranges, across the Sandy Desert and on to Alice Springs; that was if it had enough blow left. Now it's been turned due south, straight for us and it's travelling around 200km/h."

"I thought we were travelling at 230km/h. That should keep us ahead of it."

"You would think so...but don't forget I've been climbing all the time. When you climb, you not only lose speed, you lose distance as well."

"So eventually this thing is going to catch up to us?"

"By Jove, he's got it," Joe replied sarcastically.

Martin didn't like the way Joe was taking his own anxiety out on him. He was the expert in this situation, so it was up to him to get them out of it."

"So what do you intend doing?" Martin shouted.

"All right...all right...I'm sorry. Everything is under control. Operations advised me to climb above the storm front if I couldn't fly around it. And by the looks of it down there I have no option but to climb to 5000 feet."

Joe pulled back on the control column and the Cessna started to climb.

Martin turned to his window and looked down below the wing. What was once a wispy collection of scattered cloud and open patches allowing a fleeting glimpse of the landscape they were flying over was now a dense mass of turbulence. It was as if the storm front had suddenly rushed into the space the small plane had vacated when it left 2000 feet for its objective of 5000.

It was like being on a rollercoaster; bouncing off the undulating clouds. It was a boiling mass below them. The earlier 1000 feet ceiling had been surpassed and it felt as if there was no limit as Joe held the control column close to his lap.

Joe's earlier moderate climb over a period of time to save fuel and relieve Martin of his anxiety was now a rapid climb; one that would get them out of trouble as quickly as possible; which it did. When the Cessna reached the designated height Joe levelled out and they found themselves in a different world. Martin was astonished. They were flying just above the cloud layer with a massive blue sky above; the first clear sky since they'd taken off.

"Isn't that a lot better?" Joe exclaimed, sounding a little surprised.

Martin had to agree, still looking out of the window. The monster had reached its limit. He was looking down on a miasma of swirling, bubbling froth. There seemed no break in its relentless passage across the Sandy Desert and it seemed drawn to the plane's heading, with no sign of weakening.

The atmosphere in the cockpit had changed dramatically. The tension had gone and a sense of normality had returned, although Martin was not completely sure they had seen the last of their nightmare. Insufficient information was always his nemesis. He needed to control the situation to feel confident, despite the expertise of the person in charge of the situation. It was important to him.

Joe was playing with his instruments again, only this time he was more preoccupied with a pad of numbers. A calculator came to mind, but Martin was sure it was not as simple as that; it looked far more complicated.

"What are you doing now, Joe?" Martin asked, hoping for a straight answer.

Joe continued for a moment without replying until he stopped biting his lip and relaxed back in his seat. "I've been trying to sort out a little problem we have."

"What? Another?"

"Afraid so…during the early part of the storm I noticed we were being blown off course. Nothing unusual…I just kept correcting the inaccuracy and brought us back on our heading each time. Now… with this new turbulence, I find we are seriously off course and it's not as simple as turning into the proper heading; to do so I would lose height and you know what that would mean."

"I thought operations said you could change the heading when you've cleared the storm. What's different?"

"They were assuming I was going to fly around the

storm; not climb above it or have to fight this side wind. I'm so far out now, the further I travel on this heading will mean I will have to make up fifty or a hundred kilometres."

"Oh Joe…I can't understand this aviation lingo. I trust you've worked something out…just do it before anything else crops up."

"Sorry, Martin. I got the impression you needed to be kept in the loop. Just relax. I'm going to get us back on our heading…I just need to do it in stages."

Joe eased the control column to the left and the Cessna's left wing dipped slightly putting the plane into a gentle turn. At the same time Martin watched the altimeter needle drop below 5000 feet. As it did so the plane caught the upper limits of the storm and began shaking dramatically. Joe straightened the control column again, pulled back to gain height and the shaking stopped.

Joe turned his head. "See what I mean. That was only a one-degree change."

By the time Joe had carried out a further three of the manoeuvres to get the plane back on the correct heading for Site 21, each time putting the plane through an agonising shaking, Martin noticed it had gone seven-thirty.

"I hate to distract you, Joe, but shouldn't we be arriving at the site by now?"

"I know…I've been keeping my eye on the distance we've travelled. By my calculations, bearing in mind we lost a lot of forward speed and distance while I was climbing and fighting this wind, we have about a fifteen-minute leeway. The trouble is, I need to see the landscape. I've flown this route so many times I hardly need a heading to fly by if I'm in the right area."

Martin glanced out of his window. It was something he had avoided for some time, but to his eye it looked a lot friendlier. "Is it wishful thinking on my part, or do the clouds look as if they've lost their turbulence?"

"You're right…I thought that the last time I side-slipped," Joe agreed. "What do you say? Do you feel like having a go?"

"If you have to see the landscape we have no choice."

"Okay. I'll do it gently. A couple of side-slips should do. Let's just pray the cloud base stops around 1000 feet."

Martin could see by the way Joe stiffened his posture in his seat that this manoeuvre was going to test his expertise and he did the same. He wasn't sure what Joe was doing exactly, but he noticed his knees move up and down as he turned the control column left. Martin expected the plane to turn, but it did not, the wing tip dropped and the plane simply slid off to the left. As it did the control column began shuddering, but thankfully the plane maintained a smooth descent until Joe reversed the controls and they began sliding to the right.

Martin returned his attention to the clouds they were now flying through. They seemed tame in comparison to earlier. They had lost their bite.

Everything was going to plan and for some reason Martin felt calm and that somehow they were going to come out of this. They would break out of the clouds and Joe would miraculously know exactly where he was.

Then suddenly there was the loudest bang imaginable. All hell let loose. Joe was struggling to stabilise the plane's altitude as he checked what had happened. Warning lights flashed threateningly as the plane careered out of control.

Then they saw the mass of blood and feathers pressed up against the windscreen.

Lumps of shattered bird carcasses broke away from the windscreen as Joe frantically joggled the throttle trying to clear the dead bodies free of the propeller and the air vents into the engine. He kept his head while Martin lost his, screaming, "Oh my God…Is this it? Are we going to drop out of the sky?"

"Quiet…for Christ's sake," Joe shouted. "We're still at 3000 feet."

He switched on the radio as he struggled with the control column and called. "AMINCO CENTRAL. MAYDAY...MAYDAY. VICTOR HOTEL... ALPHA, TANGO, ZULU. BIRD-STRIKE...BIRD-STRIKE."

Suddenly the engine started to splutter. Joe pumped the throttle to clear it, but it was no good. The engine coughed and finally stalled. There was no response. Then the instruments died. There was nothing – not even a warning light.

"What does that mean?" Martin questioned Joe.

"I don't know Martin...for Christ's sake...I don't know everything."

"You should know more than me...you're the pilot."

"Sorry, Martin. This has never happened to me before. The battery should be enough to keep the radio active... but it's dead. Even the emergency back-up's dead."

"We'll be dead too if you don't do something."

Joe tried to start the engine again, but there was no response.

"Think yourself lucky you're not in the Lear Jet you like so much. It would have dropped like a stone. Not the Cessna. She can hang on the wind."

Martin suddenly realised they were not dropping. The Cessna was rising and falling with the wind like Joe said. It had become a bird, just like the ones that put them in this position. "You're right," Martin said. "Can you fly her?"

"Of course I can. It was a long time ago, but I still remember when my instructor switched the engine off at 2000 feet and told me to glide the plane down to 1000 feet and start the engine again."

"And you did?"

"I'm still here, aren't I?"

Martin nodded as Joe stiffened himself for yet another series of side-slips.

In hindsight some might think it was coincidence or even bad luck when a flock of Red Knots had left the Arctic, curved their way down towards Siberia, onward to Japan and Indonesia on their migration in time for a winter residence on the Eight Mile Beach in Western Australia. The bad luck was their path to avoid the storm coincided with the Cessna's. It is called a 'Bird Strike'. The impact was so sudden the birds would not have known what happened.

Joe was still side-slipping without any indication of how high he was when suddenly the Cessna dropped out of the clouds. Surprised, he immediately levelled the plane and attempted to ascertain how high they were.

From his experience, judging the horizon relative to the lower edge of the wings, he guessed the plane was at 1000 feet, give or take a hundred or so. The trouble was there was little wind at this height to give him lift and the landscape below was rushing up to meet them at an alarming rate.

"We seem to be dropping a lot faster now," Martin said.

Joe shot Martin an angry glance.

"In the cloud we had some density to keep us aloft. Down here the air is affected by the heat coming off the desert."

"I once read that birds use the hot thermals to give them lift."

"That's correct...that's what I'm looking for now."

Joe began a slow circular route, which, if nothing else, brought him closer to the ground. He was getting anxious until suddenly he picked up a thermal. They could feel it. It lifted the Cessna dramatically. It actually soared several hundred feet putting Joe in a better position to survey the landscape for a good landing sight.

He traversed the thermal in an elliptical circuit to judge its capacity to give him a five- or six-hundred-metre landing site. He knew, if he was lucky, and the thermal lasted all the way to the ground, he would be able to glide down to the surface like a magnificent eagle and land safely.

He found the site, made one more circuit and turned into the thermal.

"Brace yourself," he warned Martin. "Here we go."

"I hope you can remember how to glide this thing."

"No problem. It's just like riding a bike."

"But you're flying a plane."

They laughed and Joe eased the control column forward.

Martin kept quiet as Joe surveyed the terrain within his manoeuvrable space. He was used to this country. He could read it like a book, as he often did, imagining one day he might have to land on it; not expecting for one moment he would actually have to. As he pointed out to Martin earlier, it was scrub country: a mass of spinifex clusters with the occasional acacia shrub and small trees to give shade to the varied Sandy Desert marsupials.

On his second circuit he noticed a narrow band of clear ground with only a scant covering of spinifex. It looked like one of the many ancient riverbeds that were prolific in the northern part of the desert. He was gambling it would have a firm gravel base with a shallow layer of sand covering it. The last thing he wanted was undulating soft sand.

By now his choices were limited. He had only a hundred metres to position the Cessna in line with the bed, take advantage of the thermal to drop into a stall attitude and gently place her down on the ground. The last thing he wanted was a fast landing.

Everything was dropping into place. He was now

down to fifty metres, turning into the narrow channel when suddenly he lost the thermal. He lost the lift he needed to glide the Cessna into a smooth landing. He was still too fast.

Joe tried to lift the nose to put the plane into a stall. It was a risky manoeuvre that failed miserably. Instead he made a three-point landing: all three wheels at the same time; at a speed far beyond their capability.

The nose wheel went first, buckling under the body and dipping the propeller into the riverbed. That slowed the plane down dramatically, but in doing so, it slewed the plane sideways, snapping the left wheel and digging the wing into the ground. Instead of allowing the harness to do its job, Martin instinctively braced himself with his right arm against the doorframe. His forearm took the full impact.

The Cessna continued sliding sideways along the riverbed for another twenty metres or so until it finally stopped in a massive cloud of dust. It was so fine it seemed ages before it eventually settled and Martin could see out of his window. His head was spinning. His body was leaning in Joe's direction, still hanging in his harness, and he could taste his own blood in his mouth.

At first he thought he was all right until he tried

to turn to see if Joe was conscious. Something was wrong with his arm. A sudden, excruciating pain exploded in his wrist and ran all the way up to his shoulder. He was familiar with this pain. It reminded him of the time he'd broken his leg.

"Joe...are you all right... Joe?" Martin called out.

It was Martin's right arm that was injured, so he stretched his left arm out towards Joe's seat. He made contact with Joe's arm, shook it and heard a low rasping sound. Joe was alive. He coughed a few times and continued rasping.

Martin tried again. "Joe," he shouted, shaking his arm.

"Oh God...don't do that, for Christ's sake!" Joe called out.

"How bad are you?"

"Heaven knows. My whole chest feels as if it's caved in."

"Don't say that, Joe...how can I check you out with a broken arm?"

Joe let out a rasping laugh, coughing in the process. "Everything was going to plan. If only the thermal had stayed with us right to the ground it would have been a perfect landing. And now we're stuck out here without a radio."

Martin relaxed his body to ease the pain and let out a long sigh, looking down at the watch on his wrist. "We should have arrived by now. The warning bells will be ringing. They'll be sending out a helicopter to look for us."

"And where are they going to look? We're off course... Remember?"

CHAPTER 5

When Joe's channel remained silent, they presumed he had climbed out of trouble and they would not hear from him again until he had put the storm behind him. On hearing the Lear Jet had just landed, Philip left the operations room and made his way to the executive lounge adjacent to the main hanger, expecting Larry Kingston to be disembarking and waiting to be brought up to date on the current situation.

Only the pilot was there. He had poured himself a stiff whiskey from the mini-bar in the kitchen and was casually sipping it in an easy chair when Philip arrived. "If you're looking for the boss, he made straight for the sleep-over."

"What for?" Philip questioned the exhausted pilot.

"As you can imagine we had a hell of a flight from the top end. I was trying to outrun a cyclone. Just managed to beat it here; in the process scaring the pants off His God Almighty. He rushed off into the private room over there."

"For how long? Did he say?" Philip asked.

The pilot finished his drink and went back to the bar, looking as if he was about to pour himself another. "I have no idea. He just rushed off."

"Was it bad?" Philip continued. "I've got a plane up there at the moment."

"Then I feel sorry for him. I hope he's flying in the opposite direction."

"So do I," Philip replied; then turned on his heels and left.

After listening to the pilot's encounter with the cyclone, instead of returning to his office to wait for his boss, Philip decided to return to the operations room to warn everyone to be ready for Larry Kingston's grilling on the storm.

Philip's eccentric technicians were not used to dealing with company 'Big Wigs' and he made every effort to separate the two. However, since Larry Kingston apparently had just experienced his first storm of this category, he was bound to head straight for the operations room as soon as he recovered.

Josh Mackenzie was waiting for Philip as soon as he came through the door, and there was a look of apprehension on his face that stopped Philip in his tracks.

"All right. What's happened now, Josh?"

"Sorry, boss…we've got a Mayday."

"What?" Philip shouted, disturbing the other two, who were busy bent over the table studying the chart of the area where Joe went down.

"Two hours was not enough of a window," Max said in his defence.

"What did Joe say?" Philip finished his outcry.

Josh joined Philip as he walked over to the table, "It was only short. Not enough information for us to get a bearing on him."

"What did he say, Josh?" Philip questioned a little calmer.

Josh lifted a piece of paper to read from. "After his call sign, all he had time for was: 'BIRD-STRIKE… BIRD-STRIKE', and then nothing but static.

"Is that all? No heading, height or status."

"No, boss…and no more calls since. They'll be down by now."

"Don't say that. They could still be in the air. Their radio could be out."

"Philip," Bryce interrupted. "It's a bird-strike. What chance would they have of surviving that? They have to be on the ground. Joe's a good pilot. If the engine stalled he would glide the Cessna down. We just have to find them."

Philip made no comment. His mind was

absorbing Bryce's scenario as he moved closer to the table and scanned the situation. He could see they had already laid out a pattern for the search planes to follow. None had left yet without his permission and a complete agreement that their assumptions were correct.

Bryce could see the determined expression on Philip's face and since the layout was based on his calculations, he decided to take responsibility for the search.

"I haven't finished my calculations yet, Philip, but this is how we see it."

In the interim since the message had come through, they had cleared the chart of the strings indicating the storm's path and substituted a sheet of clear plastic, which they had already started drawing lines on in different colours. Bryce started to explain.

"Okay, Philip. This blue line from the AMINCO airstrip leading to Site 21 is the heading Joe was to take under normal conditions. Now I calculated by the time of Joe's first call, about the state of the weather, he would be about here," Bryce said, pointing to where the red line started. "That's considering he was travelling at his nominal speed of 230km/h. So...using that point as a radius, I calculated the wind would have changed his heading by approximately four degrees up to the point when we received his Mayday call." He placed a piece of string at the radius point and drew a curve from the last contact.

"That's all very well, Bryce, but does it pinpoint where Joe is?"

"No, Philip. This is not where Joe is…it's only the most likely search area."

"I see. Okay, continue."

"Right. Up to the end of the red line we can be pretty certain of Joe's course. It's this bit at the end of the red line that's uncertain. If we imagine he added another four degrees to his heading when he climbed to 5000 feet, I reckon that would put him about here when he had the bird-strike." Bryce pointed to the Mayday marker. "From then on I reckon you could add another two degrees."

Philip studied the pattern Bryce had laid out on the plastic sheet. "That's very good, Bryce. That gives us a six-degree search pattern from the original heading," he said, still studying the area. "There's just one thing that worries me…how far would you guess he drifted before he crashed? I mean I doubt if he just dropped out of the sky. We could be talking about another twenty kilometres from that height."

Bryce never got the chance to answer. The door crashed open and Larry Kingston entered the room with his usual flamboyance. A Texas-born American, he came across as a self-confident individual who knew only one code: the survival of the fittest. Amongst like-minded businessmen he was a dominant personality, but put him up against intelligent characters, regardless of whether they were introvert or extrovert like himself and he buckled.

He was one of those millionaires who bragged constantly about how he dragged himself out of poverty against all odds, imagining it was that alone that marked him as an alpha male. Individuals like Philip, Bryce and Max frightened him, but he would never admit it; instead he would hide behind his position and the flamboyant facade he assumed.

Philip was always suspicious of his English name. His dark hair, sallow complexion and brown eyes pointed to a South American, Spanish heritage. But regardless of that he was always immaculately dressed.

You could hear a pin drop when he walked out of the shadows into the lighted area of the chart table where all three of his nightmares stood together.

"Okay, you guys...what's going on?"

Philip turned to face him, "I hear you had a rough journey," he said.

"Worst I've had in a long time...I can tell you," he replied strongly as he parted the group and moved closer to the table. "So... What's going on?"

He was oblivious of what was in front of him.

"That storm you caught the edge of has brought down one of our planes," Philip said, directing his attention to the area they were studying.

"I mean, what's going on with Site 21…has he arrived yet?"

"Martin Dexter's on the missing plane."

"You mean no one's fixing my problem. I'm losing 250,000 dollars a day."

They just looked at the man.

"What about the two men in the plane? They could be dead for all we know," Philip shouted, trembling with rage at the callousness of the man.

Kingston stared at him with a wild, open-eyed expression, until his glare changed to a more composed smile. "Look, Philip…yes, it's a tragedy and I pray the men are okay, but I've got a company to run, while you and your guys have got to search for that plane. It's what we do. We can't get at cross purposes on this."

In the wider sense Philip could understand the man's single-mindedness. That's how he's got to where he is today. He is happy with the decisions he has to make, but one day it will drag him down.

"You don't have to worry, Larry; I've already transferred Eddie Kent from the Northern Territory site. He was just about to return anyway."

"Now that wasn't so hard, was it, Philip? That's all I

wanted to know. I've got to report to Hubbard shortly and you know what he's like; he fires you first, and then asks questions."

"Everything is under control, Larry."

"That's not good enough, Philip. When is he going to arrive?"

"In this weather he'll arrive when he arrives."

"God damn it, Philip. I'll be up to a million on this job before I know it."

"That's how the cookie crumbles. Is that what you Americans say?"

Kingston let out a gasp. "I'm not in the mood for jokes, Philip."

He glanced at his watch. His call to the States was due about now and he needed answers. He turned back to the chart they were studying as if he knew what he was looking at.

"Do you want an overview?" Philip asked. He leaned on the table and nodded.

"Bryce...will you take Larry through your plan?" Philip said.

"Okay, Mr Kingston. The blue line represents the heading from here to Site 21, which I am using as the control." He pointed to the first break. "This is where the pilot made his first call about the weather conditions. The red line is where I calculate he might have gained a four-degree variance when I advised him to climb to 5000 feet above the storm." He moved on to the next marker along the red line. "This is where he had the bird-strike…"

"Bird-strike…I thought it was the storm that brought him down?" Larry interrupted, shaking his head.

"Indirectly it did," Bryce continued. "When he felt it safe to return to his original height he ran into a flock of birds doing the same thing. They were all trying to get round the storm."

Larry grunted his partial acceptance of Bryce's explanation. "Very well…what happened then?"

"We received a Mayday call, which was terminated before the pilot was able to give us his heading and there's been no response since," Bryce continued.

"And you think he's gone down in this area?" Larry said, pointing his finger at the small arc drawn across the red line.

"That's my best guess for the search planes. We can send one out along the original heading as far as the arc in the off-chance he managed to get back, and another along the red line. We'll know more when the first plane arrives."

Philip could see Larry was looking for something else to say when the phone rang. Max picked it up, listened to the other end and then, covering the mouthpiece, he relayed the message to Larry. "That was

Elsie, sir; your call from America is coming through now. You can take it in the VIP lounge."

"Right, thanks. Er…it's Max?"

"Yes, sir," he replied, putting the phone down.

Larry Kingston left the room. He made no closing remarks, just nodded his head and left. Philip guessed he was about to put on his other hat. He was about to eat craw, as they say in America; but this time in private.

"That's the last we'll see of him for a while," Philip said, rubbing his hands together. He checked his watch. "Good heavens…it's eight-twenty already. That idiot has lost us valuable time. Right…by the time you get the planes away we've got about eight hours of daylight left…plenty of time to test your theory, Bryce. Max…you check the weather and make sure we've got a decent window."

They both nodded as Philip turned to leave, "What are you going to do?" Bryce questioned as Philip reached the door.

"I'm going back to my office and will contact CASA. I'll let them know we have things under control at the present, but if we have no luck by the end of the day, they can take over tomorrow."

Max screwed up his face. "I don't fancy the Aviation people taking over just yet. Surely we can give it a couple of days."

Philip considered his point. "Okay, Max...two days. Oh, and have a word with Josh. You know how he gets upset when he's left out of things."

As Philip reached his office he leaned into Elsie's room and called out to her, "Is 'you know who' still talking to America?"

She looked up from her desk with a smile on her face. "Yes, he is. I listened in on the first few minutes and Hubbard doesn't seem happy."

"Good. It's about time Larry got some of his own medicine. Can you get me CASA on the phone?"

"All right...are you in your office?"

"I shall be in two seconds," Philip said, as he stepped through his door.

As Elsie picked up the phone and was about to dial CASA's number she heard a loud shriek from Philip's office.

"Oh my God. Damn it, damn it!" he shouted.

Elsie rushed through thinking he had tripped, but he was sitting on the corner of his desk. "What's wrong?" she cried.

"Oh Elsie...I forgot to ring Kate. I should have contacted her straightaway when she was at home."

"Where will she be now?"

"She starts at the Education Council at eight o'clock."

"How do you know that?"

"Oh, it was something Martin said about the strange hours the civil servants work; something about being in line with the school hours. Oh hell… that bloody Larry Kingston distracted me. Going on about losing money."

"Wasn't he bothered about the missing plane?"

"Not in the least…he was more concerned about who was going to take Martin's place at Site 21. And I can't ring her. I have to tell her face to face."

"Look…you can't leave now, not when he's here and you have to talk to CASA. Why don't I go and speak to her? It might be better coming from a woman."

Philip's not-so-keen expression mellowed into one of compliance. He had no choice, assessing the situation. Not with Larry Kingston about.

"Very well…thank you, Elsie. You get off to the Education complex and I'll contact CASA. Bring her back here. She's sure to want to know all the details and what we're doing to find her husband."

"Okay…leave it to me," she replied, turning back to her office. She grabbed her coat and car keys and left, waving to him as she passed his room.

The rain had stopped and the dense clouds had broken up into patches while the offending cyclone had disappeared and was heading north towards Indonesia. Elsie entered the airlock of the circular door, passed through into the spacious lobby and walked across to the receptionist sitting behind a huge desk.

"I would like to see Mrs Dexter, please," Elsie asked.

The attractive girl looked at her, as receptionists do, saying, "Do you have an appointment?" This surprised Elsie. She had no idea Kate was that important.

"No, I don't. This is an emergency."

"What sort of an emergency?"

"There's only one type of emergency," Elsie shouted.

The girl jumped, looked flustered and picked up the phone.

"I have a woman down here who wants to speak to Mrs Dexter. She says it's an emergency...I know...I asked that."

Elsie snatched the phone out of the girls hand and spoke into the mouthpiece, "Who am I speaking to?" she shouted in a frustrated manner.

"I'm Mrs Dexter's secretary. What's this about an emergency?"

"I have to speak to Mrs Dexter. It's about her husband, Martin Dexter. And don't say anything to her until I see her."

"All right...take the lift to the third floor...I'll be waiting for you."

"Thank you," Elsie said politely to the girl as she handed her the phone.

Elsie followed the secretary's directions and she

was waiting for her outside the lift. "What is your name? I need to introduce you."

Kate had arrived in a sad state. She had battled through the pouring rain to deliver Jennifer to her university and then she'd gone on to her office. The sun was shining through her east-facing window, making her feel alive again. She was less concerned with Martin's welfare and ready to tackle the day's workload.

There was a buzz on her intercom. "Yes, Susan?"

"I have a Mrs Danzig here. It's urgent."

"Danzig...I don't recall that name."

"She says it's urgent."

"If it's urgent, show her in."

Kate's secretary showed Elsie into the room. As soon as Kate saw her and recognised her as Philip's secretary, her jaw dropped. There could only be one reason she had been sent to her office. Something must be wrong.

Elsie moved into Kate's office and closed the door behind her, despite the secretary wanting it left open. She tried to look casual.

"What's wrong, Elsie?" Kate cried, getting out of her seat and walking around her desk. "What's happened...please tell me."

"Philip has asked me to bring you back to the

airstrip. In the storm we lost contact with Martin's plane. There was a bird-strike. When the plane went silent on our radio, we tried to get them back. There was no response."

Kate sat back on the corner of her desk and clasped her face. "Oh God…he knew there was something wrong when he got up. What are you doing to find him?"

"That's why we want you at the airstrip. So Philip can explain."

The secretary heard Kate scream and rushed into her office. She was sobbing in Elsie's arms. She made a move to console Kate, but Elsie intervened.

"Not now," she said. "I need you to contact the appropriate people and tell them Mrs Dexter's husband has been in an accident and I have to take her to the company where he works."

"He was flying out this morning. I heard Mrs Dexter telling a colleague. Does that mean his plane has crashed?"

"Not a word about this…understand; he's just had an accident. We don't want the press getting hold of this. You're the only one who knows, so I'll know where to come if I see it on the news."

"I won't say a word…I promise."

Elsie turned back into the room and could see Kate was about to scream, but was trying so hard to maintain her composure, save for a tear running down her cheek.

"Martin knew something was wrong this morning. I wouldn't listen to him. I thought it was just because he didn't want to fly in that small plane."

"Kate...he's only out of contact at this moment. He's probably in the desert somewhere trying to get the radio working."

Kate hardly heard a word. She looked up at Elsie and said, "I should have listened to him...he knew this was going to happen."

CHAPTER 6

Joe's rasping gasps for breath subsided into a rhythmic wheeze; he had drifted back into unconsciousness. Martin tried to move his arm to see how bad it was. The pain sharpened his senses. He looked around the hazy cockpit. In the silence of the aftermath, he took notice of its layout for the first time. Nothing appeared to be working; the instruments were dead and every loose object, large and small, was strewn about the interior.

Then his senses were assaulted by all manner of strange anomalies; a pungent smell was hanging in the air; it was alien to anything around him. It reminded him of the smell when he blew a fuse trying to install a light above the balcony. It was not part of the dust that also hung in the air and coated the surfaces; it reminded him of burning Bakelite. The dust was everywhere; covering his face and hands.

He licked his lips and immediately his mouth was full of grit.

He reached out for the water bottle and screamed in pain. He forgot for that instant that his hand was paralysed.

"What's going on?" Joe called out, just coming to again.

"Oh Joe...I knew something bad was going to happen this morning."

"Rubbish," he muttered. "You were mad about the Cessna. And what did I tell you...she got you down all right."

"Yes...and in what condition? We're both wrecks."

Joe was suddenly aware of the smell.

"Can you smell that?" he asked.

"Yes...I noticed it straightaway. Like a burnt-out fuse."

"It's electrical...that's for sure. It can't be serious or the plane would have burst into flames straightaway. But it might be the reason why the radio is out of action. We have to check...see if it can be fixed."

"What do you mean...we? You don't look as if you can get out of that seat and I certainly know nothing about aircraft electronics."

Joe tried to move, coughed a couple of times and when he attempted to lower his seat he let out an almighty scream.

"Oh Joe, that sounds bad. Here, let me see if I can find anything."

Martin turned left in his seat and dragging his arm over his stomach, he leaned across the centre console against Joe's right arm. He undid his harness, draped it down the side of the seat and unzipped his leather jacket. He then swivelled in his seat so that his left arm was free and gently felt around Joe's stomach and chest. As soon as he reached his lower ribs Joe let out that scream again.

"It looks like there's something wrong with your ribs, Joe."

"I could have told you that."

"I can't see any blood, so you haven't broken the skin anywhere. Maybe you just need strapping up."

"Don't kid me, Martin. It's more than just a few broken ribs."

"I'm not a doctor, Joe. All I know is a rudimentary level in first aid."

"Never mind about that; we have more important things to worry about."

"And what does that mean?"

"I can tell you what to do, Martin, but I'm afraid it's all up to you now."

"What, with this arm?"

"That's your first priority. Get that fixed and you're fit to go."

"I don't know…but I'll do my best."

Joe had forgotten the first thing Martin had to do, and that was step outside the plane. It was around nine o'clock. He wasn't sure because his watch was broken. That was hardly his worst problem. In the desert the sun was their clock: sunrise in the east was morning, sun directly above was lunchtime and sunset in the west was time to sleep; everything in between was incidental.

At least Joe was still cognisant enough to outline the jobs Martin had to attend to in order of importance. As he'd said, Martin's first duty was to see to his arm. Outside there should be enough wreckage to find something to make a splint. He was to bring it back into the cockpit where Joe would help him bind it to his arm. Martin soon found a shredded part of the right wing support, but before he returned he thought he would reconnoitre the crash site; Joe was bound to ask.

On returning to his seat, Joe opened his eyes and looked surprised.

"I said there would be something out there…that's perfect. Now get the first aid bag, it's behind one of the rear seats."

Martin had to pull his seat forward, step into the back and rummage behind the seats until he found the bag with a big red cross on the flap. He brought it back to the front, rearranged his seat and started checking what was inside. It was a surprising collection of medical bits and pieces: several parcels of varying-sized bandages, swabs, packets of painkillers, bandaids, assorted creams for bites and sores and a small box containing a syringe, scissors, tweezers and a scalpel.

"Bring it closer," Joe said. "Now get out the pack containing the widest elastic bandage...not the gauze...and while you're at it, see if you can find something for this pain...I can hardly breathe."

Martin did what he asked, laying each item on the seat while he kneeled down on the floor. Joe tore open the bandage pack, put it to one side with the piece of aluminium, and then brought out the box with the instruments in.

"Right Martin...take your jacket off. Throw it over the seats. I doubt if you'll need it, and lay your arm across the seat." Martin, wincing, took his jacket off with difficulty.

Joe examined Martin's arm, running his hand down the full length, all the time watching his reaction and when he reached the spot where the ulna joined the wrist, Martin jumped.

"You're lucky. You haven't broken your arm...you've fractured your wrist. However, I shall have to splint your arm to keep the whole thing rigid."

Martin nodded. He could see Joe was much more

advanced in first aid than he was, so he relaxed, allowing him to place the splint and start wrapping his arm including the damaged wrist. Joe paid particular attention to the wrist and hand until he opened the box, took out the scissors and cut the bandage. He then took out one of the small bandage fixings and secured it in place. Joe was pale and struggling to move without severe pain.

"There you are...that should keep you until a medic can look at it."

"Thanks, Joe," Martin said, now able to lift his arm with no more than a slight twinge. He reached back into the bag and pulled out a box of painkillers. "I think I need one of those also." Joe nodded, with a wry smile.

As Martin expected, Joe asked him if he noticed what state the plane was in. He laughed, telling him he knew that would be his first question. In layman's terms, Martin tried to describe what he'd seen outside: The right wheel had collapsed under the body, taking with it the wing on that side and as it had impacted with the ground it buckled at an angle of maybe twenty degrees. The rest of the plane seemed okay except for the bent propeller, and the nose buried in sand.

Martin passed him the water bottle to take his tablet. He took two.

"I thought as much," he said. "A lot of mess by the

sounds of it. Anyway, you've got some work to do before that sun is overhead. The priority is to find out where that smell's coming from. So get at it. If it's what I think it is we might have a radio working before the day is out."

"I don't know anything about electronics," Martin said.

"You don't have to. Just get that cowling off the nose and have a look at the engine. You might have to clear a few dead bodies out of the way, but let your nose lead you to the damage."

"Then what?"

"Just tell me what you see...okay?"

Martin started to ease himself up from his kneeling position and realised he was now carrying a dead weight. He raised his arm, "And what about this?"

"Oh, sorry...bring it here?"

Martin returned to his position and Joe, groaning quietly, picked up the bandage again, wrapped it around Martin's arm like a sling and tied it around his neck. He cut it off, straightened it on his arm and put the scissors back in the box. Joe was looking grey now from all of the effort.

"How about that?"

Martin straightened up and found his arm was neatly hanging against his chest. "That's great...I should be able to manage things now."

He eased himself out of the plane and made his way around to the nose. As he'd told Joe, it was buried up to the propeller cone, so he had to clear the sand away before he could get at the cowling. Fortunately the leading edge of the wheel housing was lying nearby. A perfect scoop he thought and started digging away the sand. Before long the whole area of the nose was uncovered and he looked for some way of removing the cowling.

"Joe...this thing's screwed down."

"No problem. Go round the side of the plane; you'll find a small hatch. Lift up the latch and open it. Inside you'll find a toolbox. Oh, and while you're there you'll see a large blue tarpaulin. Bring it out and I'll tell you what to do with it later."

"I hope I don't have to keep going back and forth in this heat."

There was no comment from Joe and Martin could see it was going to be a long day and by the feel of it, a hot one. He opened the hatch, found the toolbox straightaway and took out a couple of screwdrivers, hoping one would fit. It did and before long he had all the screws out and the cowling off.

His nose was immediately assaulted by another, more horrendous smell: the birds were cooking on the hot engine and the stench was masking the electrical smell. It took a while, but he finally cleared the offending carcasses and continued his search. He didn't need Joe to tell him that a bunch of wires torn out of the side of a black box was the cause of the trouble. He tried shouting to Joe from where he was, but all he got was a distant mumble.

Martin bent down under the damaged wing and worked his way along to Joe's door. It appeared intact and he pulled the latch. It opened and he asked if Joe was okay. He said he was, if not a little surprised, and Martin told him about the wires. Joe seemed happy. It confirmed his suspicion and he told Martin what to do.

Martin undid the retaining clip, lifted the plastic cover and had no difficulty finding the long metal busbar. He knew this from his encounter with the one in his fuse box that it was the main electrical input, although he'd never had to meddle with the wires. Joe told him it was the battery relay and the birds must have ripped the wires out. All he had to do was clean the connections and replace them.

"How do I know I'm putting them in the right place?" Martin shouted.

Clutching the loose wires, Martin waited for Joe to answer. It seemed to take ages, as if he was summoning his strength. "Just match the same coloured wire with the screw on the bar," he rasped. Martin hoped for the best and started replacing each wire. He had no idea he was doing the right thing until he heard a muffled cry. He rushed back to his open door and saw Joe pointing to the red light on the instrument panel.

When Martin got back to the cockpit Joe explained the light was the ignition. It was telling him Martin had connected the battery and all they had to do now was switch on the radio. Martin leaned forward and did just that. Another light came on, accompanied with the most beautiful sound to their ears – glorious radio static.

"Shall we try the radio now?" Martin said,

"Not yet, Martin. It will be noon before long and there's something else I want you to do before we get fried alive."

"What's that?"

"I want you to put that tarpaulin across the plane. It has to go a certain way; corner to corner in a diamond formation. You know…just like the sunshades you hang from the wall of your house to a pole in the garden."

"I know what you mean, but what do I use to tie the corners down?"

"You'll find some rope where the toolbox is. There's a knife there too."

It took Martin a while with one hand. His first problem was how to open the large bundle, let alone cover the plane. Then he remembered helping his next-door neighbour erect his new shade-sail over his barbeque area. It was hooked up, corner to corner from the house to a pylon in the garden. The trick was to secure the first corner. Using that as an anchor, the rest was easy.

Martin opened out the tarpaulin in front of the plane, turned it round so that it was a diamond shape following the line of the fuselage and decided his anchor point would be the tail. Getting it there was another problem.

Studying the situation he realised he had his three points: the tail and the tip of each wing, even if Joe's was a little bent. Martin threw the rope over his shoulder and climbed across the damaged wing, along the fuselage and all the way up to the tip of the tail. He found a suitable hole to thread the rope through and climbed back down. He then looped it through the eyelet and walking away from the plane, he pulled the corner up to the tail.

Now he had to secure it there. That done he turned to secure the other corners using the trailing edge of each wing-flap to tie them down. Moving across the wing he noticed a large bump above the windscreen and remembered the antenna Joe had mentioned. He took out the knife and cut a long slit in the tarpaulin big enough for the antenna to poke through. One last check, he thought. Everything looked okay, and Martin eased his way back down to the ground.

As he returned the rope to the hatch he noticed a cardboard box. Down one side were the words, 'Emergency Rations'. Food was something that had not been discussed yet. The thought of being found before the day was out had turned their minds to the immediate problems. But Joe must have had other ideas. Otherwise, why would he be concerned with the heat frying them in the plane?

When Martin returned to the cockpit he was about to question Joe on what their chances of being spotted today were when he heard him repeating the Mayday call. He looked frustrated, and after gesturing for Martin to get back in his seat, he started again. There was no response; just the usual waveband static.

Martin had removed his headset to go outside; there was no use for it anymore, and when he returned he noticed Joe had changed dramatically. He looked paler, and clammy, as he passed Martin the headset.

"Here…put this on," he said. "You can do the radio now. Nothing fancy, I think the battery's going. Just say Mayday a few times."

Martin did what Joe asked. He repeated Mayday several times with a few seconds' gap in-between in pace with Joe's finger. Still there was no response.

Joe let out an exhausted gasp. "I don't think we

have enough power. And don't ask me why because I don't know. The only thing we can do now is hope a local station picks us up. That's all we can try."

"How do we do that?" Martin asked.

"Next to the radio you'll see a dial marked waveband. Click it round to a different frequency, each time saying Mayday a couple of times. Let's hope someone out there is monitoring the frequencies."

"Martin switched the dial away from their standard frequency, calling Mayday each time as Joe had asked. There seemed to be an awful lot of frequencies, but he continued, on and on. He had almost completed a full circuit when the static suddenly stopped and he heard a faint voice. Joe came to life and turned up the volume.

"HRT 700…what's your problem…over."

Joe took over. "This is ALPHA, TANGO, ZULU from AMINCO CENTRAL calling a Mayday…over."

"I read you…what is your status? Over."

The radio began crackling again and Joe shook his head in desperation.

"Crashed…7:30…126 degrees…over."

The static continued. There was a faint reply. "Repeat…you're breaking up."

CHAPTER 7

When Larry Kingston tapped on the door and walked into Philip's office, he looked as if the weight of the world had collapsed in on him. He slumped down in the chair opposite Philip's desk and looked as if he wanted to say something.

"How did it go with Hubbard?" Philip asked.

"You know, that man sits in his plush office in Dallas without the remotest idea of what's going on in the field."

"Sounds familiar," Philip replied sarcastically.

"What? Oh yeah. Anyway, he wants a detailed report emailed through to him by two o'clock. Who would be the best to do that?"

"I thought he asked you."

"I don't know all the details...you see to it."

Philip screwed his face up and nodded. As he leaned across his desk and picked up the phone to call Bryce, he noticed Elsie walking across the car park with a distraught-looking Kate.

He returned the phone and turned to Larry. "Looks like Mrs Dexter is about to arrive. Do you want to see her? Tell her about her husband?"

"Me? Oh no. I can't get involved at the moment. You explain the situation to her and I'll drop in and see her later."

"We'll be in the VIP lounge," Philip said, as Larry left the room.

Elsie brought Kate into his office. He jumped up from his desk and walked over to her. His instinct was to take her in his arms and let her cry it out, but he settled for his arm around her shoulder.

"Martin knew something was going to happen," she said, wiping her eyes with a tattered-looking tissue. Elsie pulled off several from a nearby box on Philip's desk and passed them to her. "What's happened to him, Philip?" she continued.

Philip took the used tissue and threw it into his waste basket then guided her towards the door. "Not here, Kate. Elsie will take you to the VIP lounge; you'll be more comfortable there. I'll join you in a few moments."

As he left his office he told Elsie he was going to call in at the operations room to see if they had any more news; then he would join them.

Kate was sitting nervously in one of the easy chairs clutching onto a mug of tea Elsie had made for her when Philip entered the room. She eagerly searched his expression for a glimpse of good news.

"Have you found them yet?" she cried out.

Philip glanced at Elsie with a pleading expression and they sat down either side of Kate. Elsie took hold of one of Kate's hands that had been tightly clenched together on her lap.

"I'm sorry I had to ask Elsie to bring you here, but I thought it would be the best place to explain what's happened. We're still trying to gather information. We don't know much, but I'll tell you what we do know. And let's hope we hear something before the day's end."

Kate wanted to scream her head off at someone. She picked up her mug from the coffee table and clasped it for a moment and then took a sip.

Elsie took it from her hand and stood up and said, "I'll freshen that for you."

Philip felt uncomfortable. Normally, once he grasped a situation, he could pass the information on in every detail. But once an emotional element entered the debate he found himself going over the content in his mind looking for the simplest approach. By the look on Kate's face, he guessed any information would satisfy her need. So a formal account would be best.

"Right…as I'm sure you already know, the storm front was not due over Broome until around eight-thirty. That way Martin's plane would almost certainly have made Site 21 before it arrived. Unfortunately a cyclone suddenly appeared in the Timor Sea, collided with our storm and turned it into something far worse."

"What do you mean, 'far worse'?" Kate interrupted.

"Just let me finish, Kate, and it will all become clear," he said kindly. She nodded and he continued. "This connection made the storm much stronger, meaning it was able to catch up to the plane around seven. We know that because Joe radioed in to find out what was happening. He was advised to climb above the storm. Around seven-thirty we assume he returned to his original height so that he could see the ground and fix a new heading. That's when he ran into a flock of birds."

"Oh my God! Is that what brought him down?"

"We don't know that, Kate. We received a garbled radio message saying he had a bird-strike and nothing else. No information on where he was or what condition the plane was in. The radio just went dead."

"You mean the plane fell out of the sky," she cried out. "Go on…be honest with me…they're dead… aren't they?"

"No, Kate. Calm yourself. The Cessna would not

have fallen out of the sky, even if the engine stalled – which is what we think happened. It was quite capable of gliding to the ground. What we think is the radio or some part of the electrics was damaged when the birds hit the plane and were probably sucked into the cowling."

Kate's expression turned from panic to resolve. The thought that the plane could have survived the fall and Martin was still alive gave her new hope. It also provided her with a new fear: how long would he survive the heat of the desert before they were found?

"Have you sent planes out to find them?" she asked.

"They left as soon as the storm was declared over. It should take them about an hour and a half to reach the area they're in."

"So you know where they are?"

"No, but we've calculated a small triangle where we think the plane came down. It's only a matter of time."

"Oh God…now we wait," Kate said. Elsie handed her the fresh mug of tea and Kate smiled for the first time and nodded her thanks.

Philip was expecting Larry to walk in any moment, but he was conspicuous by his absence. A timid knock on the door alerted Philip. He went over to the door and opened it. It was Josh; he looked uneasy, not wanting to enter the room and Philip asked what was up.

"Sorry boss, but I've just had a radio ham on. He asked if we've lost a plane."

Philip was speechless at first. Contact with the plane was what they were waiting for, but not from some amateur radio ham.

"Kate, something's come up. I won't be a moment."

She nodded; never thinking for one second it was about Martin.

On the way to the operations room Josh told Philip as soon as he noticed the incoming transmission was an unusual frequency he decided to record it. It was just as well. When he attempted to re-establish a connection, all he got was static.

"How was that?" Philip questioned, as he pushed open the door.

"It's not unusual. The waveband is a freaky place. You can be on a scheduled frequency one minute and suddenly get music from Indonesia. In this case I think we were lucky…or it was a message from God. I was surfing and there it was."

"Good…let's hear it."

By now the others had gathered around Josh's small enclave as he switched on the recording. "Calling AMINCO CENTRAL. This is HRT 700 out of Port Hedland."

He went on to say he had picked up a bad

transmission from a crashed plane in the Sandy Desert, copied its call sign and the last heading before it stalled.

Philip listened to the recording several times, noting certain details, "So we have the last heading, the time of transmission and a new coordinate to add from Port Hedland. How good is that, Bryce?"

"Say no more…I'm onto it," Bryce said, and dashed off across the room.

After several tries the radio sounded as if it was getting weaker with every attempt. Joe seemed to have lost interest and Martin sat sweltering in the midday heat, watching the little red light flutter.

He decided to switch the radio off in the event they might need it later on or it hopefully may renew its strength with non-activity. Joe seemed asleep, the best thing in his condition, and Martin decided to check the box of emergency rations.

Suddenly Joe started speaking. "Do I look Italian to you?" he said.

Martin glanced in his direction. His eyes were still closed, so he thought he might be dreaming or worse, hallucinating. He asked the question again as if it was serious and Martin had no idea how to answer him. It was like one of those questions when someone asks if you think they're fat.

"Australian Italian…I'd say," was Martin's reply.

Joe started laughing and Martin joined in. It seemed appropriate at the time until Joe began coughing again. Martin offered him a drink. He refused with a wave of his hand. "No use wasting water on a dead man," he said.

"That's ridiculous," Martin shouted. "You'll be dead if you don't drink."

Joe was oblivious to Martin's comment and continued the discussion. "It's all right you saying that with your blue eyes. All my brown eyes got me was a derisive 'Wog' everywhere I went. All I got was 'Wog Boy'."

Martin tried to look amused.

"That's nothing. When I arrived in Australia they called me a 'Pom'."

They laughed again and Joe coughed again, only this time Joe's anguish was far worse. He seemed to be drifting into the bad elements of his life.

"I wish I could help you, Joe," Martin said, "but I can't. I don't know anything about medicine. I'm an engineer. Now if you had a broken pump—"

"Don't worry, Martin," he interrupted. We needed an engineer when you fixed the battery relay. Look… we made contact with a radio ham. He's sure to contact AMINCO for us. They'll have a better idea where we are now."

"You keep going on about where we are, Joe. Surely one of those planes carrying tourists will spot us soon. And the planes and helicopters AMINCO must have sent out. They should be here by now."

"Not out here, Martin," Joe replied.

"You said that before. What do you mean?"

"Civil airlines have corridors; this is not one of them. That's why AMINCO chose this heading: it would be free of heavy traffic."

"But they fly at thirty-two-thousand feet; nowhere near us."

"Don't ask me how AMINCO make their decisions."

That seemed the end of their discussion and Martin turned back to the box.

It looked like one of those official boxes. The type you see on the television documentaries about UN aid in Africa. Only this cardboard box had the name 'AMINCO' printed on each side in black letters, along with 'Emergency Rations'.

Using the small knife he'd brought into the cockpit in case he needed to share out the rations, he sliced through the broad plastic tape across the flaps. As he opened them out he came across an A4 piece of paper. It was covered with instructions in the usual four translations: English, French, Spanish and Asian. The English was only short, detailing the contents: Twenty packs of 'Hard Tack' biscuits, ten small sachets of honey or peanut butter, a packet of salt tablets and to his surprise a large box of 'Mars Bars'. He could have expected a block of hard, dark chocolate; the type they had in the Second World War, but not Mars Bars.

Although there was a triangular corner of the tarpaulin draping across the windscreen, Martin could still see enough to know the sun was now directly above the plane. The sun was shimmering along the shiny aluminium cowling, working its way along the edge of one of the propellers, and sparkling highlights were dancing across tiny metal fragments scattered across the desert floor.

Knowing that made him feel hungry and he opened one of the Hard Tack packs. He burst the sealed end open and pulled out one of the oatmeal coloured slabs inside. It appeared there were ten segments to a pack, times twenty packs, which meant he had two hundred biscuits. He nibbled one corner and sat trying to decide what it tasted like. It was too bland to come to a decision. Probably that was why it needed some honey or peanut butter to give it taste.

He checked the packet again. There was a mass of ingredients; mainly vitamins and minerals, but little or no actual substance; except items like oatmeal, starch and rice powder.

Martin nudged Joe. He opened his eyes and looked around him.

"What's happened? Has that Ham called back?"

"No, Joe…I switched the radio off to save the battery, remember?"

"Yes…That's a good idea. We can try later."

"It's lunchtime, Joe…would you like to try one of these Hard Tack biscuits.'

"I see you found the emergency rations. Be careful, Martin."

"I know…they taste terrible," Martin said.

Joe tried to move. He must have been sore from sitting in the same position, but as soon as he did he let out an agonising shriek. "Oh God," he said, falling back into his original position. "I think I'll have another painkiller, Martin."

The pain in Martin's arm had eased to a dull ache, so he decided his need was not as great as Joe's. He reached down to the centre console and opening the box he took out a tablet and handed it to Joe. He then passed the water bottle to him.

"Be careful with that. We don't know how long we'll be here. Did you find the box of water bottles in the hatchway?"

"No, I didn't," Martin said, deciding this time he had better have a proper look in the cargo space behind the back seats.

"You'd better bring them into the cockpit. There's plenty of room."

"I will, Joe, after you've had something to eat."

"You have to be careful in case we're here for a while."

"You've already said that, Joe."

"Did I...well listen now, in case I can't tell you tomorrow. We've got to plan our meals as if the food has got to last. Not as if we're reacting to a normal meal time. At the beginning, your body has plenty of protein and fat to sustain you, so your hunger is only a habit. Ignore it. It won't harm you to miss a meal or two, or at least eat only a fraction of what you would normally eat.

"Water is different. In this heat you need water. Dehydration is far worse than hunger. But drink little and often; a few sips is as good as a couple of gulps. Check how much we have first. Analyse how long a bottle lasts and then you'll know how many days we've got."

"You seem to know all about survival, Joe. Has this happened to you before?"

"No, but as part of my initial training with AMIN-CO I had to go on a week-long survival course. They dropped us off in the Durack Ranges with a bunch of SAS men and they taught us how to survive on minimum rations."

"That sounds good."

"It was. It taught us how to ration ourselves, eat the right food at the appropriate time and only eat and drink what we needed – not what we wanted."

"I'm in your hands, Joe."

"No, you're not. They also taught us about the survival of the fittest. You have to take charge now. I'm too weak. I've told you everything you need to know, except one thing. Hard Tack biscuits are okay in cold climates but deadly in the heat. Up till now you've only nibbled that biscuit, by the time you finish it you'll be gasping for water and no matter how much you drink it won't quench your thirst. So leave them until the last moment. That's when you'll really need them."

"So what do we eat now?"

"You'll notice a box of Mars Bars in there. That was my idea. Take one out and cut it into quarters. Sucking a quarter every three hours will sustain you for a couple of days at least. It will also train your stomach; less food, less intake."

Martin took out the box of Mars Bars and returned the emergency rations to the rear of the plane. He opened the box. There were a dozen bars inside and he undid the wrapping on one and cut the bar into four. He popped one portion into his mouth and another he passed to Joe. He had a terrible urge to chew it.

With his watch broken Martin had no idea how long he was sucking the piece of Mars Bar. It took a while to get through the top layer of milk chocolate, all the time slowly allowing the melted liquid to pour down his throat, but when he reached the inner core of caramel and fudge it was absolute heaven. Why he had never thought of this before he was amazed. It was the best way of savouring a Mars Bar.

When he eventually finished he expected he would need a drink, but he was not thirsty. Altogether it must have taken him the best part of fifteen minutes to finish one quarter, which normally would have gone in five. That done he decided to venture outside and see what the temperature was like so he could check the hatch again and bring back the box of bottled water.

He opened the door and was immediately assaulted by an oppressive heat. It felt thick and searing. He took out his hankie, draped it over his head and held it down with the arms of his sunglasses. He stepped outside and quickly closed the door. It was a different world to anything he'd experienced previously. He stopped under the wing. It was cooler, but before long he knew he would have to brave the elements of the Sandy Desert.

Strangely the heat and sand reminded Martin of a holiday he'd had with Kate in Tunisia. Their hotel had felt like an exotic oasis within a town that had not changed since the biblical times. Young boys, each dressed in a fez, waistcoat and bright blue pantaloons, swished around the pool with an endless supply of ice-cold drinks, while the energetic tourists waited for their next excursion. It had been idyllic. The Sandy Desert, he was sure, was not.

After a few moments Martin stepped out into the blazing sun and quickly made his way around the nose of the plane, across the broken wing and back under the part that was still above the ground. He rested with his back against the fuselage. He was fighting for breath. The heat had decimated what little oxygen there was. It reminded him of his first trip into the outback; for an English pom it was terrible.

It took some time for his body to absorb enough oxygen for him to continue. He opened the hatch and leaned forward to study what Joe had stored inside before the flight. There was the rope, of course; he decided it would be better under the wing in case he needed it later. Next was the toolbox – that could stay where it was – and several mail bags and a box of a dozen bottles of water. It felt heavy as he pulled it forward.

Martin managed to drag the box to the edge of the hatch and then bent down and lifted it onto his shoulder. After shutting the hatch with his backside he made his way around to his door and stopped, wondering what he was going to do now. He dropped the box onto the ground, opened the door, pushed his seat forward and, one by one, placed ten bottles behind the rear seat and the other two he placed on the shelf above his feet. Joe stirred. He looked worse than ever and Martin noticed a smear of blood on his lips and cheek as he must have coughed and wiped his mouth.

Martin opened a bottle and let him sip the cool water. "You got it then, I see."

"Yes... It's hot out there."

"I told you. You'll be glad you put the tarpaulin over the plane."

Joe was right. Without it there, survival time would be greatly reduced. He could see the sun clearly now as it started its descent into sunset. In a few hours it would be too dark for the planes to see them. Perhaps they would have better luck tomorrow. It had to be tomorrow. Their survival depended on it.

CHAPTER 8

By mid-afternoon with still no news, Kate was feeling composed enough to speak to Jennifer on her mobile. She had no intention at this stage of telling her what had happened, just that she had called in at the airstrip to see if Martin had arrived and would be a little late picking her up. Elsie volunteered, but Kate shook her head; she wanted to wait until they were home before she broke the bad news.

She was almost through when the door opened. She immediately thought of Philip, hoping he could set her mind at rest, but it was a tall well-dressed man. She recognised him straightaway as Martin's boss, Larry Kingston.

"I must go, dear. Get a taxi home and I'll see you soon," she said, finishing her call and looking up at a nervous expression.

"Sorry if I interrupted something," he said, sitting

down opposite her. Elsie asked if he wanted a drink and he shook his head. "I just thought I would come in to see how you're doing. You must be devastated."

"I'm better now," Kate replied. "It's the waiting that's worse."

"I know. We've got two planes and a helicopter searching the Sandy Desert. They should be there by now, so we're expecting to hear something any time soon."

"Thank you...that's reassuring."

He looked as though he was floundering. He had no idea what to say. It was the first time the company had lost a plane and he had no reference point.

"I gather this latest contact has narrowed the search, but I'm afraid it's still a lot of desert to cover." With the same breath he realised that was not what she wanted to hear and there was a slight lapse of communication until the door opened again and Philip walked in. The relief on both their faces was quite obvious.

"Oh, here you are, Larry," Philip said, joining the group. "I see you've met Martin's wife, Kate."

"Oh yeah," he said, easing himself up off his seat. "We'd already met at the company party...remember."

"You're right...I forgot about that," Philip acknowledged.

Larry finally worked himself upright and took

hold of Kate's hand. "I'm sorry I can't stay any longer, but you take care now. If there's anything you need, just let Philip know and we'll do our best to sort it out. A moment, Philip."

They walked over to the door and after a short discussion Larry left and Philip returned to the easy chairs.

"What's the new information?" Kate asked, as soon as he sat down again.

"I'm sorry, Kate. I was on my way back to tell you. That idiot likes to take credit for the slightest information, when all the time he has no idea what's going on."

"So there isn't any news?" she interrupted.

"Sorry again…there is. When I was called away, it was to tell me a radio ham had contacted us. Apparently he picked up a radio message from Joe's plane."

"Oh, marvellous," she shouted. "So they're alive."

"It was only a short message, Kate. They're down and we have another coordinate to fix their position. I've radioed the planes already searching, so keep your fingers crossed; they might even spot them before they leave."

"What do you mean, before they leave?"

"You don't need to know all these details, Kate."

"But I have to…what else have I got?"

"All right, Kate…you have to understand the crash

site is nearly three hundred kilometres away. It takes almost two hours to get there and they have to leave two hours before it gets dark. But if we don't find them today, they'll be out there again first thing in the morning."

"I know, Philip," she said, with a sad finality in her voice. "I know this is in no part the company's fault; it was just one of those days. And I know you're doing everything you can, thank you."

Philip took hold of her hand. "Kate...you and Martin are family."

She glanced at her watch, "I think I'd better make a move, Elsie, if you don't mind. Jennifer will be home by now and I have to tell her."

"Yes, of course, Kate," Elsie replied. "Would you like me to come home with you; just in case you need any information?"

"No, thank you, this is one of those private things. A lift to my car would be fine; I'll manage from there."

She stood up and Elsie and Philip followed her back to the entrance. "What about Adam, your son?" Philip asked before she left.

"Yes, I know...that's another call I have to make."

Jennifer was standing by the lounge window waiting for her mother when she pulled into the drive. She rushed into the hall and opened the front door. She could see by her mother's puffy face and red eyes that something was wrong and was impatient for her to step into the house.

"What's happened?" she cried out.

Kate refused to answer until she had removed her coat and settled Jennifer into one of the easy chairs. For her own part she needed a stiff drink. She went over to the drinks cabinet, took out the bottle of scotch and poured herself a double. Then she returned to the chair opposite Jennifer and swallowed a large mouthful.

"There's no easy way to say this, Jennifer. Your father's plane crashed in the Sandy Desert this morning in that terrible storm."

Jennifer looked blank. She heard what her mother said, but her brain seemed not to accept it. Then when it did finally sink in she let out an awful scream. Kate jumped up, took the couple of steps to her daughter's side, and sitting on the arm of her chair, put her arm around her. She had cried herself out earlier, but still had space to absorb Jennifer's sobs.

"Sorry you had to hear it like that. I had to and I know what it feels like. They contacted AMINCO after the plane went down so they're on the ground. Now they just have to find them."

Still sobbing, Jennifer looked into her mother's eyes. "It's a big desert, Mum; how are they going to find them all the way out there?"

"I spent all afternoon with them. They know what they're doing, and they've narrowed the search area down considerably. They'll find them."

"What about Adam?" she questioned. "You've got to tell him."

"I know, dear. Just one more drink and I'll ring him straightaway."

Following another agonising discussion with her son, Adam, Kate was beginning to become exhausted. Supported by another drink, she spent the rest of the evening explaining to Jennifer exactly what had happened during the storm that had merged with an unexpected cyclone. Jennifer was insatiable. Her appetite for detail was difficult for Kate to satisfy as she didn't have the information required. They filled the evening with one scenario after another. Despite a need for sleep, they were waiting for Adam's plane to arrive. The Red-Eye was due in at 3:00 am.

It had been six months since Adam's last visit during mid-term break and he looked different. Kate spotted it straightaway as he left the arrival gate. It was like looking at a young Martin: the same mop of light-brown hair above a pale narrow face, slim athletic build and that loping gait. It was plain to see he was his father's son, even down to the nervous tic in his cheek.

Jennifer ran towards Adam the moment she saw him, flung her arms around his neck and gave him a great big kiss. As they walked back to Kate, she could see Jennifer was crying and Adam was holding her close. They separated and Adam dropped his holdall on the ground and embraced his mum. He held her as tightly as he could and tears burst from Kate's eyes. Jennifer joined in and the three stood for moments hugging each other in the middle of the airport lounge.

Feeling conspicuous, they broke apart, walked out of the airport complex and headed for the parking area.

"I heard about the cyclone," Adam said, getting into the car. "It was all over the news. Even the bit about it merging with your storm; it must have been a terrible experience. Did it do any damage to the house?"

"Not that I've had a chance to notice," Kate said, stopping at the car park kiosk and paying the fee. She drove out and turned left into Old Broome Road.

There was no traffic on the road at that time, except the car behind her. They separated at the roundabout. She turned left onto Gubinge Road and it went straight on. Adam had been distracted for the moment and as soon as she headed for Cable Beach he relaxed; he knew where he was.

"What time did you get the news?" Adam continued.

"Not now, Adam," Kate said. "Let's get home first, make some drinks and something to eat if you're hungry and I'll tell you everything."

"Sorry, Mum…I know it must be terrible for you."

Kate pulled into the drive, clicked the remote to open the garage door and proceeded on inside.

"That's new," Adam said, as she switched the engine off and closed the door behind them. "When did you have that done?"

"Good heavens you're wide awake," she said, nudging Jennifer as they got out of the car and opened the door to the hall.

"Sorry…it must be the adrenalin."

"For your information, your father had a man install it last month. He said it was his Christmas present to himself," Kate said, walking through to the kitchen and switching the kettle on.

"It's a bit early for Christmas," Adam said, dropping his bag onto a chair.

Kate stopped by the sink and started crying again. "He made a silly remark when I said the same thing. He said, 'I'll get it now…just in case something happens before Christmas.' Wasn't that a silly thing to say?"

Adam and Jennifer both hugged their mum.

Breaking away when the kettle popped, Jennifer sniffed and said, "Of course we all know he was talking about how expensive it was at Christmas."

Kate started preparing the mugs for their tea. "Oh dear, you look terrible," Kate remarked to Jennifer as she picked up her mug.

"Yes, I feel it. If it's all right with you two I think I'll get off to bed."

Kate, then Adam, kissed her on the cheek, after which Jennifer tiredly left them.

"What on earth possessed Dad to go on that small plane?" Adam questioned casually as he sipped his tea.

"Can we change the subject, Adam, please? I know you love your dad; we all do, but I've been crying most of the day and I would just like a rest."

"Sorry, Mum…why don't you go off to bed?"

Kate looked up at the kitchen clock. "It's 4:30 am… who's going to sleep at this time after all that's happened today."

"Jennifer obviously can."

Kate reached across the table and took hold of his hand. "Thank you for coming, Adam. I need you both around me at the moment."

"Where else would I be? I shall stay here for as long as it takes and tomorrow…sorry, later today, I'll go with you to the airstrip and we'll find out what they're doing about finding Dad."

"No, Adam…they know what they're doing. They don't want hysterical relatives under their feet. Philip, that's the Operations Manager, said he would keep me in the loop. He'll ring me when they have some news."

"I just thought you'd like to be there when it came through."

"I spent hours there yesterday and every time the door opened or a telephone rang, it was terrifying. I know I'll be pacing the floor here, but it won't be as bad. Now please…can we change the subject?"

"Are you sure you don't want to lie down?"

"No, I don't. Anyway…how is this going to affect your studies? You're not missing out on any exams, are you?"

"No, Mum…except for an exam in January, I'm all finished."

"I thought it took seven years to become a doctor."

"This is only the written part of my tests, Mum; I now have to move on to the physical side and then, if I pass all my exams, I do my internship in a hospital."

"And you're doing all right?"

Adam nodded his head. "Professor Slater has high hopes for me. That's what he says when he sees me slacking off."

"You don't do that often, do you?"

"No, Mum…I'm fine. Don't worry; you'll have a doctor in the family before you know it. Well, at least in the next three years."

Kate left the table, placed her mug in the dishwasher and made her way out of the kitchen and into the lounge. Adam did the same and followed her. She was standing by the drinks cabinet. The earlier drinks had worn off and she poured a generous glass of whiskey. She glanced back at Adam in one of the easy chairs and lifted her glass at him to see if he wanted one. He nodded.

As she passed him his drink she sat down opposite and took a gulp and sat back, expecting a response. He just looked at her lovingly and sipped his drink.

"That's the first alcoholic drink I've served you," she said.

"Well, I am twenty-two, Mum. I've been drinking for some time. Mark you, I don't usually drink neat whiskey. I'm a Bacardi and Coke man."

"There's plenty of soda if you want it."

Adam was about to continue the conversation when they heard a loud bang. It appeared to come from upstairs and he jumped out of his seat, placed his drink on the coffee table and rushed out of the room. Kate took her last gulp and followed him.

He was already on the landing when there was another bang, louder this time and it came from Kate's bedroom nearby. He rushed into the room just as Jennifer was about to open one of the doors onto the balcony. He could see a large crack in the glass and an overturned metal chair leaning up against it.

"Don't open the door," he shouted.

He was too late. As Jennifer slid the door back she was caught in a blast and thrown back into the room. Kate had just arrived, and screamed, "What's going on?"

Adam picked Jennifer up, saw that she was only shaken and went directly to the partly open door. The force of the wind blowing into the room almost took him off his feet until he grabbed the bedrail. He used it to lever himself onto the dressing table next to the door and then onto the doorframe. He stood there clutching on for dear life and Kate tried to reach him.

"Stay back, Mum. I'm going to try and get these chairs inside."

She sat on the bed next to Jennifer. They could feel the force of the wind coming through the door as Adam inched his way onto the balcony. It was furious outside. He could see papers and shredded vegetation whirling about in small spirals in the pools of light from the street lights. A man in a white van to his right had been attempting to deliver his papers, but had now given up and was just parked.

"Careful, Adam," Jennifer called out.

Fearful that he might be sucked over the railings, Adam spread his legs and hung onto the door with one hand while he manoeuvred the first chair into the room.

Kate jumped up and pulled it out of the way. He then grabbed the other chair and dragged that inside also. The small table was something else. It was too large to go through the gap, so he tipped it on its side and once back in the room, he pulled it in after him and quickly closed the door.

He fell exhausted onto the floor, lying there gasping for breath.

Kate kneeled down beside him brushing his damp hair out of his eyes. "I didn't know it was raining as well," she said, beckoning Jennifer to get a towel out of the en suite. Then they heard a rattling cascade of torrential rain.

"Listen to that," Jennifer said, returning with the towel.

As Kate kneeled down on the carpet she brought her hands up to her face and started sobbing. It was deep and uncontrollable. Jennifer and Adam tried to console her. She leaned against them in a wretched state. "Oh my God," she let out, "it's started all over again. How are the planes going to take off in this?"

CHAPTER 9

When Martin slowly opened his eyes there was only the barest glimmer of sunrise breaking through Joe's window. The plane was lifting slightly on one wing. He thought he was dreaming; reverting back to that last moment they were in the air before the Cessna ploughed into the Sandy Desert.

He could still hear the crumpling of metal, the propeller blades digging into the ground and then the deathly silence. Only this was no dream. There was no silence; only the whip-like cracking of the tarpaulin striking the windscreen.

Martin turned to Joe. He placed his hand on his neck and felt a pulse, but Joe looked terrible. His skin was pale and waxlike. His breathing was shallow and Martin noticed there was blood on his lips again. He picked up the hanky he'd left with him and wiped his mouth. Joe stirred. His eyelids fluttered. He was alive.

123

"What time is it?" he rasped, with a rustling chest.

"I don't know," Martin replied. "My watch was broken in the crash."

Joe chuckled, "That's not all we broke."

"By the look of the sky I'd say dawn's not far off," Martin said, loud enough to be heard above the racket outside."

"What's going on?" Joe said, seeing the tarpaulin lashing the windscreen.

"I think the wind's picking up," Martin said.

Joe went silent for a moment. He seemed to be listening.

"It sounds as if we've got another storm coming through. You'd better get out there Martin and tie everything down; or it will tear that tarpaulin to shreds."

Martin looked outside. It was fierce and inhospitable. He wondered if Joe was just overreacting. Then the next jolt of the plane proved his instinct was still good. He knew the heat would come back and they needed the tarpaulin.

Martin unlatched his door and tried to open it. He was pushing against a force far greater than the energy he had left. He sucked in a deep breath, pushed against the door as hard as he could and it opened; not all the way, but far enough for him to ease himself out into the maelstrom. He was immediately assaulted by every piece of small debris, vegetation, gravel and any shard of wreckage light enough to be carried by the wind. He jumped towards the wing strut and hung on until he'd gathered his breath to move under the wing and grab the propeller.

He visually checked the three tied-off corners of the tarpaulin; they all seemed to be firm enough. He could see the wind was tugging at the corners, but they held; it was the loose flap hanging down across the windscreen that was making all the noise.

He remembered the rope he'd decided to drop under the wing in case he needed it.

Now he needed it. The loose end was within reach. He grabbed it, pulled it towards the flapping corner, and holding it down, he threaded the rope through the eyelet and tied it off. Once sure he had made a secure knot, he wound the rope around one of the propellers and tied that off as well.

Holding onto the propeller Martin decided to look out towards the east where the first sign of light was outlining the horizon. The colour was wrong. It was tinged with burnt orange, almost mauve. And as he slowly scanned the line off towards the south and back to the west, he could see something else. If he could have relied on his eyesight, he would have said it was a bank of cloud close to the ground. Whatever it was it looked dangerous and he returned to the cockpit.

"You stopped the banging then," Joe said. "What was it?"

"Just one of the corners... When I tied the main three I decided to leave the one over the nose in case we wanted to look out of the windscreen. It's okay now. I've tied it down to the propeller."

"That's good," he mumbled, "but there's still a lot of noise."

"I know, I checked. I think another storm's coming in. There's a long line of cloud rushing across from the horizon."

"Is it close to the ground?"

"Yes...why is that?"

Joe grunted. "It's not like the other storm...it sounds like a sandstorm."

"Is that bad?"

"It's bad enough to stop any planes looking for us."

Martin tried the radio again. It was still set on the radio ham's frequency.

"I wouldn't bother with that. You won't pick up anything in this. Try later when it's fine again. By then there might be some planes about."

Martin switched off the radio and decided to go back to sleep.

It was nine o'clock and Broome was battening down for their second storm in as many days. Adam had found some tape in the garage and was just finishing off the cracked glass panel in the door when Kate walked into the bedroom with a hot mug of tea. She smiled at him like mothers do. It was good to have him home.

He stopped what he was doing and held out his hand. "Oh, I could kill for one of those. What time is it?" he said, taking a sip.

"What about your watch?" Kate said, sitting on the edge of the bed.

"I haven't worn a watch for ages. I use my mobile."

"Well, I never," she said. "Your dad and I have had mobiles for ages and have never thought to use their clocks. It makes sense in this age."

"I use my mobile for just about everything."

"What do you use?" Jennifer said, walking into the room."

"We're just talking about mobiles," Adam answered her.

"Sorry, dear," Kate said, "did you want something?"

"You're not going in to work then?"

"No, dear. I rang the Head Administrator earlier and told him what had happened and he said I was to stay off until something was settled."

Jennifer shook her head, "Isn't that just like the bureaucracy – until something was settled? What about how are you coping?"

"It's all right. He means well; he just doesn't know how to deal with people in emotional situations. So what about you? You're not going to university?"

"Not likely. Can you imagine me concentrating on anything today? And what about the weather… would you go out in this?" she joshed.

The phone rang. Luckily there was an extension in the bedroom and Jennifer passed it to Kate. "Hello?" she answered.

"It's Philip, Kate. How are you?"

"Hello Philip…I'm still hanging on. Have you got any news for me?"

"I haven't, Kate. I thought I'd ring to let you know that the weather has grounded the planes. But we'll get them up as soon as this storm clears."

"As soon as I saw it come through this morning I knew it wasn't a good sign. Has meteorology given you any idea when this lot is likely to pass?"

"They think it will be somewhere around three; they're not sure."

"Oh dear…if you need a four-hour window, that means today is out."

"I'm afraid so, Kate…unless it moves earlier. However, the other reason I rang you was to say his lordship, Larry Kingston, has decided to renege on his quick tour. He has decided to stay until we find the plane."

"Is that good?"

"Oh yes, it's what I've been badgering him for. It means the Lear Jet is available to join the search."

"Another plane must be good. Thank him for me."

"No, Kate, that's not it. It means the jet can search twice the distance. It can go up and down our search area covering a much narrower heading."

"Oh, I see...that's marvellous. Please let me know when it leaves."

"I will, Kate. Keep your chin up. I'll ring again later. Bye."

"Bye Philip...and thanks."

She handed the phone back to Jennifer. "Who's Philip?" she said.

"That was the Operations Manager. Unfortunately, the planes are grounded."

"I gathered that," Adam said. What's this four-hour window?"

"Oh, that. Apparently it takes the planes two hours to reach the crash area and two hours to get back...so that's the minimum time they have."

Suddenly a gust of wind buffeted the glass door again and a torrential downpour swept across the balcony. Adam rushed over to the glass panel and checked his handiwork. "The tape seems to be holding," he said, running his hand up and down the crack. "I hope this stands up to the storm until we get it repaired."

Kate was far away, thinking of Martin and Joe huddled in the cockpit of the tiny Cessna. "I wonder if this storm is as far reaching as the one that brought their plane down," she mused. "Imagine what they must be going through."

The sandstorm was upon them. Every loose item on the plane was rattling violently. The Cessna seemed almost to the point where Martin expected it to break apart any minute. There was nothing to see other than a swirling mass of sand mixed with anything that the whirlwind could pick up in its relentless journey.

It peppered the windscreen with the force of a sandblaster. And the noise; a whining roar that filled the cockpit despite the headsets they returned to their ears.

Joe had been resting quietly up until the first strike. It was he who suggested they cover their ears, but it only reduced the whine a fraction.

Then the motion started as the epicentre of the storm arrived. It was the same feeling Martin had experienced just before they'd taken off, when a sudden gust lifted the plane off its wheels and dropped it back again with a thump. This had a different effect; probably due to the broken wing. The floating sensation was not there. Martin's side of the plane, which was intact, lifted almost to the point of the wheel leaving the ground, while Joe's damaged side held the frame back, scraping and wrenching, until the plane crashed back again.

At one stage he thought the storm was about to take hold of the good wing and flip them over and maybe over and over again; like an empty cardboard box. He reached for Joe's harness and snapped the buckle into its slot. He did the same with his own and braced himself for the possibility.

The sandstorm raged for what seemed hours. Martin was becoming exhausted, just bracing himself with every cycle of assaults, waiting for the final one that would end it all. On and on it went: ferocious one moment, drained of power the next. But it persisted, lolling them into a state of torpor.

Eventually the whine ceased. It was so sudden Martin hardly noticed the difference; it was still ringing in his ears. The power had moved on leaving the remains of a spasmodic breeze that kept sand in the air, pattering against the windscreen like an irritating shower.

Martin decided to take this lull to prepare what was left of the Mars Bars. They'd missed breakfast, so this would be a late lunch. They had to make the most of it. The next meal would be Hard Tack biscuits and according to his calculations they only had six bottles of water left. It was almost the end of the second day and Martin speculated on how long that would last.

Joe had managed to sleep through the worst of the storm, bumps and all, and when Martin finally managed to stir him he was surprised he was in his harness again.

"What's this?" he said, tugging at the broad straps across his chest.

Martin undid the harness and folded it back. "Just a precaution, Joe."

He looked about the cockpit. "Why...was the storm that bad?"

"It was terrible, Joe. It almost lifted the plane off the ground. But she hung on. I think it was the damaged wing that saved us."

He looked towards the windscreen as Martin handed him his quarter of Mars Bar and unscrewed the top off a new bottle of water.

"How are the rations going?" Joe asked.

Martin wondered if he should tell him the truth, then he thought, 'What the heck. When they're gone, they're gone.' "This is the last Mars Bar and we only have six bottles of water left."

"We can survive on the biscuits, but we'll have to ration the water."

It was getting late. The shower of sand that was pep-
pering the windscreen had stopped and the sandstorm had moved on. They could see by the reflection
on the engine cowling that there was an orange glow
to the west, which meant another sunset was almost
upon them. Joe stirred again, trying to find another
easy position.

"Do you think you could get me another painkiller?"

Martin reached for the box, took out a tablet and
passed it to him.

"I can do without the water," he said, swallowing
the tablet. "I hate to say this, Martin, but I think you
should check the plane before it gets dark."

Martin needed no explanation to understand the
sandstorm may have done some structural damage
that could threaten them later. He opened the door
and stepped out into the late evening light. He stood
for a moment under the wing listening to how silent
the desert was now. It was a deathly silence. No distant sounds, no cries from animals about to search
for food; just the sense of another hot night ahead.

The first thing he noticed was how soft it was under
foot. The sandstorm must have dumped at least a
hundred millimetres of sand as it passed; but not
evenly. It was like the snowstorms he'd experienced
in England: in the open spaces it might be six inches

deep, but up against structures, where the snow drifted and collected, it could be as much as several feet. And when it had become too heavy for the angle of the roof to maintain, Martin had been faced with a mountain of six feet or more to clear.

He moved around to the front of the plane. As he guessed the sand had covered everything he'd removed the previous day, and more. There was a heap that reached up to the propellers. It stretched all the way round to the other side, burying the lower portion of the damaged wing up to Joe's door, and all the way along the body to beneath the tail. Surprisingly the tarpaulin was still intact.

"Everything all right," Joe said, as Martin returned to his seat.

"As far as I can see, except for a few piles of sand under the plane, the storm had no effect on us. Even the tarpaulin is still in one piece."

"Good. Check the radio again."

Martin switched it on. The light was still bright and the familiar hum led him to believe they were still capable of transmitting a signal. He put his headset on and spoke into the mike. "Mayday…Mayday… ALPHA, TANGO, ZULU calling."

If he got through to the radio ham's set he did not respond.

Broome came to life again when the storm passed over, despite the sun edging closer to the surface of the Indian Ocean. On reading the latest meteorological report, Philip Hastings had gathered his pilots together, including the captain of the Lear Jet, to brief them on an early start in the morning.

"First of all I would like to let you know Larry Kingston has given permission for us to use the Lear in this operation." There was a noticeable acknowledgement.

"I don't need to tell you how much of a difference that will make."

He turned to the captain. "What sort of ceiling do you want? I presume you intend flying a full complement of passengers with binoculars."

"I do…I've already arranged that for a five-thirty take off. I intend flying at 2000 feet unless we see something, in which case I shall descend to 1000. If your planes fly at 3000 feet until they reach the search area, I shall have plenty of leeway."

"That sounds great. Any questions so far?" Everyone shook their heads and Philip passed on to the new detail marked on the chart. "Now I've already explained what the headings are for the blue line and the red line. The new green lines are the different headings the Lear will fly. He's not only going to cover the gaps, he's going to do it in half the time. So keep your eyes open. I don't want you straying into each other's area. Finally, I can't emphasise how important it is for you to keep contact with Josh. A call every fifteen minutes with your position will let him know where each plane is at any moment. If anyone spots something, make your call straightaway; then Josh can coordinate the nearest planes to join the search."

"And try to stay on your headings, no matter how tempting it might be to explore another area. You can catch that spot on your way back," Bryce said.

Philip looked around for any comments before he continued.

Josh interrupted. "Sorry, Philip. I just want to repeat the fact that you must use your new call signs. Forget about the usual procedure; I must know to whom I'm talking. Each call sign is designated to an individual plane."

"Thanks, Josh," Philip said, "I forgot that. Now make all the checks you need to and let's hope the weather gives us a go for first thing tomorrow."

One of the pilots raised his hand. "As a point of interest, Philip, what happens when we find the plane?"

"After you radio it in and fix its position, Josh will radio the rescue helicopter and direct it to the site. Our first priority is the welfare of Joe and his passenger. The plane is of no interest at this stage."

"I'd like to say something," a voice rang out from the back of the room. It was Larry Kingston. He made his way towards the chart table and stood next to Philip. "I don't have anything to add to Philip's briefing other than to wish you all a successful day tomorrow. I'll be watching your progress with the guys here and waiting eagerly to congratulate the plane that finds them. We're a family at AMINCO. We look after each other, so go to it, guys; go and find our men."

There was a loud roar of applause and Philip smiled and wondered at the man. As usual, he stood back until the last minute and then stepped in with a few words to grab the moment; and in turn the engendered applause. That was what he was good at. That was his motivation.

CHAPTER 10

On the third day Martin woke to a strange silence. His head was swimming and he found it difficult to concentrate. He was facing a mass of blue, two distinct blues in fact; a dark triangular shape pointing towards the instrument panel and a lighter blue surrounding it. He thought it strange and studied the phenomenon for several seconds until he remembered how silent it was.

He was used to the rasping rhythm of Joe's breathing, the occasional cough and his mumbling of past issues. Martin shook his head and began to rouse himself. His first task was to check Joe; to find out if he was any worse.

"Come on, Joe…rise and shine. Let's see how you're doing."

Martin was awake by now and he stared at the motionless figure next to him. The silence in the cockpit was because Joe was silent. No rattling in

Blood Brothers

his breathing, no irritating jerky movements and no signs of pain to disturb his sleep.

The implication stunned Martin. He could do no more than sit and stare at the man he had spent two days with. Then panic took over. He jabbed his fingers into Joe's neck and felt for a pulse. There was none; no matter how many times he searched the side of his neck. He undid his shirt front and placed his hand on his chest, but felt nothing until he suddenly realised Joe's skin was deathly cold.

"Come on, Joe. Don't die on me," Martin cried out.

Martin rubbed his forehead. His usual grasp of challenging situations had stalled; the cognitive processes were out of synch, floating irrationally through his mind without cause or reason. He shook his head to kick-start the process, but still there was a blank space in the middle of his forehead.

He paused for a moment; took his mind away from the problem by switching on the radio. The little red light fluttered and he remembered what Joe had said about draining the battery. He also remembered what he was doing: he was checking Joe's condition. He went through the process again and suddenly it all came back to him.

"Oh Joe…please don't be dead. I'll be all alone out here in this godforsaken place. What will I do when the planes come?"

He studied Joe's waxen features.

"They're not coming...are they?"

Something happened to Martin in that moment of realisation. It was another day. Joe said the first thing they must do each morning was to switch the radio on and scan the frequencies. They might contact the radio ham again or even one of the planes searching the area.

He flipped the switch and the red light came on again. He picked up his headset, put it on and cleared his throat: MAYDAY...MAYDAY...ALPHA, TANGO, ZULU CALLING. He tried again. Joe said to do it twice and move on.

"See, Joe...I'm doing what you said. There's no answer...so I'll move on." He turned the dial and then looked back at Joe. "What was that, Joe? We haven't had breakfast yet. I know...I was going to see if the radio worked first."

The light had gone out and Martin had not noticed. He switched the radio off and turned to the packet of biscuits he'd brought out the night before. He pulled back the wrapping and took out the slab of oatmeal and vitamins he'd already started, broke it in two, placed the fresh side on the console between them and bit into his half.

It crumbled in his mouth. It was dry and he desperately wanted something to wash it down. He remembered what Joe had said earlier.

"I know, Joe, but this is all we have left. It's no use you going on about how dry they are, and how much extra water we'll use. I know all that, but what are we going to do? You said they would keep us alive at the end."

Martin went silent. His brain was trying so hard to remember what Joe had said about surviving. "We're not going to...are we, Joe? We're nearly out of water. When that goes, how long will we survive then?"

Martin remembered the honey and peanut butter sachets. "What about these, Joe...they should help?" Martin said, reaching out to the shelf in front of his knees. "What do you fancy, Joe? Honey or peanut butter?" Martin laughed. "Yes, I agree...peanut butter might be too dry. Honey it is."

Martin pulled back the tab and opened the sachet. He poured half onto his biscuit and placed the sachet on the console next to Joe.

"Umm...it's still not perfect, but it's a bit more palatable."

As Martin slowly ate his biscuit, another of Joe's measures for drawing out their meagre rations, he noticed the state of the windscreen. The sandstorm had left a swirling haze on the glass; probably the reason for his unusual blue vision when he'd awoken this morning. It might stop him from seeing a plane when it passes over.

He jumped up, opened the door and grabbed his jacket from behind the rear seats. Using the broken wheel-arch he'd used to dig out the sand when they'd first crashed, he turned it over and used it as a step to allow him to reach the windscreen. Rolling his jacket into a ball he started scrubbing the frosted glass. It was a fruitless exercise. Each alternative way he rubbed the glass, it made no difference; it was still blurred. It was a little cleaner, but still sandblasted beyond repair.

Martin returned to the cockpit, tossed his jacket behind the seats and sat down again beside Joe. He realised he was sweating and turned round to look outside his window towards the east. He hadn't noticed when he was in front of the plane. The sun was now level with the tail. Soon it would be above the plane and he knew he was going to fry.

By mid-afternoon in Broome, Philip Hastings was pacing the operations room floor listening to the radio chatter. Josh kept shaking his head and Bryce was busy plotting each report of no contact. Outside another plane landed to refuel while an earlier landing was taxying onto the runway for another last circuit before they called it a day. Philip kept checking his watch, wondering whether or not he should give Kate a ring and try to explain their failure to find the plane.

Bryce could read him like a book. "Did you actually expect us to find them straightaway?" he said. "They've still got three hours."

"Yes, I know, Bryce...I can count, and for your information that's only one hour over the search area; unless they're lucky and spot them on their way back."

"I thought the Lear would make a difference."

"It's made a difference by covering more ground. Look at your chart. There are more green lines filling the search triangle than anything else. And still they haven't spotted anything; why do you think that is?"

An awkward expression crossed Bryce's face, "To be honest there's only one explanation; we're searching in the wrong place."

Philip looked aghast, "The wrong place...I thought you were so sure of your calculations. That's what all this lot was about," he shouted, waving his finger over Bryce's immaculate chart.

"I told you, Philip...it would only take a variance of a couple of degrees to throw us off by twenty kilometres."

Philip walked around the table looking at it from every angle before he answered Bryce's bombshell. "That's almost like saying that after three days we have to start all over again. What do I tell Martin's wife?"

"You don't, Philip. You use your usual charm to

explain that we shall extend the search area tomorrow and hope for the best."

By five o'clock, when Kate knew the planes would be returning, she phoned the number Philip had given her. It was his personal mobile, so there was no way he would be engaged elsewhere.

"Hastings," he replied.

"It's Kate, Philip. I know by now you would have rung me if they'd found anything, but I'm going mad here...have you anything for me?"

"I'm sorry, Kate. The time just got away from me. I've been here in the operations room all day listening to the chatter and watching Bryce plot each plane's search pattern. There's been no contact so far, and they've covered almost every section of the search area."

"Maybe you're searching in the wrong place."

"That's just it, Kate; how do we know? As I explained to you, we have no fixed point of contact. We just have headings. Martin's plane could be anywhere."

"I thought the jet was going to help?"

"So did I, Kate."

"But it's been three days, Philip. How long can they last?"

"CASA is going to join the search tomorrow."

"What's CASA?"

"It's the Civil Aviation Authority. It means more planes."

"You didn't answer my question."

"I don't have an answer, Kate. They have enough emergency rations to last some time. I don't know about the water."

The line went quiet. Philip suspected she was trying to hold back her tears and he gave her a moment; but there was nothing else he could say.

"All right, Philip…I'll speak to you tomorrow. Goodbye."

"I'm sorry, Kate. I'll…" The phone went dead, and he cursed.

Whether it was because of sitting beside Joe's dead body or the result of hunger and thirst, Martin had begun hallucinating. It was late afternoon and he switched the radio on again for one last attempt to catch any planes in the area. He was unaware that the red light had not come on and continued with his usual Mayday broadcast.

"Hi Dad, it's Adam. Thanks for the money, it really helped me out. I'll be getting my grant soon so I'll be able to pay you back. Give Mum my love. Bye."

Martin did not question his son's reply and changed to another frequency.

"Martin," Kate called out to the chair he had set up

on the patio, "when are you going to fix that drain. I've got dishwater backing up here. And while you're on, you might as well see to that sticking gate."

"Sorry, dear," Martin replied. "Just finishing this crossword; shouldn't take more than a couple of days."

Martin snorted and switch to the next frequency. "Come on, Martin," Joe said, shaking him. "You can't loll about all day; there're jobs to do if you want all those planes to spot us. Get the tarpaulin out of the cargo space and spread it out in front of the plane. And sprinkle some sand in a giant SOS; they won't miss that."

"Yes, Joe, I'll do that now," Martin said, switching the radio off.

He took off the headset and was fumbling with his harness, wondering why it was undone, when he heard a sound like someone rapping on the window. He turned in its direction and saw a face peering in at him. It was Kate. She was shouting at him, telling him to get on with his jobs.

"I am…I am," he said. "For heaven's sake, give me a chance, woman."

He only turned away for a second, still fumbling with his harness when she rapped on his window again, only this time much louder. He turned to give her a piece of his mind, but she had disappeared.

In her place was a large black face with a broad mouth of white teeth. He was saying something and Martin opened the door.

"Hey you fella…come with me."

"I can't. I'm waiting for a plane."

"You won't live that long…you'll soon be like the dead fella."

"What dead fella? This is my friend, Joe. Say hello, Joe."

"You not right in the head, mate. It's the heat in here."

In his unstable state Martin had not realised how hot it was inside the plane. Although it was still hot outside, it was a lower temperature and a breeze was beginning to stir the spinifex as the sun dropped further towards the horizon.

The young Aboriginal boy opened the door to its full extent, leaned in and placed his hand over Martin's forehead. "How long him been dead then?" he said.

The change in temperature and the presence of another human being seemed to revive Martin's cognitive ability. He was still feeling weak, and he suddenly remembered his arm, but the sight of an indigenous native bending over him brought him back to reality.

"Oh Joe…I found him like that this morning."

"You won't last long with dead man. He's starting to smell already. You have to leave plane. Come with me to cattle station nearby. They look after you and see to your arm," he said, helping Martin out of the plane.

What Martin was not aware of was that 'nearby' to an Aborigine was two days away.

After sitting Martin down on the good wheel, he gave him a drink of water from a gourd hanging from his shoulder. It was different from Martin's bottled water; it was coarse and bitter, like the water he and Kate tasted from a natural spring in Tasmania. He was sitting on a rocky outcrop while Kate cooled her aching feet in a nearby pool. Martin laughed and the Aboriginal boy shook his head in despair, thinking he had lost his mind.

The boy looked over towards the west. There was no time to lose and he checked Martin over, seeing if he was fit to make the journey across rough terrain. Martin would not survive in city clothes. He climbed into the plane to see if there was anything he could use. He brought out the emergency rations, remaining water and the first aid bag and dropped them at Martin's feet before going back to check behind the seats. He returned with Martin's jacket and his hold-all carrying the work clothes he used on the sites he visited.

"Is this everything?" he said.

Martin was not sure until he saw his jacket next to his feet. When he picked it up and attempted to put it on, despite its state after wiping the windscreen, the boy snatched it away from him.

"No good for desert," he said, throwing it to the ground.

Martin stared at the jacket lying at his feet for what seemed ages and as he did so the recent events began to clarify in his mind. The jumble of images he was experiencing suddenly began to make sense as if a curtain had been drawn back.

He bent down to his jacket again. The boy made a move to stop him and Martin waved him away as he went through his pockets for his wallet and anything he thought he might need. The boy continued to unzip the bag and started pulling out the work clothes. Martin wondered why he would be interested in them, noticing he was nodding his head in approval.

"Take your things off," he said. "City clothes too hot for desert."

"What everything?" Martin asked.

The boy laughed. "You can keep your shorts on. Change into this."

He handed Martin his lightweight overalls. They were all in one with a zip up the front and he pulled the legs on, stood up and slipping his good arm in first, turned and looked at the boy. He shook his head, and then his mass of white teeth opened in a broad smile. Reaching into the small pouch he was carrying he took out a knife, slit the other arm off the suit and pulled the rest up Martin's chest so that he could zip it up to his neck. He then turned back to the bag, brought out the hard-hat that was mandatory on mine sites and placed it on Martin's head.

"No one is going to miss me out here in this!" Martin said. The fact that the hat and overalls were bright orange made no impact on the boy.

The boy finally came across Martin's desert boots. It was a fashionable term; not that they were really designed for the desert. Martin found them very comfortable on the rough terrain he was used to rambling over, and the thick, tyre-like soles gripped the slippery surfaces of the mine tunnels.

The boy tossed them over to Martin. Told him to remove his city shoes and put them on instead. That done, the boy gathered up the clothes and his smart new shoes, and stuffing them into the holdall, he threw it into the plane.

He then turned his attention to the first-aid bag. He seemed to know what it was when he opened it and examined its contents. Satisfied, he picked up the two remaining bottles of water, placed the unopened one in the bag and poured the half-empty one into his gourd. He then picked up the box of emergency rations and took out the pack that was already open. He bit into a biscuit, chewed it a couple of times and spat it out with a fierce grimace. He tossed that inside the plane also. Martin seemed amused and chuckled to himself.

Satisfied there was nothing more of value, the boy picked up his spear, boomerang and shoulder bag and walked off around the plane. A silly thought crossed Martin's mind that he was going to leave him there; that the whole charade with the clothes was for his amusement. Martin shook his head to rid it of such thoughts. His mind was becoming clearer and he was done with such fantasies.

With the arrival of the Aborigine something happened to Martin. He had little recollection of what state he was in, but he knew enough to realise he was not far off joining Joe. He still felt weak, fearful of whether or not he was capable of making it to this cattle station Willy had mentioned, but his thoughts were clearer now.

The boy returned after his inspection of the plane and Martin noticed he had found the rope he'd used to tie off the tarpaulin. It was coiled up and slung across his head and one shoulder as if he was about to climb a mountain. But there were no mountains out here in the Sandy Desert.

"We go now…day nearly over," he said.

"Hang on," Martin called out.

He reached into the breast pocket of his overalls for the small black book he'd retrieved from his jacket. He tore out a page and scribbled a note with the pencil in the spine. The writing was a bit shaky with his left hand. He then stood up, leaned into the plane and placed the note in Joe's hand.

"God Bless, Joe," he said, touching the cold hand. "Thanks for everything."

The boy looked impatient. The small ritual meant nothing to him, yet his time with the white ranchers had taught him their ways.

"Come now," he said. We have a way to go before sunset."

As Martin stopped in front of the plane, he noticed the boy heading off into the setting sun. Martin turned and looked back for one last glance up into the sky to see if the cavalry was about to arrive at the last moment. The sky was empty.

CHAPTER 11

Martin was not a religious man; he spurned the Protestant faith he had been christened in, yet he crossed his heart before starting his journey. He was still shaky when he left the plane and he had no idea how far the Aboriginal boy intended taking him, but as he turned to follow, he noticed the boy had stopped.

He was waiting for Martin to catch up and seeing him at a distance suddenly brought home to Martin who his new companion really was. In the past five years in Australia, Martin had not come across a native Aborigine. He had seen them on the television, in books and on his visits to outback mining sites, but those Aborigines were Aussies. They were dressed like any other miner, ate the same food, drank the same beer, but they were not natives; the Aborigine standing in front of Martin was.

He looked majestic. But for a small loincloth and a mass of white slashes decoratively placed all over his body, he was naked. He was standing like a statue with everything he needed to trek through the Sandy Desert. He was holding a long slender spear, a boomerang was slung in the braided bands around his waist alongside his water gourd and a small leather pouch hung from his shoulder.

He looked impatient and Martin placed his one good hand around the bottom of the first aid bag and shuffled away from the riverbed and the plane he had so maligned, yet which had served him well for the last three days.

Martin had no idea why the Aboriginal boy was walking off into the desert so near sunset. Watching him stride away from a relatively clear sandy area into what looked like rough country confused Martin's already taxed mind. He consoled himself with the thought that, come sunrise, he too might be dead and when the planes finally arrived they would only find two corpses.

Was he wise to allow this juvenile to take him from the apparent safety of the Cessna's cockpit to a night in the wilds of the desert? He had to trust him. He would know how to survive in the desert. And he would also know when it was the right time to stop. He appeared to be looking for something; scanning

156

the country ahead, first one side then the next. The sun was setting opposite Martin's right shoulder, which meant they were travelling south-west. Then the boy did stop, turned full on into the huge ball of vermilion and continued.

Martin soon found out what it was he was looking for. They were approaching a group of trees or shrubs; they were so small. They were surrounded by a mass of spinifex. Martin knew that much and when the boy finally dug his spear into the sand and dropped his boomerang alongside, with his gourd, Martin was sure he knew what the trees were. They were the indigenous acacia; prolific in some parts of the Sandy Desert, along with the spinifex.

He was exhausted watching this gangly native move about with such agility.

Before Martin had a chance to settle, the boy had broken off several branches, and removing his fire-stick from his pouch, he soon had them alight. As they were burning he collected a few spinifex clumps and tossed them onto the fire and before long they were ablaze also.

Martin was amazed at how quickly he set up the camp. He started by shredding branches of their leaves onto the fire; then, sticking the bare branch into the ground, he made a small windbreak. He next took fresh branches and wove them horizontally in and out like a skilled craftsman following the traditions passed down from father to son. Finally he added more spinifex clumps to support them. A few moments' work had provided them with a shelter.

The sun had dropped down below the horizon by now and Martin saw the stars for the first time in ages. They were not as bright as above the Indian Ocean from his balcony at home; the remnants of the vermilion rays had not been overcome yet by the darkness of night, but they were just as beautiful.

The boy had finished and he beckoned Martin over to the fire. The day's heat was rapidly dispersing and Martin was experiencing his first cool night in the desert. As he approached the small enclave he noticed the boy had scooped out two shallow hollows with his boomerang and when Martin settled into his, it felt warm. The sun had been heating the sand all day and it passed as a warm bed.

Sitting cross legged in his hollow, the boy picked up his leather pouch and removed a small package. From where Martin was sitting it looked as if it was made of fine bark and the boy had unwrapped a selection of beef jerky. Martin was familiar with jerky from his many dealings with miners who found it easier to handle underground than sandwiches. He called it beef jerky, although he knew it could well have been kangaroo, crocodile or any other form of dried meat.

As the boy offered him the delicacy, he had no idea what meat it was, but still accepted it. He had survived on Mars Bars and Hard Tack biscuits for three days, and even though it was hard and dry, the taste of real meat was wonderful. It was the ideal food for travelling light. It took ages to macerate the dried meat into a chewable state; all the time swallowing the rich, concentrated juices. He washed it down with another mouthful from the boy's gourd. It still tasted bitter.

"Tomorrow we shall eat fresh food," the boy said. "Good game from now on."

"Did you get that water from a stream?" Martin asked.

"No. It was ground water."

"So that's why it was so bitter."

"Not water. My crazy dust," he replied, reaching into his pouch again and pulling out a smaller leather bag and taking out a pinch of a green substance.

It looked like the herbs Kate added to her so-called 'Cordon Bleu' preparations, but Martin knew this was different. He sensed it had a medicinal use.

"Why do you call it crazy dust?"

"The desert can make you crazy with the heat. The Aborigines use this for many generations. It clears the mind."

"So I was crazy, was I?"

"Oh, you big-time crazy," he said, with a big smile. "I got you just in time."

They laughed and Martin felt they understood each other. But he could not keep thinking of him as the Aboriginal boy; he had to have a name."

"What do they call you, or more to the point, what can I call you?"

"They call me Willy at the cattle station."

"That's not your Aboriginal name."

"You can't say my real name."

Martin was going to have to get used to Willy's stunted sentences. They made sense, but they had little real meaning. Was the reason Martin could not say his name because it was hard to pronounce or that his culture would not allow a white man to use the words? Martin had little understanding of the Aboriginal culture, but his experience with indigenous miners had opened a small window to a highly diverse set of beliefs and taboo subjects. He would just have to tread carefully.

"Okay...from now on I'll call you Willy and you can call me Martin."

He flashed those white teeth again and repeated his name a few times. "Martin...Martin. Yes, I like Martin."

As they sat in their warm hollows watching the sparks float up into the night and disappear just as quickly, Martin tried to clear his thoughts by asking Willy the question that had been on his mind since they'd first met; or at least since he had been able to understand what was going on.

"What are you doing out here in the middle of nowhere?"

Willy remained silent for a moment as he placed more wood on the fire, then he turned and faced Martin.

"I'm proving good with my ancestors," he answered.

"I don't understand."

Willy looked surprised. Although he had a reasonable grasp of Australian English – enough to make him understood – Martin's statement seemed to trouble him.

"Why don't you understand?"

"Well…what are you trying to prove to a bunch of people that died generations ago. No offence meant."

Willy was either unable to explain or had a reason not to as he sat silently raking a stick through the embers, kicking more sparks into the night.

"My tribe no good with our traditions; they say they good Aborigines…but all the time they live off station food, medicine and money, and they call me no good Aborigine because I learn Aussie ways at school."

"So you have a school on the cattle station?"

"Yes…good school. I learn the three Rs."

"And your people say you're not a good Aborigine just because you went to school. Why would they say that?"

"They want me to stay a stockman. The pay's good and I won't get any fancy ideas from stuck-up Miss Gerry."

Martin could see the conflict between old ideas and new.

"And what sort of fancy ideas have you got in mind?"

Willy looked as if he found it difficult to put his dreams into words. It had to be in that part of his ancestral background that he was trying to break away from. The part of dreaming that was expressed in images, not words, and Martin hesitated from expressing those words for him.

"What do you do?" he finally said.

"Me? I'm an engineer."

"You mend cars?"

"No, it's a lot more complicated than that," Martin replied, noticing he was not getting through. "Have you seen any mine sites?"

"Only what I saw on television; it was a gold mine in the Kimberley."

"Did you see any of those giant machines that dig the rock out of the ground, or the conveyors that bring it to the surface?"

Willy still looked vague. Martin was being too technical for him. "I saw men driving big…machines. Was that what you said?"

"That's good enough. Well, I mend them when they break down."

"You were going to mend one of those things when you crashed?"

"Yes, I was. It was an emergency as well."

Willy's face lit up. There was a look of recognition on his face. "That's what I want to be: an engineer. It sounds good."

Martin stopped himself from laughing by pushing a burnt ember back onto the fire. It was a distraction that made him realise his amusement was not because he thought Willy was stretching his dream too far, but because he had reduced what was within his grasp to one goal, and not the best of achievements in his opinion. There was a whole world out there with a wealth of opportunities for him to choose from and helping this young boy suddenly crossed Martin's mind.

The heat of the fire must have affected Martin's arm. He was listening to Willy but all the time he was rubbing it. The pain had returned for the first time since before Joe died. Martin reached into the first aid bag for a painkiller. He thought about whether he needed water, thought better of it and swallowed the tablet dry.

As the pain subsided Martin realised they had digressed and turned the conversation back to his original question.

"So why walk out here in the middle of nowhere?"

"So I go walkabout. Show them I'm good Aborigine."

"But why here?" Martin asked, determined to find out what had brought Willy to that exact spot in the desert where the plane had crashed.

Martin was feeling tired, but did not want to go to sleep until he was satisfied there was a simple explanation. He could still feel Joe's presence. He was fearful of dying in his sleep like Joe did. When his time came it was the way he wanted to go, but not now; not out here. He shook off the dullness that was creeping back.

"So you just came across the plane by chance?"

Willy took his time to answer. He was staring into the flames again. They seemed to have an effect on how he put his words together. "No. You were in the sacred place. And I found you. I was meant to find you."

"You're losing me again, Willy."

"I was following the ancestors' journey; the original walkabout. Not the walkabout the stockman use when they sick of working, but the journey in the dreaming. The journey they take when the seasons change, to find fresh food and water. And as they travel the four points of the heavens, they name sacred places."

Willy suddenly looked uncomfortable. He knew he was entering the realm of sacred words. He was trying to tell the story without naming those words.

"You shouldn't be telling me this...should you?" Martin said.

"It belongs to the dreaming. It's not meant for telling."

"Is this to do with Aboriginal painting?"

"Yes. It's not for telling," he repeated.

"Just tell me in white man's words...not what it means."

Willy picked up the remnants of a half-burnt branch on the edge of the fire and cleared a space in front of his crossed legs. He then stabbed it into the flat area and started talking. "This is my ancestors' traditional camp on the banks of the Oakover River, east of Port Hedland." He traced a line above and marked out several crosshatched strokes, "They left the river and walked two days to the marsh land to hunt for eels and frogs, then east to the riverbed you crashed in." He drew a line to the right and then changed it to a wavy line and stopped. "This is sacred land. I can't tell you why. Then they turned south to the Sandy Desert and Lake Waukarlycarly." He scratched another line in the sand with an oval at the end.

Martin could see it all now drawn into the sand. It was a round trip of many kilometres, always turning into another quadrant after each stop. Willy finished his pictogram by finally turning west back to where he started.

Willy looked pleased. He had managed to tell Martin how he'd arrived at the crashed plane without divulging any Aboriginal secrets. But Martin was even more anxious about those shadowy areas of ancient beliefs and customs. He was a long-standing agnostic with unwavering views on the supernatural and anything to do with ordained occurrences. The possibility that something from the past guided Joe's plane to the very spot where Willy was heading for was beyond his belief.

"Joe, that was my pilot, said this was an ancient riverbed when he was looking for somewhere to land. And your ancestors just happened to visit this place?"

"I don't know. It has no name. It has always been known as the dry riverbed."

As Willy continued with his explanation, Martin's eyelids suddenly became very heavy. He tried to keep them open, but in the darting, hypnotic flames of the fire it was difficult. All he could think about was the strange coincidence that Joe should pick the very sacred riverbed that Willy's ancestors visited thousands of years ago. And, more significantly, that Willy should travel to the very spot where the Cessna had crashed.

In mythology a believer would account for such a coincidence by saying an ancient race, many thousands of years ago, seasonally visited the same flowing river for its abundance of fish until an oracle predicted a great occurrence, when a giant magical bird would fly down and drink all the water. From then on the ancients would make their seasonal pilgrimage to the river to extol the bird's arrival.

Martin never completed his analysis. A mythological veil fell across the campsite enveloping them in a long sleep.

CHAPTER 12

It was six-fifteen in the evening, three days after Martin's plane had gone missing in the Sandy Desert. Kate was sitting on her balcony, sipping a glass of riesling, watching the smouldering orb of the sun sink into the Indian Ocean. She was continuing a ritual she and Martin had started the first day they'd bought the house overlooking Cable Beach. On that occasion it had been champagne, an expensive practice they had to compromise on. Yet they vowed to continue.

It was Martin's idea. He had been on a mining site in the Kimberley hills for two days and it was late afternoon when he'd returned to Broome. He felt guilty leaving Kate on her own all that time and bought a bottle of champagne at the airport. When he walked into the house he found Kate sitting on the balcony watching the sunset, exhausted after moving into the new home. He placed the bottle on the table with two glasses he'd found in the kitchen. It was not how he'd planned their first evening, but the champagne and the sunset changed everything.

By the time Jennifer and Adam returned from the local takeaway they found the house in darkness and their mother sitting on the balcony silhouetted against the orange horizon.

"What are you doing sitting out here?" Jennifer asked, walking onto the balcony and noticing the bottle of wine. "Drinking isn't going to help."

"Sit down, have a drink and watch the sunset," Kate answered her.

"Didn't you hear me?" Jennifer said, sitting down.

"I heard you…and I'm not just drinking as you say. I'm sitting here quietly, as your dad and I have done every night since moving here."

Jennifer noticed the glass of wine in front of her; the glass that was meant for her father."

"Mum…you're talking as if Dad's dead."

The sun was no more than a thin orange line stretching across the horizon as Kate switched her attention to Jennifer. It was a harsh look, the sort of look that said you are entering sacred territory; beware. But as usual a gentle smile replaced the scowl and she stood up, looked around and asked where Adam was.

"He's in the kitchen getting the meal ready…

remember? We went out to the takeaway. That's what I came up to tell you."

"Then we had better get downstairs before it gets cold."

"Oh, there you are," Adam remarked, switching the kettle off.

"I'm sorry, dear," Kate said, wandering into the kitchen. "I bet the food's all cold by now. What did you get?"

"I hope it isn't…not when I went to all that trouble, dragging Dad's portable fridge with us. You should have seen the look on their faces."

He lifted it up onto the end of the table and undid the catches.

"I thought it was just for keeping things cold," Kate questioned.

"No, Mum…it's a thermal box. You put ice cubes in to keep things cold and empty to keep them hot – or at least at the temperature they were served at."

Kate was leaning over the box when Adam removed the lid and she had to admit she actually felt a warm, sweet smelling current catch her face.

"I don't think your dad was aware of that…I'll have to tell him."

Adam made no comment when he brought out his mum's fish and chips, Jennifer's lasagne and his own beef balls and noodles.

"Is that to madam's liking?" he said, pouring the tea.

"I had no idea you liked Chinese, Adam."

"That's what happens when you go to university in Sydney."

Jennifer laughed. "You don't have to be in Sydney."

It had just gone seven when Kate walked into the lounge and switched on the television. It was news time and she had the ridiculous notion there might be a mention of the missing plane, despite Philip saying it would not be broadcast.

Just as she picked up the remote to find the channel she wanted the phone rang. She dropped the remote and rushed to pick it up but Jennifer had beaten her to it and was nodding her head listening to the caller.

She had a pensive expression as she cupped the mouthpiece and looked at Kate. "It's Philip," she said, passing the phone to Kate's outstretched hand.

Kate held the phone to her chest for a moment while she composed herself. She sucked in a deep breath and answered, "Philip...I didn't expect you to call so late. I expected all the planes to be back by now."

Adam walked into the room and stood next to Jennifer with a puzzled look on his face. Jennifer shook her head.

"It is late, Kate," Philip replied. "And, yes, I've just been de-briefing the pilots on another wasted day. That was until the Lear Jet just radioed in—"

"I thought they all had to be back before sunset," she interrupted.

Kate was beginning to shake and Jennifer put her arm around her.

"The Lear has clearance for night flights and the pilot decided to stretch his time over the area to the last minute. Kate...he found the plane."

She burst out crying and shook the phone in front of Jennifer's face as if she could not bear what was to follow. Jennifer took the phone and explained to Philip what had happened.

"Jennifer, that's the best news we've heard in four days," Philip said.

"What did they see?"

"Tell your mother the plane looks intact. He flew over it a couple of times but there was no activity. But that doesn't mean anything. They had a tarpaulin over the cockpit to keep the sun off, so they're alive."

"What happens now?"

"I've already arranged with CASA to send their rescue helicopter out at first light tomorrow, so we should hear something about seven...seven-fifteen."

"Shall we come to the airstrip about then?"

Philip paused before he answered her. The

possibility of bad news was very likely under the circumstances and he had no wish for them to hear that
in the operations room. It would be far better if he
collected all the information first.

"No, don't do that. I can't tie CASA down to an
exact time. I'll ring you."

"All right, Philip…thank you."

Jennifer replaced the phone and Kate grabbed her
hand, covering her mouth to prevent herself crying
again, with her other hand.

"Well…what did he say?" Kate asked.

"The plane looks okay. They even set up a sunshade,
would you believe?"

"Did they come out when the plane passed over?"

"No, Mum…but you can't read anything into that.
The Lear is very fast, it was almost dark and they may
well be too exhausted to leave the plane."

Adam joined in. "She's right, Mum. At least they
know where they are."

Kate left them and made her way upstairs to her
bedroom.

There was no discussion about the helicopter arriving in the morning; no questions about what else
Philip had said. It was as if Kate already knew.

Adam shook his head and wandered into the
lounge where the television was playing to itself. Jennifer was a little more concerned about her mother's

state of mind and followed her upstairs. She walked into her bedroom. There was no light on. The sun had finally disappeared on the other side of the Indian Ocean, but there was still an orange glow radiating from the horizon; enough to light the room.

Kate was standing in the eerie light with her back to the chest-of-drawers. She was holding what appeared to be a present.

"What's that?" Jennifer asked.

Kate turned her head with a vague expression.

"Pardon?"

"It looks like a present."

Kate continued fondling the package wrapped in silver paper covered with little drummer boys. "It is… It's your dad's birthday present."

Surprise crossed Jennifer's face. She had obviously forgotten.

"Sorry…I forgot," she said. "When is it?"

Kate turned round and put the present back in the top drawer. "This Friday."

"Oh dear…how old is he?"

"Fifty-five," she answered, and let out a low chuckle. "I was worried about the wrapping paper; it was all I had after wrapping young Stephen's present last week. I was worrying for nothing." Kate sat back on the bed, and there was a whimpering sound as if she was trying to stifle her cries.

"Dad's going to be all right, you'll see…he's a survivor. And when he gets back we'll have a big party with a cake and fifty-five candles. And believe me, he'll laugh at all the drummer boys."

"Maybe so, but no candles. Your dad has a thing about his age."

Jennifer took hold of her mother's hand, "He's not the only one."

By seven-ten the following morning the Sikorsky Rescue helicopter arrived at the Cessna's coordinates. The pilot spotted the crumpled silver cross covered in the blue tarpaulin. He circled several times expecting someone to come out of the plane and wave their arms skyward, but there was no sign of life.

"I don't like the look of that," the pilot said, turning towards his co-pilot and giving him the nod.

Helicopters, especially ones as big as the Sikorsky, had a problem landing on soft surfaces; their rotors created a downdraft that lifted the dust, or sand as in this case, into a swirling cloud that obliterated the landing site. So it was his co-pilot's job to open the door and stand on the rail to inspect the site and guide the helicopter down to the surface.

"Out you go, Baz," the pilot shouted over the intercom.

"Oh, I hate this bit. Can't you just set down here?"

"What and end up like them, and wait for someone to come and get us?"

Baz unhooked his harness from the seat, worked his way across to the large door and hooked himself to the frame. By now the pilot had found a likely spot a few metres in front of the plane on the gravel of the dry riverbed. He switched on the green light above the door and Baz slid it open.

As the helicopter hovered over the chosen site, the loose material began to rise in the downdraft and Baz stepped out on the side-rails to guide him down.

"Three metres...two metres...one. Hold it...left a bit...a bit more."

As they dropped lower the rotors formed a spiral of swirling sand. This was the bit Baz hated: not hanging out of the door on his harness, but being surrounded by masses of flying stones and small fragments. The dust got in everywhere, despite his sealed helmet, overalls and gloves.

"Okay, you're down," he shouted, watching the heavy bulk settle onto the ground; he unhooked himself and jumped down.

As the cloud of sand settled and Baz slid shut the door, the pilot switched everything off, opened his hatch and climbing down the rungs he jumped down beside him. Their first priority was to walk around the helicopter to make sure it was secure and ready to take off when they had completed their mission. Satisfied everything was in order, they made their way to the crash site.

They'd landed on the damaged side of the plane so they were curious to see it leaning badly to one side with the crumpled wing covering the door. They continued on around the nose. Baz touched the propeller and ducked under the good wing.

"This side's all right," the pilot commented.

As they reached the door they were surprised to see how fogged the windows were. But not as surprised as the shock they got when they opened the door. The smell hit them first; it made them step back and almost retch. It was a familiar smell. A sweet, stomach-retching smell that often made them consider if they were in the right job; until they realised this was why they were in Rescue.

The knowledge that there was a dead body inside was bad enough, but when they realised it was their good friend, Joe, and he was still sitting in his seat; it made them turn away and move under the wing.

After the smell had cleared, Baz realised someone had to identify the corpse. He returned to the open door, leaned across the passenger seat and placed his fingers on Joe's neck to confirm he was dead. At the same time he checked the tag on Joe's leather jacket. He nodded his head: it read 'Joe Cirano'.

"Mike…I thought there was supposed to be a passenger," Baz questioned.

Mike was leaning against the wing having a smoke to clear the smell that lingered in his nostrils. He reached into the pocket above his knee and took out a pad with the details of the crashed plane, its occupants' names and coordinates.

"According to this the pilot is Joe Cirano, we know that, and a Mr Dexter."

"So where's Mr Dexter?" Baz asked.

"Is there any sign of him in the cockpit?"

Baz looked around noticing the mess. There were empty water bottles, Mars Bar wrappings, a half-eaten Hard Tack biscuit and a tablet. He then swung round and checked the rear seats. That was interesting. He found Martin's holdall with all his clothes inside, a crumpled jacket and the emergency rations carton.

That was it, he thought, until he picked up the jacket and went through the pockets. Nothing – they were all empty. Then, as he was about to toss it back with the other stuff, he noticed a tag inside the collar. It read Martin Dexter.

"I've found a jacket with his name inside, so he was definitely on the plane. And get this…so were all his clothes. He checked the holdall again.

"Anything in there," Mike said, finally poking his head inside.

"Just the clothes I mentioned and here we are...a work sheet, a clipboard with some technical specs on it and a pair of goggles."

"Wait a minute," Mike said. "This is his work bag. He's changed his clothes."

"I don't know...maybe he messed himself." Mike finally had to look in Joe's direction. "What's that in his hand?" he asked Baz.

Baz reached to the small rolled-up piece of paper in Joe's clenched fist, withdrew it and opened it out. "Well, I never," Baz let out in surprise. "It appears our passenger was found by an Aborigine."

"Does it say where he's taken him?"

Baz passed the note to Mike, "No. Just that he's out of water."

Mike shook his head, put the note in his breast pocket and stepped out of the plane. "Okay. You see if we can get Joe out of his door while I go and radio the news to AMINCO headquarters."

"Why do I always get the dirty jobs?"

"Because I'm wearing the wings."

Back in the AMINCO operations room Philip was patiently waiting for news from the helicopter. He kept checking his watch. It was nine-fifteen; they should have found the plane by now. Then out of the shadows he heard Josh's voice calling him. He walked the short distance into his small enclave. Josh turned to face him with a sombre expression on his face.

Philip stared back at him, "It's bad news. Isn't it?"

"A bit of both, boss," Josh replied, handing him the message. "Joe's dead and Martin was not in the plane."

"What do you mean he's not in the plane?" he shouted, snatching the paper from him. He read what it said just as Josh was reciting the words.

"An Aborigine came and took him with him."

Philip read it twice looking for an explanation, "Took him with him?"

Josh shrugged his shoulders.

"Is the pilot still on line?"

"Yes, boss," Josh replied, flipping a switch and handing Philip the microphone. "Just press the button and speak."

"This is Philip Hastings, the Operations Manager; who's this? Over."

"Mike Spelling, the pilot. Over."

"Good…can you expand on your last message that an Aborigine took Mr Dexter? Took him where? Over."

"I have nothing to add, Mr Hastings. That's all the note said. Over."

"Have you any idea which way they went? Over."

Before he replied there seemed to be a commotion near him. "Sorry about that. It appears there's a weather front moving in on us. We'll have to leave. Over."

"What about my question? Over."

"Oh yes...sorry about that. We reconnoitred the immediate area and came across two sets of footprints heading west – a boot and a bare foot. Over."

"Can you check the area? Over."

"That's a negative. This bad weather is heading in our direction. I can't afford to hang around. We'll have to pick up the search later. Over and out."

"Hello...are you there? Over." Philip called out.

"That's it, boss...he's switched off," Josh said.

"Damn, damn," Philip cried out, walking back to the chart table to see what was west of the plane. Bryce joined him.

"I heard. This doesn't seem to get any better."

Philip picked out the point where Bryce had marked the plane's position and studied the open terrain to the west. "He can't be taking Martin to the coast."

"I have no idea, Philip. If we can get the helicopter back up when this weather front has moved on we might spot them before they get too far away."

"What have you got on this so-called weather front?"

"By the looks of the satellite radar it's a broad band heading their way. I'd say it's one of those mini-tornados. They call them willy-willies."

"Can you have a mini-tornado?"

"They're categorised as a spiralling dust storm actually."

Philip sat down by the table and buried his head in his hands." What on earth am I going to tell Kate?"

"Just tell her how it is, Philip."

"Oh, that's fine. Sorry, Kate, we've found the plane but your husband's not in it. He's gone walkabout with an Aborigine."

"Look on the bright side, Philip. At least he's still alive; not dead like poor old Joe. Now you are going to have a problem with his mother."

Philip's panicked expression gave way to an even worse look of horror. "Oh my God," he uttered. "I forgot all about Joe." He turned and shouted back to Josh, "Are they bringing Joe's body back with them?"

"Yes, boss…I thought I told you."

"Thanks, Josh," he replied, and turning back to Bryce, he said, "They'll be here in no time. I'll have to make arrangements with the morticians."

"Won't CASA have something to say about that?"

"You're right, Bryce. I forgot about them."

CHAPTER 13

I t was the fourth day when Willy shook Martin. His black silhouette was standing above him with the red ball of the sun just above his shoulder. It was an amusing sight. A little more to the left and the sun would have been behind his head, making him look like a saint.

"Why is the sun so red?" Martin asked.

"Bad sun," Willy replied, handing Martin another strip of jerky and his gourd of water. He was in a different mood this morning. He seemed in a hurry.

"What's your hurry, Willy?" Martin said, as he was lifted onto his feet.

"We must hurry...find shelter before it comes."

"Before what comes?"

"Before that comes," he shouted, turning Martin around to face the wall of dust heading their way.

Martin was in no mood for more disasters. His

head was aching, his arm was giving him hell and despite a full night of sleep, he felt exhausted. He suspected his afflictions were due to lying on the ground, regardless of Willy digging a bed for him.

Despite not seeing so well, there was no mistaking the swirling mass heading in their direction. Willy had already set off and Martin turned to follow him. He was setting a brisk pace, too brisk for Martin to catch up, so he decided it was enough to keep him in view. He had no idea where he was going to avoid the storm and wondered why he had left the trees, until he realised Willy was heading for a small mound in the distance. Under normal circumstances it would be insignificant, but out here, where you can see to infinity, the slightest bump becomes important.

When Martin finally arrived at a small outcrop of sandstone slabs, Willy was already digging furiously between two upright rocks. On the surface they were no more than a metre high; hardly a worthwhile barrier against the raging mass that was almost upon them. But below that, Willy was up to his waist.

Martin kneeled down, removed his hard-hat and began scraping away the sand Willy had already excavated. It had begun to fall back into the hole and Willy nodded his approval as he continued to dig.

"You pile all this sand up like a wall over there,"

Willy said, climbing out of the hole and walking over to the scattered trees nearby.

Although Martin vowed he would not look at the approaching mass, his curiosity got the better of him. The swirling miasma was almost upon them and as he continued frantically building the wall he shouted at Willy, "What the Hell is that thing? It doesn't look like the sandstorm I was in the other day."

Willy returned with a handful of branches. "We call it a willy-willy," he said, digging the branches into the bank Martin was making.

Martin had to laugh, despite the situation. "Don't tell me that's something to do with your name."

"Sometime I'll tell you the story," he said, walking back to the trees.

As soon as Willy had thrust the last branch into the embankment, which now would act as a shield to protect the hole, he helped Martin into the bottom close up to the rock he had been digging against and jumped in himself. Once inside, he pulled the shield over them and they waited.

It was an agonising wait. They heard it first. An express train that Martin was sure was about to tear them apart. It seemed to have the same ferocity as the one that had attacked the plane. But there was a difference. With the first one Joe and Martin had the protection of the fuselage to save them; here, all Willy and Martin had were a couple of rocks, a few acacia branches and each other.

At first Martin felt a suffocatingly warm blast of air that popped his ears and took his breath away. According to Willy, it was the desert air that was being pushed out of the way. Then there was a short calm and as Martin closed his eyes and prayed, the corkscrew hit them.

The sound was unbelievable. It was what Martin imagined it would be like in a washing machine without the water. Although he was not tumbled about as he had the rock to hold onto, a force beyond his description was trying to suck him out of the hole. Every piece of loose material was spinning around the hole with them. Martin had to bury his face in his free hand whilst trying to hold onto his hat. Willy was trying his best to protect Martin's arm and at the same time hang onto his own belongings.

The willy-willies came in waves. No sooner had one passed, another followed, with the only consolation being that with each successive attack they grew weaker. They were blowing themselves out until eventually the swirling mass was reduced to no more than a normal sandstorm. That was bad enough, as Willy found out when he tried to see outside the hole.

"No good yet," he said, spluttering and spitting out sand.

By late afternoon, when the express train had passed and the cacophony had diminished, Martin still had an irritating ringing in his ears. Willy was trying to say something, but it sounded far away and muffled. He resorted to sign language. He was attempting to get Martin out of the hole.

"Now it's good to leave. We must make camp."

Apart from the bottom of the hole being full of sand up to his calves, his upper body was entangled with the branches. Willy wriggled his way clear and freed Martin from the branches. He then reached down for Martin's waist and dragged him out of the hole.

The sight was amazing. The sky was bright blue again and as Martin turned a full circle he regained his position with the sun. It was to his right, well past the overhead position but not yet heading for sunset in the west. He could hear Willy but not see him. He was rummaging about somewhere amongst the group of rocks. He had taken his spear with him and there was an occasional sound of digging.

Martin left the edge of the hole and followed Willy's footprints. On the other side of the largest of the rocks, he came across a campsite. Willy had been busy. He had cleared an area up against the rock with the same type of windbreak he'd made the night before, laid a pile of branches ready to light about two metres in front and as he expected there were two hollows for them to lie in.

Martin, who had already chosen his hollow, took out a painkiller and washed it down with a mouthful of his own bottled water from the first aid bag when Willy returned. He looked as if his rummage in the rocks had not been successful but after stabbing his spear into the ground he dropped two small creatures beside the fire. Martin could not see what they were from where he was, but the idea of small animals being good eating offended him.

Without a word Willy started the fire, went off a short way for a handful of spinifex and returned to stoke it. They were facing west. The trees were in front of them and the sun was just clipping their spiky tops. He put the first spidery ball in the flames, tamped it down with a branch and waited until the first embers formed. Then he picked up the tiny bodies and tossed them into the flames. Straightaway they began to hiss and crackle and Martin turned his head. During the whole episode Willy did not talk to Martin; he was in his own world.

Martin had no idea how long they would take to cook or if he would be able to eat them without being sick, but he knew one thing – he was hungry, and at this moment anything would be better than jerky. Martin was so tired. He closed his eyes and visualised the last time he and Kate had gone to the restaurant at the end of Cable Beach. It was their wedding anniversary and the sky had been the limit. The seafood plater looked inviting and they agreed on that: a whole lobster cut in half surrounded with scallops, prawns, shrimps and mussels with a side dish of tossed salad in Hollandaise sauce.

Martin heard a sound close by. He opened his eyes to see Willy standing over him with his spear. He knew he was annoyed with his catch, but he had no idea he would take it out on him. He was motionless. His knees were bent, his spear raised and his attention was focused on something just above Martin's shoulder.

As quick as lightning, his spear left his hand, passed Martin's head too closely to think about and a wriggling mass shot across his shoulder. It was a huge snake, the back end still thrashing across Martin's chest. It was covered in reddish-brown and cream stripes and was about as thick as his arm at its widest part.

Willy grabbed his spear with the coiling snake still alive and lifted it over Martin's head. He placed it on the ground with his foot over the snake's neck, removed the spear and thrust it once or twice again into its large head. It struggled for a few moments until it went still.

"No trouble from him no more," he said, with a broad smile on his face as he tossed it on the fire. "Good tucker tonight. You have fat belly at last."

By the time Philip had spoken to the man from CASA and determined they would deal with the formalities regarding Joe's body, witnessed his remains transferred from the helicopter to the waiting ambulance and sat in on the debriefing of the men who inspected the crash site, it was late afternoon before he left to see Kate.

After another long day Kate was back in her usual spot on the balcony overlooking Cable Beach waiting for the sunset. As she took another sip of wine her attention was diverted to a strange car slowly pausing for a moment outside each house until it stopped opposite hers.

She was not familiar with Philip's car but when the grey-haired man got out and casually looked up at the balcony, she knew it was bad news. She stood up, walked into the bedroom, checked her hair and dried the tears that were beginning to form in the corner of her eyes, and then she walked out onto the landing.

Jennifer was standing at the bottom of the stairs and just as she spotted her mother she called out, "Oh Mum...it's Mr Hastings."

Kate took in several deep breaths, prepared herself

for the possibility of bad news and walked down-stairs to the lounge. Philip was standing talking to Adam. He turned to face her as soon as she entered the room and she studied the expression on his face. He too looked as if he was attempting to mask his true feelings. He had a pleasant smile – one that sent out the message that this was just a casual visit. But she could see it in his eyes; they were full of pain.

"What's so important a phone call wouldn't do?" she questioned. "It's bad news, isn't it? They're dead, aren't they?"

"No, Kate. As usual that mind of yours is racing ahead. For the past four days you've been one step ahead of me all the time and in each case your suspicions have been wrong; like they are now."

A glimmer of relief crossed her face. He was right. Already, before he had a chance to tell her why he was here, her thoughts had created another outcome. She braced herself for the true reason a phone call would not have sufficed.

"I'm sorry, Philip. Why don't you sit down and tell us why you're here?"

He did that and everyone sat down in the small group of easy chairs.

"After leaving at first light, the helicopter landed at the site around seven and found no activity. Inside the plane they found the dead body of the pilot. Martin was not there and by the condition of the cockpit, he had left some time earlier."

While Adam and Jennifer were evidently bursting with questions, they held back. Kate was almost gagging with the shock and took a moment before she replied.

She cleared her throat and wiped the beginnings of a tear from her eye; then she blurted out her question in a sudden outburst. "What do you mean, Martin was not there? He had to be...where else could he go?"

"They found a note in Joe's hand. Apparently an Aborigine found Martin dying of thirst and, as it said on the note, he took him away."

Adam could not hold his tongue any longer and while his mother came to terms with her shock he interrupted. "Didn't they investigate the site for any clues as to where this Aborigine took my father?"

Philip reached into his inside pocket and removed the notebook he'd brought with him for such questions. He flicked over a few pages and stopped at the page that covered what the pilot had said about the site. "They didn't say a lot...apparently they were in a hurry. According to the radio message, they did inspect the crash site and found two sets of footprints leading away towards the west."

"Why were they in a hurry?" Jennifer asked. "I

thought you said it was only seven. They had plenty of time to take off and head in that direction."

"Jennifer, don't you think I asked the very same question? The pilot's reply was that there was a serious-looking weather pattern closing in on the site and they had to leave before they were caught in it—"

Kate suddenly jumped into his explanation. "Do you mean to say Martin is out in the desert with this… weather thing, about to hit them?"

"Kate…I'm only the messenger."

Kate stared at Philip for what seemed ages until she finally came to terms with what he'd said. "Oh, sorry, Philip…this is all getting too much."

"Look, Kate…as I see it, if the Aborigine hadn't come along when he did, Martin may well have died of thirst and the helicopter would have been bringing two bodies back. As it stands, he will be safe with the Aborigine. The Sandy Desert is his country and he must be taking him somewhere."

"What is CASA doing now?" Adam asked.

"As soon as the weather clears the helicopter is going back to see if they can pick up their tracks. That's all I can say at this point."

CHAPTER 14

With the strong, gamey taste of the death adder lingering on Martin's palate, Willy offered him a mouthful of his bitter water before they set off. Martin noticed, by the position of the rising sun over his left shoulder, that Willy had changed course again; they were now heading south-west.

He ran his furry tongue over his teeth in an effort to clean them, but the taste still remained, only now it was competing with the bitter gourd water. Martin shook his head and wondered why he bothered to react to all this stimuli. The snake had provided a sizeable meal. There was enough left for at least two more meals, so the taste was going to be a recurring dilemma. He supposed that the small chunks of white meat that Willy kept feeding him last night until he was fit to burst were from the two small animals.

There was something different about Willy's new

direction. Yesterday, before the willy-willies came through, there seemed to be more open sandy territory, but now Martin was constantly stubbing his toes on grey and black rocks that looked distinctly like iron pyrites. This was mining country by the looks of it.

"Willy," Martin called after him. He stopped and waited.

"Do you want to rest?" he asked.

Martin was panting but thought better of stopping just yet.

"No… Not yet. I should be able to last out till noon. What I wanted to know was…is there a mine near here?"

"Not for a long time. All this rubbish they left behind."

That settled, Willy continued and Martin trudged on behind.

With no watch to constantly refer to, Martin became conscious of the position of the sun. When Willy made his first change the sun was low on his left shoulder; now it was beating down on the side of his helmet. Rivulets of sweat were forming on his eyebrows and once they were saturated, droplets poured down his cheeks and he soon discovered the collar of his overalls was soaked and beginning to irritate his neck.

Despite his indigenous coalescence with the high temperatures in the Sandy Desert, Willy sought refuge in another small copse of acacias nearby. When Martin finally stumbled into the shade and collapsed alongside, Willy had already laid out his bark bundle containing the death adder's remains.

Martin retrieved his bottle of water, took a mouthful to ready his mouth for the strong meat Willy was about to serve him, and seeing the bottle was almost empty, he offered it to Willy. He shook his head and poured it into his gourde.

"I have to look for water soon," he said, passing Martin the snake.

"How soon?" Martin cried out. "I thought we would be there by now."

"Don't forget we lost a day in the willy-willies."

When they finished their meal Willy agreed to a short rest and Martin leaned back against the trunk of an acacia tree. It was too hot to sleep, so closing his eyes he became one with the desert. He'd had no idea the desert had a smell. It was the smell of nature: the acacia that afforded them shade, the nearby spinifex that pervaded the area with a pungent scent that reminded him of Kate's aromatic containers of dried flowers. Even the stifling heat had a smell.

It was like Sunday afternoon in his garden. Lying on his recliner with his straw hat over his face, listening to the bees going about their business, competing with all the other sounds: The after-dinner fly looking for a tasty morsel, the high-pitched whine of the midge, ready to drain the blood from any unprotected skin and the drone of something much bigger. Another sound had entered the chorus.

Martin had opened his collar to dry it in the sun and, as a consequence, had made his neck an open invitation for the insect making the sound. It was no more than a tickle at first. He couldn't see what it was, but as soon as he raised his hand to brush it away, he felt an excruciating pain.

"Bloody hell," Martin screamed out.

He was jumping up and down, waving his arm about like a madman. Whatever it was, Willy had no English word for the striped insect attacking Martin's neck as he instinctively lunged forward, sweeping it away. Willy then placed his hands on Martin's shoulders and eased him back down onto the ground, opened his collar further and pushed his head to one side.

Willy could see the swelling forming on Martin's neck as he took out the knife he'd used to skin the snake and moved closer.

"What are you going to do with that?" Martin shouted.

"This only way to get bad stuff out," Willy replied.

"Not with that thing, you don't," Martin said, reaching over for his first aid kit and placing it on his lap.

He opened the bag and brought out the plastic case containing the variety of surgical instruments. Willy's eyes opened wide. Inside was a scalpel and spare blades, a pair of small scissors and a curved needle attached to a small spool of fine thread. Martin took out the scalpel. But first he took out a large plastic bag of folded lint, a sterile pack of gauze, a small bottle of Iodine, a bag of cotton wool balls and a larger bottle of surgical spirits.

"Now Willy, unscrew the cap off the bottle and put some on one of those cotton wool balls and wash your fingers with it."

Willy was not impressed with the smell, and after replacing the cap he started laying out each item on the plastic bag across Martin's lap.

"Good," Martin said, handing him the Iodine. "Now cover another cotton wool ball and rub the Iodine over my neck – gently now."

They were words that had no meaning for Willy as Martin gritted his teeth. That done, Martin pulled the lint out, placed it on the plastic and cleaning his own fingers with the surgical spirits, he picked up the scalpel and handed it to him.

"Here, use this. And make sure it's only a small nick; I don't want to bleed to death over a sting," Martin explained, backing away slightly.

Without a shake of his hand, Willy started to cut. It took several strokes of the sharp blade and Willy's probing fingers and it was done as he stood up with a broad smile on his face. Then handing the scalpel back to Martin he took the plug out of his gourd and quenched his thirst with a mouthful of water.

"That's good, Willy. Now wipe the wound down with Iodine again."

"Not finished yet," he said.

Before Martin had a chance to ask why, Willy bent his head over his neck, put his mouth on the wound and as Martin struggled, he started sucking. It was a vicious suck, to the point of hurting and when he'd finished, Willy stood up and spat the contents of his mouth on the desert floor. It was bright red. He had drawn blood and Martin could see his blood on Willy's lips.

"All done," he said. "No more bad stuff."

"You've got my blood on your lips," Martin pointed out.

Willy laughed, and wiping it away, he said: "You and me blood brothers now."

After Martin's ordeal he signalled to Willy that he was ready to continue their journey. Although the sun was directly above by now, Martin got the impression Willy had changed course again. Instead of walking away from the copse in the direction they'd arrived, he followed the scattered acacia trees' path.

It was yet another surprising sight in this ever-changing desert. What he thought was an isolated group of trees as before, turned out to be one copse in a long line that seemed to stretch into the distance. From the air, Martin would have imagined he was following another ancient riverbed that had long since drained off to one of those subterranean aquifers.

Willy was following this new source of shade and branches to build his nightly shelters. His attention was now drawn to the trees themselves. Within a few hundred metres he stopped, sat Martin down in the shade and continued on a short distance, tapping the ground with his spear.

Eventually he stopped, kneeled down with his face close to the sand and apparently satisfied, began digging a hole. It looked like a big hole. Martin's curiosity was too much and he stood up and wandered over to see what Willy was doing. By now he was a good half-metre down and Martin noticed the walls of the hole were much darker, the lower he went.

Then to Martin's amazement, Willy stopped and sat back as if he was waiting for something to happen. And it did: suddenly the hole began to fill with water. Within seconds the water had risen sufficiently for him to lower his gourd. It sank below the surface, and as Willy scooped the loose debris out of its way, Martin watched a series of bubbles rise to the surface.

"Plenty water now," he said, lifting the gourd out of the hole, replacing the wooden peg and slinging it back across his shoulder. "We go now."

It was the hottest part of the day and Martin was beginning to feel drowsy, despite the cover of trees protecting them from the severe sun. He felt different somehow. He was now rehydrated; his belly was fuller than it had been in days, his arm had stopped aching and the ground they were walking on seemed less severe. Yet his head was throbbing, his clothes felt wet and he was beginning to shake.

Willy had put some distance between them or Martin was slowing down. He had stopped looking back. He seemed preoccupied with something up ahead. Martin's eyesight had become blurry; that was another symptom of whatever it was that had taken hold of his system.

Martin eventually caught up to Willy kneeling behind an acacia shrub. He gestured for him to sit down and gave the sign for him to be quiet. Willy looked furtive as he dropped his spear, boomerang and pouch beside Martin. Staying in a crouching position he slowly made his way through the trees. He took the rope from the plane off his shoulder, made a loop in one end and tied the other end around his waist. He then continued his panther-like prowl through the trees.

Fascinated by Willy's performance, Martin focused his attention on a spot amongst the trees about fifty metres in front of Willy. It was difficult to see at that distance, with his eyesight beginning to fail, but Martin suddenly realised Willy was watching a small group of horses nibbling on new acacia shoots.

What took place next amazed him. He saw the Aboriginal boy's character change before his eyes as he reverted to his native state. He appeared to take on the habit of the horses. He bent over and slowly walked with the horses, even grazed with them. He had become one of them and they hardly noticed him. Then he was amongst them. Brushing up against them as horses did, until he seemed to find what he was looking for.

It was a fine-looking red horse with a long mane and he moved up alongside it and stroked its flank; then, he moved his hand along its back and up its neck and calmly placed the noose over its head. The horse suddenly realised what was happening and raised its head above the others. Willy instinctively took hold of the horse's mane and leaped onto its back, alerting the rest of the group, who reared their front legs and raced off across the desert taking Willy with them.

Martin lost sight of Willy and the horses in a cloud of dust that obliterated the scene. It seemed confined to them and he watched the ball of dust disappear into the distance. He was astonished at what had just taken place and for a moment or two sat looking into the distance wondering what was going to happen next. He glanced down at Willy's cherished possessions, knowing he would never leave them behind and his thoughts returned to his throbbing head.

Some time later Martin looked up towards the shimmering waves rising from the desert floor and saw something else shimmering in the heat. The image seemed to hang in the air getting larger with every minute until finally Martin saw Willy riding towards him on his red horse. They looked as if they belonged together; it seemed different from the other wild horses. Willy stopped the stallion in the shade beside Martin. He jumped down with no concern that the horse would bolt. It seemed calm, at home with Willy's casual hand movements across his back.

"Why did you pick that particular horse?" Martin asked.

"It's one of ours," he said, pointing to the brand on his rump.

It was a large G within a circle. "What does it stand for?"

"It's the Galene brand. We go there."

Martin was too tired to ask any more questions. He assumed this was going to be their transport from now on, as he watched Willy remove the noose and fashion it into a more suitable bridle. A wave of emotional relief ran through Martin's body. He was now convinced someone up there was looking out for him. He knew, despite anything else that might come their way, he was no longer able to place one foot in front of the other.

Willy lifted Martin to his feet, handed him his spear and boomerang and hanging his gourd across his shoulder, led Martin and the horse a few metres on, towards an old stump. It was high enough for Martin to step up and climb onto the horse's back. Then Willy climbed on behind Martin, took hold of the loose end of the rope and wound it around their waists, binding them together in case Martin fell off. Once settled, Willy made a clicking sound and the horse moved off.

"Why is he so calm?" Martin asked as they continued following the trees.

"Him belong on station...I broke him in."

"So he knows you."

"Him good horse; he just gets restless...like me."

Martin wondered why, of all the horses, they had to run across this one.

It was an effortless journey; Willy hardly needed

to correct him. He seemed to know where he was going. That was reassuring and as soon as Willy felt the horse was comfortable with two on his back he began increasing the pace. It was as if they both could smell the cattle station. And before long, without any prompting, the horse broke into a trot.

The constant bouncing on the horse's back must have lulled Martin into a state of torpor. Occasionally he opened his eyes and saw the back of the horse's neck rising and falling, but little else until the horse slowed down and resumed his earlier canter. The sun was back above his right shoulder, but this time the heat had dissipated. His head was too heavy for him to look up and check, but he guessed it was late and expected the reason they had slowed down was so that Willy could select a camping site for the night.

In reality, it was late afternoon and Willy was entering the stockyards of Galene cattle station. At first no one paid any attention – a stockman on horseback was a common occurrence – until someone shouted "Willy"; then they all looked up. All the way past the horses' enclosure, the cattle pens and on to the outskirts of the cattle station buildings, men were looking up and shouting to Willy.

Willy was sitting 'high in the saddle', as they say, although he had no saddle, and he had gathered a crowd behind him. They looked as if they would follow him until the Aboriginal stockman boss walked out into the middle of the dirt road and raised his hand to stop Willy.

"Who's this fella then?" the stockman asked.

"He's my blood brother, Martin," Willy exclaimed proudly.

As the old stockman rubbed his hand across his grey stubble with a questioning look, another commotion stirred the crowd.

The old stockman boss swung around, lifted both arms above his head and bellowed at them, "Clear off you lot; back to work! It isn't sundown yet."

As they separated and returned to their tasks, a white-coated figure pushed his way through the last of the stockmen. It was the cattle station's doctor. News of Willy's arrival had preceded him and the doctor was anxious to see if he was the man everyone was looking for.

Willy unravelled the rope and took charge of his spear and boomerang so that those who were left could help Martin down from the horse's back. The doctor could see he was in a serious state. Willy had not noticed Martin's decline as he'd focused on reaching the cattle station before nightfall.

"Okay you lot," the doctor called out. "Carry him into the clinic."

Everyone except Willy seemed to know Martin was a celebrity on television. The last few hours the CASA rescue machine had gone into action, spreading the news of a downed plane across the radio bands as well as the media.

But there was no mention of the one who'd actually saved Martin's life. As the group disappeared into the clinic nearby, Willy, realising his moment of glory had passed, slowly turned his mount and headed for the horses' enclosure. At least the red stallion was going to get his reward: a good rub-down and a bellyful of hay.

CHAPTER 15

Philip was sitting in his office sipping a large double whiskey. Darkness was overtaking Broome and he sat there with only the automatic light from the hall. Elsie walked into the open doorway and stood there for a moment.

"Do you want me to switch the light on before I leave?" she asked.

Philip looked up from his thoughts. "What? Oh no, Elsie, leave it."

"I suppose you're relieved now CASA has taken over. Did you see the media coverage on the television?"

"No, I didn't. They told me what they were going to do to narrow down the new search area. I was just thinking of the effect it would have on Kate."

Elsie was about to reply to him when Josh walked up behind her. "Oh Josh. Don't creep up on people like that," she said, moving over.

"Sorry darlin'. I thought Philip would like to hear my latest news."

Philip finished his drink. "And what news would that be, Josh?"

"They've found Martin."

"What…already?"

"Yes, boss…that's the power of the media for you."

"How? Where?"

Josh referred to his message sheet. He stepped back into the light to read it.

"The Aborigine took him to a cattle station about twenty kilometres south-west of the crash site," he said, walking into the room and placing the paper on Philip's desk. "Luckily they have a doctor there. He radioed in the news."

"Have you informed CASA?"

"Bryce took care of that, boss. He also cancelled all the flights."

Philip looked relieved. He poured another drink, saw the expression on Josh's face and took out a glass and poured him one too.

"What about Kate?" Elsie questioned.

Philip put his glass down and shook his head. "You're right. I should get down there before CASA does."

"What about Mr Kingston?" she reminded him.

"Oh yes, Elsie," he said, glancing at his watch.

"We've got a meeting in ten minutes. That's why I was having a drink."

"Or two," she reminded him again. "You can't drive down to Cable Beach smelling of whiskey."

"Is it that bad?"

"It will be if a policeman pulls you over," Elsie said, noticing the dilemma on Philip's face. "Why don't I go and see her on my way home."

"You live on the other side of town," Josh interrupted.

"I'll go the long way round."

After being alerted to the earlier news broadcast about the plane crash, Kate was sitting in the lounge waiting for the seven o'clock news when Elsie arrived. She thought Elsie had called to ask if she'd seen what CASA had put together about the story and welcomed her in to hear the broadcast.

"Did you hear what they said, Elsie? I missed it," Kate said.

"They've found him, Kate," Elsie replied.

"Yes. I'm waiting to hear. Sit down."

Adam and Jennifer were amazed and rushed over to hug her.

"What?" she said.

"Didn't you hear Elsie, Mum?" Jennifer said. "They've found Dad."

Kate looked shocked. Her wide, watery eyes were darting from one to the other in disbelief. "They've found him?" she said, looking at Elsie.

Elsie nodded her head and took hold of Kate's hand. "Yes, Kate. We just received a radio message from a cattle station saying the Aborigine brought him in."

Kate's face lit up. "Is he all right?"

"We don't know much yet, but it was a doctor that sent the message."

Kate took hold of Elsie and hugged her. "Thank you, Elsie. I don't know how I was going to get through another night. And thank Philip for me."

"I will. He apologises for not coming himself but he was stuck in a meeting with the big American. Among other things, they're working out the details about Joe's death. So you can imagine the state he's in."

"Oh, I forgot all about poor Joe," Kate said. "Has he left a wife and children?"

"He was divorced some years ago. Luckily there are no children, but he has a mother in Sydney. He was all she had."

"I would like her address, when you have the time."

"I will, Kate. Now I must go. Philip will speak to you tomorrow."

"Let me show you out," Adam said.

Adam walked Elsie out to her car and stood by the

CHAPTER 15

open door. "Have you any idea what's going to happen now?" he asked.

Elsie smiled at him. "I don't really, Adam. I'm only a small cog in the works, but I would imagine they'll try and get your mother out to Martin."

When Adam walked back into the house he was surprised to hear raised voices coming from the lounge and even more surprised to see his mother and Jennifer opening a bottle of wine.

"Come on, Adam," Kate called out, taking hold of him. "We're celebrating your dad's return." She noticed his surprised look. "What's wrong?"

"Mum, it's great that Dad's alive and safe, celebrate that, but he's not going to be home in a hurry. We don't know how bad he is or how long it will be before he can travel. And how are they going to get him back?"

"What do you mean?"

"He's out in the middle of nowhere."

"What did Elsie tell you?"

"Nothing, Mum…she's only a secretary. Philip will tell you what's going to happen. But it won't be about Dad coming home soon. Probably they'll be making arrangements to get you out to see him."

Kate paused, still holding the bottle of wine. "I never thought of that. I'll have to make arrangements. When do you think I'll be going?"

Adam looked exhausted and Jennifer took the bottle out of her mother's hand and sat her down. "Mum...slow down. You won't know anything until Philip rings. He does have other things to take care of; you heard Elsie."

"Yes... I'm sorry. It's just that I want your dad home again."

It was late. Adam and Jennifer finally turned in and Kate was sitting at her dressing table staring into the mirror contemplating the highs and lows of the past five days. She found herself opening doors in her memory that she always tried so hard to keep shut; like Martin's near-fatal car crash. But he'd survived, she thought, and kept brushing her hair.

She glanced at the reflection of the bed and Martin's empty space.

She smiled, remembering him watching her brush her hair and remove the make-up from her face. It had become a nightly ritual he enjoyed so much; so often a prelude to a night of love. Then she frowned. It hadn't always been that way. When they were young and she misunderstood his emotions, she did something that almost ended their marriage.

She ran her fingers through her hair and the painful memory flooded back. She questioned why now? Why were these past memories of another time in their life together of particular importance? Martin was not dead and he was not about to die; yet that one silly incident filled her thoughts as if it was yesterday.

They were getting to know each other. Exploring likes and dislikes, in particular, the signals that stirred each other's emotions. In Kate's naivety, she misunderstood Martin's innocent attraction to a young film star who had short blonde hair. Her solution was to cut hers and style it to look the same.

Martin's reaction terrified Kate and it took ages before he would talk to her again. Eventually he softened. He even began to like her new look, and when she decided to let it grow back again, he told her to leave it; it suited her. He had no idea why and she was not about to tell him; she was only happy she had him back again.

By mid-morning the following day there was no word from Philip, and Kate looked as though she was going to spend the rest of the day next to the phone. Jennifer had to call in at the university to receive her end-of-year results and Adam decided to get his mother out of the house.

"Come on, Mum...let's go into town and have lunch and do some Christmas shopping before the stores get busy."

She looked up at him with a surprised expression

on her face. "Good heavens. I'd forgotten all about Christmas," she said, glancing to where the tree usually stood.

It was yet another trigger for her tears.

"Why are you crying, Mum? I should think you would be happy."

"Sorry, Adam. It's just that your dad usually has the tree up, ready for me to decorate, by the second week in December."

"Then that will be my first job when we get back."

"Get back?"

"Oh Mum…you're not listening to me. I said let's go out to lunch and do some shopping before the shops get busy. I don't think Philip's going to ring today."

"Yes…you're right. It looks a nice day, so let's do some shopping."

It was Larry Kingston's sixth day at the AMINCO headquarters and he was driving everyone mad. Philip was doing everything he could to keep him away from operations, but since the planes were stood down from the search, he had resumed his original task of checking into the efficiency of the team.

With due respect Philip knew he would probably have been less inquisitive if it hadn't been for his American boss Hubbard checking up on him. Normally Kingston would approach things with a more relaxed attitude; preferring to use his trip to enjoy sight-seeing in Australia than work.

Sitting in Philip's office, he was reading the report he'd asked Philip for; the one he was supposed to provide for Hubbard. Philip had a smirk on his face as he watched Larry wade through the massive document. He had asked Bryce to pay particular attention to detail, to enlarge on the different aspects of AMINCO's operations in this area, and to make sure he dotted the I's and crossed the T's. Bryce was particularly good at reports; especially long ones.

Larry read the five-page summary, then flicked through the rest, before turning to Philip. "Very good...I'll finish that off in the Lear when I fly to Sydney."

"You're taking the Lear?" Philip questioned.

"Of course...why?"

"It's just that I had arranged to send Mrs Dexter to the cattle station to see her husband, and if he was fit enough, bring him back to Broome."

"That's all right. She can use the Piper Navajo. I understand it's scheduled to fly down to Site 21 tomorrow morning. It can easily continue on to this cattle station. In fact she can have it as long as she likes."

Philip couldn't argue with that. "Fine...I'll make the arrangements," he said. "By the way...when can we expect you back?"

"I'll only be a day in Sydney. I'm attending Joe Cirano's funeral on behalf of the company; then it's Melbourne the next day and back here the following."

"It's a pity his mother hadn't lived with him here, then the whole AMINCO team could have shown their respects at the funeral, instead of just flowers."

"Yeah...pity. Still, I shall be taking all your cards with me," Larry replied in his offhand manner. He was about to leave when he stopped. "Oh, by the way did CASA say when they would be finished with the Cessna?"

"I have no idea. They're at the crash site now. I doubt if it would take them more than a day, knowing it's in the middle of nowhere. Why the concern?"

"It was something Hubbard said last night. Apparently he's been talking to CASA and they seem to think the damage is only superficial."

"I wouldn't call a broken wing, left undercarriage and wrecked engine superficial," Philip replied. "He's not thinking of flying it out of there?"

"No way. I think he's more interested in its spare-part value."

Philip laughed. "If the crash had happened here I would suggest it could be repaired. But out there, it would have to be stripped down and transported piece by piece. That would cost a fortune. I don't know if the Sikorsky could do it."

"I see your point. We'll have to go into it when I get back. In fact that's something you and the guys can look into. Give me some figures."

Kingston picked up his hefty report and left the room without as much as a discussion about Philip's arrangements tomorrow for Martin's wife. Once he'd gone Elsie walked in with her notepad.

"Is there anything you want me to do?" she asked.

Philip looked at the reports and worksheets in front of him and looked up at Elsie's comforting face. "Oh Elsie…that man is going to drive me mad before he goes back to Dallas. Thank goodness he's going to be away for a couple of days."

"I don't suppose you want to look at the worksheets now."

He flicked through the top one, then laid his hand on top, "Not really Elsie. If it's all right with you I'm going to see Kate to sort out her trip tomorrow. Then I'm going home to surprise my wife, and relax with my feet up."

"Good idea…that lot can wait till tomorrow."

As fate would have it Philip arrived at Kate's house and found no one was home. He left her a note telling her he had arranged for her to visit Martin tomorrow. As it was a long flight, a car would call for her at five o'clock so that the plane could take off at six. She would stay at the cattle station overnight and if

Martin was fit enough, they would leave for Broome the following day. He thought that was enough information for a short note and left out the bit about Martin going to hospital.

CHAPTER 16

At half past three the following morning Jennifer was woken by an unusual sound behind her head. She sat up on one elbow and listened. The sound was coming from her mother's bedroom on the other side of the wall. It was a clinking sound, followed by grunts and sighs.

Jennifer rolled out of bed, put on her dressing gown and slippers and trudged half asleep out onto the landing. She stood for a moment to make sure it was not a dream that had woken her up and saw a light shining through the gap under her mother's door. She opened it and stood in the doorway, amazed at the turmoil.

Kate was standing by the wardrobe in her underwear holding up a dress in front of the mirror. Not satisfied, she discarded it onto the pile of clothes lying haphazardly across her bed.

"What are you doing, Mum?" Jennifer whispered.

"It's all right, dear. I decided to get up early…"

"Mum…it's three-thirty," Jennifer interrupted.

"I know," she said, discarding another garment onto the bed. "I couldn't sleep, so I decided to see what I could wear on the flight."

"You're going into the bush, Mum. You don't wear good clothes in the bush."

Kate flopped onto the bed looking distraught.

Jennifer sat down and placed her arm around her. "It's all right, Mum."

"I'm so nervous, Jennifer. I don't know what I'm going to find when I get there. It's like your dad's crash all over again; remember? No one would tell me anything and when I walked into the emergency and saw him lying there with tubes coming out of everywhere, I couldn't handle it. If it hadn't been for you and Adam to cling onto I think I would have passed out. Oh, I don't want to do that with strangers."

"I wish we could go with you."

"So do I. I asked, but Philip said the company couldn't take responsibility for an entire family. They weren't that happy about me going. It was Philip that argued to get me a seat," she smiled. "I think Larry Kingston felt guilty too."

"Who's Larry Kingston?"

"He's the big American boss."

Jennifer jumped up and walked over to the wardrobe and started flicking through the hangers. "Here," she said. "Wear your linen jacket over a nice blouse and these jeans. Oh, and make sure you wear some sensible shoes; ones with flat heels. You'll be walking on some rough ground; they don't have pavements in the bush."

"You keep saying bush, dear, I thought it was the desert."

"Bush…desert, it's all the same, Mum. It's uncivilised."

Kate laughed. "You're right. Thank you."

"Now get dressed. Five o'clock will be here before you know it," Jennifer said, turning to leave. "I'll go down and put the kettle on."

Kate stood up and walked over and gave her a big hug. "Oh love…I don't know what I'd do without you and Adam. I bet he's fast asleep."

"He is, Mum; I can hear him snoring from here."

"Leave him. We don't need to disturb him till the last minute."

"No. We don't want him fussing about."

Kate nodded and started changing into the clothes Jennifer had chosen. She had already showered, packed her overnight bag with a change of underwear and fresh pyjamas; all that was left were her toiletries and makeup bag. She glanced at the mirror in the wardrobe door and shook her head. "To heck with it," she said. "I'm going into the desert; who's going to know the difference out there?" She hesitated, thought better of it and tossed the makeup bag into the holdall.

By the time Kate dropped the bag in the hall and walked into the kitchen she heard the bread jumping out of the toaster. Jennifer had a hot mug of tea waiting and a small bowl of cereal ready for Kate. "You shouldn't have bothered, dear; tea would have been fine. There'll probably be something on the plane."

"Mum, this is not Qantas Airlines. There won't be air hostesses walking up the aisle serving refreshments. This is a company plane you're going on."

"I keep forgetting. I hope I don't get one of those small planes like your dad did. I would hate that. It looked so tiny and fragile on the runway."

"I think it will be bigger than that. Not as big as an airliner, but big enough to take those men to Site 21… remember?"

Kate nodded her head and started her cereal.

Without any prompting, Adam walked into the kitchen, said good morning and poured himself a cup of coffee. He was still half asleep. He just assumed the water was hot and sat down opposite Jennifer and his mum.

"I suppose you were going to wake me," he said, sipping his coffee.

"Is that all right?" Jennifer remarked.

"It's fine. I like it tepid."

Kate finished her cereal and buttered a slice of toast. "You know I couldn't leave without saying goodbye to my big boy," she said, mussing his hair.

It made little difference. His hair looked as if it had not seen a comb in years. He took a piece of toast and smiled at Kate. She looked nervous and kept checking the clock on the wall behind him.

"Five o'clock will be here soon enough, Mum," he said.

It was four-forty-five. She finished her last piece of toast, washed it down with the tea and leaving the table she placed her dishes in the dishwasher.

"I seem to remember someone doing the very same when they were waiting for their taxi to take them to the airport last year," Kate rebuffed him.

"I know, Mum…I was just making conversation."

She walked out of the kitchen and into the lounge and started pacing in front of the window. They followed her; neither one wanting to tell her to calm down. They knew it would make no difference.

"Have you got everything?" Jennifer asked.

"Now you ask me," Kate replied, running through the items she'd packed into her overnight bag. Then there was her money, although why she would need money out there she had no idea.

Adam walked over to the window. "I wonder what this big black limousine is doing pulling up outside our house."

Kate turned back to the window. "Where?" she cried out. "Oh my God, look at the size of it! Fancy sending a car like that."

Jennifer rushed to the door and waited for the man to ring the bell. Then she sucked in a deep breath and opened the door. A smart middle-aged man in a black chauffeur's uniform was about to ring again. He looked indifferent; not about to become involved in idle banter.

"Is this Mrs Dexter's bag?" he said, noticing it in the hall.

"Yes," Jennifer replied, surprised at his brevity.

Without another word, he picked it up and returned to the large black car at the bottom of the drive. Kate and Adam arrived in the hall expecting him to introduce himself and make some comment about their journey.

"Where is he?" Kate said.

"He just picked up your bag and left," Jennifer said. "I got the impression he was in a hurry, Mum. You had better get moving."

"All right," she said, hugging and kissing them both. "I'll give you a ring when I arrive. By that time I should have calmed down."

Adam kept quiet. He had no intention of telling her there were no mobile towers in the desert. They said their goodbyes and she hurried down the drive to the waiting car. As she approached, the chauffeur got out of the car and opened the door for her. She looked back with an excited smile on her face and stepped into the luxurious interior. She had the whole back seat to herself. It was warm and she sank into the soft beige leather upholstery.

When the man returned to his front seat he turned and slid the dividing glass panel back. "Fasten your seat belt, Mrs Dexter; we'll be about half an hour."

Kate nodded with a cautious smile and looking out of the window, she waved at Jennifer and Adam as he pulled away from the house, turned into Gubinge Road and headed north. The scented fragrance of the car made her want to close her eyes. For once she had no sense of the journey, the roundabouts or the sub-urbs just passed by. She had half an hour to relax and enjoy the luxury.

It was too short. Before long the car slowed down and she felt the tight right turn and the bump onto the different surface as it entered the AMINCO air-strip. She opened her eyes and glancing out of the window was surprised to find the car was not in the car park, but negotiating some buildings on the edge of an open area. She soon recognised the lighted windows of the lounge she was in when Martin left.

The car stopped next to the embarkation lounge. Philip was there to open her door and as she stepped onto the concrete she looked out towards the twin-engine plane standing on the runway. Its shiny surface was picking up the first traces of orange light from the rising sun behind the trees in the distance. And despite the difference in planes, she sensed she was experiencing the same feeling Martin had that fateful morning.

"Oh Philip, thank you. You're here early."

"It's what I do, Kate," he said, taking hold of her elbow and guiding her towards the plane. He handed her a thin folder with the AMINCO logo on the front. "Here's something for you to read on the flight."

"What is it?" she said.

"If I told you there would be no point in giving it to you," he said, stopping at the plane's steps. "Sorry it's a rush. Say hello to Martin for me."

The chauffeur had put her bag on board and was leaving the plane. He tipped his hat and Kate thanked him for a smooth ride. Philip helped her up the steps and she waved goodbye.

Kate's company taxi did not run to the Lear Jet, but thank goodness it did not mean a dreaded journey in a small tin box either. According to Philip, her transport was a twin-engine Piper Navajo. She was none the wiser, only being used to jets when they went on holiday. The interior was much the same only shorter and the young man, who closed the door, ushered her down the aisle.

The rear of the plane, next to the door, was taken over by a group of young men playing cards. They acted as if this was just one of their usual flights; a bus ride to work in fact. They looked up and smiled and the young man continued on down the aisle to the pair of seats behind the partition with a narrow door in it. Kate chose the window seat and the young man leaned towards her.

"Philip told me to give you this seat. He thought you might want to catch up on your sleep, away from that lot at the back."

"Thank you. This will be fine."

"Don't forget to fasten your seat belt. The toilet is at the back of the plane, your bag is in the overhead compartment along with a bottle of water and if you need anything just push that button." He pointed to the red button above her head.

The young man turned away and disappeared through the small door into a dark confined space full of brightly coloured lights. She realised she was sitting in front of the engines when the first one on her side roared into life. Then the one on the other side did the same until for a moment there was a high-pitched crescendo.

Kate closed her eyes and relaxed into her seat. It was not a reaction to the small Piper Navajo; she felt the same panic each time she left the ground in much bigger aircraft; it was just one of those things. Martin was the same. But once she was in the air and heard the thump of the wheels retracting into the plane, she felt peculiarly at ease again.

As soon as she felt the plane rise steadily above the trees at the end of the runway she opened her eyes and looked out of her window. The top edges of the woodland below were tinged with orange from a sunrise she could not see until the plane began its slow turn to the south. As it did, the low fiery ball gradually moved from window to window along the left-hand side of the plane until it disappeared beyond the window alongside the young men playing cards.

They seemed oblivious of the event, other than masking the momentary glare from their cards. As she turned away to read the report Philip had given her, she heard a voice calling her name. She looked round and caught sight of a young man in a blue nylon windcheater and matching trousers. On closer inspection she could see it was a uniform. Not a military uniform; more like that of a security guard.

When he stopped at her seat and reached out his

hand, she noticed a large round badge on his upper arm, but could not read what it said.

"Hello," he said. "I'm Chris Isles, the paramedic that's going to travel back with your husband to the hospital."

"Oh…" Kate exclaimed, as she shook his hand.

He took her by surprise for the moment, and as he dropped into the seat next to hers, she found it difficult to acknowledge what he said. She had no idea Martin warranted a paramedic, let alone that he was going back to a Broome hospital. Then she glanced at the shiny folder on her lap and realised that must be part of the information Philip had supplied in his report.

"I'm sorry Chris, you caught me by surprise. As you can see I was just about to read what AMINCO has in store for my husband. I had no idea they included you escorting him to a hospital on our way back."

"I won't pre-empt your read. It'll be a good way to spend the next couple of hours. But I will say AMIN-CO has a strict procedure regarding injured personnel. It's all to do with insurance. You know what the Americans are like about covering their arses when it comes to possible liability. So…my job is to check your husband out when we reach the cattle station, not interfere with the doctor of course, but simply record everything that has taken place, including the crash and subsequent time in the desert. That will mean I might have to commandeer some of his time, I'm afraid. Then if I think he is capable of making the flight back, I shall monitor him all the way to the private hospital in Broome."

"Private hospital?" Kate exclaimed.

"Oh yes. AMINCO's insurance caters for the best."

"What I meant was, why does he have to go back to a hospital?"

Chris pointed to the folder on her lap.

"As I just said…the insurance demands he is physically fit and has no subsequent underlying problems. They're very thorough."

"So if my husband is fit enough to travel, what happens then?"

"Since there will only be three of us returning to Broome, they'll be able to knock down two seats into a bed for your husband. And when he lands, there will be an ambulance waiting to transport him to the hospital."

"I'm amazed the company are going to so much trouble."

"They're very good like that. As I said…they have to be."

"Have you contacted the doctor? Do you know how my husband is?"

"That's out of my province. I know there's been

some contact, but I won't know any more until I speak to the doctor. Like you, I'll know when I get there."

"I suppose something's been arranged for our stay tonight."

"All I know is the station owner has that organised."

"I'm glad to hear that. I feel a lot better."

The young paramedic stood up and turned to leave. "I'd get on and read that report if I were you, Mrs Dexter; then you can settle back in your seat and try and catch up on that missing sleep."

"Thank you, Chris…and by the way, my name's Kate."

He nodded and moved back along the aisle to where the other men were deeply engrossed in their card game. She turned back to the folder and decided she had better read what Philip had put together for her to digest during the flight.

She opened the stiff cover and immediately saw that it was the work of a good secretary like Elsie. She may not have been the author, but she most certainly was responsible for laying it out. There was a short introduction outlining basically what he'd said to her before she boarded the plane, followed by a personal note that he hoped Martin was on the mend and her unusual flight was a good one.

The contents list that followed surprised her; it

seemed to cover everything: from the plane's flight to Site 21 where they would drop off the young men, a short stop and off again to the cattle station. It went on to list the people she was to meet before spending time with Martin, her stop overnight at the owner's homestead and the preparation to take Martin back to Broome the next morning. That, of course, depended on whether he was fit enough for the journey.

She was a little confused that there was no mention of the hospital. She flicked through the following pages until she reached the section about the preparation to leave and there, in the last paragraph, Philip mentioned the private hospital Martin would be taken to on his arrival in Broome. As Chris had said, there was the usual statutory blurb regarding the requirements of the insurance company and that it was compulsory for the patient to be checked over before he was discharged.

Being a Senior Civil Servant, Kate was quite familiar with the complexities of insurance claims and the fear of being sued. She smiled and returning to the front of the report again, she thought she had better read every word.

By the time she'd finished and placed the folder to one side, she found her attention had wandered to the scene outside her window. It was an interesting landscape; one that she had only seen on documentaries of the Australian outback. At the time the diverse desert had little interest for her, but now, since this was the terrain that had almost killed Martin, she was drawn to the desolation.

Watching the spasmodic outcrops of spinifex pass by below was a mesmerising experience. She had no idea till now what Martin must have gone through: flying over the same scene one minute and being down there the next.

So this was the Sandy Desert, she thought; not at all what she'd envisaged. Although it was the colour of sand, it bore no resemblance to deserts like the Sahara. Instead of rolling dunes, it looked more like an ocean of scrub.

The unfriendly environment went on and on, with the only relief being the changing colours. Martin would know what the different shades of sand meant: from the rich coppery-orange to the varying hues all the way down to the common ecru. Yet it was a desolate place. No sign of life except the sparse vegetation; not even a kangaroo. And Martin had to run across a godsent Aboriginal boy. Kate was looking forward to meeting the one who'd saved Martin's life.

"Mrs Dexter...Mrs Dexter," Chris Isles called out, as he gently nudged her shoulder. He had to nudge her again.

It took a moment, but Kate slowly turned her head and opened her eyes.

"Oh dear," she said, blinking her eyes and shaking herself awake. "I must have dropped off for a moment there."

Chris Isles laughed. "I think it was more than a moment, Kate," he said. "We'll be landing in ten minutes."

"Are we there already?"

"It's not big enough to see from here," he commented. "You won't know you're there until he starts to land. That's why I woke you…so that you won't get a shock."

"Thank you," Kate said. "I can ready myself." Then she realised. This was only the first leg of the journey. "Oh my…I'm not getting off here, am I?"

"I hope not," he said, leaning over her seat and looking out of the window. "There, you can just see it now. I'd better get back to my seat and buckle up."

Janet looked out of the window at the small collection of buildings. She had no idea what Site 21 stood for. She should have paid more attention to what Martin was talking about. She only knew it was south-east of Broome, with the crash site somewhere between this place and the cattle station further west. It hardly made any difference. All the jargon she'd overheard about headings and bearings left her more confused than Martin's simple explanation had that morning in the kitchen.

It was all to do with the points of the compass. Once you knew where north was, all you had to do was turn left for east and right for west. And knowing the sun rose in the east, the rest was dead easy.

As the plane circled the small airstrip, she could see by the long shadows pointing away from her that they were landing towards the west. She closed her eyes and waited. Once again she was gripped with a sickening panic. It started as soon as she heard the whirring noise of the wheels lowering, then a different sound when the flaps dropped into place. And after an excruciating pause, the thump as the wheels touched the ground. Only then did she feel easy again.

CHAPTER 17

There was that high-pitched engine sound again as the plane turned around and started to taxi back towards a vehicle parked near the runway. She saw no reason to open her eyes; the ramshackle mining site Martin described was of no interest to her. Once the engines stopped ringing in her ears, she just sat listening to the scuffing sounds of the young men leaving the plane.

She heard voices outside. She heard doors banging and the sound of a vehicle driving off. Then, just as quickly there was a variety of scuffs, scrapes and metallic clunks; people were working under the plane and she just had to look. She stood up, opened the locker above her head and took out the bottle of water and started unscrewing the cap as she checked the windows.

"They're checking the plane before we take off,"

Chris said, walking back down the aisle. "It won't be long now."

Kate glanced at her watch. She was surprised: it was only eight-fifteen.

"I had the feeling it was much later," she said, removing the cap and taking a drink. "What time will it be when we arrive at the cattle station?"

"Oh, it's only about another hour."

Chris was stretching his legs. He smiled and continued back up the aisle. Kate had satisfied her curiosity and returning to her seat she prepared herself for the next onset of panic. She heard Chris buckle his safety belt and she did the same; then she heard the thump of the door being closed, followed by a metallic click. Next was the ear-splitting noise of the engines starting up, the jolt as the brakes were released and the plane slowly taxied to the end of the runway, did an about-turn and started its high-speed run. With her eyes closed and her jaw stiffened, she clenched her teeth; then before she knew it they were airborne again and heading west.

Being all alone at the end of the plane, Chris wandered down to where Kate was and stood with his hand on the seat next to her. She had just opened her eyes and although she was aware of his presence, she was still surprised at his closeness. She looked up and realised they were the only ones left on this second leg.

"Do you mind if I keep you company?" he asked politely.

"Of course not, Chris…why don't you sit down?"

Kate undid her safety belt and thought this would be a good opportunity to find out as much as she could about the young man who was going to look after her husband, and, according to the report, have a lot to say about the time that Martin left for home. She soon found out how informed he was when he gave her an immediate explanation of what she was to expect when they arrived at the cattle station.

She found herself unwittingly drawn to his personality. He was certainly enthusiastic, all the time giving her the impression he was an old hand at this sort of procedure, when she guessed he could hardly be old enough. More likely this field trip was as new to him as it was to Kate. He looked too clean. His skin looked as if it had never been exposed to any harsh desert sun. There were no squint lines on his brow or around his eyes and his uniform looked as new as the day it was handed to him. No, she thought. His carefully rehearsed bedside manner was straight from his training programme and she was his first opportunity to practise.

"I gather you work for AMINCO," she commented.

"Yes, I do. There are six of us: four on site at any one time and two on standby like me. We get all the interesting jobs instead of being locked down for four months on one assignment."

"That seems an awful expense to go to," Kate replied. "I mean, six full-time medics and all the supplies you must need."

Chris tilted his head to one side in acknowledgement.

"That's the Americans for you. They seem paranoid about being sued. Apparently it's become a way of life in the States. And would you believe I have to sign a waiver every time I enter what they call a designated area?"

"What's that?"

"Your husband would know. They have this enormous chart of north-western Australia on the wall in the operations room. They probably have one of each state they mine in. Anyway, ours is broken into different-coloured sectors. Each colour representing a safety hazard category: red for extreme and blue for low; you get the picture I'm sure. And along with that goes a thick folder, laying down all the risk factors, the liability allotted to that and the appropriate action to be taken should an accident occur. My section is in there, and I have to know it by heart."

Kate laughed at his casual acceptance that he may only be employed as a protection against the workers taking the company to court.

"They sound very mercenary," Kate remarked.

"Oh no, don't misunderstand what I just said. They're a great company to work for: they pay top wages, they go to great lengths to keep their workers happy and as I just explained, if you have an accident, you get the best care."

"Why shouldn't they?" Kate commented. "I mean, who's going to work in the middle of nowhere for months on end?"

"There is that, I suppose," he had to agree.

Kate turned back to her window. The desolate landscape looked just as desolate as it had fifteen minutes ago and she tried to imagine what it was like down there for Martin. She knew almost nothing about Martin's ordeal; it was going to be one of her first questions, but her acute imagination was enough for her to sense it had to have been unbelievable. She turned back and looked at Chris.

"It looks so desolate down there," she voiced her fears.

"I know…I've often thought that myself," he agreed sympathetically. "I wouldn't like to be stranded down there…" Then he realised what he'd said. "Oh, I'm so sorry, Kate. I wasn't thinking."

"It's all right. I know it was a casual remark. I was thinking the same."

"Yes, well, it's all over now. He's safe. Thanks to that Aborigine."

"Yes. I must find out who he was and thank him."

It was an awkward moment. A silence followed when they were both trying to find some way of changing the subject and Kate spoke first.

"I bet it's a tedious job for you."

"It can sound like that, but really I don't get the time to worry about the isolation. It's usually non-stop all day and when it's finished I just want to have a good meal and drop into my bunk."

"Is that so?" Kate commented, wondering if she had misjudged him.

"Oh yes. The mining sites and rigs are dangerous places. You'd be surprised at the amount of accidents I have to deal with every shift."

"I can understand the companies need to make sure they look after their men."

"Now you can understand the reason for all the insurance procedures."

"I assume you're going to be looked after on the cattle station?"

Chris had to cast his mind back to what Philip had said.

"I'm told the pilots and I are going to bunk in one

of the chalets. Apparently they're rented out for jackeroo holidays."

"I haven't heard of jackeroo holidays," Kate laughed. "I haven't heard of jackeroos. Are they kangaroo hunters?" she said as a joke.

It was Chris's turn to laugh now. "No. A jackeroo is a junior stockman, just as a jillaroo is a female one. I don't know much about it, but it seems young people actually like the idea of a holiday working cattle on a real station. I've seen the ads on the Internet; they're not cheap. You fly to the cattle station, stay in one of these chalets and chase cattle about just like the real stockmen."

"Are they trying to learn ranching or is it just a bit of fun for them?"

"I have no idea...perhaps I'll find out."

Kate was grateful for Chris's company. After sleeping through most of the flight to Site 21 she was wide awake and eager to find out more about her companion. Just as she turned to speak to him she felt the plane bank slightly. They headed west when they took off and she naturally expected that was the direction to the cattle station, but now the pilot had made a correction to the right, which meant he was turning north. It was only a small correction. Before she had a chance to see the sun start its run back along the right side of the plane this time, it was levelling off again. They were now heading north-west.

Now she had the bright sun cascading across her shoulder from the window behind her. Chris could see it was catching her right eye and he stood up, crossed in between the seats behind her and closed the blind.

"Oh, that's a lot better," she said. "Thank you, Chris."

"We can't have that bothering you for the rest of the journey," he said, sitting down next to her again.

Kate had decided the site must be further south than the cattle station.

"Is this our final direction?"

"To be honest with you, I haven't the vaguest idea. I'm hopeless with directions. If I went for a walk on one of the sites I'm sure I would get lost."

"Has that happened?"

"No. That's why I never leave the site precincts."

Kate let out a low chuckle and once again, as she turned to say something, she was distracted by a folder on his lap, much like her own. "Are you boning up on your exams?" she asked, nodding at the folder.

He looked down. "Oh no. That's all finished, thank goodness. No, this is a company manual I grabbed before we left this morning to do with transportation procedures." He picked it up and waved it in the air. "One of those dreaded policy edicts I was telling you about."

"You mean when we take Martin back to Broome?"

He nodded his head as he flicked through the pages.

"Exactly. I already know the procedure for transporting a patient in an ambulance, but this is my first time in a plane."

"Is it that different?"

"I don't know…that's what I want to find out. Either way I will have to be led by the doctor's wishes. He's the one who will ultimately decide if your husband is fit to travel. I doubt whether it's much different from an ambulance, except…" He suddenly stopped and checked the index for something that came to mind.

"What is it?" Kate interrupted.

"Oh, it's nothing really. I just wondered if there was a problem with him travelling in a pressurised cabin."

"And is there?" Kate asked, as curious as he was.

It was a long index but he soon found what he was looking for.

"According to this, apparently not; unless your husband has a problem with his lymphatic system," Chris said, shaking his head. "He doesn't, does he?"

Kate had a blank look on her face. "I have no idea. He obviously had no problem flying out on other occasions."

"It doesn't matter; that's the doctor's province. I only have two areas to worry about: first to make sure I have detailed everything that happened to your husband during and after the crash, and second, to follow the doctor's instructions, maintain him in a stable condition and keep him secure during the flight."

"Well, let's hope the folder will do that," Kate commented.

"To be truthful, it's more about covering the company's assets."

"You certainly seem to know a lot about those," she said. "By the way are you a natural Australian or a resident like us?"

"No, I'm an immigrant, but I can't remember much about it. I seem to have been here all my life; I only have vague memories of England."

"Where was that?"

"Northumberland, I think. I'm not sure where; maybe Durham, that strikes a bell. Yes, I remember my mother talking about the cathedral once."

"That's odd. We came from Yorkshire, just below Durham," she commented, thinking how small England really was, "And how old were you?"

Chris pursed his lips. He had to think, showing how little his heritage meant to him. "I think I was five or maybe six. I know we were on the plane for an awfully long time. We stopped in Singapore. My mother wanted to see what Asia was like. All I can remember was how hot it was…even in the night."

"I know what you mean," Kate replied, casting her

mind back to their terrible experience and another long trip across Australia. "And that journey across the centre of Australia to Melbourne. All we could see was masses of orange; no green."

"It was different for us. We went to Sydney."

Kate could not help letting out a stifled laugh.

"Isn't that amazing. Just about everyone I've spoken to in Broome said they came from Sydney. Apparently it's the most common place for immigrants."

Chris laughed, "Except for the Greeks and Italians."

"You know about them?"

"Oh yes. When I took up my studies to be a paramedic, I went down to Melbourne. And before you ask, why Melbourne, I met my girlfriend in Fiji on holiday. She was from Melbourne and she was studying to be a paramedic. I was at a loose end in my career, so I thought, why not; it sounded a good occupation and what I saw of Melbourne when I went down to a game, I liked."

"I like that," Kate said. "You have a spontaneous spirit.

"So I'm told. It gets me into trouble at times."

"And did you marry your girlfriend?"

"No. It didn't work out in the end."

"Oh, I'm sorry. Maybe you were just meant to meet so that you could find out about being a paramedic. Life's like that."

Chris turned and studied the expression on Kate's face. "You know, you're just like my mum. I don't mean age-wise. I mean in the way you view life. She's always analysing what I do; saying this was meant to be, I may not know it now but I will in time and all that stuff. I bet you're into horoscopes as well."

Kate laughed, Chris sounded just like her Adam; in fact, looking at Chris, there could not be much difference in their ages. "Yes, I am…and tarot cards, runes, clairvoyants and just about anything about the future. Martin goes mad."

"I bet you didn't see this coming? Sorry. There I go again."

"You're right. But I prefer to say I missed the signs."

Kate's strategy worked. The next hour went by before she knew it as Chris occupied his need for information by reading his manual, all the time conversing with Kate on certain points that had a direct bearing on her husband; and her thoughts wandering each time, inwardly contemplating what Martin would say or do.

The landing at the cattle station was much different; the airstrip seemed softer than the mining site. As the plane touched down, a cloud of red dust filled the air, obliterating any sign of what the cattle station looked like, except Kate occasionally caught sight of a large vehicle keeping pace with the plane. It was only a short contest; the car stopped and the plane continued on to the end of the runway, turned like it did at Site 21, then slowly taxied back to the waiting car.

"Here we go, Kate," Chris said, jumping up and walking back along the aisle.

Then the cockpit door opened and the young man Kate had seen earlier walked out and went straight to her overhead locker. "Everything all right, Mrs Dexter?" he said, looking down at her with a big smile on his face.

Kate stood up and stepped into the aisle. "Yes, thank you. That was a good flight. I look forward to as good a one when I collect my husband."

"Don't worry, Mrs Dexter. Everything will be organised for him."

He took hold of her bag and she followed him down the aisle. As Chris and Kate waited, he opened the door and there was a sudden blast of hot air. They stood back and waited for the atmosphere to equalise.

"Oh dear," Kate let out. "I knew it would be hot, but not this hot."

"Sorry about that," he said. "It's forty-three outside. It feels hotter because you've been travelling in a comfortable twenty-six degrees for the past three-and-a-half hours. Once outside your body will soon adjust."

Kate gave him a wry smile, thinking you don't know me and the sun.

As the two men stepped down the short ladder onto the red dust airstrip with the bags, Kate stood in the doorway for a moment surveying her new environment and as the young man said, acclimatising her body to the heat.

It was totally different to anything she was used to. Her senses had been assaulted by the biggest blue sky she had ever seen; supported by a mass of burnt red country. She looked for the sun to get her bearings just as Martin had taught her. It was almost overhead.

She knew from past experience that it was going to burn her up. Chris had already donned a blue desert hat supplied by the company and she too was prepared. She reached into her jacket pocket and brought out the foldable canvas trilby she bought when they were in Spain and pulled it down over her head.

As she stepped down onto the ground she instinctively looked for the car. It was almost parallel with the plane, but still some distance away. It was an olive green Land Rover, she knew that much; her next-door neighbour had one.

There was a tall man leaning against the car with one arm casually draped across the roof rack and the other down by his side. His long jeans-clad legs were crossed as if he was not in any hurry to meet them.

Kate thought he had to be one of the stockmen; he was too scruffy to be the owner. She walked over to where Chris was standing with her holdall and his medical bag slung over his shoulder.

This appeared to be a signal for the distant stockman. He kicked the toe of his cowboy boot into the red dust and headed their way. Like the blue sky and the desert, he looked part of the land; one with the Great Sandy Desert that provided him and his family with a steady living.

Kate had no experience of outback stockmen other than what she saw on television, but judging by them, he was from the same mould. He was big; she could see that. He needed to be if he was going to handle cattle all day. His face was covered by the shadow from his crumpled, tattered, broad-brimmed hat that had probably seen more roundups than Kate had hot dinners; likewise, the long sleeved blue-chequered shirt he was wearing.

"Mrs Dexter?" he called out, when he finally arrived; touching the tip of his hat in an old-fashioned way, and thrusting the other huge hand in her direction.

"Oh yes," she said, relieved as his cultured voice could only mean he had to be the owner. "Call me Kate," she added.

"Right…and my name's Jeff."

His eyes quickly moved onto the immaculate

young man in the blue uniform and he shook his hand also. "You must be the paramedic," he said, taking Kate's bag and turning back to the car.

"I suppose it's a bit obvious…my name's Chris."

When they reached the Land Rover, Jeff opened the back door for Kate and helped her inside. He then went around to the rear, opened the boot and dropped her bag inside, before returning to the front. Chris was already sitting in the passenger seat. As soon as Jeff was behind the wheel he turned to Kate. "I'm sorry you had to walk all that way," he said, starting the engine. "The pilots don't like the four-wheel drive digging up the runway."

"Is that right?" she said.

"Yeah…they don't like the ruts."

Jeff slipped the Land Rover into gear and moved away from the runway onto a wide dirt road that headed towards a group of buildings in the distance. Within a few moments they were passing through an area of fenced-off spaces. Kate recognised it straightaway from the documentary she'd seen on television. They called it a stockyard. There were no cattle in the pens at present; they were probably out on the range, but the next group of closed pens they passed were full of horses.

Jeff slowed down as he caught sight of one old stockman waving at him. He stopped and switched off the engine. "Sorry," he said. "This won't take a moment."

He left the car and walked over to the old man. He seemed irritated about something, waving his arms in all directions until Jeff playfully slapped him on the rump and pushed him back in the direction he'd come from.

"Can you smell that?" Chris questioned. "You can tell it's a cattle station."

"All I can see is a lot of horses," Kate said, not impressed.

"They don't keep the cattle on the station; they're out grazing on the range. All those pens are for when they bring them in before they go to the market."

"So what do the stockmen do?"

"Most of them will be out on the range, mustering and chasing up strays."

"And those, sitting on the fence over there?"

"That's a pen for wild horses. They're taking turns breaking them in. Then they shift those into another area and use them as stock horses."

"You seem to know an awful lot about a cattle station."

"Not really. I'm one of those people who like to know what I'm dealing with. So when I found out I was going to a cattle station I got a book out of the library and read all about it; well enough to know what not to do."

Kate laughed. "That sounds like AMINCO training to me."

Chris did not get the chance to answer. Jeff returned to the car, started it up and drove on along the dirt road. "Sorry about that," he said. "You'll find, Kate, I might have to leave you on occasions, but I'll find you."

"I thought I was going straight to see my husband."

"I'm taking you to see the doctor first. Then in between that and you seeing your husband, the teacher wants to see you."

That sounded awfully strange.

CHAPTER 18

Kate glanced at her watch. It had taken the best part of fifteen minutes to finally leave the stockyard area and return to the undulating dirt road heading towards a large weatherboard building with a tall metal-framed tower standing alongside. It still seemed some distance away, giving Kate the idea this was a huge cattle station.

As they neared the building she could see the tower was supporting an antenna and one of those round dishes. She recognised it straightaway from the neighbour's dish two doors down that was supposed to give them better reception. She took her mobile out of her jacket pocket and flipped it open, speed-dialled her house, hoping to surprise the kids, and waited, but nothing, except a message saying no signal. This needed investigating, she thought.

Looking at the tower, Kate had not noticed that

the road ran by the group of buildings at an oblique angle, positioning the first weatherboard so that it blocked her view of the others. As the Land Rover turned alongside she was surprised to see a wooden boardwalk stretching for some distance in front of a long line of similar buildings. All that set them apart was their size. Some corrugated roofs had weathered differently from others, but generally they were like peas in a pod, reminding her of the towns in the old westerns.

Jeff continued on for a short distance and stopped outside what appeared to be the longest building and Kate was suddenly filled with apprehension.

He switched the engine off and turned to Chris. "This is the medical clinic, Chris," he pointed out. "Would you like to introduce yourself to Dr Fitzgerald?"

"I thought I was going to see Martin straightaway," Kate interrupted.

"All in good time, Kate," Jeff answered her with a reassuring smile. "I need to bring you up to date with what happened." He could see how bewildered she was. "It's okay, Kate. Believe me. The doctor just wants to have time with Chris to see if he's happy with the plan to take your husband back to Broome tomorrow."

Kate did not look at all happy. She had thought of

nothing else since she'd got up this morning and now, when Martin was so close, she had to wait. "I understand," she said. "It's early after all. The day has only begun."

"That's fine," Jeff said, waiting for Chris to leave the car. Obviously Chris was waiting for Kate to accept the situation and he stepped out onto the boardwalk, gave her a reassuring smile and closed the door.

"Where to now, Jeff?" she said brusquely.

He turned round in his seat with a furtive expression, "The doctor asked me to have a word with you. Apparently he doesn't want you raising a lot of questions with Martin, about what happened in the desert or the crash for that matter. If he brings it up, that's fine, but for now he needs to get over the trauma of sitting with a dead man for a day. He still talks to him, you know. At times he thinks he's still waiting for the plane to come and rescue them."

That was something Kate had not expected. She was all prepared to walk in on him sitting up in bed with a few bandages and his arm in a sling. She knew that much. But Jeff was right. She needed to know a lot more.

"Thank you for telling me that; I'm ready for that talk," she said.

Jeff looked much happier. He was not about to tell her he objected to this preparation discussion with her. He would have preferred his wife handle that; woman-to-woman sort of thing, but for some reason she thought Kate might control her emotions better with a man. His wife was an outback woman, not into city women's talk or hysteria. He stepped out of the car and opened Kate's door for her; something he hadn't done in years and escorted her into the smaller building at the end of the Medical Clinic.

As it turned out, Jeff decided she would be more comfortable in his office while they wait for Chris and the doctor to settle their business. As they entered the building Kate had the distinct feeling she was stepping back in time: to the Victorian period by the looks of all the old furniture. A young girl, no more than in her early twenties, stood and walked round her antiquated desk.

"This is my daughter, Ross," he said, opening the only other door in the room and leaving it open so that Kate could follow him inside.

"Don't take any notice of him," the girl said, shaking Kate's hand. "You're Martin's wife? I bet you thought my dad's a real grump. He means well though. You just have to realise he's more used to dealing with surly stockmen."

"Actually he's been a perfect gentleman with me. And the name's Kate, by the way," she said, hearing the sound of someone coughing next door.

Ross nodded with her head tilting towards her father's office and Kate walked into his room. It was another tableau from the past. He was sitting behind an enormous mahogany desk; one of those with drawers on either side, as if it belonged in a museum along with the rest of the furniture.

Just as she sat down in a beautiful chair with velvet upholstery, Ross poked her head around the architrave and said, "Tea or coffee, Kate?"

"Tea please, with milk and one sugar."

Jeff let out another of his small coughs, signalling he was ready to bring her up to date. He looked uncomfortable and Kate noticed he had a sheet of paper in front of him. She guessed it was his written prompts, probably composed by his wife, and sat quietly, ready to hear what he had to say.

"Right, Kate. I've already told you of the state Martin was in when the Aboriginal boy brought him in, the fact that he must have spent at least a day with the dead pilot, according to remarks he made, and I might add he is still a little delusional. The doctor says he can see no signs that might indicate a head injury, but he can talk to you about his medical condition when you see him. I'm just alerting you to the fact that it has been difficult discussing the crash with him. As soon as anyone mentions anything to do with that period right up to arriving at the cattle station, he goes into some kind of time warp."

"I'll try to avoid that," Kate said, just as Ross brought the drinks in.

She set the tray down on the end of Jeff's desk. "Thanks, Ross," he said. Kate also thanked her and she left, closing the door behind her.

Kate took a sip of her tea. It was very strong and she wondered if it had anything to do with being out there. She then asked the question that was on the tip of her tongue. "You mentioned the Aboriginal boy who brought Martin in." He nodded, as if that was all he was. "I would like to speak to him if that is possible."

"You should run into him," Jeff commented, taking two gulps from his mug. "He's been hanging around the Medical Clinic since he brought Martin in. He seems to think he's bonded to him in some way. He's another one who doesn't seem to want to talk about the two days they spent together," he digressed slightly. "But he can talk when he wants to; the trouble is getting him to shut up."

Kate laughed. "I know. I saw all those men sitting on the railing shouting at the riders. It was a wonder they could hear each other."

"Oh, they could hear all right. They were betting on how long the rider could stay on the horse. They're gambling fanatics. They'll bet on two ants crossing the track in front of them." Jeff laughed. "In fact it's the only way I can get them to do some work. All I have to say is, I bet you can't do something."

"You seem to be well organised here."

"You're looking at several generations of hard work. This is the Estate office. Everything is run from here and this is where everyone comes if they have a problem, want to order anything, get paid or need to contact a family member. Next door is the Medical Clinic which you will visit shortly; further up is the General Store, then at the top of the street there's a non-denominational church and of course we have our small school. On the other side there's the machine shop where we maintain all our equipment and build new if we need it and further up we have three well-equipped chalets for our paying guests that come to visit each season."

"Yes, Chris, the paramedic, told me about your jackeroos."

"It was a good idea of my wife's. It helps with the finances and, if they come up to scratch, it also helps out during round-up time."

"You said your church was non-denominational." He nodded. "What about the Aborigines? What do they worship?"

"That's an area I stay away from. Although they

love the church, they just like the singing and listening to all the biblical stories. I don't know if they understand them or even relate to them. I think they just like stories; after all, that's what their culture is based on."

"And where do they live?"

"The main tribe lives about nine kilometres away beside the Oakover River, but the stockmen I employ live here on the property. They live in the stockman's shed. That's what they call it, not me. It's a big barn-type building down by the stockyard. It has two levels, reasonable quarters, a games room and television."

Kate suddenly remembered her mobile.

"That's what I was going to ask you," Kate interrupted. "How is it you get television but no mobile service?"

"There's no telephone or mobile out here; we communicate by radio. We have specific contact points around Australia and the medical and teaching authorities have regular channels to us and all the outback stations. As for the television, I had three dish towers put up and they manage to pick up most Australian stations, although it's a good day when we get anything from further afield."

"You're quite an isolated community out here. How do you manage with food and supplies? And what about the mail?"

"Every week a plane comes in from Port Hedland with the mail and whatever we need to keep the General Store topped up. And of course we get the occasional flight, such as yours and the jackeroos in season. My wife always has a standing list of incidentals so she can place an order to be brought in on that flight. You'd be surprised what your plane brought in."

"I'm looking forward to meeting your wife."

"And she also, but I think it's time you met our doctor."

When Kate followed Jeff out of his office onto the boardwalk she noticed a young Aborigine sitting on the step leading down to the dirt road. He looked to be a lonely individual – unlike all the other stockmen she had seen so far, jesting with each other and busy with their business. He had a slouched appearance, with his gangly legs splayed out and his arms hanging over his knees. She tried to see his face, but it was shrouded below the broad-brimmed hat pulled down over his forehead.

As Jeff opened the door into Dr Fitzpatrick's office the boy looked up at her. It was a furtive glance; more of an exploratory inspection. Kate sensed that he knew she was Martin's wife and she hesitated.

Jeff took hold of her elbow and escorted her inside.

"I can't let you speak to him just yet. He's in limbo until I can sort things out with his tribe."

Kate said nothing. The last thing she wanted to do was get involved in an Aboriginal feud; if that's what it was. She could make her point later, even if it meant going through a mediator. She stood to one side as Jeff stepped forward and punched the bell on the corner of an antiquated desk.

The small room was the same as his office. It too appeared to be stranded in the Victorian period. It was as if she had stumbled into a village from that time that had stayed unchanged till now. Other than a chromium trolley in the corner, containing white enamel dishes covered with green napkins, a small ancient computer with a companion printer, certain personal items on his desk and what looked like a sterilising unit next to a bed against the opposite wall, everything else was made of dark polished wood.

The only person in the room was Chris. He was standing by the open drawer of a wooden cabinet, going through some of the files by the look of it.

The only other door in the room opened and a small middle-aged man wearing a long white coat entered the room. He looked harassed until he saw Jeff, his first eye contact; then he immediately turned to Kate and a smile broke out across his face. Chris closed the drawer and left the room through the same door.

"This must be Mrs Dexter," he said, holding out his hand.

Kate shook it and smiled back. "Call me Kate, please," she said.

"Is it okay, Doc, if I leave Kate with you?" Jeff said, taking hold of the door handle. "It's only I've got a lot of problems today," he laughed. "You're not one of them, Kate. Mine are all four-legged."

"I understand, Jeff," she replied.

"I'll keep a check on you...don't worry," he continued, then left.

The little man walked around to the other side of the desk and dipped his head to look over his glasses before he sat down. "Please Kate...sit down. We'll have a little chat before I take you in to see Martin."

Although he seemed pleasant enough, Kate could feel her apprehension returning as she sat down opposite him. Despite his name she could tell he had been in Australia for a long time. You don't get sallow, wrinkled skin in Ireland. And the small brown spots on the back of his hands made her think he might probably be older than she'd first thought.

He still had his stethoscope around his neck. He placed it on his desk, went across to the wooden filing cabinet Chris was standing by, took out a file and returned to his seat. He opened the file and looked up at Kate.

"I'm sorry if all this seems a trifle melodramatic; I know you must be anxious to see your husband. But I don't want you to get the wrong idea when you meet him. I want you to be fully informed of his condition."

"I understand, Doctor, thank you."

"Firstly, to put your mind at ease, Martin's condition is stable."

Kate tried to smile, but his words did not help.

"His condition can be broken down into three categories: firstly he broke his lower arm and wrist in the crash. According to Martin the pilot helped him set his arm in a splint; quite a good job really. We only had to change the bandage for a plaster cast. I don't have a lot of information about the pilot, but it sounds to me as if he had severe internal injuries; but I'll return to him later. Secondly, they spent several days cooped up in a small space, in extreme temperatures, with very little food and even less water: I understand they had a few Mars Bars and some Hard Tack biscuits, whatever they are. They could not have survived for very long."

He reached over to a small tray with a jug of water and glasses on the end of his desk. He poured a drink and nodded towards Kate. She nodded back.

"If it hadn't been for the young Aboriginal boy stumbling onto the plane I fear you may well have lost your husband. He had a day at best. As it was, the boy gave him water, which I understand contained an Aboriginal potion to combat heat prostration and it helped Martin's condition immensely. Enough for the boy to get him out of the plane and walking the twenty kilometres or so to our cattle station; although, I must admit the boy was clever enough to catch a horse in the latter period, which helped enormously. I have to add at this point that the boy inadvertently infected your husband. He arrived with a high temperature and a badly infected wound on his neck. Apparently Martin was stung by something. He had his first aid and told the boy what to do to keep the sting sterile, but at the end he had to use the Aboriginal way of sucking the poison out."

"And he gave Martin blood poisoning?"

"Yes…but don't worry, I had some antibiotics on hand and everything is under control. His temperature is back to normal."

"That's good," she said. "You mentioned a third category?"

"Are yes. In fact it's probably the most important at the moment. Something I'm not capable of treating. It's something the hospital in Broome will have to look into." He saw the look on Kate's face. "Don't alarm yourself, Kate. It's just that I don't have any experience in psychiatry."

"Psychiatry. What does that mean?"

He glanced at the open folder in front of him. "According to observations, he has been showing signs of delirium. At first we thought it was a product of his high temperature. Then we examined the potion the boy gave him; he said he reacted to it strangely before he improved, but it turned out to be nothing more than a mild sedative. Now that he is fairly stable physically, I can see no reason for his ramblings, other than he is suffering some form of paranoia brought about by the traumatic ordeal he went through."

"What ramblings?" Kate exclaimed.

"I said I would come back to the pilot. He seems to be Martin's main preoccupation at the moment, along with the young Aboriginal boy. It all seems to relate to how he bonded with these two during his hallucinations."

"And how does it manifest itself?"

"For one, he still thinks the pilot is alive. He talks to him all the time. I think he calls him Joe."

"Yes. That's right."

"And he looks upon the Aboriginal boy as his saviour."

"I really want to speak to the boy, but Jeff says he's having trouble with his tribe. Do you know what's happening?"

Kate could see by the awkward look on the doctor's

face that he was going to be as difficult as Jeff had been and she gave him her pleading expression.

"It's Miss Gerry, the teacher, you want to talk to. She knows everything about the Aborigines. She'll get to the bottom of it," he said, standing up. "Anyway, I think I've put you in the picture, so it's about time I let you see Martin. But don't forget: don't be too alarmed at what he might say. At first he may not be the Martin you know, but seeing you might just bring him round."

Kate stood up when he came round the desk and opened the door leading into the hospital side of the clinic. She stepped inside and he followed.

She had entered a long room with the first three metres taken up by a small room on either side. The one on the left was marked Toilet and the opposite one was marked X-ray. Beyond that the room was unhindered, except that it was split into small cubicles by curtains. Most were drawn back exposing an old style hospital bed with a wooden cabinet alongside in each. Directly behind the X-ray wall, the first space was taken up with a nurse's station consisting of a small desk and chair, another wooden filing cabinet and a trolley covered with a cloth.

Sitting at the desk, going through some charts, was a young Aboriginal girl in a white uniform and a blue plastic cap. Chris was sitting alongside. He smiled, stood up and disappeared back into the doctor's office. As soon as Kate and the doctor entered the ward she jumped up and smiled. She looked nervous and walked round the desk to introduce herself.

"This is Nurse Jackson," the doctor said. "If you want me at all I'll be next door. Oh, and nurse... explain things to Mrs Dexter."

The nurse nodded politely and as he left she moved closer to Kate and offered her hand. "I'm Mini," she said, looking calmer now he was gone.

Kate took her tiny hand and shook it. "I'm Kate, Martin's wife."

"Yes, I know. He keeps talking about you."

"I thought he was rambling."

"He has his lucid moments. Seeing you might make them longer."

"Doesn't the doctor call you Mini?"

"Oh no. That would be too personal. And before you ask, we all have English surnames. No one could pronounce our Aboriginal names. I got mine from the English female actor...you know, Glenda Jackson. I thought she was so gracious in the film about Queen Elizabeth. I was going to call myself Elizabeth but at school they called me Mini because I'm so small."

"I like the name," Kate said. "You were going to tell me about Martin?"

"Not really, I suppose the doctor did that."

Kate sensed she was conscious of what she said.

"He didn't tell me anything personal."

"No, he wouldn't. We did try and find out from Martin if he had any allergies, but it's too late now; we had to go ahead with the antibiotics. Eventually AMINCO came through with his details."

"To be honest it has never come up before," Kate answered.

Mini had one more question before she let Kate see Martin. "Did you bring any fresh clothes with you?"

"What happened with the clothes he left in?" Kate asked.

"I'm not sure," Mini replied, checking some notes in his file. When Willy found him he was in a state and the clothes he was wearing were not suitable for walking across the desert," she said, referring to her notes. "Anyway, Willy found some lighter clothes in a bag—"

"Oh, those must have been his overalls," Kate interrupted.

"It says here they were like an all-in-one jumpsuit. Orange coloured."

"Yes, they were his overalls."

The nurse smiled, "They were in a state also. You should have seen them; I had to cut them off him." She noticed the shocked look on Kate's face. "It's okay, I was discreet."

275

"That's all right; we're women of the world after all."

They laughed. "Anyway, if you didn't bring any clothes we shall have to visit the General Store in the morning – as long as you don't mind jeans and a shirt."

"No, Mini…as long as he's decent."

Before she escorted Kate to Martin's bed she opened a drawer in her desk and took out one of those plastic resealable bags. It was his personal belongings: his wallet, the little black book he used to write the note in, his mobile and an unusual piece of stiff paper.

"What's that piece of silver paper?" Kate asked.

"Oh that…I forgot all about it. I think you should read it first."

As the nurse disappeared into the X-ray room Kate dipped her hand into the bag and brought out the wrapper from a packet of Hard Tack biscuits. Strange, she thought and instinctively turned it over. She recognised Martin's scrawl straightaway. It was like shorthand to her. Like the numerous notes he would leave all over the house to remind him of something he had to remember. As Kate read his message, tears formed in the corner of her eyes and slowly ran down her cheeks.

The scrawl was an abridged version of Martin's will and ended with the words: 'Tell my wife Kate I love her dearly, and that I'm sorry I could not keep my promise to be with her forever.'

Kate wiped away the tears, folded the piece of paper and just as she placed it in her bag the nurse left the X-ray room and looked at Kate to see if she was ready.

Kate said, "Can I see my husband now?"

CHAPTER 19

A s Kate followed the nurse down the ward she was intrigued to see the small hospital ran to twelve beds: six down each side. The first three beds on one side were taken up by Aboriginal patients, probably stockmen, and Martin was in a bed at the far end.

The nurse was quick to point out that she'd placed Martin there so that he would not be disturbed by the boisterous relatives of this lot; she nodded to the three smiling individuals they'd just passed.

When they arrived at Martin's bed Kate could see he was reclining against several pillows, with his head turned away from them. It was difficult to see if he was asleep or 'just resting his eyes', as he'd often said in similar situations. The nurse walked around to the other side of the bed with a mischievous look and bent down close to his face.

"Martin, look who I've brought to see you."

His only response was a slight movement of his legs.

"Martin," Kate called out from the other side.

He opened his eyes and stared at Mini's beaming face.

"Willy? What are you doing here?"

The nurse stood up, shrugged her shoulders and looked perplexed. Kate was horrified and tapped Martin's good arm.

"Martin, it's me…Kate. Look at me."

Martin turned in her direction. She thought he recognised her voice, but wasn't sure he recognised her face; he just stared at her with a vague expression, as if she was a stranger. Then his eyes opened wide and a big smile crossed his face.

"Kate. Is that really you?"

The nurse left with a satisfied look and Kate sat down in the chair next to the bed. She took hold of Martin's hand as she leaned across the covers. "Yes, Martin, it's really me; how are you feeling?"

"I saw you earlier looking at me through the windscreen, but when I called out, you had disappeared; where did you go?"

This was what the doctor had warned Kate about and she felt like screaming. When Jeff and the doctor first mentioned Martin's lapse, past memories filled her with panic. It was starting again and she dared not say anything. It was 2010 all over again, when she'd nearly lost him in that near fatal car crash. The doctors said his head injury had caused him to 'turn in on himself' and there seemed little chance of a recovery back then. But somehow, by a miracle, he'd found his way back.

"Martin sweetheart, I'm in the hospital. Remember? You're on the cattle station. I've flown down to visit you."

In the space of a few moments the expression on Martin's face changed several times. He looked as if he was struggling with the simple question of what was real: what he could see or what was in his head. Then, to Kate's relief, he settled on what he could see and he gripped her hand tightly.

"Oh Kate…am I glad to see you. It's been terrible. I told you that morning that something wasn't right. And when I saw that plane, I just knew…I knew something bad was going to happen."

"I know, dear," she said, squeezing his hand.

Deep down this was what Kate wanted. She wanted him to face up to his demons and talk about what had happened. That was the problem with the car crash; he'd lost all recall of what had happened. To this day those three months have remained a hole in his memory. One he constantly tries to resurrect. She can't allow another black hole to form.

So she sat patiently and allowed him to relive that traumatic week. The detail that was spilling out of his mind was unbelievable; if she had asked him he would not have been able to recall such minutiae. Yet he did. And over an hour later he was still recalling every instant, until he reached the morning he woke and found Joe dead. The actual word was not used and at this point Kate should have stopped him, changed the subject – done anything to distract him from what she quickly found out was one of those dreadful triggers.

She had been warned about it the first time; but then they had no idea what they might be. But the doctor had told her: stay away from any mention of Joe or the Aboriginal boy.

"They won't tell me how Joe is," Martin said, glancing towards the curtained-off cubicle between him and the end of the building.

His relapse took Kate by surprise. Up till now Martin had been lucid enough for her to understand every detail of what led up to Joe's death. That now took him back and she had to break that by changing the subject.

"Adam's back in Broome by the way. He hopes you're feeling better and will be fit enough to fly back tomorrow. It's a nice big plane this time; not as good as the Lear, which I know you like, but still pretty swish."

Martin had returned his attention to the curtain, stretching his plastered arm out to see if he could snag the material, but it was no good. "They won't pull the curtains back. I know why." Kate smiled as if she was interested. He continued, "He's too ill…the commotion might be too much for him."

"Is that so, dear? Did you hear what I said about Adam?"

"What? Oh yes," he said. "Go and have a look. See if he's all right…he's been very quiet lately. Say hello; he'll remember you."

To keep him happy Kate got up and walked over to the curtained cubicle and opened a small gap and peered inside. There was no one there. The bed had been turned into a storage space for fresh sheets and pillows. They were neatly stacked like a wall of bricks. She shook her head in desperation and turned straight into the enquiring stare of the nurse, Mini.

"What's going on?" she whispered.

"Would you believe I've had a good hour or so of sane conversation. Martin was telling me all about his ordeal. I didn't prompt him, he just led into it on his own steam, until he arrived at the moment he found Joe."

The nurse nodded her head and smiled. "And he asked you to check on Joe?"

"Yes… What could I do? I don't want to get into a discussion about his death."

"Leave it to me," she said, moving back to Martin's bed.

He seemed oblivious that she had arrived and focussed his attention again on Kate. "Well…is he all right?"

Kate glanced at the nurse who shrugged her shoulders in a gesture that obviously meant 'It's up to you'. And Kate took the easy course.

"He's asleep, dear," she said. It was a half-truth.

As Martin settled back into his pillows, satisfied his friend was resting peacefully, the nurse pulled Kate to one side. "The reason I came along was to let you know Jeff was sitting outside. He said if you want a break he would take you to see Miss Gerry, the teacher. Otherwise he could come back later."

Kate was beginning to feel a little fragile and thought she could do with a break. She felt guilty leaving him like that, but he seemed peaceful enough.

She turned to the nurse and smiled a thankful smile. "That's a good idea," she said, bending down and giving Martin a kiss. "I'm going outside for a while, dear. I won't be long." He looked up at her as if he hadn't heard a word.

Outside the ward Jeff was talking to the doctor. He

looked up. He seemed a lot more relaxed than he had an hour ago.

"Sorted out your problems, Jeff?" Kate asked, for something to say.

His sun-burnt face cracked open with a half-hearted laugh. "Until the next catastrophe! I swear...the next man who walks through that door and asks for my help, I'll string him up and let him bake in the sun."

Within a hair's breadth of Jeff finishing his sentence the door opened and Chris walked in, asking which way it was to the jackaroos' chalets. They all burst out laughing. It was an unusual sound under the circumstances; enough to bring the nurse out of the ward wondering what all the commotion was.

"What did I say?" Chris exclaimed, looking mortified.

Jeff just shook his head, too bemused himself to comment. He turned to Kate as he went for the door that Chris was still holding open. "Come on, Kate... I'll take you to see Miss Gerry," he said, as he shook his head again at Chris.

CHAPTER 20

As Jeff left the Medical Clinic he was still chuckling to himself. He'd seemed to take pleasure in upsetting Chris, as if it was some recompense for the hassles he must have encountered so far today. Kate decided to treat him with respect from now on, in case she too caught the whiplash of his strange humour.

He instinctively went to the Range Rover and opened the door.

"Is the school that far?" Kate asked him.

"I just thought you wouldn't want to walk that far," he replied.

Kate looked past the end of the clinic, Jeff's office and the General Store towards an open space. It did not seem that far and she was willing to have a go.

"I've been sitting down all day, Jeff; a walk would be nice."

"It's still hot to be walking about."

Kate looked above her head. "I've got a canopy shading my head all the way, Jeff, and the air is not so hot that I couldn't bear it until I get into the school."

"Okay, Kate, that's fine with me," he said, closing his door and stepping back onto the boardwalk. "But shout out if it gets uncomfortable."

Kate nodded and they started walking along the boardwalk. From the outside the clinic appeared longer, as she found herself counting the windows. At the end there was a small gap of a metre or so, with steps down to the dirt alley between.

Then before she had a chance to see where it led she was outside the Estate Office and then onto the next building; the one that was called the General Store. It could have been taken for a duplicate of Jeff's office; one window and a door. Only this door was open and she stopped for a moment to look inside.

"Do you want to go in?" Jeff asked her, hesitating for a moment.

It was a store by name only. It bore no resemblance to what she was used to, with no more than a long wooden counter in front of a wall of shelves. The shelves only displayed food and supplies. Where the clothes were she had no idea. She would know more tomorrow.

"I'm supposed to be going in tomorrow with the

nurse to find something for Martin to wear; I'll leave it until then."

"Old Pertwee keeps the clothes in the back; that's if you're not particular about style. Otherwise you do what my wife does: order from a catalogue."

There was another building past the store, which she missed. It was another small structure with only a door but no window. Across the door in bold black letters on a dirty white background was the word, Generator. There was no explanation needed and she continued on.

Finally they came to the end of the boardwalk and the start of the open space. As she looked across the dirt path, the border of a white picket fence and what looked like a large garden, she caught sight of a small stand-alone building with a pitched roof of corrugated iron. The tall wooden cross in the centre of the garden meant this was the non-denominational church Jeff had mentioned. It looked more like a church hall and Kate decided she would investigate tomorrow and thank God for saving Martin.

As she passed the picket fence towards the other building that was obviously the school, her attention was momentarily drawn to the church garden. She stopped and looked more closely at the plants.

"We don't go in for flowers out here. Water is too

scarce to waste. So as you can see we grow vegetables instead," Jeff enlightened her.

"But I'm sure I saw a vase of flowers on your daughter's desk."

"You did. My wife has a small patch that she waters with dishwater."

Kate nodded and continued her journey along the fence.

The school was hardly bigger than the clinic, with two smaller buildings tagged on as if they were afterthoughts. There was no recreational equipment in what looked like the playground. It was just an irregular oblong of dirt with an occasional wooden bench for the children to sit on and have their lunch. There was no reason for Kate to imagine that – several Aboriginal children were already gathering outside.

"Do they sit out in the hot midday sun to eat their lunch?" Kate asked.

"Some do. Aborigines aren't affected by the heat like we are."

There was no fence around the school like the church. The unremarkable building was on the edge of the open part of the station. It looked unfinished, a work in progress; maybe that was why it had no fence, Kate thought. As they made their way across the dirt playground the door opened and an old-fashioned-looking woman stepped out to greet them.

She stopped to correct a couple of boisterous boys and, looking seriously at Kate, she offered her hand. As soon as their hands met Kate felt this woman was a kindly spirit with a warm heart. It radiated from her as if she had not been contaminated by modern living. But looking at the wisdom in her eyes Kate knew that was not true; this woman had vast experience.

"Miss Gerry, this is Kate, Martin's wife," Jeff said, when they met.

"I'm sorry we have to meet under such circumstances," Miss Gerry replied, linking Kate's arm and guiding her into the school. "I hope you've got time for a nice long chat," she continued, glancing in Jeff's direction.

"You're okay, Miss Gerry; I've got to go over to the Maintenance Shed for a while. Say half an hour?"

"That will be fine, Jeffrey. Now get on with your business."

Jeff smiled back at her in the fondest way and turned back to the main street and whatever he had to attend to in the Maintenance Shed. Miss Gerry turned back to Kate, still holding her arm, and they walked into the school. Kate was immediately drawn to the similarity with the Medical Clinic. It looked as if it had been designed by the same person, except this building had a small lobby coming off the front door. It was just like any other school lobby, with a large map of Australia on one wall and an equally large pin board on the other.

Directly opposite was a corridor with a closed door on one side and an open one opposite. Miss Gerry entered the one that was open. It looked exactly the same as the doctor's office. Kate hesitated before she followed her and peered through the glass panel in the door at the end of the corridor. It was the classroom, with no more than twenty desks, some occupied by Aboriginal children. She quickly scanned the room for any white children. She only counted four.

"Shouldn't you be teaching?" Kate asked, returning to Miss Gerry.

"My assistant is finishing off for me. It will be lunchtime shortly."

Kate sat down opposite. This was her opportunity to study someone she considered to be a unique woman. Being used to dealing with modern teachers, the name Miss Gerry conjured the impression of a formidable woman with her grey hair drawn back in a bun on top of her head and a floral dress. The age was right but the image was not. This Miss Gerry had short grey hair, a chequered shirt and jeans.

"I hope you don't mind, but I'm an educational administrator in Broome and I have more questions than you could possibly answer."

"Slow down, Kate. Why don't we start with one?"

Kate stared into her penetrating hazel eyes and sensed straight off that she was dealing with a woman of intellect. But why was she here?

"My first question must be an obvious one. You called Jeff, Jeffrey."

"It's a sign of endearment. I've known him a long time and Jeff seems so curt. And back then people used proper names."

"But he calls you Miss Gerry...that must be a nickname."

"You're right, of course. My proper name is Geraldine Hunter. But in Australia they had to shorten it. Anyway, the children call me that."

"You teach mainly Aboriginal children I see."

"Yes, I do. Except for Ralph Bellamy's children, all the other workers are Aboriginal. All the Aborigines choose western names, don't ask me to explain why; it's far too complicated."

"Is that why the Aboriginal boy who saved my husband's life is called Willy? The nurse told me if I wanted to know about him I had to ask you."

She could see the perplexed look on Kate's face and she laughed.

"I know what you must be thinking. It has a different connotation in the Mardu tongue. It's a derivation of the term 'willy-willy', which is a whirlwind.

The Aborigines choose names that fit the character and Willy certainly is a whirlwind. He can't keep still. He's always on the go and he never stops."

"Why do I have the feeling there's more to it than that?"

"You're right…it's a comical turn of events; although the boy doesn't think so. Anyway…one day a twelve-year-old naked Aboriginal boy ran into the stockyard and climbed up onto the top rail of the enclosure to watch the horses being broken in. A few minutes later a middle-aged woman caught up to him and tried to drag the boy off the fence. The head stockman walked over wanting to know what all the commotion was about, because she was spooking the horses. She told him she was the boy's aunt and he'd got away from her. He asked what she called the boy. Maybe using his name might help. She said he runs about so much, we call him Willy-Willy, like the whirlwind. The old stockman became serious for the moment. He studied the boy, noticed he hadn't been initiated yet and broke out laughing. Then he said, from now on I shall call him Willy and walked off laughing. From that day on, the young boy who grew up to love horses was called Willy."

Kate was fascinated by the tale but a little confused, not being familiar with Aboriginal customs. "What did he mean, initiated?" she asked.

Miss Gerry laughed again. "The boy hadn't been circumcised yet."

"Oh…" Kate let out. Then regaining her composure she said, "Well, he doesn't seem much of a willy-willy now. He's just sitting on the office steps looking as if he's lost something."

"Yes, I know. It's a complicated story. I suppose I'm partly to blame for his situation. You see the Aborigines who live on this land try to maintain their traditional way of life a few kilometres away on the Oakover River, but being so close to the modern way of life makes it difficult. Jeffrey tries his best to respect that, at the same time offering them all the benefits the station can provide."

"Such as?" Kate questioned.

"Everything we enjoy. Food, water, medical treatment and the schooling I provide for the children. And I might add some of the adults."

"Including Willy?"

"Exactly…that's the problem. The clan are happy to accept the things they want and even the teaching of the children to speak English, but they draw the line at filling their heads with grand ideas of a better future. They want them to continue sitting round a camp fire on the ancestral lands. I can see their point. They fear losing their heritage. They say, one day the Aborigine will be gone."

"I know what they mean. I have the same problem with the Asians in Broome. The old generation can't see a future when the young can grow with the times and still acknowledge their birthright."

"And that's how my involvement in this has muddied the waters. I could see straightaway his brain was like a sponge. He was desperate for more knowledge and when he reached the limit of this school's curriculum, I just had to start tutoring him privately. I know now that was wrong. But what could I do? His clan wanted him to follow the other boys and be a stockman. He wanted to go further."

"So what happened?"

"When he told them what he wanted, his clan disowned him. They accused him of disobeying his ancestors. He was no longer an Aborigine. That's when he made the decision to go on the ancestral walkabout to prove that he could still be an Aborigine and you know the rest. That's when he found your husband."

"And doing all that, as well as saving someone from sure death, had no effect on the clan? I mean, surely he proved his point? And I might add possibly brought more benefit to his people than just a stockman's wage."

"Silly…isn't it?"

"We need to do something, Miss Gerry. I'm in a

position to help Willy. It's what Martin would want and I'm sure Willy would. But I don't want to cause trouble for the station, not when they've been so good to us. And I want to help you also. I don't know whether you are aware of the Indigenous Education Grant, but I can help your school there. Just let me know what you want and I'll look into it."

"I know what you mean. I saw it on the television, but never thought a small school like ours would qualify. It would be a great help if you could."

"I can do something, but I need to know I have the full backing of the clan and I might add, the cattle station. I'll have a word with Jeff later."

"No, Kate…the one to talk to is his wife Marge; she's the driving force in that family. I know Jeffrey takes care of all the stock business, but Marge is the one who organises all the daily routine. She was the one who continued his grandfather's dream for a self-contained community in the outback."

There was so much to do. Miss Gerry had inspired Kate in much the same way she must have driven Willy to greater ambitions. Then there was Martin. It was not so much in what he'd said, but the way he'd described Willy as his saviour; and Miss Gerry had indirectly had a hand in that. It was just another link in the chain of events that had led to Willy finding the plane, as if it was meant to be.

Kate's suddenly remembered the first thing that had crossed her mind. "Miss Gerry, don't misinterpret my curiosity, but how did all this come about? And how did an English girl end up teaching Aborigines in the Sandy Desert?"

"Don't worry yourself, Kate. I know exactly what must be going through your mind; it has occupied mine for the past thirty years." She answered her. "Firstly, let me correct your notion that I'm an English girl; I'm a born and bred Australian. My parents were English. They emigrated from a small town in Sussex in 1953. They were both teachers and for whatever reason, they felt they could do a lot better in an emerging country like Australia. You have to remember, back then it was very much like England. They followed the same way of life, except for the heat of which England was short. They had the same units of measurement, the same currency; even roast beef on Sunday. The transition for them was almost unnoticeable."

Kate commented, "I heard of those days; it sounded almost like Utopia. I researched a lot about Australia before we took the plunge. It was very different in 1982."

"Yes…we were well into multiculturalism by then. Anyway, my parents decided to settle in Perth, worked their way through the different levels of the education system; giving birth to me in the process. I had a privileged upbringing.

"By that I mean educationally. I had good mentors and after university I spent the following years teaching overindulged, spoilt children whose lives of luxury had already been mapped out for them since their birth. I suppose it was that experience that encouraged my need to work in an orphanage at first; then I moved on to schools for the underprivileged and finally this cattle station."

"But how did you find out about the cattle station?"

"I never had a family of my own; I suppose I preferred being a single woman. It's not something that controls my life; my teaching does that, but I met a young girl some years ago…oh, it was so long ago now. Anyway, she was obsessed with the natural life. She rambled in the bush, climbed mountains, and lived rough in hostels; probably because of her tendencies also. We met briefly when she was lecturing at one of my schools. She imparted her experiences about the isolated places in Australia; she even wrote a book. It was during that time she told me about this cattle station and how desperately the Aborigines needed help. She was going back there."

"She sounds fascinating. What happened to her?"

"Shortly after her last visit to Perth, when she told me about this place, she became ill. She was diagnosed with cancer and died eleven months later. It was her death and the mass of notes she left me about the country surrounding the Sandy Desert that convinced me I had to find this place. That was thirty years ago. It was only half the place it is now. There was no school; I had to teach the young Aborigine children on the bare earth. I would sit on a wooden box with the children forming a circle. I had no school books, just scraps of paper the Palmers gave me. Then one day the old tight-fisted patriarch came over to our circle and said, 'You're an eyesore in my new town, Miss Gerry; I had earned my nickname by then. You and these black kids get in the way of my cattle, so I'm going to box you in, out of harm's way."

"Oh dear," Kate exclaimed. "That sounded harsh."

"From him it was what one expected. He was an old-style rancher. He was fair, but he dealt out harsh justice. The next day a horse and cart arrived with a mass of timber and ten Aboriginal stockmen followed with the gang boss. He was young then – he's an old bugger now – but he took me to one side with a big brown ledger, opened it to a new spread and placing a pencil in my hand, told me to draw out my school."

"Oh…how lovely," Kate said, with tears forming in the corner of her eyes.

"Yes…I couldn't believe my ears. He said keep it

simple, only basic to begin with…and I did. I drew out the main classroom first, added a small office for myself and a cloakroom-come-toilet. They were separated with a square lobby and that was it; they started straightaway and within the week I had my school."

"Just stockmen built this?" Kate said. "No architect or skilled builders."

"Good heavens no. You don't have those luxuries out here. Everyone learns how to do everything for themselves, otherwise you wouldn't survive."

There was a knock on Miss Gerry's door. It was open and Kate could see the young Aboriginal assistant standing outside.

"Yes, Penelope," Miss Gerry called out.

"You told me to remind you when lunchtime came, Miss Gerry."

"Oh yes, dear, thank you. I'll be along shortly."

Kate glanced at her watch. It was twelve o'clock. "Is it that time already?"

"Yes, I have to see to the children that don't go home for lunch. They live in the camp. It's a long walk just for lunch, so I provide some sandwiches here."

Kate stood up and shook Miss Gerry's hand. Holding onto it for a moment she looked grateful for this meeting. "You don't know how much I've enjoyed our talk. Now I meant what I said about Willy and the school. How can I keep in touch with you; particularly for all the information I need?"

"Letters are too spasmodic out here. Your best bet is the radio. When you see Marge, talk to her about it. She'll know what to do. She'll set you up with a radio call sign and all the paraphernalia to do with specific times."

"Fine," Kate said, satisfied with that. "And if I have time tomorrow morning before I leave for Broome, I'll try and pop in and see you."

"That sounds good, Kate; I'll look forward to that. She stood up and walked with Kate to the front door and they stood for a moment embracing each other. "Now you get off to your husband and have some lunch, and don't worry, we'll find a way to sort something out for Willy."

CHAPTER 21

Kate had forgotten all about Jeff when she walked out of the school onto the dusty playground. There were a few children outside by now and she smiled at them. They seemed curious about the white woman visiting their Miss Gerry and gathered around as she walked towards the main street.

She looked for Jeff, thinking he might be waiting for her. He was not about. Not even down the board-walk by his Land Rover. A small Aboriginal girl took hold of Kate's hand. It surprised her and she looked down into her big brown eyes.

"You looking for Mr Jeff?" she asked.

"Yes, I am," Kate replied.

"He's in the big shed over there," she said, letting go of Kate's hand.

"Thank you. If you see him will you tell him I'm in the clinic?"

A big smile broke out across the little girl's face. "I'll tell him white lady," she said, and ran off across the playground to her friends.

As Kate slowly walked down the boardwalk towards the clinic she suddenly realised her day had been completely turned inside-out. She had planned her meeting with Martin in such detail that when it had finally taken place it had been totally different. She expected him to react as he usually did, but he didn't; he was a stranger.

Now she was faced with the same struggle; trying to get him to remember her without venturing into the ordeal he had just encountered. It was a catch-twenty-two situation; whichever way she approached him, she was sure to confront his nemesis: what happened to Joe? And why was he so silent?

As soon as Kate opened the door to the clinic she noticed Dr Fitzpatrick's door was open and was confronted by the sombre stares of two hot-looking individuals. Despite a small, old-fashioned-looking air-conditioner, the small room was an oven; probably why the door was open.

Chris Isles was sitting next to the doctor going through the report he had prepared for AMINCO and Kate's presence appeared to have something to do with that. They looked up at her with anticipation.

"Ah Kate, we were just talking about you," the doctor said, standing up politely. "Come in. Take a seat for a moment."

Chris half left his seat, then sat down again. He had a pen in his hand and he had an open folder in front of him.

"It seems I returned just in time," Kate said sitting down. "Why was I part of your discussion?"

"Nothing dramatic, Kate," Chris answered. "We have almost finished the details for the hospital in Broome, a copy of which will go to AMINCO for their insurance people to look through. We were just wondering if you could show any light on Martin's mental state. Anything that might give the hospital an insight into his present condition; it's quite strange."

Kate was not surprised. It was the first thing that had crossed her mind when she'd heard of Martin's dilemma. Its similarity had prompted her to confide in the doctor.

"As a matter of fact I was going to mention Martin's car crash three years ago; although I would have thought that information would be in his AMINCO file."

"I'm sure it will be," Chris commented, turning over to a fresh page and scribbling a new heading at the top. "I wouldn't know, of course. My job is simply to take down the facts of the incident; I have no details of his medical history. However, I'll jot down some details if you don't mind and pass them over to the hospital so that they can treat him as soon as possible." He looked up at Kate with his pen in hand, ready to take notes.

Kate had no idea where to start. He obviously had no intention of getting involved with the traumatic events that had led to Martin's long recovery. All the relevant information was in the hospital files and Chris had asked her to keep it simple.

"As I said, Martin was involved in a car accident. It left him with serious leg and head injuries, as well as the usual minor abrasions. Because of his head injury he was in a coma for two weeks and following that he was disoriented for a further month. All this is on file at the hospital. A Dr Felix Grossman in Psychiatry took over the case once he left the surgical ward. I suggest he is the best person to contact. He is familiar with Martin's history."

Chris was frantically making notes, drawing particular attention to the doctor's name with a circle around it.

"This disorientation you mentioned, was it similar to Martin's present condition?" Dr Fitzpatrick asked.

"Medically I have no idea; that's why I mentioned Dr Grossman to you. From a personal perspective…I think so. The obsession is different, but the inclination is exactly the same."

"In what way?" Chris asked. "I need to get my facts right."

"I'm no psychiatrist, Chris. Like the other event, he seems preoccupied with the past, but for different reasons."

Chris looked down and started writing again.

The sombre expression left the doctor's face and was replaced with a gentle smile. He looked like a man who had suddenly been relieved of a burden. It was a satisfied look and he turned to Chris, who was still busily writing.

"I think this Dr Grossman is the one you should turn your attention to when you get back to Broome… don't you?"

Chris finished with a look of accomplishment and nodded as he closed his folder. "I agree," he replied, looking up. "I'm only a messenger here. My main task is to see that Martin gets the best attention straight-away. In fact I shall go now and put in a call to Philip. Fill him in with this information and see if he can contact everyone concerned and have them waiting for Martin's arrival tomorrow."

Chris jumped up from his seat, grabbed his folder and left without waiting for a comment from either the doctor or Kate. They could see he was too preoccupied with what he was going to say to Philip.

The doctor looked across to Kate and shook his head. He picked up the conversation. "I don't know... these youngsters. They're always so full of energy. I remember when I was like that; there was never enough time in the day to do all the things I wanted to do."

"I know what you mean, Doctor," Kate sympathised, hoping she could get back to Martin. She seemed to be constantly distracted.

Then the young nurse entered the hall outside, as if she had been listening at the door. The doctor looked up across Kate's shoulder and his persona changed.

"Yes, Nurse...was there something?"

"It's past lunchtime, Doctor. I was just wondering if Mrs Dexter would like to have sandwiches with her husband?"

His eyes darted back to Kate. "I'm sorry," he said, glancing at his watch. "You must be starving. How long is it since you had anything to eat?"

Kate had to reflect on his question. What with all the commotion and different people she'd met this morning, she had forgotten about food. She realised it must have been hours; not since her breakfast of toast and cereal.

"Not since my breakfast."

"The nurse will soon put that right," he said.

"Mr Dexter isn't on a full meal yet," the nurse commented. "He seems perfectly happy with a sandwich. In fact, he loves our beef sandwiches. Of course I could arrange for you to have a meal if you'd like that."

"No, Mini…er, Nurse, sandwiches will do fine," Kate replied.

"I'll get the cook to make up an assortment."

Kate nodded with a smile. She had felt uncomfortable about introducing a personal note into their relationship.

"My usual, Nurse," the doctor said sharply.

There was something strange about the doctor's attitude towards the Aboriginal nurse; yet here he was managing a clinic that mainly served the needs of Aborigines. Maybe she was wrong. Maybe it was not a racial prejudice, but simply a case of the need for senior recognition.

"Have you been on the station for long?" she asked him, bringing his scowl back to a pleasant smile.

"I was thinking about that the other day, in fact. I don't know why, but I woke up to a raging sandstorm. Probably the same one Martin was talking about; I lose track of time these days. Anyway, I finally figured out it had been twelve years. Can you imagine suddenly realising you had lost track of twelve years?"

Kate gathered that he was probably a tactless person. "You're not unique in that, Doctor. I have to remind myself how long I've been in Australia quite often."

"Chris told me you were an important civil servant in Education."

"Important was not the right word; more like a dictator."

"Dictator... Oh, that can't be right," he responded.

"Not as in a tyrant, of course," she corrected. "It's the humorous nickname they gave me. I'm the person that formulates the management procedures for the Education Department; the person who's often blamed for all the politically correct clauses in the working manuals for each department."

"Oh dear," the doctor exclaimed with a snigger. We had one of those on the Medical Board, although I never met him or her."

Dr Fitzpatrick had cleverly steered Kate away from her questioning of him and she turned the conversation back to his life on the cattle station. "So...did you come out here as a vocational thing like Miss Gerry?"

"Hardly," he said, with that short tone again in his voice. "She is a true saint, whereas my motives are a lot less vocational as you say. I'm afraid I'm one of those fallen icons. You know, the ones with feet of clay."

"And that's it…you're not about to tell me."

"Oh no… To the contrary, everyone knows about my shady past. It's stamped across my medical certificate. It's like being bankrupt. I can only be employed under certain conditions; which meant I drifted from one medical practice to another, slowly getting more menial posts until I finally gave up and applied for this job. You might say I decided to opt out of the civilised world for the isolation of the Sandy Desert."

Eureka…Kate had discovered his Achilles Heel. "And what was so terrible?"

"I was an alcoholic. Fortunately I wasn't a surgeon or anything as vital as that; I streamed my career towards a consultancy in Biochemistry. I did very well. Too well in fact…it went to my head and I started to drink. It was the old story; I couldn't handle the stress. Then the Board of Ethics decided I could not be trusted to work on dangerous drugs. I was still able to practise general medicine."

"And here you are; out of harm's way."

"I wouldn't quite put it that way, but yes, I suppose you're right."

Kate felt sorry for the man. Instead of fighting to beat his habit and get his position back, he simply had taken the easy way out. "It sounds like that to me. You can drink as much as you like out here. I mean, you're only working on Aborigines; who's going to oversee you out here?"

Dr Fitzpatrick expression changed to one of solemn acceptance, yet there was still a spark of defiance in his eyes. "The Palmers are my judge and jury out here. They are the supreme overseers and won't tolerate any deviation from the path they have chosen to run this cattle station. And for your information I haven't had a drink for ten years. Jeff Palmer saw to that when he found I had one drink two years into my contract. He came straight to the point; he said he only gave people one chance and I had just used that up. So…for the last ten years I have lived on a knife edge, but it's one I wish I'd had back in Perth."

Kate felt she had misjudged the doctor. She had been the judge and jury before she had heard all the facts. She was still against his manner of taking his past out on others, but now she understood.

"I didn't really mean everything I said," Kate responded. "I just wanted to find out what was responsible for your mean streak."

"Mean streak," he let out. "I've treated you with the utmost courtesy."

"You have; and in my opinion you've looked after my husband in a most professional way. It's your manner with your staff that offends me."

He could see Kate was not a woman that minced

her words or one you would bandy words with. In fact he thought 'The Dictator' was an admirable nickname.

Before he got a chance to defend his attitude, the nurse returned with a large tray covered with a red-chequered tablecloth.

"I hope everyone's hungry," she said, noticing the tense atmosphere.

After she placed a plate covered with a napkin in front of the doctor and he reciprocated with a forced smile, she ushered Kate out of his room and into the ward. She placed the tray on her desk, lifted the cover and took sandwiches over to the three Aborigines who were banging on the side of their beds. She put them straight with a few well-chosen Aboriginal words and returned to Kate.

"What did you say to them?" Kate asked, peeping under the cloth.

"You don't want to know," she said, picking up the tray and heading down the aisle towards Martin's bed.

Kate followed and sat down beside him. He opened his eyes immediately and looked at Kate. "I told you I wouldn't be long," she said, brushing a piece of hair away from his brow. "Now let's ease you up and you can have your lunch."

The nurse placed the tray on the small table

running across the bed on trolley wheels and moved it towards his chest. By now he was sitting up and staring at Kate.

"Have you been away?" he said.

"Never mind that," the nurse said. "I've got your favourite sandwiches."

She pulled back the cloth and pointed to the beef sandwich specially prepared for Martin. All the sandwiches were made out of outback style bread. It was coarse-grained dough with a heavy crust, but on Martin's the crust had been removed. Kate studied the different sandwiches.

"His digestion can't handle anything heavy yet," she pointed out to Kate, but he loves the beef. He won't eat anything else. I think that's because Willy fed him nothing else in the desert. First with the jerky he carries in his pouch and when that ran out, he cooked small critters and even a snake," she laughed. "The same one that almost killed Martin."

She realised she had told Kate something she hadn't known when Kate's eyes moistened.

"Heavens," Kate cried out. "How many times did my husband come near to death? The plane crash, running out of water and now a snake."

"Oh no, Kate," the nurse interrupted, realising that Kate needed to be told more about Martin's ordeal, "You forgot the sandstorm, the willy-willy, the sting from an unknown insect and Willy's silly blood poisoning. The doctor spent all night working on Martin. We lost him twice, but he punched his chest and got his heart going again. If you ask me, Martin wasn't meant to die; someone was watching out for him."

Kate was flabbergasted and suddenly felt guilty about the way she'd treated that poor man. Then she remembered Martin. He was looking hungry and she offered him his sandwich. The nurse was right; he attacked it with gusto. She then turned her attention to the tray. Despite what the nurse had given already to the three Aborigines and now Martin, there were still piles of sandwiches. Kate noticed they were arranged in neat rows, if rough-looking sandwiches could be neat.

The nurse stepped forward and pointed as she described what the cook had prepared. "These are beef and pickle, those are tomato and lettuce and the ones at the end are cheese and tomato; that's if you like goat's cheese."

"They all look lovely, Mini. I'm sorry I started calling you Nurse in front of the doctor, but I got the impression that he didn't like me calling you Mini."

"That's all right, Kate. It's our fault really. He thinks the clinic should be run strictly...and I agree. The patients, and I must admit, us assistants, tend to treat life a bit more relaxed. So it's hard for us...with our background."

Martin finished the first sandwich and Kate gave him the next. He reached for his water and she helped him with it. "I think you might find the doctor a bit less rigid from now on," Kate remarked.

"We'll see," Mini said. "I'll get you both some tea."

She walked off down the ward, bantering with the other patients and switched on her water heater, while Kate turned her attention back to Martin and her choice of sandwich. He seemed to be coping all right and she decided she would risk one of the goat cheese varieties. She took a small mouthful at first; she was surprised by its delicious flavour and texture.

Nurse Mini returned with the tea and Kate asked her to sit down and keep them company. She pulled a chair over from the empty bed next to Martin's and as they finished the sandwiches, washed down with a mug of strong tea, Kate probed the young Aboriginal girl about her entry into medicine.

The more she got into her life, which seemed to parallel Willy's, and how Dr Fitzpatrick had taken her under his wing and groomed her to take a radio correspondence course to be a registered nurse, the more Kate felt guilty. She had branded the man as a washout who could not face up to the peer pressure doled out to him in a society that had a lot to answer for itself.

She was too familiar with the same struggle women

had with the hierarchy in her own career. But the difference between her and the doctor was she did not choose alcohol to solve her problem. Then again she had to admit there was more than one side to this story. Within her own domain, she had the same difficult task of dealing with an alcoholic; only in her case, with a little digging, it was found she had lost a child, a traumatic event. It did not absolve her from her habit, but it did explain her problem.

Despite the doctor's strict line between his level and hers, Mini would be eternally grateful for the opportunity he had offered her. Under normal circumstances her life had already been mapped out for her in the role of an Aboriginal woman.

"My parents had me bonded with a young man from the tribe on the other side of the river; they were just waiting for me to come of age. I'd never seen him. He didn't work for the cattle station; he was a traditional Aborigine. I didn't want that."

"So what did you do?" Kate questioned.

"I was working for the doctor as a clerk…is that what they call someone who looks after the records?" she asked, not certain. Kate and Martin both nodded. "I told him what was wrong when he asked me. I was crying a lot."

"That's my girl," Martin suddenly uttered, to their surprise.

"And that's when he helped you become a nurse?" Kate asked.

"Not just then. He had a word with Mr Jeff and he spoke to my parents next time he went for water by the river. I don't know what he said, but they agreed to let me become a nurse. I was looking after the Aborigines after all."

"What Aborigines?" Martin spoke again.

Up till now he had not drawn any distinction with between himself and Mini or those on the ward. Kate thought this could be due to his frequent encounters on the mining sites; maybe the overseers never referred to them as Aborigines.

"Willy is an Aborigine," Mini answered him. "You remember Willy; he's the Aborigine who found you in the plane."

Kate shuddered. Mini had entered the taboo area and she waited for Martin to revert back into his imaginary world. If he remembered the plane, he would most certainly remember Joe. He went silent. His eyes rolling this way and that searching through his memory until recognition took over.

"What happened to Willy?" he asked.

Kate looked relieved for the moment. Mini had suddenly remembered her instructions and held her breath. Martin waited for an answer.

"Willy's back on his job as a stockman," Mini

answered. "He was asking after you; wanting to know if you were doing all right."

Martin was still mulling over his experience in the desert. "He saved my life, you know. We've got to help him. He doesn't want to live as his Aboriginal family does all his life. He wants to be an engineer like me," Martin rambled on. "I said I would help him," he said, staring into Kate's eyes. "We can help him…can't we?"

"Yes, dear. I've already talked to someone about that."

"Good," he said, nodding his head in approval.

As the two women talked, Martin began to converse alongside. It was a natural process; he was not dragged into the discussion. He was allowed to become interested in what they were talking about, particularly when Mini filled Kate and he in about the small community of the cattle station, about which they knew very little. Kate had barely scratched the surface so far.

To get away from the plane Kate had turned her questions to the station. "You know what I thought was strange, Mini – when Jeff was driving me past the stockyards, there were no cattle, just horses."

Nurse Mini laughed. "They're not here, Kate; they're out on the range. They only come in during branding and before they go to market."

"Funny, that's what Chris said, but I thought I'd misunderstood, and I haven't had a chance to find out since," Kate said. "But how can they feed in the desert?"

"The desert is only a small part of the station. Most of it is south-west, bordering on the Oakover River. It's not rolling grasslands, but they fatten up good and when they're really thirsty they head for the river; there's always plenty of green stuff there. One really hot summer he found them all the way over by Lake Waukarlycarly. Mr Jeff was really mad."

"Why do you keep talking about a cattle station?" Martin interrupted again.

"Sorry, dear," Kate answered him. "That's where you are now."

Martin's world was no more than a bed in a small ward and one amenable nurse as a companion. There was no mention of Joe at this point and they did their best to occupy his attention enough to avoid that. He had no idea he was on a cattle station or what it looked like, and most likely would leave this place tomorrow without ever finding out.

The door opened at the top of the ward and they both turned around.

It was Dr Fitzpatrick. Nurse Mini glanced at her watch. "Oh dear," she said, standing up. "It's time for Martin's antibiotics."

As she rushed back up the ward, the doctor sauntered down to have a word with Kate. He stood at the bottom of Martin's bed and checked his chart.

"Has everything been all right, Kate?" he asked, walking round to her side to check Martin's pulse. She moved her chair back.

"Yes, Doctor, he's been very good this afternoon. Is he still on antibiotics?"

"He should be on this course for two weeks, but that won't be possible if he leaves tomorrow. I'll give him an injection now and one tomorrow morning. Chris said he'll give the hospital his chart and then it's up to them."

The nurse returned with the injection in an enamel bowl. "Here you are, Doctor. I'm sorry I was a little late."

"That's all right, Nurse," he said, taking hold of the syringe, flicking it a few times as he adjusted the dose while the nurse rubbed alcohol on Martin's arm. He injected him as Martin looked at Kate affectionately. "Martin usually has a nap afterwards. I have no idea why; it's not a sedative. So maybe you'd like to come back later. Mind you, he seems to sleep through most of the evening."

"He's had a long day and tomorrow is going to be an even longer one. Thank you, Doctor. If it hadn't been for you saving Martin's life, I don't think that we would be having this discussion. You have my eternal gratitude. I think I'll let him rest; I'm looking forward to some of that myself." Kate stood up, bent across Martin's bed and kissed him on the cheek. He opened his eyes and smiled at her; then closed them again.

CHAPTER 22

Once again Kate stepped out of the clinic to find Jeff's Land Rover still standing by the boardwalk, empty. She remembered what the little girl had said about him being in the shed – obviously she'd meant the Maintenance Shed he'd pointed out to Kate earlier. She stepped onto the dirt road and walked diagonally across to the large building. It was her second experience of how hot it was away from the shade.

It had to be the biggest she had seen so far, or at least a close second to the clinic, and as she neared the huge open doors she could hear the sound of metal hitting metal. It was the sound she would have expected from a metal worker, although she had never seen or heard one before. Just as she'd never come across a smell like the one that seemed to pervade the very ground she was walking on.

The closer she got, the stronger it became; it seemed a mixture of all things. Her senses were assaulted by an overall smell of oil, the type you get around cars, with a hint of something burning, and above all that, a familiar aroma of nail polish. Of course it would not be nail polish, but one of its ingredients, acetone.

As she entered the noxious building and stood just inside the doorway, she heard Jeff talking to someone out of view. She spotted him standing in front of an old vehicle; the other person must have been behind it. Jeff looked up.

"Oh, I'm sorry, Kate. I got carried away. Have you been waiting for me?"

"Not at all, Jeff," she said, stepping a little closer out of the heat. "Your community kept me informed as to where I might find you."

"My community?" he asked, a little puzzled.

"Yes...Miss Gerry and a small Aboriginal girl."

He laughed and a mass of unkempt grey hair popped up from behind the vehicle. The rugged-looking workman must have been listening and Jeff's outburst had been too much for his curiosity. "This must be Martin's wife," he said in a distinctly Irish accent.

"Yes...I'm Kate," she said, offering her hand across the bonnet.

"Ah, I won't shake hands with you just now, dear

lady; I'm covered in grease," he replied with a big smile. "I hope the husband is feeling better for seeing his beautiful wife. Is he improving?"

"I think so. Enough to take him home tomorrow."

He looked surprised. "And we're not going to have the pleasure of your company after tomorrow?"

"All right, Sean, I'm sure Kate has better things to do than listen to your overtures," Jeff spoke out. "You'll have to forgive Sean; he's a bit of a romantic."

The burly man walked out from behind the vehicle rubbing his hands on a cloth just as dirty and Kate hoped he was not about to shake her hand. In fact he was an awful sight in his long leather apron, tattered shirt and what she could see of his jeans and huge leather boots. But what caught her attention most was the unusual leather leggings he had strapped to his legs.

He noticed her downward look straightaway. "Do you like them?" he said, sporting them for her benefit with a stunted jig.

"They look like something I once saw in a documentary about the 1914-1918 War." She hesitated to recall the instance. "Yes…they called them gaiters."

"That's where I got the idea from. Out of an old magazine I found."

"He's talking about my grandfather's collection of magazines from that period. He had them piled up in the corner over there. This used to be his old shed where he fiddled with his inventions, like our water truck here," Jeff said, patting the old vehicle they were leaning against.

"Do you mind?" Sean interrupted. "I was telling the lady about my gaiters."

Kate smiled and refocused her attention on the blackened and burnt-looking objects around his lower legs.

"Sorry...I'm sure," Jeff replied. "Carry on."

"I should think so," he bantered. "For that I shall definitely accept your dinner invitation tonight. I'll put the fear of Almighty God into Marge."

"Why would you do that?" Kate said.

"Is this a conspiracy or something?" he blustered, looking angry. "Here I am trying to tell you about me gaiters and you keep changing the subject. I'll come to Marge in a minute." Jeff just shook his head and turned to one side. "Now, dear lady, can you imagine the suffering I had to endure every time I used that old welding equipment over there? I used to burn the bottom of my jeans every time and my ankles into the bargain. Then one day I was looking through this old magazine I'd come across about the First World War and saw the soldiers wearing these strange leggings. Just the thing I thought, and cut myself a pair from some leather, a few old belts and here you are – no more burnt ankles."

"That's all very well, Sean," Kate jumped in, "but what about Marge?"

"Oh, very well… When Jeff has an argument with Marge he invites this scruffy fella to dinner, knowing Marge will go crazy worrying about her fine furniture."

"Who's this scruffy old fella?" Kate asked, glancing at Jeff.

"Why me, of course," Sean shouted. "I'm the scruffy old fella."

They all laughed, including Kate, not sure if she was being joshed.

Kate turned her attention to the shiny-looking vintage vehicle Jeff seemed particularly proud of. But what drew her attention back to it was him calling it a water truck. It caught her interest as she realised water, especially when there were bushfires, could be an issue in the Sandy Desert.

"So tell me about this water truck," Kate asked them.

"Now you're talking," Sean started. "She's a beauty."

"It was something my grandfather started but never finished," Jeff took over. "Back then he was trying to convert it to a water truck. We're only nine kilometres from the Oakover River, which is only a short drive; certainly not enough to use up a lot of petrol. It was very scarce back then…still is, really. Anyway that was before I had all the bores put in, so we didn't really need it."

"Not until the fire," Sean interrupted.

"I was getting to that," Jeff corrected him. "Sean's right. When we had our first bad fire back in 2000, we found the pressure from the bores was not enough to beat the fire. We lost three buildings. That was two years' hard work up in smoke."

"Can I speak now?" Sean asked. Jeff nodded. "You have to understand this was a 1929 Ford Station Wagon. It had a wooden back on it, and it was stored in one of those buildings. Jeff's grandfather had done no more to it since he'd found it in some old barn, than get it started again. And the fire destroyed the wooden back. We hauled the burnt-out wreck over here with the intention of rebuilding it. In the process Jeff had the brilliant idea of putting a water tank on the back. I don't think we could have rebuilt the wooden back-part anyway. We kidded ourselves we could, but we just didn't have the carpentry experience."

"You speak for yourself," Jeff interrupted. "I've done a lot of renovation on the old house. It's looking good now. Especially all the work I've done on the staircase...and what about the veranda? That took a lot of doing."

"I'll grant you that, Jeff," Sean acknowledged. "But the tanker idea was much better. I know we haven't had a fire since to test it out, but for keeping all the tanks topped up and watering the vegetable gardens it has proved its worth in gold."

"What does it actually do?" Kate asked.

They both stared at her thinking it was so obvious, but to her it was not.

Jeff took the lead. "Look, Kate, the bores are holes we have drilled into the underwater aquifers. They're enough to supply us with drinking water and a low-pressure tap water. We pump it up to large water tanks. That improves the pressure a bit with gravity, but it means we have to keep the tanks topped up. We can't rely on the meagre rainfall, so we had to cart it from the river. That was very labour intensive and time consuming. Then Sean came up with the idea of using the pump we'd built into the tank on the back of this fire-truck. He fitted a reversal valve to it and now we can drive down to the river, suck up enough water to fill the tank and then hose it back into the water tanks on the station."

"A job, I might add, that can be done by two," Sean boasted.

"So you've found a use for her after all," Kate pointed out.

"That's what I keep telling him," Sean said, nudging Jeff's side.

"Ah…but what about the petrol situation?" Kate

questioned. "You'll be going back and forth to the river more often now."

"That's no longer a problem since the Cattlemen's Association agreed to a collective in this region on petrol delivery. Now we have a regular tanker delivery every two months. He sets off from Port Hedland and does the circuit to Newman and back, cutting off on the dirt roads to each cattle station on the way."

"And I suppose you have a storage tank for that as well?' Kate said.

Jeff's face broke out in a broad smile. "We sure do," he said, glancing at his watch. "Good grief…have you seen what time it is?"

Kate checked hers. "It's only five-twenty."

"I promised Marge I would help her with the roast," he said, taking Kate's elbow. "I'll see you later, you old reprobate," he remarked to Sean.

"You will that."

Jeff walked Kate back across the road to the clinic and stopped on the boardwalk by the car. "What do you want to do, Kate? Stay here for a while with Martin or come home with me? I can always bring you back later if you want."

"No, Jeff, Martin's exhausted me today. He's nodding off anyway. So if it's all right I'd rather come with you. I'm dying to meet Marge."

"She's going to be busy getting this evening's meal

ready, but I'm sure she can speak to you at the same time. She usually does with everyone else," Jeff replied, as he opened the car door for Kate.

She decided to sit in the passenger seat this time, "Am I right in thinking Sean is going to be there tonight?"

Jeff started the car, pulled away from the clinic and left the station's outbuildings, driving in the opposite direction. "Yes, you heard right," he answered her when he cleared the last building and headed out into the open country.

"That must make for an interesting evening," she said.

"It's interesting every night at the homestead. Marge nearly went mad with loneliness when we first arrived on the station, despite my father being around. He had just lost my mother, so he wasn't much company and I had to spend most of the day doing all the jobs he'd let go. So...being the hardy individual she is, she decided to keep the homestead alive with people all the time. And that includes scruffy layabouts like Sean."

"I hope he washes his hands before he comes. That's if he can get all that grease off; and the caked-in dirt under his fingernails."

Jeff laughed as he increased his speed. "Believe me, Sean will be leaving the shed about now and heading for his chalet and he'll spend the next hour or so scrubbing himself raw. You won't recognise him when you see him later."

Kate was surprised how the departure from civilisation to the wide open space of coarse scrub and the occasional acacia was so abrupt. It was like a film set, with wooden shacks on one side of the road and desert on the other. Then Jeff turned left onto another track that was barely noticeable. There were parts where the sand had blown over the track obliterating it completely, but Jeff seemed to know where he was going. It was an instinctive sense Kate thought until she noticed he was heading for an isolated hill up ahead. From her perspective it was no more than a hump in the middle of a flat plain. It looked as though it had just been dumped there millions of years ago. And then, what looked like scrub from a distance suddenly became an oasis of small trees, too neat to be part of nature.

As the dirt track joined what appeared to be a circular road following the base of the hill, Kate noticed tall chimneys poking their ornate heads above the trees. Then, just as quickly, a large Colonial house appeared in the middle. As Jeff neared the open area in front, Kate could see the house was not unlike the Colonial houses in Broome, all built sometime in the 1800s.

The double-storey dwelling looked identical, right down to the shuttered windows and delicate fretwork on the pillars supporting the corrugated canopy that curved across the eaves to the edge of a deep veranda, shadowing nests of rattan chairs and tables.

Jeff pulled up in front of a wide set of steps and Kate noticed a woman standing at the top. Kate took her for Jeff's wife Marge. She was everything Kate expected of a woman in the outback; just as everyone described her.

As Kate stepped out of the car and walked towards the steps, Marge walked out of the shadow. Kate guessed she was in her forties; greying light-brown hair, weathered Anglo features, little make-up, country-style blouse and jeans and of all things, cowboy boots.

By now Jeff had retrieved her bag from the boot and was urging Kate forward, and as she climbed the six steps to the boarded veranda, Marge took hold of her arm and led her through the double front doors to what could only be described as a vestibule; it was too big to be a lobby.

"Now then," she started, in a motherly way. "If you don't already know, my name is Marge and I know you're Kate. Don't look surprised. On the two occasions I had to visit the station today, everyone was talking about Martin's wife, Kate; so I know more about you than you think."

Kate let out a snigger. "And for what it's worth I know all about you too."

They both laughed as Marge led Kate over to the grand staircase.

"Now, don't you think I'm being impolite, but I bet all you want to do right now is flop down on a bed. What time did you start this morning?"

"Three-thirty…and you're right; I'm exhausted."

"I knew it. Well, I've got a dinner to prepare…" She scowled at Jeff returning down the stairs after dropping Kate's bag off in her room. "That's when someone butchers the meat. So why don't you have an hour to yourself."

"I think I will, Marge, although I would like to freshen up first."

"I understand. It can get real dirty out there on the station. The bathroom is on your right at the top of the stairs and your room is on the right at the end of the corridor. You can't miss it. Jeff had the bright idea of putting a slot on the guest room door so that he could put the guest's name in it."

"What if you have more than one guest?"

Marge laughed. "That's not very often out here. But if it does occur, we just let them know the one with his name on the door is more important."

"I'll see you later," Kate said, climbing the stairs.

"Oh…when you come down, just walk through to

the lounge here; there'll be someone about. And if you fall asleep, I'll give you a shout about six-thirty."

Kate nodded and continued on up the stairs. There was a long landing either way at the first level and she turned right. She popped her head into the bathroom, expecting if anything that it would be modern, but it was far from that. The bath, basin and toilet looked straight out of a vintage magazine. They were white porcelain, not enamel and they were covered in Victorian-style flowers. She lifted the lid of the toilet. It looked normal enough, but made her wonder where the contents went, and how efficiently, after what Jeff had said about the low water pressure.

Now for her room, she thought. It was only two doors along at what looked to be the corner of the building. There was a small window at the end of the corridor and she checked what it was like at the back of the house. She was looking down on a small courtyard paved with irregular slabs of stone. Over on the far side she could see Jeff's Land Rover standing in front of a weatherboard building that looked like a garage. On the other side there was a large open patch of earth. It was black, just like ordinary garden earth, which surprised her, and it appeared to be planted out with vegetables like the open ground in front of the church.

She turned and faced her door and there was her

name in big capital letters just as Marge had said. She opened the door and her eyes opened wide. It was beautiful – straight out of a period movie: an antique dressing table with a huge mirror that had flowers cut into one corner, a massive mahogany wardrobe, matching chest-of-drawers and a bed that had to be seen to be believed.

"Oh my God," Kate uttered when she looked round the door and saw the bed.

It was the biggest, fluffiest bed she had ever seen. When Kate walked over to it the mattress came up to her waist. How she was going to climb into it she had no idea and she looked around for some steps. And when she pressed the floral eiderdown cover, her hand sunk all the way to her elbow. She soon realised this was not an inner-spring mattress; it was either stuffed with lamb's wool or old-fashioned feathers. Then again it could have been straw.

Kate then looked for her bag wondering if she should change for tonight. She could wear the same clothes tomorrow. No one would notice on the plane; especially Chris – he would be too occupied with Martin. As she swung round to see where Jeff had dropped it she noticed it was standing next to a small Victorian en suite in the corner. It was a white cabinet with a basin in the top, a towel rail on the side and hot and cold taps. This surprised her because in the period there would have been no taps, just a bowl and ewer on a shelf behind a door in the front. Out of curiosity she tried the taps and to her further surprise the water was at least warm.

This she just had to ask Marge about. She knew about the generators that supplied electricity to the buildings and the water tanks, but how did they get rid of the waste from the toilet and heat the hot water. Kate finally washed the thin layer of sandy dust from her skin, managed to climb up onto the huge bed and, sinking back into it, she lay there staring up at the ornate ceiling. The day had rushed past quicker than she'd expected, she thought, and then she continued thinking about her journey back to Broome with Martin tomorrow.

CHAPTER 23

Kate opened her eyes. For the moment she struggled to capture a dream that seemed tantalisingly close; but like quicksilver, it was soon gone. The orange light that filled the room confused her; at first she thought this was the dream and she was back in Broome. But as her senses cleared she knew that was not so; her bed did not face the orange light. It came through the balcony doors on her left.

Suddenly everything came back: the early morning flight, the tour of the cattle station and this magnificent house. She rolled out of bed, just remembering she had been twice as high as in the bed at home. She went over to the window. She hadn't realised it before, but the house was facing west. On her right the terrain was open and flat, to her left in the distance there was a mountain range and just where it rose out of the flatland, there was the sunset.

She glanced at her watch in the bright light; it was ten past six and Marge would be calling her soon. Fortunately she had washed and changed before she'd lain down on the bed, so all she needed to do was straighten her clothes and comb her hair. Then she stopped for a moment as she became aware of something else; there was a strong smell of roasting meat. It was stronger over by the door, and when she opened it the delicious aroma greeted her.

She checked her reflection in the mirror; she would have to do.

At the bottom of the stairs Kate remembered the lounge was to her right. It was not difficult to miss the large antiquated room through the wide opening with a wooden arch of radiating spindles at each end. She walked through and down one step into the past – beyond the timeless oil lamps and antique furniture, the walls were galleried with oil paintings, watercolours and engravings, echoing the station's ghosts.

The present, she noted, was allotted to all the surfaces of the furniture in an array of photographs from different periods that stood as a record of the new Palmer dynasty. Presumably starting with the old man standing beside the car, Jeff and Sean had told her about, continuing on to Jeff's father and other people Kate guessed were Marge's family, and finally the new Palmers. Kate took particular interest in these pictures, mostly taken on the station (except the ones of teenagers standing in front of a large modern building).

As she walked across the polished wooden floorboards Kate just had to reach out and touch the nearest wall. It was covered with flock paper in a classic Greek design. She had heard about it, even had seen it in the Broome museum, but had been too far away to actually touch it. It felt like nothing she had experienced before; an upper-class Victorian home.

It was plain to see the old house had not changed in ages. It was the sort of house in which she expected to hear the sound of children running about, curious to see who the new female guest was. But the house was almost silent, except for the distant sound of a television. Kate guessed so, when she heard the familiar sound of a commercial. They always had a sound of their own, when everyone jumped up to visit the toilet or put the kettle on for tea.

The sound seemed to be coming from another room on the other side of the lounge, through another decorative arch. It was half the size, split in two by a large dining table set out as if Marge was about to have a banquet.

The other half looked unusually modern. With an open fireplace on one wall, an old-fashioned cabinet-style television on the other and the space between taken over with an assortment of plush easy chairs that was obviously a new addition.

Kate could hear Marge talking to Jeff somewhere close by in another space and decided to look for them, when she was stopped in her tracks by the sight of an old man in one of the easy chairs watching the television. He looked familiar in some way, but unfamiliar in another. His grey hair was combed back across his head and parted in the middle. It looked shiny, as if it had been plastered back in place with hair-cream. He looked flushed, uncomfortable in fact, in a green-striped shirt, buttoned up to his neck, grey tweed jacket and dark-blue jeans.

He was suddenly aware of her presence and turned his head in her direction.

"I was wondering where you were until Marge told me you were having a lie-down. Do you feel better for that?"

Kate stared at the impudent old man until something in his voice clicked. "Sean…is that you, Sean?"

"Of course it is…who else would it be?"

Kate couldn't believe her eyes. "You look so different," she said, almost on the verge of laughing. "You look so clean. Oh, I'm sorry; I didn't mean it to come out like that. You look smart…like a country gentleman."

"I know, isn't it terrible? This is Marge's fault. She

won't let me in the house unless I'm looking all spick and span. I even had to shave, do you know? It took me weeks to get that stubble. That's how long it's been since I was last invited over."

"Don't believe a word the old bugger says," Marge said as she came into the dining half of the room carrying a tray of steaming tureens.

"Can I help?" Kate asked, walking over.

"No, you don't," Marge ordered. "You sit down until the table's ready."

"I told you. She's a hard woman," Sean mumbled.

Marge walked over to him with a wooden spoon in her hand and he cowered in his chair. "You be good or I won't let you sit at the table in your shirt sleeves or cut the outside of the meat for you."

"Oh Marge, I was only having a little fun with the darling girl. Do you not want me to enjoy myself in me old age?"

She bent down wagging the wooden spoon at him. "And there'll be less of the familiar talk. Kate might get the wrong idea."

Marge walked back to the table looking back at Kate with a smirk on her face and a twinkle in her eye.

When she left the room and Kate sat down in an easy chair next to Sean, he turned to her. "I didn't mean anything by it, Kate, it's just my way. I've never known anything different since I left Dublin."

"I bet you were a right lad with the colleens in Dublin," Kate jested.

"That would have been a miracle, Kate," he said, with a grin on his face.

"I can't believe that."

"Then would you believe I left Dublin orphanage when I was eleven and sailed off to Australia?"

Kate was shocked. She had heard about all the children from England and Ireland that were shipped over to Australia to a 'better life'. That was true for some, but not for others.

"I'm sorry, Sean. I hope it was a move for the better."

"Ah…it was and it wasn't. I just left one Catholic orphanage for another."

Kate's insatiable curiosity got the better of her. "And where did you go?"

"We landed in Sydney. It was all right, at least the weather was better and on the voyage I hooked up with this lad from Rathmines. We got on well."

"Did you go to the same orphanage?"

"Yep…even managed to sleep in the same dorm. He swapped with another boy and we spent the next few years sleeping next to each other."

"Then what did you do?" she asked. By now she was so interested in his story, she was facing him with her elbow resting on the arm of the easy chair and her chin in her cupped hand.

"Ah you know, it was a typical tale in those days. The orphanage was getting worse and there was not much work about in Sydney, so Paddy and I – that was what I called him, he didn't know his real name and the priests called him a biblical name he hated – bunked off. Took what little we had and left."

"What did you do then?"

"It was strange. The old orphanage gardener used to fill our heads with all sorts of tales about how he roamed Australia with no more than a swag. When we were old enough to understand that song we thought he was dreaming, but out on the road for real, we got thinking. It didn't seem a bad life, so that's what we did."

"You started travelling around Australia? What did you live on?"

"Believe it or not, we had a better life than we did in the orphanage. Before long we became part of a group of travelling men. Each new man we met told us about a different spot. It didn't matter what it was, on the rail lines, building roads and even cattle stations, I've done it all."

"And how did you come to stay here?"

"Paddy and I stopped on this station a few times; it was a circuit thing. By then we had mastered a few skills and Jeff's father kept asking us to stay; he needed skilled men he could trust. But we still had itchy feet, so we kept moving on. That was until Paddy's accident. It was a cattle muster. We were driving twenty-thousand head from Alice Springs up into the Kimberleys to get them fattened up for the market. We camped overnight and Paddy just had to play cards with a couple of newcomers. They were taking him for everything he had when the cattle stampeded. Silly thing it was. The cattle were spooked by a sudden thunderstorm. Paddy just didn't get out of the way quickly enough."

"I'm so sorry, Sean. I shouldn't have asked."

"It's all right, darlin'…sorry, Kate. It's been a while since I brought the tale out for an airing. If there was any consolation; the men who'd kept him occupied, died as well. Our priest would say they paid the price for their wickedness. Anyway, when I'd finished the drive I made my way back to the station, and I've been here ever since."

It was the type of story that is always followed by a long silence. Kate and Sean turned back to the television. Neither knew what they were watching and turned their heads with eager anticipation when Jeff walked in bearing a huge beef joint. They could still hear it sizzling from across the room as he rested it gently on a large old salver Marge placed on the table. The silver tureens she already brought in were warming over each one's individual candle. She followed with two more; one full of roast potatoes, the other gravy juice from the roasted meat.

"Come on you two, don't let it get cold," Marge said, as Jeff started carving.

"That's enormous, Marge," Kate said. "What are you going to do with it?"

As they all sat down and Marge started filling the plates, making sure Sean got his outside cuts, she said, "Yes, Sean you can take your jacket off at the table," and then she turned back to Kate. "After we cut a few slices off for our dinner and some for tomorrow, I shall pass the rest over to the cook when I take you down to the plane in the morning, so that he can warm it up for the school children's dinner, along with lunches for the hospital and anyone else until it's finished. We never waste anything here on the station. Even the scraps go to feed the pigs."

Kate looked bemused as she started on the roast potatoes.

Recalling the photographs Kate had seen earlier in the lounge, she broke the silence with a question. "I gather from the pictures in the lounge you have children?"

Glancing in Jeff's direction, Marge let out a chuckle. "I'd hardly call them children. Steve, our eldest is twenty-nine. He's out on the range checking on the new calves. That usually takes a couple of weeks. And as for our other two, Billy and Sarah, they're both away at High School in Port Hedland."

"How does Steve live out there?" Kate asked.

Jeff looked up from his plate and answered her, that side of the station being his business. "They go out in a team of four in a campervan and with two motorcycles. The cattle are collective animals; they wander in groups, so when Steve comes across a group, which I might add could stretch for a kilometre or more, he stops the van and takes off on the bikes. Two of the team are stockmen, the third is a general handyman, capable of repairing any damage to the bikes and the fourth is the cook."

"Ah…what would we do without cooks?" Sean commented.

"Exactly," Jeff continued. "He also sets up and dismantles all the home comforts they need out in the desert."

Marge's stern expression softened. "Most of the time we're all alone in this monstrosity of a house. Steve seems to feel more at home out there amongst the spinifex and the occasional kangaroo. Except the daily invasion from the station to see Jeff here," she said, glaring at Sean totally engrossed in his roast.

He looked up, as if he could sense her piercing stare. "What? Why am I always singled out as the villain?"

"Because you live here most of the time," she said.

"All right, Marge, not in front of our guest," Jeff reminded her.

Marge turned her attention to Kate. "Sorry, Kate. Don't take what you hear literally; we argue like this all the time. It's better than television."

As Marge and Jeff cleared the table, telling Kate to go on through to the lounge, she noticed she was alone. Sean had disappeared, probably duty bound to help his benefactors with the dishes as payment for his meal.

She felt bloated after such a fine spread and contemplated whether this was how they ate out here in no-man's land. She dropped into the first comfortable-looking easy chair she came across and found herself facing a whole new tableau. She was facing back towards the open arch and her first view of the lounge had missed what was behind her as she entered the room.

She was looking at an enormous open fireplace, with giant brass andirons supporting two huge logs. Where the logs had come from she had no idea, and why such a large fireplace in the desert? It was built of stone with a slate mantle standing two-thirds up the wall. On top was another array of small silver and brass frames with older photographs of Victorian relatives. They had to be. The men looked stiff and grand with their walrus moustaches and the women, dressed in sombre finery, could have been clones of Victoria herself.

It was then that Kate's attention was drawn to a large wooden scroll about half a metre higher on the wall. It had a rustic look that reminded her of a Swiss holiday she and the family had enjoyed before they left England. It was a final round trip of Europe before they went 'down under'. They stopped at a small village at the base of the Alps with chalets that looked like the cuckoo clocks they were selling. They had scrolls or plaques as they called them, with names carved on each, hanging above the front door.

This one was the same. She had to half close her eyes from that distance to read the name and decided it said 'Galene'. It was an odd name; something else she would have to ask Marge about.

She heard the others arriving, it sounded like another mild argument; something about the beef would have tasted better with a little mint. Of course Sean's Gaelic voice was uppermost, until Marge settled the matter as they entered the lounge with the fact that mint only went with lamb.

"In Ireland we do things differently," he said.

"Well, you're not in Ireland now."

Marge chose the chair next to Kate either because she wanted to talk or it was her favourite seat. Kate hoped it meant the latter.

"Did you enjoy the dinner?" Marge asked, giving the other two a stare that they obviously understood. They huddled for a moment then made their way out of the lounge, through the arch.

"I did," Kate replied. "I think I've eaten too much."

"Think of it as stocking up for tomorrow. Heaven knows when you'll get a proper meal again. What with the plane flight and getting Martin settled in at the hospital. I could make up some beef sandwiches if you like."

"No, thank you Marge…I think it's going to take a good twenty-four hours to get over this lot. My figure might take ages to revive."

"We don't bother about figures out here. In fact, we don't bother about much."

"I'm sorry. I got the impression you were in an idyllic lifestyle."

"Oh Kate. At the end of the day I wouldn't really change my life for what you must endure in the city. Don't misunderstand me; I'm not criticising your way of life. I suppose it's what you've been brought up to."

"I understand; sometimes the grass is always greener."

"Exactly. It's like this house; sometimes I could curse all this old-fashioned furniture when I watch television; then in the next instant, I wouldn't part with it. I don't think many people could say they were living with four generations of their family. Although these are Jeff's ancestors, I look upon them as mine."

"Don't you have any ancestors here?"

She looked hesitantly towards the fireplace. "That's all I have on the mantelpiece. Funnily enough I have no pictures of my mother and father, or cousins. I was an only child and at the time, my parents came out here when I was a baby, they left everything behind. These pictures were sent to me by an old aunt before she died; apparently there was no one left in England."

"At least they weren't thrown away," Kate remarked to a distant Marge. "By the way…I was wondering what the scroll was up there?"

"Oh, that. It was one of Jeff's great, great grandfather's endeavours. I gather he fancied himself as a woodcarver, among other things."

"What does it mean?"

"Galene…that's the name of the station," Marge said, standing up and gesturing for Kate to follow her over to the two oil paintings she'd noticed earlier. They were of a feisty old man and a beautiful woman several years younger. "This is Jeff's great, great grandfather, Merril Palmer, and his wife, Galene."

"What a beautiful woman," Kate commented.

"Yes, she was. He was so depressed with the land he bought for them to settle on, he said, 'At least it should have a beautiful name,' and he named it

Galene, after his wife. She was the one who started the Palmer dynasty."

"What a lovely story," Kate said. "Does her name mean anything? They usually did in the Victorian times."

Marge had to think for a moment. "Yes, it does. It means the Goddess of Calm Seas. Her father was a sea captain."

"I can see by the picture that she was a refined woman. I wonder how she coped with this country back then, and, of course, the terrible sea voyage beforehand. I read about such times: a lot died on the journey and if that didn't kill them, the wagon trip to their destination usually did."

"Well, this woman was made of sterner stuff. She survived everything."

"I bet it was hard for you, Marge, even with a fine house to come to."

"This country is hard on all women. You've only been here one day and I can see already you find it difficult. The heat, the flies, the difficulty getting what city folk take for granted and above all, the isolation."

Jeff and Sean returned, hesitating for a moment under the arch; then seeing the smile on Marge's face, they entered.

"All right, you two, you can come in. Did you have a good game of snooker?"

Blood Brothers

"He beat the pants off me as usual," Sean commented. "Not literally, of course, ladies, but near enough; I
have to clean out the shed for a week."

Marge glanced at the large mahogany clock on the
sideboard. "It's late enough for some drinks. So make
yourself useful, Sean, and bring in the trolley."

"Oh, those are the sweetest words I've heard tonight,
dear lady," Sean said, scampering off into the dining
room.

"And you, dear husband, can come and sit down
and continue with the family history for Kate before
she leaves us tomorrow."

CHAPTER 24

Jeff settled himself in the easy chair on the other side of Kate after moving the coffee table to make room for Sean and the trolley. He arrived and Jeff pulled it closer. Sean sat on the other side and brought out his favourite bottle of scotch.

"What will it be, Kate? A whiskey if you're frisky, a brandy, some sherry or what about a liqueur?" he asked.

"Is that a bottle of white wine I see?"

"We've had that for ages, Jeff," Marge said. "Will it be all right?"

"Of course it will. If anything it'll be stronger now," he said.

"White wine it is, dear lady," Sean said, breaking the cork and pouring her a drink in a long glass. "And your usual sherry, Madam?" he said to Marge. And looking at Jeff he continued his charade. "Finally, a whiskey for Jeff and the barman."

Jeff fussed with his drink, twirling it around, taking a sip, and considering Marge's scheme to drag him into the conversation. He was a conservative man – a rock in emergencies or tending to men's business – but ask him to play the host at a party or explain the facts of life to his children, he would shy away.

"Who's interested in our history?" he questioned in a sullen manner.

"Kate is for one," Marge answered back. "She happens to be interested in how the Palmer dynasty managed to build up this cattle station."

"You've started so you might as well continue," Jeff replied, finishing off his whiskey and pouring another. "You're the one who keeps all the records and decorates the place with photographs."

Marge knew as soon as he started a second drink it was a sign that he was feeling pressured. And that was never something she did intentionally.

"Oh, very well; it's just that I thought you would be better placed to cover the recent past, seeing we're talking about your family," she mumbled. He grunted and she continued. "I suppose I have to start with how we arrived at the station."

"Kate doesn't want to hear about how we got together," Jeff interrupted.

"I wasn't going to. That's why I asked you to tell the story."

"Oh, for Christ sake, Kate will be on the plane before you start," Sean said.

"And you stop taking the Lord's name in vain," Marge snapped back. She took another sip of her sherry and turned to Kate with a frustrated look. "Jeff and I were living in Perth at the time. We met on a course for Animal Husbandry and Agriculture and got married shortly after. We did that because Jeff's father had an idea he would marry the daughter of his friend on the next cattle station. Anyway, with our certificates in hand we moved to the station hoping he might come round.

"He didn't. He was a difficult man since Jeff's mother died. He was an old cattleman that didn't like change, especially if it was something modern, and the two of them fought constantly. He thought of nothing but his cattle, the station and of course the Aborigines. I think he thought more of them than he did his own family."

"That's a bit of an exaggeration, Marge," Jeff butted in.

"Oh, come on, Jeff…you remember that time. He would disappear for days on end. And you'd always find him with the stockmen on one of their corroborees," she said, taking another drink. "Sorry, I'm getting carried away. He was one of those old pioneers like his father and his grandfather before him—"

"I can see there's a lot of heritage in this house," Kate interrupted.

"It only goes back to my great grandfather," Jeff responded. "He rebuilt it after the original wooden house almost fell down in 1923."

"Yes…well your father was the end of the line as far as true cattlemen were concerned. He wouldn't listen to any of Jeff's ideas to improve the property. 'It would cost too much,' he would say."

"That's true," Jeff agreed.

"Even when Jeff told him there were government grants and low interest loans to help improve the property, he still wouldn't have any of it. Then when the old man had his accident in the stockyard, bless him, Jeff took over as manager until his brothers finished their time at university." She reached over and placed her hand on Jeff's. "They never did come back to the station…did they?"

Jeff looked over to Marge and gave her a pinched smile. "No…they never did. I had to buy them out, and we're still paying for it." Jeff answered her with a faraway look, as if he was still thinking about his father's death. "The cattle station is not a place for old men. My father was only fifty when he died; my great, great grandfather lasted the longest at seventy; and my great grandfather and grandfather were lucky to reach their sixties."

"You know as well as I do, Jeff, they were average life-spans in those days and your father's death didn't count," Marge reassured him.

Kate felt she was beginning to understand this remarkable couple. Yet she wondered how two diverse people like Marge and Jeff ever made it to marriage, parenthood and owners of a successful cattle station like Galene.

Jeff was the typical patriarch cattleman with generations of hard men behind him; a significant background to emulate. Yet when he let his guard down, the gentle, considerate man took over. Marge, on the other hand, was the opposite. She came across as a woman that was all for her family. Then again, whether by necessity or because of the number of men she encountered in a long day, there was always that 'do or die' spirit lurking in the background. Either way, Kate felt she would have loved to have seen her with her children.

In one respect, the Palmers' way of life was something Kate admired. They were the stuff this country was made of; but sadly they were from a dying generation.

Silence fell across the group huddled around the drinks trolley and despite a few more drinks being partaken to stimulate the conversation, only Sean managed to voice an opinion, even if a little belatedly.

"I must have heard that story a hundred times and it always seems to get more fantastic with each telling," he commented, waving his glass in the air. "What about you, Kate? Have you as interesting a tale to tell?"

Kate was not prepared to expose herself as much as Marge and Jeff had. She thought a modern life was not folklore material like theirs was. However, from the expressions on the faces turned in her direction she felt something was warranted, if only as payment for the Palmers' genial hospitality.

"Oh dear…I don't know where to start. Our mundane life has no bearing on your colourful experience. I only asked you because I could never imagine people actually did live like it has been portrayed in legends."

"Hold on, Kate…I hope you're not comparing our life with what you might have read. Let's face it; it was a terrible time. That's why those writers romanticised that period. Very few wrote about all those who died horrible deaths."

"I'm sorry, Marge. I didn't mean it to come out that way."

"Of course you didn't. I just don't want you leaving here tomorrow with the wrong idea. We're ordinary folk trying to get on with our lives. There are no massive fortunes here. We simply live from day to day and take what comes."

"It seems our families are exactly the same. We have two children, Adam and Jennifer, who are also at university; Adam, the oldest is studying to be a doctor in Sydney, while Jennifer is just trying to graduate in Science. They've broken up for Christmas and are at home at present waiting for their dad to come home."

"He was a lucky man, surviving a plane crash," Sean spoke up.

"Yes, Kate. How is he doing?" Marge continued.

"The doctor's not so sure. His injuries are under control, I understand."

"Are you saying he has a mental problem?" Marge asked.

"I suppose you can't keep things quiet on the station."

"That's an understatement, Kate. It only takes a word and it spreads like wildfire. It's ideal if you want something to get around quickly."

"I never thought of it like that. To be honest, at the beginning I never considered it important. We were only going to be here for a day after all. But now I've got to know you all, I find it's very important. I want to leave behind a pleasant memory. Not one of two odd people who crossed your path."

"You're going to leave a lasting memory here, Kate," Marge said. "We already know about your plans to help Willy and the school. If you can pull it off you'll make an enormous contribution to the community."

"Miss Gerry asked me to talk to you about my ideas. It seems that won't be necessary now. But there is one thing; she says I shall have to communicate with her through the radio. I gather I'll need your help for that."

"No problem, Kate," Marge replied. "When I take you in tomorrow I'll give you our call-sign and our scheduled radio list. That means the allotted times we're on the air. The only problem you may have is transmitting. Have you any radio access?"

"They have a radio setup at the AMINCO headquarters. That's the American company Martin works for. I suppose they could help me."

"That's obviously your first objective. Sort that out and you're home. If they're a big operation as the doctor guessed when he contacted them, they should be able to help you. I'm sure they will. I understand Martin's an important man."

"Good heavens, you do know a lot. I didn't realise how important he was until the crash. Just goes to show how we sometimes take our husbands for granted."

"Hear, hear," Jeff exclaimed, with what looked like a fresh glass in his hand.

"I think you've had enough," Marge said. "You have an early start tomorrow."

"Not on my behalf, I hope," Kate said.

"No, Kate, it's all right. I shall be seeing to your arrangements tomorrow. He's got to get out to Steve with a spare part for the campervan."

"How did he know?"

"We have walkie-talkies for the stockmen to carry when they're out on the range. They were an expense we just had to pay. They've been a godsend since we got them and they run off batteries that we keep charged in the radio shack."

"I seem to have strayed a bit, I'm sorry," Kate said.

"That's okay, Kate," Marge said, glancing over to the other two, lying back with their eyes closed. "Isn't it, lads?" she called out.

"I can hear every word, Marge," Jeff muttered. There was no reply from Sean.

Marge laughed. "We already know quite a lot, even if some of it is slightly exaggerated. "I know you're both English, but why did you leave all that culture to come out to one of your colonies?"

"I don't think we really class Australia as one of our colonies; I suggest that's all on your side. To us, Australia is another country, like any other. If I was to sum it up simply, I'd say we emigrated because of the terrible weather and the state of the country back then. And, yes, we miss the culture, but it was a small price to pay for all the advantages we have here."

"Why choose Broome?"

"We didn't. We landed in Melbourne. We had relatives there who made our integration that much easier. I fitted in fine with my credentials in the educational field, but Martin was the one who had difficulties. His area of engineering was not catered for as it had been in England, so he had to lower his sights."

"That can be very hard for a man. His job is everything."

"Yes, he had a bad time for a couple of years."

"So how did Western Australia come into it?"

"He saw an ad for an Engineering Consultant's job for an American mining company in Broome. Although, at the time he didn't realise he wouldn't actually be working there. He was to be a travelling engineer."

"Didn't that put him off? I mean it's a long way to travel for a job if it's not what you really want."

"He was bedazzled by the dollar signs. For a start the salary was twice what he was getting, all the removal expenses were paid for and on top of that they provided a low interest house loan. It was manna from heaven."

"You didn't mind that? You must have been settled in your job by then."

"That's just it, Marge. When the American company found out about my qualifications they contacted the Broome Educational Authority and lined up an excellent opportunity for me. Subject to the interview, it was in the bag. And when they found out Martin was hesitating, they flew the whole family up to Broome on an all-expenses-paid holiday. We were able to have our interviews and enjoy the beautiful weather at the same time."

"Of course you still had all the hassle of selling your house in Melbourne."

"No, Marge. That was the icing on the cake. They hired an agent to take care of everything. That's what it's like dealing with these giant American companies."

"I don't know, Kate. I mean I'm glad for you and your family, but it sounds like you're selling your soul to them."

"There you are," Jeff interrupted. "You sound just like my father. He didn't want anything to do with the government aid and low interest loans. He said once that the government's got hold of you, they own you."

"That was a different situation, Jeff."

"How different? We're still in hock to the bank."

"Don't pay any attention to him, Kate; he still blames his father for getting the station into such a mess. It had nothing to do with money. He was too easy on the Aboriginal stockmen. He let them do what they wanted."

"You soon sorted that out," Jeff spoke up again. "Now I have to work twice as hard just to keep things working. If it wasn't for those jackeroos every season I don't know what we'd do."

"And whose idea was that?"

"All right, you two. Can a man not get any sleep?" Sean uttered.

They all laughed and Marge shook her head, "Kate must think we're a terrible lot, arguing all the time. We don't mean anything by it."

"I know, Marge. It reminds me of home. I miss not being able to talk to the kids. I keep checking my mobile, but all I keep getting is the 'No Signal' sign; when are they going to put some mobile towers out here?"

"And where would they put them, Kate?" Jeff asked. "The Great Sandy Desert is an enormous place. Then you have the Gibson Desert and following that the Great Victoria Desert, which takes up half of Western Australia."

"I suppose you're right. In America the mid-west is just the same."

"Yes, but they've got around their problem with satellite phones. That's what we need to do; get ourselves one of those satellite dishes."

"And add more expense to our bank account," Marge reminded him.

Kate never did finish her tale of the Dexter family's progress when they reached their new environment in Broome with the extreme difference in the climate, only two seasons instead of four, and not seeing Martin for days on end. There were too many interruptions and the evening was drawing to a close.

She had not taken into account the different lifestyle of the inhabitants of the cattle station on the verge of the Sandy Desert. Early to bed and early to rise was their regime. Like country folk everywhere, they measured their day by the rise and fall of the sun, the dry season and the wet season. They were a God-fearing people; if he could not help them, no one could.

By ten o'clock they were preparing for bed. Sean said his farewells and left for his permanent guestroom, Jeff surprisingly embraced Kate and wished her a safe journey and that Martin would soon recover in Broome. Then he left the room for an early start in the morning. Tomorrow was just another day to them.

Marge stood up, bent over Kate and kissed her on the cheek. "I won't say goodbye just yet. You and I have an early start tomorrow, getting Martin ready for the plane, having our chat with Miss Gerry and with my little lesson on the radio. So I'll leave my goodbyes till then. If it's too early, you can watch television if you like. It's not much good though."

"Good heavens no, Marge," Kate said, standing up. "If we're getting up early in the morning, I'll need all the sleep I can get; although I doubt if I will sleep. I'll be thinking about how Martin is going to cope on the plane."

CHAPTER 25

Kate opened her eyes wondering what had woken her. The room was still dark, and reaching for her mobile she discovered her alarm had not gone off yet. She lay there going over her discussion with Marge as they had climbed the stairs, about a four o'clock call, so that they could leave for the station at five. It was only three-thirty.

Then she heard the thump of a car door, a man's voice and another thump. She eased herself out of the bed and went across to the window. It looked still and lifeless with only the barest of light creeping around the corner of the house. It was too early for sunrise, until she remembered her window was facing west. Then two brilliant beams of light shot out across the dirt forecourt, getting longer and narrower until a dark shape appeared behind them. Kate was not sure, but she guessed it was Jeff's Land Rover. It turned left.

The beams disappeared behind the shape, with only a glow outlining it until it turned right at the conjunction of the circle and the long beams lit the track as it headed towards the station.

As Kate started to return to her bed she caught the smell of cooking. She opened the door. Marge was up, probably pottering in the kitchen after making breakfast for Jeff and Sean. There was no point in going back to bed now, not when Marge would soon be knocking on her door. Kate tiptoed across the landing to the bathroom, switched on the light, had a quick wash down and dried herself.

Back in her room she switched on the light, put on the clothes she'd worn the night before, packed her holdall and saw to her make-up. She checked herself once more in the mirror and nodded. One last check of the room to see that she was leaving it tidy and she switched off the light and made her way across the landing and down the stairs towards the lounge.

There were two table lamps on in the lounge, which cast a glow across the shiny wooden floor all the way to the foot of the staircase. Going only on the pervading smell and her recollection of Marge and Jeff's movements with the food last night, Kate headed into the dining room and turned right towards a lighted doorway, and as Kate walked into the huge kitchen

Marge looked up from a table she was sitting along-side, finishing her breakfast.

She glanced at the clock on the wall opposite. "You're up early, Kate. I was going to let you sleep on till four."

"I woke early for some reason, so I decided to get up."

"Probably those two oafs banging about...I told them to be quiet with your room right above the garage area, but it's like dealing with children some-times. Anyway, don't stand there holding your bag. Drop it over there and sit down."

Kate did what she asked and sat down opposite. Marge was just finishing what looked like a hearty breakfast. She had a drink from the mug she was holding and, looking Kate in the eye, asked her if she was ready for her breakfast.

It was almost four o'clock in the morning; the thought of eating anything at that time made her shudder. Then she noticed the white plate at the end of the table opposite the huge black stove. On the plate was a sausage, two slices of bacon, a chopped tomato and alongside the edge of the plate was a brown egg.

Kate looked at Marge with a frown. "You don't expect me to eat all that, do you? Not at this time in the morning?"

"We always start the day with a good breakfast

inside us. You can't run a cattle station on an empty stomach. You never know when your next meal will be."

"I don't have to run a cattle station, Marge."

"No…but you are going on a long flight."

Kate held off her reply for a moment, contemplating whether or not the plane would furnish refreshments during the flight. "Instead, would you possibly be able to make up some of those beef sandwiches you mentioned earlier, please?"

Marge looked disappointed for the moment, and then she smiled and returned the plate to the large old-fashioned icebox standing in the opposite corner of the room. "Very well," she said returning to the table. "I'll make you an assortment. You might get sick of just beef."

Before she started, she made Kate a mug of tea as she toasted some of her homemade bread by the open stove and left Kate a dish of butter and a pot of blackberry jam. Kate hesitated, asking her where the blackberries had come from.

"As you may have noticed from your window, I have a small garden of sorts," Marge answered as she got on with the sandwiches. Passing Kate two pieces of toast, she continued, "Anyway, amongst the essentials I treated myself to a blackberry bush; I had it sent down on the mail run. It took a year to mature, but eventually I got enough berries off it to make some jam. Now get on with your breakfast, we'll have to leave soon."

"One last question," Kate said, "How do you heat the water?"

Marge smiled and pointed to the large black stove she cooked on.

After breakfast, Kate sat in one of the rattan chairs on the veranda waiting for Marge to bring her car around from the garage. It was surprisingly warm for five o'clock; not hot of course, but not chilly either. In Broome, close to the open sea, there would always be an early morning fret that left the garden lathered with a layer of dew. It soon disappeared when the sun climbed above the distant hills; by which time Kate would be just starting her day after Martin's early start.

Once again a pair of beams turned in front of the house. Marge got out of her earlier model Land Rover and climbed the steps for Kate's bag. She threw it on the back seat assuming Kate was going to sit beside her in the front. She did, and with only a reminder for Kate to put her seat belt on, she set off along the circular track back towards the main route to the station.

Kate could see lights in the distance. The station

had already been awake for over an hour. She turned to Marge, her blank expression highlighted by the coloured dashboard lights, wanting to chat.

"It must be a long day for you, Marge," she said.

"Oh, it's not that bad once you get used to it. Yes...I have to get up early, but by six-thirty...seven, the day's mainly my own... Except today. Apart from seeing you off, it's accounts day. I go round all the different sections of the station and sort out their expenses and mark it all up in the ledger."

"I wouldn't have thought that was necessary out here."

Marge laughed. "Oh dear, I wish. Not only do I have to balance how much of our collaborative supplies each outlet is using; there's the tax man to satisfy."

"The tax man?" Kate exclaimed.

"Oh yes... It might only be once a year, but we still have to justify what profit or loss we make on the end-of-season cattle sales."

Kate shook her head in amazement, "Isn't that just the thing? I never thought you would be bothered with all the paraphernalia of the outside world. But I suppose civilisation does have a long reach."

By the time Marge pulled up in front of Jeff's office, Kate could see the sunrise lighting up the stockyards further on towards the east. They looked gaunt and spidery against the orange glow and the silhouettes of the stockmen, leading out the horses ready for another day, were like marionettes on a rustic stage.

Kate expected Marge to stop outside the school for her last-minute talk with Miss Gerry, and just as she was about to turn and say something, she saw the old teacher walk out of Jeff's office. She was standing on the boardwalk when Marge pulled alongside and switched off the engine, and she waved to Kate.

"I got up early this morning so that I wouldn't miss you," she said, as Kate walked round to the boardwalk. "Are you all ready to go?"

Kate gave her a kiss on the cheek and when Marge joined them, they all walked into Jeff's office. Chris was sitting by the desk with his medical bag in-between his feet, with a look of apprehension on his face.

"Everything's ready, Kate," he said. "Martin's had his meds so don't be surprised if he seems a little drowsy." He checked his watch and glanced in Marge's direction. "I checked with the pilot and we have a window of forty-five minutes if you want to sort out your radio details."

Kate was amazed once again. "You were right. Everyone, even Chris, seems to know my business. "How did you find out about the radio?"

He hesitated while he ran through last night's

activities. "I don't know really. It seemed to be general knowledge. I spent some time with the doctor, the pilots, of course, and oh yes, a funny Irishman popped his head in when we were playing snooker. He wanted to talk to the doctor."

"There's your link, Kate," Marge said nodding her head. "And don't ask me how he found out…it would take too long."

Knowing she was going to spend the next three hours with Martin, Kate turned her attention to the important matters of Willy and what to do with the radio communication. She sat down in a chair next to a small table in the corner where the radio equipment was. Marge sat in front ready to explain, while Miss Gerry stood alongside. Chris left the room, presumably to see to Martin.

"If I can start first," Kate interrupted Marge, who was eager to get started. "I just wanted to ask Miss Gerry if Willy was serious about improving himself."

"He talks about nothing else, Kate. That's why he got himself into so much trouble with his clan."

"Didn't you say Jeff sorted that out?" Kate replied.

Miss Gerry glanced at Marge for confirmation. "Yes, it's all sorted."

"Good…so I can go ahead with my enquiries?"

"Well, yes, I suppose so," Miss Gerry said, nodding her head.

"I think there's going to be a lot of consultation before anything's settled, so let's sort out this radio procedure as we haven't got much time," Marge said.

Kate nodded, eager to learn another skill, although by all accounts she wouldn't actually be doing the communicating.

"Remember I said Martin's radio man will be handling the radio – that's if I can persuade them to let me use it."

"Of course, I remember you telling me," Marge answered. "That makes it much simpler. All you really want to know is our call sign and what frequency we use...they're funny about that. Then as soon as you get the okay, get the radio operator to call us and leave his call sign and frequency."

"Is that all?" Kate asked, surprised it was so simple.

"Yes...except it does take some experience to get the transmission right. But that will be your operator's problem. I'm sure they're more proficient that me."

A smile crossed Miss Gerry's face and she jumped in to say her piece.

"That sounds great. As soon as we make contact we can keep in touch and pass information to and fro until we can reach a final solution about Willy's welfare."

Marge jotted down the information on her pad,

pulled off the top sheet and handed it to Kate. She dropped it into her bag straightaway.

Just as they shook hands and hugged each other, Chris popped his head around the door. "Have you settled your business? The doctor's ready with Martin."

Kate stood up and made her way outside. The tears began to flow when she saw the nurse, Mini, waiting by the car. Kate embraced her and didn't want to let her go. But she had to, just as she had to say goodbye to all those who'd helped her and Martin. By now there was a crowd gathering on the boardwalk as Chris and the doctor helped Martin into Marge's car. Chris went in first, then Martin and finally Dr Fitzpatrick. Kate returned to the passenger seat with her window open so that she could hold Miss Gerry's hand one last time. Marge switched the engine on and slowly made her way past the waving hands of the stockmen sitting on the railings and on to the waiting plane at the end of the runway.

"Where have you been, Kate?" Martin said, in his drowsy state.

She turned in her seat and reached over to him, "Sorry sweetheart. I had to speak to Miss Gerry the teacher before we left."

"Teacher?" Martin said, puzzled.

"Don't concern yourself, Martin. I'll tell you all about it on the plane."

"What plane? Not one of those Cessnas, I hope?"

Kate gritted her teeth and turned back towards the open area where the plane stood. She just had to mention that word. It had just slipped out without her realising. It soon became silent again as Martin slipped back into his dreams. She crossed her fingers and hoped he would stay that way.

Apparently the pilot of the Piper Navajo must have conceded to Marge's request to drive her car right up to the side of the plane so that Martin only had to walk a short distance. It was just as well. A large crowd had gathered on the edge of the runway and only parted to let Marge get through before quickly closing the gap again.

One of the pilots stood by the door ready to assist Chris and the doctor when they guided Martin towards the steps. Then just as Martin's foot was placed onto the first step, Willy broke through the crowd and ran to his side with a big smile on his face and all three helped Martin into the plane.

"There you are, mate," he said, taking hold of his good arm.

"Is that you, Willy?" Martin said. "I've been looking for you."

Willy turned to leave. It was his first time inside a plane and he felt shut in. As he stepped down from the steps, Kate caught his shoulder as he passed. "Thank you so much, Willy, for saving Martin's life. He won't forget his promise to you."

A smiling Willy put his hat on his head and stepped back as Marge stepped forward and wrapped her arms around Kate. They were both crying by now and Kate could hardly speak. Even Marge was tongue-tied for once.

"Oh Marge, I don't know how to thank you and Jeff," Kate blurted out. "Or everyone on the station come to that."

Marge wiped her eyes and laughed to break the tension. "Come on now; you don't want Martin to see you like this."

Kate dried her eyes and tried to smile. "I mean it, Marge. You're all wonderful people...I'm going to miss you."

"We'll be talking before you know it on the radio. Now come on...you're holding up the plane. Have a good flight...and good luck," Marge said, as she led Kate towards the open door. For an outback woman who had braved many tense situations, this event was too much for her and she returned to her car.

Willy was still standing by the steps and she took hold of his hand and gave it a tight squeeze. "You better get a move on, Missus," he said, with a grin.

She climbed the steps into the plane. Chris and the

doctor were preparing to give Martin another injection. She moved in close. "What's this one for?" she asked.

Dr Fitzpatrick looked up. "His mild tranquiliser is wearing off now, so I'm giving him the sedative I told you about. That should keep him calm until you reach the hospital. He swabbed his arm and inserted the needle. It was only a slight prick; Kate felt it more than he did. The doctor returned the syringe to his bag and closing it, he stood up to say goodbye to Kate and Chris.

He took hold of her hand and held it for a moment. "I hope everything goes well for Martin in the hospital. He'll be in the right place."

"Thank you, Dr Fitzpatrick," Kate said, "Despite what you said, I think you did a marvellous job. I don't think Martin would have survived otherwise."

He let go of Kate's hand and glanced back to Chris sitting in the seat beside the bed they had prepared. "He's in your good hands now, young man," he said, and made his way past the pilot at the door and down the steps.

The pilot closed the door and returned to the cockpit. Kate moved over to a window seat so that she could wave to everyone when the plane left. The crowd moved back from the edge of the runway as the engines started up. A cloud of dust rose into the air, but Kate could still see them. By now the crowd was largely made up of Aborigines waving as passionately as they could. Their excitement was probably focused on the plane rather than Kate and Martin leaving, but that did not matter – it was still a magnificent send-off.

Marge, the doctor and Miss Gerry were in the Land Rover by now. Kate could not see them, but she knew they were, as it kept pace with the plane just as Jeff had done that morning when it landed. This time Kate was more occupied with the car trying to keep up to the plane than her fear of take-offs. She waved frantically, not knowing if they could see her, as it pulled to a stop at the end of the runway and rapidly dropped away as the plane climbed into the air.

Kate sat back in the seat with a satisfied smile on her face. She'd had no idea how she was going to say goodbye to all those wonderful people, but she had done it. It was a more fulfilling end to her stay at the Galene Cattle Station than she could have hoped for. She chuckled to herself. In all that excitement she had not realised that everything had taken place in a sub-dued orange light. She had been so conscious of the sunrise and sunset to get her bearings but this morning it had passed her by until now.

Kate sat and watched the sunlight follow the

windows all the way around to just behind her as the plane banked steadily towards the north-west.

Kate undid her safety belt and checked her watch. The pilot was on schedule; he'd said he wanted to leave by six o'clock and it was five past. She moved across the aisle and sat in the seat opposite Chris, alongside the bed set up for Martin. Chris smiled a confident smile; everything had gone to plan and he was satisfied.

"That was your first airborne pick-up," Kate said. "You did well."

"Thank you, although I have to acknowledge Dr Fitzpatrick's role."

"Nonetheless, you were the coordinator."

"Let's hope the landing and ambulance pick-up goes as well."

"I've been so busy I didn't think of another ride in an ambulance," Kate said.

"I must admit I was a little concerned, so I radioed Philip yesterday and he said he would organise that when the pilot gave him his ETA."

A frown crossed Kate's face. "Oh dear," she uttered. "You've just reminded me that landing in Broome is not the end of our journey. It's just the start for Martin, and we only have a week until Christmas."

"Is it that close?" he said.

CHAPTER 26

The relief that they were finally on their way had a soporific effect on both of them. Apart from the low whine of the engines and Martin's disturbed, although sedated state, all was still. Chris looked as if he was attempting to catch up on his early start and Kate felt her heavy eyelids closing. She opened her eyes again and checked Martin. He was somewhere other than in the plane. His eyes were twitching under his eyelids; darting left and right. He was fighting his demons again.

Kate reached over his chest and stroked his brow. The man she always looked up to for guidance and strength looked so frail and helpless. She wondered what the children would think; only Jennifer had seen the state he was in after his car crash. Now they both had to face the fact that this was not their father. Her touch was all he needed. His eyes stopped rolling and his body relaxed.

Kate woke with a sudden jolt as if she had rolled off her seat, but she was still sitting upright, her shoulders pushed back into the cushion and both arms lying casually on her lap. She opened her eyes. The seat opposite was empty and glancing around the cabin she wondered if Chris was talking to the pilots. Then she heard running water behind her, the click of a bolt being drawn back and he appeared in the aisle.

"You're awake, I see. You've had a good hour," he said, reaching for his bag.

Kate glanced at her watch, "I think we were both tired."

Chris placed the bag on his seat, unzipped it and brought out his notebook, stethoscope and his thermometer case. Kate was watching every move when he rolled back the blanket the doctor had used to cover Martin. Her eyes opened wide. Martin was dressed in a new pair of jeans and a grey-chequered shirt. She had forgotten her appointment with Mini at the general store to select a fresh set of clothes for his journey home.

"Good gracious," she exclaimed, covering her mouth with her hand. "I forgot all about going with Mini to the store for Martin's new clothes. She must have done it for me, bless her."

Chris laughed. "Actually she asked me to go with

her while you were at the homestead. She thought you would be too flustered in the morning."

"She was right. All I could think about was learning how to use the radio."

"He doesn't look so bad," Chris said, taking Martin's pulse.

"Good job he can't see himself. He hates jeans," Kate continued. "By the way, do I owe you any money?"

"No…AMINCO will take care of all the expenses. It's all here in my notebook. All the drugs they used, the cost of the use of the ward, Dr Fitzpatrick and even the nurse, Mini. Everything will be charged to their insurance, including whatever it costs to get Martin right in the hospital."

"My goodness, they are efficient."

Placing the book on Martin's chest and jotting down his pulse, he then continued to check his heart rate and temperature; continuing to make notes of the result. He looked satisfied and returned everything to his bag.

"I gather everything's all right?" Kate asked. "That's a turnaround from the other day when the doctor was fighting Martin's infection."

Chris nodded his head. "Yes. I called in on him last night before I turned in and everything was back to normal. The antibiotics did their job; one less complication for the hospital to worry about."

"Does that mean, apart from his fractured wrist healing and this disorientation sorting itself out, he's out of the woods?"

"Oh, I'm not qualified to answer that question. I mean we won't know what he's really like until he comes out of the effect of the sedative. For all I know his mental problem might just be related to his blood poisoning, the residual effects of being without food and water all those days and the trauma of the crash."

"But what about Joe? He still thinks he's alive."

"That was when he was fighting the infection. But I can't really say, Kate; only a physician can answer that question."

"Yes, I know. It's just that you've done so well, thank you."

"I've just done my job," he replied, returning to his bag. "Well, I never," he uttered, bringing out a small brown paper parcel. "I forgot all about this. Marge gave it to me when you arrived at the office; she told me to give it to you on the plane."

Kate was just as surprised as he was until she opened it and saw an assortment of sandwiches inside. She laughed. "Oh dear Marge. When she tried to force a huge breakfast down me this morning, I refused, asking her to make some sandwiches for the flight. I forgot all about them."

"Well, let's see what we've got in here," Chris said, peeling back one corner.

The smell was still strong. Kate could pick out the roast beef from last night, pickles and that delicious goat's cheese Mini had brought in to the ward.

"I must admit they smell nice," Kate said.

"It's been three hours since my breakfast," he commented. "What say we have a couple now? There's a hot water jug in the galley. I'll switch it on."

As Kate sorted out which she liked, Chris dashed off to make some drinks. He soon popped his head back around the corner. "There's only coffee, I'm afraid."

"That's okay... Make it with two sugars, please."

Kate went for the cheese and tomato, while Chris stuck to the beef. When they were finished there was still a lot left.

"Do you think you'll want any more before we land?" he asked her.

Kate shook her head, still trying to finish the last one. "I think those will keep me going for a while. It's not so much the filling, it's the bread."

"I know what you mean," Chris acknowledged, tearing the brown paper in half. He then wrapped two sandwiches up for later and standing up he said, "I'll see if the lads want the rest of these. Wrapping them up, he made his way up the aisle, opened the door after knocking and stepped into the cockpit.

When he returned Chris started examining what he had written in his notebook. He checked Martin's pulse again and continued writing.

"Have you been checking him all the time?" Kate asked.

"Only on this flight… All the previous notations I copied from the clinic charts. Although I've brought those with me for the hospital, I still need the AMIN-CO copies for the record. That's what I'm doing now."

"It seems a lot of extra work to me."

"I suppose it does, but that's what the Americans want."

Kate left him to it; her lack of sleep was catching up on her. She checked Martin once more; he seemed settled now and she leaned back in her seat and closed her eyes. She tried to think of meeting the kids again and telling them she was back. She even began thinking about Christmas. It was only a week away and other than Adam putting the tree up, nothing was ready. He had forced her to go shopping; that was something, but it wouldn't be the same without Martin.

The jolt that woke Kate this time was not her body waking up; it was the plane's tyres bouncing on the AMINCO airstrip. By the time she had realised what was happening they were taxying slowly past the wooden buildings. Chris was already standing by the locker lifting down the bags. He noticed she was awake and pointed out of the window to the waiting ambulance.

He looked ecstatic. "It's here. Philip managed to get the ambulance."

"Yes, I can see," Kate said.

The plane taxied onto the concrete apron opposite the embarkation lounge where Philip was waiting. The young pilot was already opening the door and lowering the steps. Two dark blue-uniformed para-medics entered the small opening carrying a folded-up stretcher. They examined Martin yet again as that was the accepted procedure.

Chris slung his medical bag over his shoulder, took hold of the bags and left the plane. Kate stood back out of the way and waited for the men to transfer Martin from the plane to the ambulance, which they did with great dexterity.

A waiting Philip walked over to Kate, hugged her, asking if the trip had gone well and how Martin had travelled. "He's still sedated...and, yes, everything went marvellously, thank you."

"That's good. Now get into the ambulance; every-thing's been arranged for Martin at the hospital. Give me a call tomorrow."

Kate wanted to talk to Philip – she had so many

questions – but seeing to Martin was more important. "Okay...thank you, Philip. I'll call you. Bye."

She kissed him on the cheek and walked over to the back of the ambulance. With Chris in the front passenger seat next to one paramedic and Kate and the other paramedic in the back with Martin, the ambulance moved off.

Kate was too concerned with what the paramedic was doing with Martin to notice the journey back into the centre of Broome. He was placing a needle into a vein in Martin's arm, to which he attached a small plastic junction and then he covered it with a gauze swab. He explained that he was prepping Martin now for any medical tests in Emergency.

"Why are we going to Emergency? I've been expecting that he will go straight to the appropriate ward."

"Until he's been thoroughly checked out and his treatment decided, we don't know where he's going."

Kate accepted this and it wasn't long before the ambulance arrived and Martin's stretcher was wheeled into Emergency.

It had been three years since Kate had walked through the flapping plastic doors, as she had done that wet morning, following the paramedics wheeling Martin into the General Hospital Emergency Department. By the time they had cut Martin out of the wreckage, she had already been on the scene.

As she followed them into a side cubicle the pervading hospital mixture of carbolic and a variety of drugs caught her sinuses. By now Martin was coming round and he looked around all the faces and curtains. Kate stepped forward and took hold of his hand to reassure him.

"It's all right, sweetheart. You're back in Broome. You slept right through the plane journey," Kate said, as a nurse placed a syringe into one of the connections in his arm. By the time he realised what was happening, she had finished.

Kate looked around to see if she could see Chris anywhere. He was standing by a small desk talking to a young woman with a stethoscope around her neck. He had his medical bag open and was handing her the notebook.

"I won't be a moment," she said to Martin. "I just want to have a word with the doctor." She kissed his cheek and walked over to them.

Chris turned when he saw her. "I'm just giving Dr Loxley here Martin's record," he said, as the doctor started to read the notes.

She looked up at Kate. "I'll need to talk to you about his past medical history; you know, his local GP, any allergies…that sort of thing."

"Yes, of course," Kate said, confused. "I thought Martin was going to a private hospital? You must have a file on him. He was in this hospital about three years ago…Dr Grossman treated him. Is he still here?"

"He will be in a private wing, Kate," Chris informed her.

Dr Loxley was suddenly alert. Her eyes opened wide as soon as Kate mentioned his name. He was teaching at the time. Maybe she was one of his interns.

"Dr Grossman, you say," she repeated, with a smile. "He's a consultant now, but I shall contact him and see if he wants to see your husband."

"Thank you, Doctor…I think you'll find he will."

The doctor passed Chris's notebook to a nurse who promptly started copying it on a machine on the other side of the main Emergency counter. The doctor then walked over to Martin and began examining him.

"How many times is my poor husband going to be examined? Don't you people ever read each other's notes?"

Chris took hold of Kate's elbow and guided her to a group of chairs and sat her down. "Don't get yourself in a state, Kate. It's what they call counter measures. They keep checking each other's notes just in case someone misses something. It's common practice and it guarantees no one makes a mistake."

"I don't believe that," Kate responded sarcastically. "The papers are always full of reports where someone in the hospital has made a mistake."

"There's nothing you can do about it, Kate," he countered.

When the doctor finished her examination she called a porter to take Martin to X-ray and returned to her little desk to make a notation down on his new sheet.

Despite Chris's attempt to hold her back, Kate stood up and walked over to the doctor. She looked up with an expression that said, 'Are you still here?' and Kate stiffened her resolve. "Why does my husband have to be X-rayed? You already have the films from the cattle station."

"Exactly...I don't know how old their equipment is, but it's not a satisfactory result. I'll get a much better idea how his wrist is healing on our own machine. By then I should have the results of his blood test and I shall be able to confirm or not this Dr Fitzpatrick's report. Why don't you go and comfort your husband?"

She walked off and started talking to a nurse.

Kate was not known for having a short fuse, but this patronising woman was just about taking her there. If she hadn't glanced at the expression on Chris's face she might have given her a piece of her mind. She took a deep breath and returned to the seat next to him. The nurse had just returned his notebook.

"That woman is infuriating," Kate said, sitting down.

"Only because you're questioning her; she's following a boring routine," Chris answered her as he made sure his notebook was intact.

"I suppose you're right. All this routine is driving me crazy. It's just the same as last time; only then he had some serious injuries. It was hours before I got home." Kate suddenly remembered the kids. "Oh dear…see what this place has done to me; I forgot to ring home."

Kate took out her mobile and as she was about to dial, Chris covered it with his hand. "Before you get all weepy and engrossed in your family, I have to leave. I have to report back to Philip; that'll take me into the afternoon. Anyway, I put your bag next to the stretcher trolley, so don't forget it."

Still gripping her mobile, Kate flung her arms around his neck and kissed the young man on the cheek. "Oh Chris, I'm so sorry to see you go. We haven't known each other very long, but I feel we're old friends. Do you have my address?"

"Yes, I have it somewhere here."

He opened his book and checked, nodding his head.

"If you're in this neighbourhood at Christmas, you must call and see us. I would love the kids to meet you, and Martin, if he's out of hospital."

"Oh, don't worry, Kate; I shall keep an eye on him

through AMINCO. As for Christmas, we'll see. It may only be a week away, but I have no idea what the company has in store for me after this."

They stood up, gave each other another hug and Chris picked up his bags and made his way back towards the flapping plastic doors. Kate sat down and returned to her mobile. She opened the flap and a big smile crossed her face when she saw she had a signal. She dialled her number and waited.

"Hello," a male voice answered.

"Guess who this is," Kate said with a chuckle.

"Mum…is that you? Where are you?"

"I've just arrived at the hospital. Jennifer knows where it is. I'm still in Emergency, so if you hurry you might still catch me here."

"Is that you, Mum?" Jennifer called out, grabbing the phone.

"Yes, dear…I landed about fifteen minutes ago. I've missed you both so much, so hurry. I can't wait to tell you what's happened."

"Adam's getting the car out. Is Dad all right? Oh, he's here now. See you in ten minutes. Is it the same hospital Dad was in last time?"

"Yes, dear…see you soon."

The hyperactivity that had surrounded Martin when he'd arrived had concluded in a silence that was worse than the flight. A nurse had drawn the curtains around Martin's cubicle, shutting Kate off from the calamity that was Emergency. It was not apparent to her when they first arrived. She was so focused on Martin getting the right attention and listening to everything Chris said to Dr Loxley, in the event he overlooked something, that her surroundings did not register. Now, in the seclusion of three curtained walls and one covered with electrical points, oxygen outlets and Martin's trolley, she could hear every trauma.

Someone was being violently sick, another was arguing about the injection they were being subjected to and there was an annoying beep coming from the next cubicle. It was one of those regular sounds; one that made you aware that it was the rhythm of someone's heart.

A small female hand entered the break in the curtains. Kate jumped, expecting it was the doctor at last, with information on Martin's condition and what was going to happen to him. The hand stayed there for a moment; someone was talking to its owner. And then the curtain opened; it was Jennifer.

"Oh Mum," she said, looking teary. "I thought they weren't going to let me in for a moment. Adam's still trying to park the car."

Martin was just coming round again. His eyes

looked bleary, but he quickly recognised Kate and then Jennifer. "Is that you, Jennifer?" he said, trying to see where he was. "And Kate…are we still on the plane?"

"No, dear, we're in the Broome hospital now. We've just arrived."

He sucked in a deep breath as he continued looking around the small space and listening to the activity outside. "I know that smell," he said. "Where's Mini?"

"Who's Mini, Mum?" Jennifer asked.

"That's the nurse on the cattle station. She looked after him."

Tears ran down Jennifer's face. She brushed them away with her hand and bending over her dad she gave him a big kiss. She looked at Kate. "Oh Mum, it's just like it was last time we were here."

CHAPTER 27

The following morning when Kate, Adam and Jennifer were preparing to leave for the hospital, the phone rang. It was Dr Grossman. He seemed surprised to be talking to Kate again since their last encounter with Martin's accident.

"Good morning Mrs Dexter," he opened. "It's been a long time since I treated Martin after his car crash. Three years, I think."

"Yes, it was, and it's Kate, Doctor."

"Of course it is, Kate," he said, sounding friendlier. "Have I caught you on your way to the hospital? Dr Loxley has contacted me about Martin being in Emergency again. An air crash this time I understand?"

"Yes, Doctor. Over a week ago. He's been treated on a cattle station till yesterday when we flew back to Broome."

"That's why I rang, Kate. I made a cursory examination of his condition and read his notes. It's a bit confusing, so I thought if you were visiting the hospital you might look me up and we can have a chat. Sort out a few details. I'm intrigued why this big American company is showing so much interest."

Kate let out a nervous laugh. "It's a long story, Doctor. What time do you want to see me? I'll be in the hospital by nine-thirty."

"Why don't we say about ten? I'll clear a space for you," he said.

Kate agreed and put the phone down. Jennifer was nosily standing alongside by now, curious to know who was ringing at this time.

"I'll clear a space for you," Kate parodied, with a snooty expression on her face. Then she saw Jennifer. "That was Dr Grossman."

"Is that what he said?" Jennifer asked.

"Yes… He was just an ordinary doctor last time we met. Now I gather he's a consultant, and he wants to see me at ten."

"What are we going to do?"

"I shouldn't think it will be a long session, so you can stay with your dad and keep him company while I see this Dr Grossman," Kate said, with a frown on her face. "How do I address a consultant? I can't keep calling him Doctor."

"What consultant? Adam questioned, as he walked into the lounge.

"Mum's got to see this Dr Grossman...consultant when we go to the hospital this morning. Have you got the car out?" Jennifer asked.

"Yes...it's all warmed up and waiting to go."

Kate stood up, "I'll drive," she said, holding her hand out for the key. "I want to get used to Broome traffic again."

As far as Jennifer and Adam were concerned, Kate had not told them about their father's aberration regarding Joe. It was the same with the car crash. She kept Jennifer out of that part of his treatment; so to her, this Dr Grossman was only treating Martin for his injuries. The last thing she wanted was his children thinking he had some form of mental condition.

The night before, Martin had been moved to a part of the hospital set aside for private patients. Chris had organised this with Dr Loxley. The last thing AMINCO wanted was Martin lingering in an Emergency cubicle for longer than was necessary.

So when the family arrived, they were surprised when the receptionist could not find him. Kate had to mention Dr Loxley and Dr Grossman's name before a spark of recognition crossed her face, and she immediately switched to another screen.

"Ah... Now I know who you're talking about; Mr Dexter, the new American patient who was flown in yesterday."

"My husband's not American," Kate said. "He works for an American company. How did you get that mixed up?"

"I'm sorry, Mrs Dexter. I can only go on what I read on the screen. But now you mention it I can see what's happened. He's been transferred to the private wing under the prefix: American, Mining Corporation. Whoever typed this up mistakenly placed a comma between American and Mining."

"That's fine," Kate said, with a smile... "As long as you've found him."

"All done," the woman said, satisfied. Take the lift on your left, he's on the fourth floor, room 26," she continued, handing Kate a plastic card.

It looked like one of those keycards for hotel doors, only this one had Martin's name on, the AMINCO details and the room number. Other than Martin having a room of his own, which surprised Kate at first, he was still in the same hospital; apparently on the floor above Dr Grossman's suite.

When they entered the room Martin was sitting upright, sinking into a mass of plump pillows behind his back. His eyes were closed and Kate could see a thin plastic tube running from the junction in his arm to a bag of clear liquid hanging from a tripod next to his bed. The first thing she did was examine the bag. She turned it around to read what it said. The bold letters were sufficient to explain they were giving him an intravenous drip of saline solution.

She also noticed he was no longer wearing his cattle station clothes. They had changed him into a pair of lightweight pale-blue pyjamas.

"I bet they even washed him first," Kate said, walking round to the side without the drip. "I mean, look at him. He looks all new and shiny. I bet as soon as they saw cattle station on Chris's notes they decided to decontaminate him."

Jennifer sniggered, "I see what you mean, Mum," she said.

"Do you think Dad's asleep?" Adam asked.

"I can hear every word," Martin said, opening his eyes.

"Oh, you fraud," Kate said, giving him a big kiss. "Here we are tiptoeing around, not wanting to disturb you, and you're awake all the time."

"How are you feeling, Dad?" Adam said.

"Better," he replied, staring at Adam. "Why aren't you at university?"

"It's Christmas break, Dad. And I had to come to Broome as soon as I heard."

"Christmas," Martin said, with a surprised look. "Christmas already?"

Kate could see the large clock on the opposite wall. It was nine-forty-five and she decided she had to go or Dr Grossman might get upset. She leaned over him again and kissed his cheek. "Sweetheart, I have an appointment with the doctor. I shan't be long. Apparently they want all the usual details about your medical history."

"Not again?" he cried.

"I'm afraid so. That's the bureaucracy for you."

As soon as Kate stepped out of the lift she thought she had pressed the wrong button. Directly opposite was a sign indicating this floor was the Psychiatric Unit. It took Kate several seconds for the implication to sink in. She knew Martin had experienced difficulty coming to terms with the trauma of his car crash, but there was no mention of it being a mental problem. This could not be right, she thought, but when she checked the floor level above the lift, she found it was. She glanced back at the sign and saw arrows pointing left and right indicating which way the numbers ran.

According to Dr Grossman's instructions, his office was the first one on the left before the glass doors leading into the main ward. His door was only a few metres further on. It was obviously his; his name stood out in large brass letters.

Kate hesitated for a moment before she entered the

room; she was filled with apprehension. Three years ago Dr Grossman had been just an ordinary doctor. She had the vague idea he had been studying to be a Psychologist, but at the time she'd been more concerned about Martin. She recollected that he was not actually his physician; he was just one of the doctors in a white coat that patrolled the ward and shared a consulting room with a colleague.

She glanced back at his shiny name on the door and entered the room. It was not what she expected. The room was a swish, modern waiting room; casually furnished with an array of easy chairs grouped in nests around coffee tables covered with magazines. Three-seater lounges occupied the walls either side of the window, with elegant prints above. Directly opposite the door sat an attractive brunette behind a long mahogany desk; she looked up at Kate and smiled.

She glanced at her computer screen. "You must be Mrs Dexter," she said.

She caught Kate off guard still concentrating on the room. This was going to be a day of surprises, she thought. "Yes, it is…I have an appointment with Dr… sorry, Mr Grossman."

"He's almost ready for you. Would you like to sit down and I'll let him know you've arrived?" she said, gesturing to the nearest group of chairs.

As Kate sat down she had the gnawing feeling this was about to be the prelude to many visits, either on her own or with Martin. No sooner had she picked up one of the magazines when the door opposite opened. A smart man walked out with an elderly woman. He caught sight of Kate and offered a polite smile. Kate was desperately trying to place him, but too much time had passed.

This man was nothing like the Dr Grossman she knew back then. This man was suave and business-like, dressed in smart trousers, a blue-striped shirt and silk maroon tie. She could see it was silk or satin by the way the light from the windows shimmered across it as he moved. His once half-shaven face, now smooth, had matured and the unruly mop of hair, not unlike Adam's, was a well-groomed, short-cropped style.

The woman finished and turned away towards the door and his attention fell back on Kate. She stood up, dropped the magazine back on the table and followed him into his consulting room. He stood by the door until she was inside and offered her his open hand.

"How nice to see you again, Mrs Dexter. Not under these circumstances, of course. Why don't you sit down over there?" he said, shaking her hand and then gesturing to yet another group of easy chairs.

The room was similarly decorated to the waiting

room except for the large desk across in the opposite corner. Kate sat in one of the easy chairs with her back to the window. It was still a while until noon, but the sun was already streaming through the massive panes of glass, despite the blinds being partially closed.

Grossman sat opposite. He had retrieved a file from his desk first and placed it on the coffee table between them. He relaxed back in the chair, crossed his legs and casually draped one arm across its back. "Mrs Dexter, I asked you to drop in so that I could talk to you about your husband's condition," he started, leaning forward and opening the folder. "To put your mind at rest, Dr Loxley has confirmed that Martin is over his blood infection and subject to his fractured wrist healing, he is physically fit. I would go so far as to say you could take him home."

Kate's face lit up. She was ecstatic about the possibility of having him home for Christmas, but she could see there was a reservation in his eyes.

"There's a 'but' isn't there, Doctor?"

"I'm sorry, there is. May I call you Kate, please? I would like you to call me Felix."

"I thought there might be," she said, her elation turning to a frown. "I recognised the same symptoms when I visited him in the medical clinic on the cattle station. He was delusional. Dr Fitzpatrick was not qualified to say whether it was due to the trauma of the crash or Martin's high temperature. But I knew he was experiencing the same reaction he had to the car crash."

Felix nodded his head as he read the notes. "Yes… this Chris Isles, the paramedic has done an excellent job in documenting Martin's condition even though he was not privy to his previous mental episode."

Kate's eyes opened wide. She knew there was something lingering from the past. "There it is again, that casual reference to a mental episode. Yet…I don't recall anything being mentioned at the time."

"Yes…I'm sorry, Kate. All I can say is I realise I have to do something I should have done the first time. It didn't impact on me back then."

"And what does that mean?" she cried out.

"Calm yourself, Kate, and let me explain. Would you like a drink?"

"No…please Felix, I want to get back to Martin. Just tell me what all this mental episode business is about."

Felix closed the folder and returned to his earlier position in the chair. "All right. My initial mistake was allowing the conventional procedure of the brain to take over the trauma by blocking it out of his memory. I was a junior doctor at the time and I should have referred Martin to a Senior Psychologist before I cleared him to be signed off and returned home. I was only clearing his physical injuries."

"You mean this is a standard practice?"

"I wouldn't quite put it like that. It's not standard, it's natural. When a person is involved in a serious accident or mental trauma, the brain often has an automatic tendency to cancel out the memory of that incident to negate any further anxiety. As I say, it is a natural process. You ask anyone if they can remember the instant of that incident and they will say their memory is a blank. They can remember the period before the incident and the period after, but not the instant itself."

"So why is Martin's incident any different?"

"Because, Kate, he was involved with a death."

Kate went silent for a moment. She remembered the crash site. Martin's crumpled car standing in the middle of the road junction and the wreckage of the other car on the opposite verge. It was so clear to her. The medic on the scene rang her on Martin's mobile. The firemen were struggling to cut him out of the heap of mangled metal, expecting him to die any moment. The other driver was already dead. There was no point in ringing his next-of-kin.

"I remember the other driver died, but I was so terrified Martin would die also, I didn't think of him. And when the police told me at the hospital that it was his fault, I simply wiped him from my mind."

"Just as Martin did. And if I had done the right

thing at the time, I would have attempted to bring that memory back."

"Why? It hasn't done him any harm. It was proved that the other driver jumped a red light. He could well have killed both of them."

"Because the part of Martin's brain that stores all these hidden memories, could well have hidden that fact as well. Has he discussed the other man's death with you since he's recovered? Has he acknowledged his own innocence?"

Kate had to cast her memory back to that time. "No, he hasn't."

"What has he said of the accident?"

"He admits he can't remember whenever it comes up in the conversation. As you said, he recalls driving up to the crossroads and nothing else until he came out of his coma. But why is this so significant now?"

"It's his reaction to the pilot's death that concerns me."

"But he still thinks Joe is alive."

"Exactly... That's what makes both these incidents so significant."

"I don't understand."

"Look, Kate, by all accounts Martin should be able to remember his pilot's death after a few days following the plane crash. In this instance his brain did not wipe the crash out of his memory. Maybe because it needed him to survive the ordeal, I don't know. So why is it messing with his memory now? The pilot died after a long struggle with his injuries. Martin knows he was badly injured; he told the doctor on the cattle station—"

"Sorry," Kate interrupted. "Martin told the Aborigine boy who rescued him and took him to the cattle station. The Aboriginal boy was the one who told the doctor."

"Oh…so we have a conflict of information. That's significant, Kate. When the Aborigine suddenly entered Martin's disoriented state, he may well have transferred the pilot's existence to the Aborigine. That's why he still thinks he's alive."

"It sounds very implausible to me," Kate said. "He knows the Aborigine in his own right. He knows his name…Willy, and calls him by that name."

"The memory can be a very convoluted thing at times, Kate; I don't have any explicit knowledge of why it does that. That's why I have to make sure Martin knows his pilot is dead. And while I'm doing that, also make sure his subconscious doesn't hold any alternative outcomes to his crash three years ago."

"How are you going to do that?"

"There is only one thing I can do; try hypnosis. I have to take him back through both accidents to make him understand what actually happened; not what his subconscious has fabricated."

413

"Will that be dangerous?" Kate asked, becoming anxious.

"What's the alternative, Kate? Do you want him to keep asking where Joe is? If you're lucky he might just forget him, like the other driver, but sooner or later it will crop up again. I guarantee that."

Kate knew the decision was not hers to make and to discuss the problem with Martin might well make the situation worse. "How do you propose treating Martin with this hypnosis? And how long is it going to take?"

"I would like Martin in a relaxed state, preferably after a week or so of home surroundings. I'd like him to think he's coming in for a final check-up, in accordance with AMINCO's insurance clearance."

"Won't they have something to say about that?"

"They already have. The paramedic, Chris Isles, was a little too detailed in his report. As you may know, they are paying for Martin's treatment and want to make sure he will be free of any side issues when I sign his clearance papers. In the meantime they drew my attention to Martin's previous accident and the possibility that it may have a connection with the disorientation in Isles' notes."

"I knew he was making notes with Dr Fitzpatrick, but I never realised they were so detailed. It never dawned on me that the insurance people would be so thorough. Is this a problem?"

"They must have consulted their own psychiatrist, because reading this young man's notes I can't see any obvious connection. As for being a problem; I don't think so. They're only covering themselves against any future litigation. So, I have their permission to delve more closely into Martin's mental state."

A glimmer of recognition crossed Kate's face. "And you want my permission? That's what all this is about…isn't it?"

"I'm afraid so, Kate. I was trying to be as subtle as possible, just as I have to be with Martin. And that means you and your family. He must not know the true purpose of my examination."

"Very well, I agree. Where do we go from here?"

"As I said, I want him relaxed and ready for his treatment. I suggest you take him home when I release him tomorrow; I need to run a few tests and I shall explain that AMINCO want a thorough, top-to-bottom medical. Then you can bring him back into hospital for a few days, it shouldn't take any longer; sometime after Christmas should be fine. Is that all right?"

Kate's expression must have said it all. She was going to have Martin back home again for Christmas, doing what he liked best. He loved watching Adam and Jennifer opening their presents in the morning, carving the turkey and strolling along Cable Beach after lunch. It was going to be a happy time. It had to be; once the therapy began he might never be the same again.

CHAPTER 28

It was two days before Christmas and to everyone's surprise, despite his arm still being in a sling, Martin was back to his old self. Kate had set boundaries for Adam and Jennifer before they brought him home. There was to be no mention of anything to do with the crash, AMINCO or his return to the hospital.

It had been a rush, but they managed to dress the tree, buy a nice plump bird and wrap all the presents. Then a frown crossed Kate's face. "I wonder what your father's going to say when he realises he hasn't got any presents for us."

Adam checked the time. "You could dash out now. I'll tell him you forgot something. We'll keep him occupied."

Kate thought for a moment. "No, Adam...it's a lovely idea, but it's just going to be another lie. I think

417

we have to draw a line. I think he'll understand he couldn't be expected to remember Christmas presents under the circumstances."

"I suppose you're right," Adam said. "We'll get round it."

Kate suddenly looked surprised. "That reminds me...I forgot all about his birthday present, Jennifer."

"What birthday present?" Adam questioned.

As Kate rushed upstairs, hoping she wouldn't disturb Martin in the bath, Jennifer enlightened Adam. "It was Dad's birthday when he was missing."

"Good grief; will it never end?" Adam said. "I completely forgot."

"Join the club."

Kate crept back down the stairs with Martin's present and dropped it amongst the others under the tree. "I'll give it to him when he comes down."

"What's with the drummer boys?" Adam asked, squatting down by the tree.

"Never mind," Kate said, leaving the room again. "It's a long story."

Martin had been some time in the bath and she began to worry. She knocked on the door. "Are you all right in there? Do you want any help?"

"Who's that," he called back.

"It's me...Kate."

"Come in, for heaven's sake."

Kate opened the door and slipped inside. "Sorry," she said.

"What are you doing knocking on the door?"

She laughed, "I don't know...I suppose it's because the kids are here."

"It never bothered you before."

She noticed he had removed his sling and was able to use both hands getting out of the bath, but that was the extent of his movement. He was unable to manipulate the towel and passed it to her.

"Dry me down, will you? I'll be glad when I can use the shower again."

"Well, you don't want to get that plaster wet."

Martin glanced over his shoulder as Kate rubbed his back. "Oh, I'm glad it's you and not that gargantuan Balinese maid or whatever they call them. I used to ache after she mauled me."

"Did she wash you?"

"Either her or the Taiwanese woman...I preferred her. She was only small and she was so gentle; I thought she was one of those women in the bathhouse."

"What bathhouse...when did you go to one of those places?"

"I was only using it as an example."

As Kate continued drying Martin, her curiosity got the better of her.

"How did they wash you? In the hospital I mean."

Martin avoided the question for the moment, trying to think of a simple answer. "Why the third degree; it was just the usual bed bath."

"Then you wouldn't mind telling me how they performed this bed bath."

Martin knew this would crop up sooner or later and hesitated before he finally answered her. "I don't know what all the fuss is about; it was over and done with before I got a chance to object...they had it down to a fine art."

"You mean there were two of them?"

"Yes...they changed over each day. While one removed my pyjamas, the other took out a large damp towel from a steam cabinet on a trolley. They then stretched it out across my body and that was when one of them massaged me. Then they turned me over and did my back and legs. Finally they changed to a dry towel and you know the rest."

"And this happened every day? It's a wonder you wanted to leave."

"Of course I did...it was embarrassing."

"I bet it was," Kate exclaimed, laughing her head off.

With that out of her system Kate looked back at Martin trying to cover his nakedness with the towel. It was a side of him she hadn't seen since the early days of their marriage. Since then he'd thought nothing of his nudity. She could kick herself for embarrassing him; he looked so vulnerable.

Kate kneeled down beside him and placed her arm around his shoulders. "I'm sorry, sweetheart," she said, kissing his cheek. "Come on…let's get you dressed. Adam and Jennifer are waiting for you downstairs."

A broad smile crossed Martin's face as he raised his good hand out of the towel and rubbed the stubble on his chin. "What about this?" he commented.

"Can you use the electric razor with your left hand?"

"I think so," he replied.

"Then why don't you try after you get dressed?"

After helping Martin Kate left him to get shaved and returned to the lounge. Jennifer was finishing off the decorations and Adam was watching the news on television. He turned round in his chair as Kate walked into the room and stood looking at the tree. Jennifer switched the lights on.

"Everything okay upstairs?" Adam asked.

"Yes…your dad's just shaving; he'll be down soon. I just want everything to look like Christmas for him."

Before anyone else had a chance to say anything the doorbell rang.

"Who could that be?" Jennifer said, standing up.

"I'll go," Kate said. "It's probably another neighbour asking after Martin."

421

As Kate opened the door her first impression was that the young man in a leather jacket and jeans was a stranger, but on closer inspection she recognised the clean-shaven face of her cattle station companion.

"Chris, I didn't recognise you at first without your uniform. What a lovely surprise. Come in and meet the family."

He hesitated in the doorway. "It can only be a short visit, I'm afraid; I'm on my way to the airport."

"Oh, what a shame…never mind, you can have a longer visit later," she said, and then taking hold of his elbow she hesitated. "Before you see Martin, I must warn you not to mention anything about Joe or Martin's mental state."

"I understand. I made a follow-up call to Mr Grossman, just to finalise my report before I presented it to the American insurance company; so I'm aware of the situation."

Jennifer walked out of the lounge. "Who was that at the—" she said, looking surprised at seeing Chris in the hall.

"This is Chris, Jennifer. You remember me telling you about the young man who accompanied me to the cattle station?"

"Yes…hello Chris. Thank you for looking after my dad," she said, shaking his outstretched hand and holding on to it a little longer than she should have.

"Come on now," Kate said, breaking them up. "Come into the lounge and you can meet my son Adam."

Adam must have heard her; he was already out of his chair and walking towards the door. "It's all right, Mum. I heard," he said, when they walked through the door. He lunged for Chris's hand and shook it vigorously. "I've been waiting to thank you, Chris. Mum told us how you smoothed the way for my dad."

"It's all right," he said, a little flustered at all the attention.

"Sit down, Chris," Kate said. "Would you like a Christmas drink?"

"Just a white wine, if you have it. I've got to drive to the airport soon and I don't want to get caught. Did you know the police have got a blitz on over Christmas; booze-buses are on all the major routes out of Broome."

"Get Chris a drink, Jennifer, please; that's a dear," Kate asked her. "So where are you flying to Chris?"

As Jennifer returned with his drink, he nodded his head. "AMINCO have given me a month off, so I've decided to fly over to Sydney and spend the time with my mother. I've neglected her a bit lately. Anyway, since it might be some time before I see you again, I thought I'd call in and wish you all a Merry Christmas on my way to the airport. Is Martin about?"

423

"Yes...he'll be down in a minute. He'll be so pleased to see you."

It was not a long wait. Martin made a grand entry, scuffing through the door with a large plastic bag. Kate was already standing and she rushed over to help him. She took hold of the curious bag, dropped it just inside the doorway by the tree and pointed out that he had a guest.

"Look who's popped in to see you on his way to the airport."

Martin stared at Chris for a few moments just as Kate had, until his face fitted that of the young man in the uniform at the medical clinic.

"It's Chris...isn't it? You were at the cattle station," he said, as it all began to filter through. "Yes...and again at the hospital here."

"That's right, Martin," Chris replied. "You look a lot better now."

Martin walked over to the couch and sat down opposite. "I feel a lot better since I've come home; I hate hospitals," he said, still trying to place why he knew him. "Why were you there again?"

Chris glanced in Kate's direction, and then returned his gaze to Martin. "I thought you knew. I'm a paramedic and AMINCO sent me to bring you home."

There was a look of comprehension in Martin's

eyes. "Oh yes! AMINCO, good old AMINCO; you can rely on them to look after you."

The conversation painfully came to an abrupt end and everyone for some reason looked uncomfortable, except Jennifer. She seemed to be taken by this new young man who had entered her life. Kate was not sure about the atmosphere she was creating. He was a few years older than her and she still had to finish her term with university. Maybe it was a good thing he was going away.

"What has AMINCO got in store for you when you return?" Kate asked.

"Indonesia, I understand. It was only a hint. I'll find out when I get back after the Christmas holidays. I'll pop in and let you know if I'm off again."

Kate looked pleased. "Well, it's all more experience, Chris."

Chris was true to his word. After answering a few of Kate's questions about his mother and finishing his drink, he left for the airport. Kate went into the kitchen to make Martin a cup of tea to go with the mince tarts and Jennifer followed her.

"What was that all about?" she said.

"What was what all about, dear?"

"All that pussy-footing about on eggshells with Chris; you could have cut the atmosphere with a knife."

"I'm sorry if it seemed that way, but Chris did not want to get into the accident. You remember our little talk after I saw Mr Grossman…Adam obviously does. You don't hear him questioning our conversation."

"Sorry…I forgot. It's all right for Adam – he's almost a doctor; these things come naturally to him."

"Let's just think about Christmas, shall we, dear? Your dad's still got all that to go through again when he goes back to hospital."

"That reminds me," Jennifer said, as Kate picked up the tea and mince tarts. "What was in the big bag Dad brought in when Chris arrived?"

Kate stopped in the doorway and looked at Jennifer. "Yes…I forgot all about that. Let's find out. I bet your dad has forgotten as well."

Kate walked into the lounge, handed Martin his tea and placed the dish of mince tarts on the coffee table in front of him; then she stood looking down at him with her clenched fists on her hips. "By the way, Martin Dexter, what was in that large plastic bag you brought in when Chris arrived?"

Martin looked up at her with a vague expression on his face. "Oh yes," he said, placing his cup on the coffee table and getting up from the couch. He walked over to where Kate had dropped it, pulled it open and took out three presents.

Kate and the other two were amazed as they

walked over to the tree and watched Martin place his presents amongst the others.

Kate was curious. "And when did you find time to buy those?"

With a satisfied expression on his face Martin told her he'd decided to buy them a month ago. It was just as well. The next week he had been told about the emergency at Site 21. As he positioned his presents in a prominent spot, moving others about to make room for his, he noticed the one with the little drummer boys.

"What's this?" he asked, picking it up.

He looked around at their beaming expressions. "It's your birthday present, dear," Kate answered. "It's been under the tree for a while."

Martin placed it back under the tree. "Well, it can stay there until Christmas day. My birthday is long gone, so it can be another Christmas present."

CHAPTER 29

It was the week after Christmas when Jennifer decided to take down the ornaments from the tree and Kate was sitting watching her as she sipped a small cherry brandy. It was one of the presents Adam bought her every Christmas; a thick warming liqueur that brought pleasure to the palate. But Kate was happy for another reason. Whether it was because Adam and Jennifer were making a particular effort to please their dad before they returned to their respective universities or that Martin was gradually settling into his old routine, Kate didn't know. But she could see that spark of happiness in him that she had missed over the past few weeks.

"Mum...what's going to happen to Dad when you go back to work on Monday?" Jennifer asked, turning away from the tree.

Kate stopped sipping her drink and looked in her

direction. "It's not what happens on Monday, dear, that bothers me, it's what will happen when your father finishes his treatment."

"I had forgotten about that. Is he going to stay over in the hospital?"

"Yes, dear. Mr Grossman says if things go well it should only take a couple of weeks. Then we might have your old dad back."

Jennifer stopped what she was doing and came round to where Kate was and sat down beside her. She was like a little girl again. Whenever she hurt herself or Adam was nasty to her, she would cuddle up next to Kate, who would put her arm around her and stroke her hair.

"Oh Mum, I hope we get Dad back soon. I'm sick of seeing him sitting on the balcony looking out to sea. What does he see out there?"

"It doesn't matter, dear; as long as it makes him happy and he's not thinking about his friend Joe or the crash."

On the morning Kate delivered Martin to Mr Grossman's Psychiatry Unit, she knew she was going to struggle through the rest of the day. Her first chore was to report to her superior. That would be followed by a grilling from her colleagues. They all meant well, but to go over the same ground time and again was more than she could tolerate. Then, as she sat at her desk, she thought of Martin and what he must be going through.

Despite Martin's aversion to hospital life, he settled back into the same room as if he was a permanent fixture. Familiarity seemed to be the key. He actually looked forward to the Balinese and Taiwanese maids' attentiveness; if not his daily bed-bath embarrassment.

For some strange reason, Martin was not nervous when Mr Grossman outlined the hypnosis procedure. The first day was going to be a simple trial to ascertain Martin's susceptibility to suggestion; because without that link, the treatment would be futile.

The sessions would be conducted in his consulting room, in an environment that did not smell of a hospital treatment room. He soon found Martin to be a good subject. He was relaxed; all his signs were as they should be and switching on the recording apparatus, Felix began. He decided to explore the possibilities of a fear fixation. He needed to know if Martin had a hidden trigger response.

"All right, Martin, I'm going to ask you a few simple questions to get you started; nod if you understand." Martin nodded. "Now…going through the notes I put together about interviews with different people, one thing Kate mentioned, I found very interesting.

431

She said you were particularly nervous the morning you were to fly... Why?"

Martin did not respond straightaway. He seemed hesitant. Either because he did not understand the question or he did not want to answer it. Then suddenly he spoke. "I had a bad feeling that morning."

"What sort of bad feeling?"

"Like a premonition. I knew something was going to happen. As soon as I knew I was going to be flying in a light plane, I had a bad feeling."

"Yet I'm told you do a lot of flying. Why this particular plane?"

"I fly in jets. They only have small windows."

"Is that important?"

"Small planes have windows all round. They're just like the Tiger Moth."

"I'm sorry, Martin. What is a Tiger Moth?"

"It's the plane I trained in, when I was in the RAF."

Martin's hypnosis session had taken a turn Felix had not expected. He was simply searching for possible vulnerabilities, and if he found any, he would explore that anomaly first. He never expected to unearth a whole new scenario.

"You say you were in the RAF; why don't you tell me about it? Not everything, of course; just the part about the Tiger Moth."

Felix could see Martin's heart rate was climbing, but it was within a tolerable level. He decided to keep a close eye on the graph.

Martin did not start straightaway. The twitches in his hands down by his side and his REM eye movements seemed to indicate that he'd hesitated before entering that world again.

"I had to pass my take-off and landing procedures in the Tiger Moth before I was ready for my solo flight later that day. It was important to me if I was going to be able to progress on to my jet trainer lessons; so naturally I was a little nervous.

"I was on my third flight when a new instructor climbed into the plane; Lieutenant Parker had taken ill. I didn't like this man straightaway. He was full of hell because he had to cancel a previous appointment. The first thing he said was: 'Come on sprog, let's get this thing over'. Usually I take off myself, but he wanted to show me how it was really done before he passed the control over to me.

"We did a few circuits and he said I'd do and told me to land the next time round. As I approached the runway we were suddenly hit with a strong wind that sucked the lift out of the plane. That's when he should have taken over. I had no experience in turbulent weather; especially sudden gusts. When I told him, he just laughed and said, 'This is what it's all about'. If

I couldn't handle the plane in all weather conditions
I shouldn't be flying.

"I was shaking like a leaf. The plane was all over the
place, but I finally managed to get it under control. I
positioned her in line with the runway; all was fine,
until, just as I was descending, we were hit with an
almighty gust that lifted the plane one minute and
dropped it the next. That's when he snatched the
stick. I could feel him taking over and I let go. It was
too late. There was another gust and he clipped the
trees at the end of the runway and flipped her over."

"What was the outcome?" Felix questioned.

"It was disastrous. After months in hospital, he was
left with an injured spine and I suffered a punctured
lung. Neither of us flew again. He was left in a wheel-
chair and I was written off as unfit to fly. He tried
to blame me, but my RAF defence proved he should
have taken control of the plane as soon as there had
been any sign of unnatural weather conditions."

Felix noticed Martin's levels were climbing fast.
He was sobbing by now and Felix told him to calm
himself and slowly brought him round. Everything
returned to normal except the wetness on his cheeks.

"What's this?" Martin said, wiping his face with
the back of his hand. "Have I been crying? Why was
I crying?"

Kate's first day back was becoming a bore. The reorganised system to accommodate her absence meant nothing was coming across her desk, and it would take time for the routine to re-adjust. She rang Professor Sinclair, her superior, and asked if she could take the afternoon off to settle things with Martin's employer.

He understood, even suggesting that Kate should take time off until Martin was cleared from the hospital. She said this afternoon should be enough. Her assistant could handle things until tomorrow.

Kate had spent a good part of the morning looking into the possibility of Willy joining the residential school, the curriculum scheduled and when an opening would be available. Her position on the Educational Council carried enough weight to guarantee an immediate space for Willy. All she had to do now was see if Philip could arrange for her to use AMINCO's radio.

After the conversation Kate had with Philip to arrange a meeting she was full of confidence when she arrived at the AMINCO headquarters. Philip must have seen her drive into the car park. He was waiting with his door open and immediately left his desk to greet her.

"It's good to see you, Kate," he said, taking hold of her shoulders and kissing her on the cheek. Kate smiled back at him, glad he was in a receptive mood.

He sat her down in one of the easy chairs in the corner of the room by the window, and returning to his desk, he picked up the phone.

"Elsie, Kate's arrived. Can we have that pot of tea now, please?"

"You shouldn't go to so much bother," Kate said.

He shook his head and asked how Martin was doing.

Kate placed her handbag by the side of her seat and replied as he joined her, "He did very well over Christmas. He's back at the hospital starting a new round of treatment," she said, with a slight snigger. "Of course you'll know all about that."

Philip tried to smile. "I'm sorry about the intrusion. Unfortunately Martin is still under the scrutiny of our insurance company in America; you can imagine what they're like. You can stop them if you wish, but you'll lose any future benefits."

"It's all right, Philip. You forget I work for the government. They're just as pedantic; maybe even worse."

The sensitive subject was put on hold as Elsie walked in with the tray. It was unusual to see a tea pot, milk jug and sugar basin. Alongside the mugs there was also a plate of assorted biscuits for good measure.

"Hello Kate," she said, placing the tray on the coffee table. "How's Martin?"

"Thank you, Elsie…he's coming along fine."

A phone rang in Elsie's office and she dashed off, leaving Philip to pour the tea. As she sweetened her mug, Philip continued their discussion.

"I think this last lot of treatment will settle matters, and then we can get back to discussing Martin's future," he said, testing his tea.

"His future?" Kate questioned, puzzled by his early remark.

"I'm sorry again, Kate. That's Larry Kingston's phrase. He's always way ahead of everyone else; it's hard to keep up with him at times," he said, sipping his drink again, expecting a response from Kate. "He has this idea that after Martin's ordeal he won't want to continue with field work. So he's come up with this idea of forming an engineering school here to train budding young engineers."

"And what has that got to do with Martin?"

"Sorry. I thought you got my drift. He wants Martin to run it."

Kate was amazed. She had no idea why Philip would raise such a question at this stage; unless he was testing the waters, thinking Martin might have confided his future thoughts to his wife.

"I must admit, Philip, I'm surprised. Martin is finding it difficult enough coping with his current problem to be considering his future."

"Of course," he replied. So…you said you wanted to ask me something."

"Yes…I did," she answered. "I was wondering if it would be possible to use your radio on occasions."

A puzzled expression crossed Philip's face before he answered. "That's a strange request. Have you a particular reason?"

"Oh yes…do you remember the Aboriginal boy who saved Martin's life by taking him to the cattle station?"

"Vaguely…his name was Willy, by all accounts."

"That's right. Well, during their time together in the Sandy Desert, Martin found out Willy wanted to improve himself. He was not happy with just living in the camp or the traditional life; he wanted more out of life. Anyway, after Martin told me, I decided to have a word with Willy's teacher. She agreed; she said he was an extremely bright young boy and deserved a better education."

"I see…and the reason for the radio?"

"It's the only way I can communicate with her; to tell her if I can arrange to get Willy into a residential school here in Broome and when that can be arranged."

"And has this Aboriginal boy said what he wants to do?"

Kate laughed. "Believe it or not, he wants to be an

engineer like Martin. I think that decision was based on his first contact with the outside world."

"He could be a candidate for Kingston's new school."

"Then you will help me sort this out?"

"Of course, Kate. Anything I can do to help the boy who saved Martin."

Kate looked so pleased. "Thank you, Philip," she said, taking out the piece of paper with the call sign information on it.

"Hold your horses," he said. "I don't know one end of a radio from another. You need to talk to our man in charge of radio communications, Josh Mackenzie. So pick up your piece of paper and we'll go and scare the pants off him."

"I beg your pardon."

"It's only a joke. Josh is one of those technicians who prefers being on his own, muffled up in his headset, listening to the ether. So he's a little shy of strangers...especially women. Come on," Philip said, helping Kate out of her seat.

He led her along the corridor, just as Martin had that fateful morning, past the lounge she'd met Joe in and on to the Operations Room. This was an area she'd only heard about. Despite its size it was claustrophobic, lit only by an array of computer screens around the walls. The occupants were not aware of her presence and Philip did not disturb them. Instead he continued on to the end of the room known as Josh Mackenzie's domain. The sign on the door, 'The Radio Shack', said everything. Philip pushed the door open and they entered.

It was not a huge space from what she could see of it. Each side of the room was divided into small cubicles, much like the listening booths in a record shop, and, as in the other room, its occupants appeared too busy to notice, except a tall burly man who stood up and walked towards them. It was difficult to see him clearly, until he stood near a white light over a small cabinet that looked like a fridge.

Working attire apparently was not important – sweat shirt and jeans seemed the order of the day – but her attention was drawn to his long ginger hair and beard.

He removed his headphones and let them fall around his neck as his blue penetrating eyes scanned the woman Philip dared to bring into his enclave, and the gap in his beard twisted in one corner as he greeted her in a coarse Scottish accent.

"It's my pleasure to meet you, Mrs Dexter. I was so sorry to hear about Martin; he's a good bloke. We always got on," he said, glancing at Philip.

"Thank you, Josh…I can call you Josh, can I? I'm Kate," she said.

"Why yes, Kate. I'd deem it a privilege."

Philip stepped into the conversation. "Josh, Kate wants to make contact on occasions with a cattle station in the desert. Can you arrange that?"

"Indeed I can," he said. "You come over here, my dear, and we'll see what we can do." He pulled out a spare chair next to the first cubicle for her to sit on.

"Is it all right if I pop next door for a moment, Kate?" Philip asked.

"That's fine, Philip. I'll be all right here with Josh."

Philip left and Josh sat down in front of his equipment. He turned to her with an open palm. "I gather you have their call sign and frequency lassie...oh, sorry, Kate, I forget myself at times."

"That's okay, Josh; we're all guilty of falling back into our native ways," she said, retrieving the piece of paper again and passing it to him.

"Aye...that's what I want," he drawled.

As he checked her information with a book of codes, Kate took the opportunity to familiarise herself with Josh's environment. It was fascinating. On the wall above his bench there was a map of Australia decorated with large pins with numbers on them. They meant little to her, except they all seemed to be in an area with little else around it, until her focus was drawn to a pin in the Sandy Desert between Broome and Port Hedland.

Josh noticed her fixed stare. "Is everything all right, Kate?"

"What… Oh yes, sorry. I was interested in your numbered pins. Is that one Site 21…where Martin was heading for?"

"Yes, Kate, that's the mine he was to inspect."

"Where did the plane crash?"

"Ah now, you don't want to be bothering yourself with that now."

"I need to put it in perspective, Josh, please."

"Ah well," he said, picking up a pencil and pointing to a spot north-west of the site pin. "It's about here, Kate."

"And where is the cattle station?"

He shook his head and begrudgingly traced the pencil tip south-west to just below the Oakover River. "I'm not sure exactly. It's somewhere in this region."

Kate seemed satisfied with that. The actual crash site where Martin nearly died was one of those missing pieces of the puzzle that dominated her sleepless nights. Now she knew where it was, she could rest.

"Right, Josh, thank you…you can continue now."

As he started to type the information into his computer Josh rambled on about the difference between the old ways ham radio was used when you had to twiddle with knobs on your set to find the frequency you wanted.

After a few high-pitched squeaks and buzzes she began to hear an excited voice acknowledging the call sign he'd dialled in. Kate was surprised when Josh's

Scottish drawl suddenly changed to perfect English. There were no dropped vowels or slurred consonants, just good old plain English.

He quickly established contact with the person on Galene cattle station, and after identifying the caller as Kate Dexter in the Broome AMINCO headquarters, he turned in his seat to an eagerly waiting Kate.

Kate's expression was astonished to say the least.

"My radio voice," he said in explanation. "Speak plainly and make sure you say 'over' each time you finish." Josh swivelled his chair to the side so that Kate could move closer when he pushed the microphone stand in her direction.

Kate looked nervous, took hold of the microphone and asked her question.

"This is Kate Dexter...who am I speaking to?" There was a pause and Josh nudged her, "Oh, sorry... Over."

"It's Marge, Kate...so you managed to get a radio? Over."

"Yes...I'm calling from the AMINCO headquarters. Over."

Josh smiled with a thumbs-up sign and she continued.

"I gather this is just a test, Kate? Over."

"That's right Marge. Over."

"Did everything go all right with Martin on the plane? Over."

Kate glanced at Josh to see if she was taking too long; he nodded with a smile.

"The whole journey went by without a hitch, Marge. Over."

"That's good, Kate. I must sign off now. In future the operator will tell you how to book your calls. Over."

"I got that...he's giving me the okay sign. Nice hearing you, Marge. Over."

"Thanks for calling, Kate...goodbye. Over."

The speaker hummed again with static and Kate looked satisfied.

"That was great," Josh said, reverting to his drawl. "Now if you don't mind I've got some calls waiting. I won't be able to go through the call booking procedure now, but I'll catch up with you next time you come in."

"That's okay, Josh," Kate said. "This was just a trial to see if it would be all right to use your radio."

"No problem, lassie...sorry, Kate. You just ring when you're ready and we'll arrange a time to go through the procedure."

"I understand, Josh."

As Philip walked back into the room, Josh started flicking switches before he returned to the computer. "Oh, by the way," he called out before she left. "It would save a lot of time and embarrassment if you had a script in front of you the next time. And don't forget to include the 'over' each time."

"I won't, Josh…and thank you again."

Philip led Kate back through the operations room, this time introducing her to Bryce and Max. Their sympathetic conversation was much the same as what she had been forced to endure for most of the day; although with these two men and the many pilots and ground staff who helped in the search for Martin, she had a special sense of indebtedness that she could never express.

CHAPTER 30

The first week of Martin's treatment had come to an end and Felix was bringing his notes up to date before his meeting with his partner, Richard Ogden. It was a practice they set up with the formation of the Psychiatric Unit: each one checking the other's notes prior to their weekly overview. That way they would catch any nuances the other missed. Or see different approaches.

When Martin drifted into new territory with his description of his first air crash in the RAF, it threw Felix's line of enquiry into the death of Joe Cirano, but he soon steered Martin's hypnosis back on course. By the end of the week Martin had reached the day just before the Aborigine found him. Joe's death must have occurred that evening or early the following day. According to Willy's statement when he arrived at the cattle station, Joe was already dead when he'd come across the plane.

Felix read his transcript of the last tape and realised he had found no reason for Martin's obsession about Joe still being alive. The trauma of the RAF crash only supported the fact that he had a fear of small planes, but had no connection with Joe; unless Martin was linking Joe's injuries in the air crash to the first pilot.

There was a tap on his door and Richard walked in. If Kate had been in the room she would have had difficulty telling them apart. They belonged to the same fraternity as the misunderstood technicians that designed most of the high-status equipment in the room. They thought alike, looked alike and were absorbed in what they did. Likewise, Richard and Felix were absorbed in their work and part of an elite group. The only major difference between them, apart from their choice of ties was Richard wore heavy-rimmed glasses.

"I gather you have a problem, Felix," Richard said, on entering the room and sitting down in the seat in front of the desk.

Felix winced. "There are too many options, really. Did you get a chance to go through my material?"

"I did. I found it very interesting, and you're right; his first encounter in the RAF bears little connection to your initial prognosis, other than the similarity with an air crash," he said, with a snort. "I would say there is more of a link with the car crash three years ago. Both outcomes resulted in a death."

"Yes, I agree. I deliberately avoided that scenario then because he had a complete loss of memory of the incident."

"Yes, but don't you see, that fact in itself points to a possible trigger."

Felix pondered on Richard's suggestion with a raised eyebrow until he too saw the possibility of a hidden connection. "You don't think his subconscious feels guilty about the earlier death in some way, and is deliberately reversing the situation with Joe to absolve himself. It's a bit of a long-term reaction."

"Felix, I recently had an old man who was still blaming himself for his mate's death in the Second World War. And in his day-to-day life he had no memory of that incident. Yet seventy years later he's suffering terrible depression."

"And you discovered this in hypnosis?"

"Yes…just like you did with this man's RAF experience."

"But you discarded that scenario."

"No, I said I couldn't see a connection. That doesn't mean there isn't one."

"Meaning it wouldn't necessarily have shown itself."

"Exactly."

Felix sat for a second studying the top page of his notes. "So do you have any suggestions on how I approach my next session?"

"I have given it some thought, Felix, but you're not going to like what I have come up with. This is where you and I may part company on treatments."

"You mean I'm not radical enough."

"You could put it like that. I see it as a matter of choices. You can leave him thinking Joe is still alive and hope he doesn't become paranoid about it. Or you can force his subconscious to realise Joe died in that plane. Of course, you might run the risk of unravelling whatever it was that triggered his brain to bury the car crash. And in turn, why all these three incidents are linked together?"

"You actually believe that, do you?"

"They have to be, Felix. If you eliminate the detail, all three incidents bear a relationship with each other: the similarities in the Tiger Moth experience, the Cessna crash and the car accident, where someone died in each case but where Martin survived. Don't you see it? Martin feels guilty for being alive."

"Surely it's not as simple as convincing him he's not to blame?"

"Look Felix… You know as well as I do, it's all immaterial when it comes to hypnosis: you set the ball rolling and see where it goes, as you found out with the RAF story. It wasn't planned; it just materialised. So lighten up. Don't direct the action, simply spread a few breadcrumbs and see if you get any nibbles."

"And what sort of breadcrumbs would you scatter?"

"Oh, most definitely toast. If you want to get to the bottom of this, throw a spanner in the works; tell him he was responsible for Joe's death, just like the other man in the car accident. And for good measure, suggest he should have landed that Tiger Moth and not wait for his instructor to take over."

"And tip him right over the edge?"

"I think this character of yours is made of sterner stuff. He may have to think about your accusation, but I think he'll deny every word."

"You tricky bastard. You want him to decide for himself."

"Felix," Richard started, as he stood up, "the quickest way to get someone to deny anything is to accuse them of doing it."

The following Monday, after allowing Martin to recuperate and enjoy his family, Felix started the second round of sessions. He also used the weekend to rehearse his radical plan to shock Martin into a clearer perspective on what had taken place in the small Cessna before the Aboriginal boy found him.

Martin was in good spirits. He said he was looking forward to his next session; even though he had no idea what had taken place on previous ones. Felix felt he was the one who was nervous and omitted his usual overview of what was about to take place, and put Martin under as soon as the equipment was set up.

"That's the way, Martin. You're in a deep sleep now, relaxing in the plane where we left off last time. You said you were preparing that evening's food ration; what happened next?"

"I was breaking up the Hard-Tack biscuits. I placed both our shares on the centre consul and asked Joe what he wanted on his – peanut butter or jam."

"Of course, Joe had no idea how much you were having. He just took what you gave him. Like the water; how many drinks did you have compared to him? Was it two for you and one for him?" Felix interrupted.

Martin's heart rate climbed and he started shaking his head.

"No... That's not right. I shared everything out equally."

"What was the point? Joe was dying; you said so yourself. So there was no point in wasting food on a dying man. If he died today instead of tomorrow, that would mean an extra day of food for you."

"Look… Joe was badly injured, but he didn't die."

"So when the Aborigine came you just left Joe in the plane."

"No… He was in the clinic with me."

"No, he wasn't, Martin. Willy said he only took you across the desert. You left Joe to die in that plane all alone. The helicopter came a day later and found him."

"That's not true," Martin said, with tears running down his face.

"It is, Martin. You starved Joe to death. You killed him, just like you did the man in that car crash three years earlier."

"What are you talking about? I had the green light. He didn't stop."

"How do you know? You can't remember what happened."

"The coroner said the camera on the junction showed him running the red light. And he had an alcohol level twice normal."

"I think your memory is playing tricks on you, Martin. With every accident you have managed to twist the facts to suit yourself. You should have landed that plane in the RAF; instead you waited until the last minute when it was too late and the instructor had to take over, crippling himself. Then you switched things around in your mind when you hit that car and killed the other driver. And now you're trying to cover up Joe's death by pretending he's still alive."

"Stop it… Stop it. I didn't kill Joe. When I woke up the next morning he was dead. Do you understand? I tried to get him to eat something, but he was dead," Martin screamed, his life signs almost going through the roof. He suddenly went quiet. Felix had to check his instruments.

Then Martin came out of the hypnosis without any assistance and said, "I couldn't get him to eat anything…he was dead. Did you hear that? It was Willy that found me, wasn't it? Otherwise the helicopter would have found two dead bodies."

"I know, Martin," Felix said, with a broad smile on his face. "I'm sorry I had to put you through that. I'm still not sure what it was your subconscious was trying to hide from you, but you were not responsible for anything."

Martin stopped crying, wiped the tears from his face with a tissue Felix passed to him and even managed a smile. "Oh God, the relief is hard to handle. I don't know what I feel but I feel terrible. Are you sure I wasn't to blame for the car accident?"

"I'm sure, Martin. The Coroner was given irrefutable evidence at the inquest, proving the other driver went through a red light."

"Yes…I remember now. I was in the middle of the

junction when I saw the car a split second before he hit me. The next thing I was being cut out of my car by a man in a yellow coat. I remember the coat. It was bright and shiny and made a squeaking noise when he moved. Then he covered my head in a plastic sheet; it was to stop the sparks from burning my face."

"That's good," Felix said, detaching the wires. "Now you won't have that black hole in your memory any more. Oh, and your RAF accident happened just as you said it did. I took the liberty of checking your record. You didn't tell me they asked you to remain in the RAF as an officer."

"No...I wasn't interested in the RAF as a career unless it was as a pilot."

"And as far as Joe was concerned, his fate was sealed the moment he crashed. He seriously damaged his spleen and liver among other things. All that time you were looking after him he was slowly bleeding to death. Only, it was internally, not externally, so you had no idea. According to the Pathologist's report, he was lucky he lasted as long as he did. Probably because you did everything."

"I panicked when I came to and found him like that. I didn't know what to do. When he came round he took over. The radio wasn't working and he told me what to do to check under the cowling. He told me how to cover the plane against the heat, find the emergency rations and share out the food and water. If it hadn't been for him I think I would have died also."

"You survived, thanks to him and an Aboriginal boy who just happened to wander onto your crash site. You owe them your life."

"I know...but he didn't just find the plane by chance. My wife, Kate, found out we crash-landed onto an ancient Aboriginal dry river bed. He was following his ancestors' ceremonial journey. Makes you think, doesn't it?" Martin said, shaking his head. "For some reason Joe had to put the plane down on that spot, otherwise Willy would have missed it and they would be mourning over me as well as Joe."

Felix laughed in a casual way. "Unless you're spiritually minded, Martin, you must not go any further with those thoughts. It's a labyrinth of what ifs and maybes that could take you down a path that has sent many theologians mad. Be thankful your guardian angel was watching over you that day."

Although in the final analysis the mysteries of the brain remained unchallenged; the outcome for Martin was a successful one. Not only had he regained his memory of three years ago, his recent distractions had been brought back into a normal perspective; that is if one ever existed.

However, Martin was not home free yet. Felix Grossman needed the rest of the week to establish this return to normality was not simply an interlude. He had to be certain that the hypnosis had resulted in Martin's psychological recovery, and that he had cast out his demons for the foreseeable future.

CHAPTER 31

For the Dexter family, 2012 had been a tumultuous year, although the worst was saved until the last month. December was a month they would never forget. Martin's crash in the Great Sandy Desert proved to be not only a litmus test of the family's love and loyalty for each other; it proved to be a catalyst.

With Martin's recovery in the New Year, 2013 felt like a change was about to take over their lives. Philip was right. Larry Kingston had read Martin's future like a fortune teller. By February he had agreed to head the new School of Engineering at AMINCO headquarters, and once he had settled into his office across the corridor from Philip, his life was finally complete.

Kate had managed to enrol Willy into one of the residential schools in Broome, arranged his flight from Port Hedland and with the help of Jennifer, established his new lifestyle. Jennifer had passed her first term exams at the university and would be continuing her Science Degree, in which she was majoring in Chemistry, so she had some free time to look after Willy's new environment. Adam on the other hand was now a doctor, starting his internship at a Sydney hospital. Although a new phase had entered his life, it was going to be a challenging one.

Like Martin, Kate had decided to lessen her stressful work load and had stepped down from her senior role in favour of her deserving assistant. She too had her sights on a tutorial role and her superiors jumped at the opportunity of retaining her years of knowledge and created a senior position for her in Management Studies; not unlike Larry Kingston had done for Martin. This gave her more time to concentrate on Willy's future development.

During his first year Willy became another member of the Dexter family. Although residing on the school's campus, he joined them regularly on weekends and leisurely excursions as he settled into making friends with other indigenous students.

This first year for him was a terrifying experience. He looked upon Jennifer as his mentor, even though there was a difference in their age. She had taken it upon herself to introduce him to the few similarities and the many differences between a city school and

Miss Gerry's remote cattle station school. She virtu-
ally had to teach him everything, with the help of his
new friends, who had suffered the same integration.

He soon realised his new environment was totally different from his life on the cattle station. Miss
Gerry did her best in the final weeks before he left for
Broome, by showing him videos on the television of
city life, but that was no comparison to the real thing.
Walking on footpaths and concrete was his worst initial problem after loose sand and scrubland. Then his
next nightmare was the traffic. He thought he had
faced every danger possible mustering cattle until he
faced a moving car or bus. His first experience in a
plane had been enough for him to endure.

As time passed he began to get used to these terrors
and venture out of school more with his new friends,
visit noisy arcades to play with the slot machines and
even sit in a cinema for two hours watching a film. He
was beginning to adjust to his new way of life, learn
to talk the way city folk talked and become interested in the way they dressed. He still wore the same
simple clothes the school had helped him with when
he'd arrived. It was different to running around half
naked. That's why he enjoyed the beach; at least there
he could strip down to his shorts.

By the end of his first year Willy thought he had
experienced everything modern society could throw

at him; but he soon found out his latest, most terrifying experience was yet to come. Each year's end was celebrated with a party; the focus decided by the monitors and everyone was expected to attend or beware of the consequence the following year.

In Willy's first year away from the cattle station, he had little opportunity to mingle with girls of his own age and members of the white community. He found more in common with the Asian students, who called Broome their home as they were descendants of the early pearl divers, than with the Yawuru students, whose tribe was not familiar to him.

Not knowing many girls was not Willy's major fear; after all, apart from a few guests outside the school environment, he knew everyone else. His problem came with the term 'A Formal Affair'. It took Jennifer to explain that it was not formal in the adult sense of black tie and dress suit, or the usual sweat top, jeans and sneakers. The party formal was a smart jacket, trousers or jeans, shirt with tie and polished shoes.

Willy had none of these items and it took Jennifer and Kate's credit card to solve this problem. To Willy, the casual clothes he was used to were sufficient; he had no need for anything else. So it was a shock to his singular belief that you were either naked or clothed to find that you could also be stylish. He never imagined that the modern youths of today dressed to suit the occasion.

It took Jennifer the journey in the car to explain that to be 'with it', you had to have different clothes for different occasions. It wasn't until she'd explained to him that his people had adopted different body designs for each ceremony that he began to understand what was expected of him.

Willy was about to have his first experience of a department store. It was a trying ordeal, as Willy had his own idea of what was good for him. The variety of choices he faced was equal to that of a child in a candy store until Jennifer put her foot down and told him what he had to wear at this formal party.

Two hours later Jennifer had finally managed to fit Willy out with everything he needed, except the jacket. Out of desperation, Jennifer rang Kate; she'd had more experience when buying clothes for Martin.

She had to wait for Kate to stop laughing. "Jennifer, bring Willy home. Your dad has a wardrobe full of suits and jackets; surely there's something amongst that lot to suit Willy."

Martin had not arrived home yet and Kate thought it would be an ideal opportunity to get rid of some of his cherished oldies. Jennifer and Willy arrived shortly after and Kate rushed them upstairs to the bedroom.

"What's the rush, Mum?" Jennifer asked.

"I want Willy to choose a jacket before your dad comes home. You know how he loves the clothes he brought from England. I've been trying to get rid of them for ages, but he just won't let go."

"Yes, but Mum, this is a special occasion for Willy. He doesn't want any old thing. He wants to look stylish for the girls."

"Believe me, Jennifer...you can't get more stylish than the seventies."

'Dad's oldies' was an apt description. When Kate opened the wardrobe, their mouths dropped open. Jennifer could not remember seeing her dad in the suits and jackets inside. They were unbelievable. As she ran her fingers across the material she could see Martin never bought anything but the best. Willy was amazed at the variety of shades, ranging from soft greys to subtle blues, but one jacket stood out from the rest as far as he was concerned; it was Martin's favourite suede jacket.

It was a natural skin, not dyed like some were in that period and when Kate brought it out and placed it against Willy, he looked a million dollars.

"Oh, the kids are going to have fits," she said. "Come on...slip it on, Willy."

The sight of it brought memories back of a younger Martin, as Willy's slim, athletic build slipped into the silk lining perfectly. He felt good in it and Willy's face lit up when he saw himself in the mirror.

"There you are, Willy," Kate exclaimed. "You look like a stud." Jennifer gave her an awkward glance. "Isn't that what they say?"

"He looks good, Mum. Leave it at that."

"What do you think, Willy?" Kate asked him.

"I like it," he said. "It belongs to the boss."

"Will you stop calling him that...he's Martin," Kate snapped.

"Sorry...I only know him as boss-man."

It was not unusual for Willy to stay over on a weekend, so when Martin and Kate retired to their balcony with a bottle of white wine to watch the sun sink into the Indian Ocean, they were not surprised when Jennifer said they were going to watch a show on television. However, she was planning to get Willy ready for a debut show of his own before the school party.

With the last orange rays leaving the horizon and the sky taking on a warm glow, Jennifer pushed Willy into the bedroom.

"Well, what do you think?" she called out.

As they swivelled round in their chairs, Kate got up and walked into the bedroom, switching on the bedside light as she passed. In the subdued light Willy suddenly looked nervous as Kate slowly examined every detail of his ensemble. Martin realised what was going on and followed.

465

Stopping in front of Willy with a surprised look on his face, he said nothing at first as he stared at the young man in the stone-washed jeans, striped shirt, patterned tie and what looked like his favourite suede jacket.

Martin recognised the jacket from the days when he had no need to watch his weight. When he had a waistline fit for an Adonis.

"Who's this fella?" he said, winking at Kate.

"It's Willy, Dad," Jennifer said.

Martin stepped closer for a better look. "No. This isn't Willy," he said sternly. "This isn't that stockman from the Sandy Desert."

Kate caught on and joined in. "Of course it's Willy. Look at all this mop of hair," she said, running her fingers through the unruly bush and mussing it up.

Martin looked closer. "Mmm. You might be right," he said, tapping Willy's forehead. "Are you in there, Willy?"

Willy was beginning to look uncomfortable and Martin knew when enough was enough. But just as he was about to apologise, Willy interrupted him.

"It's me, boss."

"Will you stop calling me boss?"

"I'm in here."

"Of course you are and you look great. I was only teasing you." A huge smile broke out on Willy's face and he grabbed hold of Martin around his shoulders and hugged the life out of him.

"Then we're still blood brothers?" he said.

"Yes, Willy…we're still blood brothers."

When Jennifer and Willy left for the party, Kate and Martin finally had the house to themselves. By the time they returned to the balcony and opened another bottle of wine that Martin had chilling in a bucket nearby, the sun had disappeared into the Indian Ocean without a trace. All that was left to hint that the sun had ever existed was a lingering salmon glow that slowly permeated the darkening sky above the foreshore.

"This is the life," Martin said, as he lifted his glass.

Kate took hold of his free hand and said; "Willy looked really happy tonight. I think we achieved our objective – the promise you made him."

"Yes…as selfish as it might seem, that's what pleases me the most."

As they sipped their wine and enjoyed the panorama of their balcony view, Kate turned to Martin and paused for a moment. "Martin…what's this 'blood brother' thing?"

Martin laughed, had another sip of his wine and turned to face her curious expression. "It's a long story. Remind me to tell you about it some time."

As a child in the London blitz, Charles Beagley distracted himself from the horror of his family's situation by making up stories or drawing. His eventual training was at Art School, which equipped him for the many years he spent working in advertising and design. He lived in London initially, did two years National Service in the RAF, worked in Ireland and Belgium and then set up a Design Consultancy back in England for twenty years.

He married and had two sons whose futures concerned him as things were grim economically in 1982 England. He jumped at the opportunity to move his family to Australia when he was offered a managerial position in design. During his years in England, his writing developed as he wrote promotional text and an occasional short story.

Since coming to Australia he has honed his skills, writing many fictional stories, mainly mysteries. *Blood Brothers* is his first published novel.